PENGUIN ~~
GENERAL EDITOR: CHRISTOPHER RICKS

THOMAS TRAHERNE: SELECTED POEMS AND PROSE

THOMAS TRAHERNE (1637–74) was the son of a shoemaker, in Hereford. It has been supposed that he and his younger brother Philip were orphaned at an early age and brought up, in part, by a wealthy innkeeper named Philip Traherne, who was twice mayor of Hereford and who may have been their uncle. Both boys received a good education, and Thomas graduated from Brasenose College, Oxford, in October 1656. In the following year he was appointed rector of Credenhill, Herefordshire, but probably did not take up residence there until 1664. He was ordained in 1660 and took his MA from Oxford in 1661. At Credenhill he is likely to have joined the religious circle at nearby Kington centring on Susanna Hopton, for whom he may have written his meditations now known as the *Centuries*. In 1669 he took his B.D. at Brasenose and became chaplain to the Lord Keeper Sir Orlando Bridgeman, in whose household at London and Teddington he spent the rest of his life. Many of Traherne's works, including the *Centuries*, remained undiscovered until the end of the nineteenth century. During his lifetime, however, he published *Roman Forgeries* (1673), which exposes the falsifying of ecclesiastical documents by the Church of Rome, and prepared *Christian Ethicks* (1675) for the press. At the time of his death he was at work on a vast encyclopedic project called *Commentaries of Heaven*, which was intended to show 'ALL THINGS ... to be Objects of Happiness'. The long-lost manuscript of this unfinished work was recovered in 1967 and identified in 1982. But his major achievements remain the *Centuries*, the poems and the *Thanksgivings*, which reveal him as among the first English writers to respond imaginatively to new ideas about infinite space. The boundless potentiality of the human mind and spirit is his recurrent theme, as is the need for adult man to regain the wonder and simplicity of the child.

ALAN BRADFORD holds a B.A. from Duke University and a Ph.D from Harvard University. He is Professor of English at Connecticut College, where he has served as department chair. Currently he is an Associate Director of the College's Center for International Studies and the Liberal Arts. He teaches courses in metaphysical poetry, Shakespeare and Renaissance drama and has published articles on Renaissance and seventeenth-century subjects in such journals as *English Literary Renaissance*, the *Huntington Library Quarterly*, *Shakespeare Quarterly* and *John Donne Journal*.

THOMAS TRAHERNE
SELECTED POEMS AND PROSE

EDITED BY
ALAN BRADFORD

PENGUIN BOOKS

PENGUIN BOOKS

Published by the Penguin Group
Penguin Books Ltd, 27 Wrights Lane, London W8 5TZ, England
Penguin Books USA Inc., 375 Hudson Street, New York, New York 10014, USA
Penguin Books Australia Ltd, Ringwood, Victoria, Australia
Penguin Books Canada Ltd, 10 Alcorn Avenue, Toronto, Ontario, Canada M4V 3B2
Penguin Books (NZ) Ltd, 182–190 Wairau Road, Auckland 10, New Zealand

Penguin Books Ltd, Registered Offices: Harmondsworth, Middlesex, England

This edition first published 1991
3 5 7 9 10 8 6 4

This edition, introductory matter and notes
copyright © Alan Bradford, 1991
All rights reserved

The moral right of the editor has been asserted

Filmset in 10/12 pt Ehrhardt [Monotype lasercomp]
Printed in England by Clays Ltd, St Ives plc

Except in the United States of America,
this book is sold subject to the condition
that it shall not, by way of trade or otherwise,
be lent, re-sold, hired out, or otherwise circulated
without the publisher's prior consent in any form of
binding or cover other than that in which it is
published and without a similar condition
including this condition being imposed
on the subsequent purchaser

CONTENTS

PREFACE	ix
TABLE OF DATES	xix
FURTHER READING	xxi
THE DOBELL POEMS	1
The Salutation	3
Wonder	4
Eden	6
Innocence	8
The Preparative	10
The Instruction	12
The Vision	13
The Rapture	15
The Improvement	16
The Approach	19
Dumbness	21
Silence	23
My Spirit	25
The Apprehension	29
Fullness	29
Nature	30
Ease	33
Speed	34
The Design	36
The Person	38
The Estate	40
The Inquiry	42
The Circulation	43
Amendment	46
The Demonstration	48
The Anticipation	50

The Recovery	54
Another	57
Love	58
Thoughts I	60
Bliss	62
Thoughts II	63
'Ye hidden nectars'	65
Thoughts III	66
Desire	68
Thoughts IV	70
Goodness	73

POEMS OF FELICITY: DIVINE REFLECTIONS ON
THE NATIVE OBJECTS OF AN INFANT-EYE 77

The Author to the Critical Peruser	79
An Infant-Eye	80
The Return	82
News	83
Felicity	85
Adam	86
The World	87
The Apostasy	91
Solitude	94
Poverty	98
Dissatisfaction	100
The Bible	103
Christendom	104
On Christmas-Day	108
Bells I	111
Bells II	112
Churches I	114
Churches II	115
Misapprehension	116
The Odour	118
Admiration	121
Right Apprehension	122
The Image	125
The Evidence	125

Shadows in the Water	126
On Leaping over the Moon	129
'To the same purpose'	131
Sight	132
Walking	134
The Dialogue	136
Dreams	138
The Inference I	140
The Inference II	142
The City	143
Insatiableness I	146
Insatiableness II	147
Consummation	148
Hosanna	150
The Review I	152
The Review II	153

POEMS FROM CHRISTIAN ETHICS — 155

'As in a clock'	157
'Mankind is sick'	158
'Contentment is a sleepy thing'	162

FROM AN EARLY NOTEBOOK — 163

'Rise, noble soul'	165

FROM A SERIOUS AND PATHETICAL
CONTEMPLATION OF THE MERCIES OF GOD — 167

Thanksgivings for the body	169
'While I, O Lord, exalted by Thy hand'	177
'Then shall each limb a spring of joy be found'	180

FROM CENTURIES OF MEDITATIONS — 185

From The First Century	187
From The Second Century	203
'If God as verses say a spirit be'	221

CONTENTS

The Third Century	225
The Approach	227
'In making bodies Love could not express'	235
'His power bounded, greater is in might'	236
On News	239
'A life of Sabbaths here beneath'	250
'Sin!'	252
The Recovery	253
'In Salem dwelt a glorious king'	261
From **The Fourth Century**	278
The Fifth Century	310
NOTES	316
INDEX OF TITLES	377
INDEX OF FIRST LINES	379

PREFACE

Although Thomas Traherne's work in poetry and prose is often seen as anticipating that of Blake, Wordsworth, Thoreau, and Whitman (among others), none of these authors can have been aware of Traherne as a forerunner. The discovery of this previously unknown seventeenth-century poet belongs to the twentieth century and is a continuing story – often a dramatic one – without a foreseeable ending.

During his lifetime (1637–74) Traherne published only one book, *Roman Forgeries* (1673) – a polemical work attacking the authenticity of certain documents on which the Catholic Church based its claims to spiritual and temporal authority. In the year following Traherne's death there appeared *Christian Ethics*, a book which the author himself had prepared for the press and which contains a few poems interspersed with its theological prose. The last of Traherne's works published in the seventeenth century was called *A Serious and Pathetical Contemplation of the Mercies of God* (1699) – not the poet's own title for this set of free-verse paraphrases and imitations of the Psalms now known as the *Thanksgivings*. Finally, in 1717, a minor work by Traherne called *Meditations on the Six Days of Creation* was published by Nathaniel Spinckes as the first part of *A Collection of Meditations and Devotions*; it was attributed to Susanna Hopton, a friend of the poet's who possessed some of his manuscripts.

Most of the poetry and all of the prose included in the present edition came to light only in the early part of this century. In 1896 William T. Brooke purchased for a few pence two manuscripts that he found on a London bookstall. One of these, a folio volume, contained thirty-seven poems in Traherne's own handwriting, followed by copious extracts from his reading that have come to be known collectively as Traherne's commonplace book. The other, though untitled, contained what we now call the *Centuries of Meditations* – Traherne's acknowledged literary masterpiece. Neither of these volumes, however, was signed, and their authorship remained a mystery until Bertram Dobell, with the help of Brooke, succeeded in identifying Traherne as their author. The clue was provided by the *Thanksgivings*, a book which Dobell was convinced had come from the same pen as the two anonymous manuscripts; it had an unsigned preface by a gentleman who, though he desired 'to pay his respects to his pious friend's memory', nevertheless thought that to mention the author's name would be 'to no purpose', as did the book's publisher, Dr George Hickes. The writer of this preface did, however, mention that the author of the *Thanksgivings* had served as chaplain to Sir Orlando Bridgeman, at one time Lord Keeper of the Great Seal under King Charles II. In due course, Anthony à Wood's *Athenae Oxonienses* supplied the information that this post had been held by Thomas Traherne, B.D., 'a shoemaker's son of Hereford', Rector of Credenhill, and author of *Roman Forgeries* and *Christian Ethics*. The last piece of the puzzle fell into place when the latter book yielded a passage of verse found also in the *Centuries*. For all practical purposes, Dobell had discovered Traherne. His edition of the poems followed in 1903, and of the *Centuries* in 1908.

Shortly thereafter, yet another Traherne manuscript – this one in the hand of the poet's brother Philip – came to the attention of H. I. Bell at the British Museum, where it had resided undetected in the Burney collection since the early nineteenth century. It contained not only many of the Dobell poems but also forty other poems by Thomas Traherne not in Dobell. Bell's edition of this manuscript, entitled *Poems of Felicity*, appeared in 1910. Together, these two compilations have provided us with the poems on which Thomas Traherne's modern critical reputation as a poet rests. They are all included in the present selection and furnish the bulk of the poetry given here.

Other Traherne manuscripts that have subsequently come to light include an 'early notebook' (shared by Thomas and Philip), the 'Ficino notebook' containing Traherne's notes on Marsilio Ficino's fifteenth-century commentaries on Plato, and a minor and derivative work known as *The Church's Year-Book*. But the most dramatic finds have been the late James Osborn's discovery of the *Select Meditations* in 1964 and the astonishing rescue of the *Commentaries of Heaven* from a burning rubbish heap in 1967 – though the latter was not identified as Traherne's until 1982. These two important manuscripts, now at Yale University and the British Library respectively, remain to be edited and published.

All in all, Traherne was not well served by the people who were, in effect, his literary executors. In fairness, however, Philip Traherne and Susanna Hopton would not have thought of themselves in that light, nor of Traherne as a literary figure. Earlier in the century, George Herbert on his deathbed had entrusted *The Temple* – a manuscript containing almost all of his poetry – to his friend Nicholas Ferrar of Little Gidding, with the request that it be published only if, in Ferrar's judgement, 'it may turn to the advantage of any dejected poor soul'. Both Philip, a clergyman like his brother, and Mrs Hopton, like Ferrar the leader of a religious society, would no doubt have applied a similar criterion in deciding which if any of the many Traherne manuscripts in their possession ought to be published – quite apart from any question of literary merit. Moreover, they cannot have been ambitious for renown on Thomas's behalf. When Mrs Hopton – a quarter of a century after the poet's death – turned over her manuscript of his *Thanksgivings* to Dr Hickes for publication, she did not see fit to contribute a memoir of her own or to insist that Traherne receive credit for having composed them; nor, apparently, did she ever inform Hickes that the *Meditations on the Six Days of Creation* were by Traherne. He assumed that she had written them and so informed Spinckes, the publisher; there may indeed be unresolved questions of attribution surrounding the manuscripts from the Hopton circle.

Philip, meanwhile, withheld *Poems of Felicity* for an even longer time – kept them 'too long in private' by his own admission – before laboriously transcribing and revising them for an edition that, for whatever reason, never materialized. If Philip's edition had appeared, its title page (included in the manuscript) would have borne Thomas's name, thus saving Dobell the need for so much detective work. Even so, Philip's prefatory matter makes clear that Christian piety outweighed either fraternal duty or cultural responsibility as a motive for publication, the desired effect of the book being its readers' salvation.

Nevertheless, Philip certainly considered it part of his job as editor to 'improve' his brother's literary performance by the standards of the Augustan age: intervening wherever fancy superseded judgement; honing (or so he thought) Thomas's craftsmanship; but above all taming the poems' radical theology. Consequently, *Poems of Felicity*, as a text of Thomas Traherne's poetry, must be regarded as irretrievably corrupt. Yet it has to be included here because it contains many of his most important poems, which are in no sense inferior to the best poems in the Dobell folio. The reader need only be warned that unless we have the good luck to recover Thomas's autograph manuscript of these poems, we shall never have them as he wrote them. It has been estimated that, in the twenty-two poems that appear in both manuscripts (Dobell and Burney) plus *News*, which is Philip's version of *On News* from *Centuries* 3.26, about thirty-five per cent of the lines have been altered by Philip. Twenty-three poems are a large enough sample that we can confidently project a similar percentage of altered lines for the remaining forty poems found only in Philip's hand.

The alterations themselves range from minor to drastic. Readers of this selection have three opportunities to gauge the extent of the damage done by Philip: *On News* and *News* are both reprinted in their respective contexts; *The Apostasy*, in *Poems of Felicity*, is reprinted with Philip's version of its fifth and sixth stanzas retained intact despite the existence of Thomas's version of these same stanzas as *Bliss* in the Dobell manuscript; and finally, the note on *The Estate* gives Philip's rendition of that poem's final stanza. This last instance shows Thomas at his most inspired and Philip (consequently?) at his most destructive: any editor capable of substituting 'And air, design'd to please / Our earthly part' for 'The air was made to please / The souls of men' has missed Traherne's main point (which was never understated). Readers wishing to make a thorough comparison of the variant readings in the Dobell and Burney manuscripts are referred to H. M. Margoliouth's standard edition, which prints on facing pages the parallel texts of the twenty-two poems that they have in common.

Editing the *Poems of Felicity* is largely a matter of damage control. The trick is to make Philip's hand disappear, in so far as possible, but there are practical limits to what can be done. Whenever Philip deletes a line or part of a line and substitutes new wording, an editor must assume that Philip is revising Thomas's manuscript on the spot. Philip's revisions, however, do not always occur spontaneously in the act of transcription; and even when they do, restoration of the original is not always possible without doing unacceptable violence to rhyme, meter, and meaning since whole contexts will have been distorted to accommodate even relatively minor changes.

No such problems occur with regard to the poems from the Dobell folio. Although Philip did make, to the manuscript, emendations which he later incorporated in *Poems of Felicity*, his handwriting is easy to distinguish from Thomas's, so that an editor need only ignore any changes made by Philip. My only departure from this principle is in accepting Philip's correction of an apparent slip of the pen by Thomas in the penultimate stanza of *The Design* (see note on that poem). Thomas himself made several last-minute changes after copying out the Dobell poems, and the present edition aims to print *all* of these final authorial corrections. In doing so, I have departed from the precedent set by Traherne's two Oxford editors, H. M. Margoliouth and Anne Ridler (she, however, included many more such changes than did Margoliouth). While this decision results in the sacrifice of some familiar readings (preserved here in the notes), it has the merit of representing the poems as Traherne would have published them if he had lived to do so.

Since the changes inserted by Philip in the Dobell manuscript also appear in *Poems of Felicity*, he must have used this manuscript as one of his copy-texts. Moreover, since his title-page implicitly promises a second volume, there must have been other poems available to him besides the fifteen Dobell poems that he had excluded from the first volume. (Some of these unknown poems are, indeed, mentioned by title in the notes that Philip wrote from time to time in the Dobell folio.) If the second volume was to be equal in size to the first one, it could have included approximately forty-seven additional poems (the exact number depending on their average length). Philip may therefore have meant to conflate as many as three independent poetic sequences in assembling his projected two-volume edition. Alternatively, he may have worked with the same manuscript material from which Thomas had culled the Dobell sequence. *The Estate* and *The Evidence*, for instance, appear to belong together, yet Thomas used only the former in the Dobell sequence; either Philip put them together in the process of forming a new sequence, or he found them together in a manuscript no longer extant. In either case, it makes sense to treat the poems that are unique to Burney as a sequence in its own right, though a less coherent one than the Dobell manuscript and probably not complete once the Dobell poems are extricated from it.

When did Traherne write the Dobell and Burney poems? All that can be inferred with reasonable certainty, from manuscript evidence, is that he gathered and arranged the thirty-seven Dobell poems (presumably written at various times) and made a fair copy of them after having composed the *Centuries* but before completing his research for *Christian Ethics*, one of his last works. Affinities between the poems in both sequences and the *Centuries* are sometimes so close as to suggest simultaneous composition: a circumstance that would be more enlightening if the *Centuries* could be dated with greater precision. My own guess is that Traherne must have been very active as a poet throughout the 1660s, during periods of residence at both Oxford and Credenhill (near Hereford). An extremely prolific writer, he is remembered in the anonymous preface to the *Thanksgivings* as 'spending most of his time when at home, in digesting his notions ... into writing'. It appears, however, that during the last four or five years of his life – his London period as chaplain to the Bridgeman household – he was exploring new pathways of expression that may have led him away from stanzaic verse towards larger and looser forms which promised more room to a sensibility that had always resisted confinement; thus the encyclopedic *Commentaries of Heaven* (in progress at the time of Traherne's death) uses regular verse, mostly in pentameter couplets, for poetic and meditative reflection on the topics of its alphabetically ordered prose articles but contains few poems as such. Scholarly analysis of the *Select Meditations* (apparently written after the Restoration but before the *Centuries*) and of the *Commentaries of Heaven* may shed further light on the chronology of Traherne's canon.

In selecting and arranging the poems for the Penguin edition, I have been governed by two objectives: (1) maintaining the integrity of the Dobell sequence because of that manuscript's textual authority; (2) representing the remainder of the Burney sequence (i.e., after the subtraction of the material it shares with Dobell) in its entirety, including *The Author to the Critical Peruser*, which both Margoliouth and Ridler promoted to the front of their editions but which is here restored to its rightful place as prologue only to the *Poems of Felicity*. The sequential nature of both groups of poems makes it worthwhile to include all the poems from each group, and the notes accordingly stress the interdependence of the poems within their respective sequences. Considerations of space have limited me to a single specimen of the nine *Thanksgivings*; the poetry selections are rounded out by three of the five complete poems found in *Christian Ethics* (which also contains three verse fragments) and an attractive lyric poem, 'Rise, noble soul', chosen from among the six poems (one of which is a translation of Seneca) attributable to Thomas Traherne in the early notebook. *Meditations on the Six Days of Creation*, which has a poem for each day, and *The Church's Year-Book*, which contains two verse translations and one original poem, are not represented here. Prose selections, all taken from the *Centuries of Meditations*, are intended to amplify the context of the poems and thus are frequently cross-referenced in the notes to the poems. Because the Third Century, as Traherne's spiritual autobiography, provides both poetic sequences with something like a narrative frame, I have included the whole of it – even the relatively unfamiliar later sections which, with their commentary on the Psalms, reveal a major source of Traherne's poetic inspiration. Readers will also find six complete poems and two large fragments of a lost poem in the Third Century, which is the only one of the Centuries that includes poems.

There are five instances in the Burney manuscript of poems paired under a common title: *Bells* I and II; *Churches* I and II; *The Inference* I and II; *Insatiableness* I and II; and *The Review* I and II. (Originally there was a sixth pair, *Right Apprehension* I and II, but the second poem in this pair is *The Apprehension* from the Dobell sequence, a single stanza which seems to be a fragment of a rejected longer poem.) These pairs may have been conceived as two-part poems, or Traherne may have followed George Herbert's practice of re-using a title and numbering the poems so designated according to the order in which they were composed. But Traherne, unlike Herbert, never uses the same title more than twice – with the exception of a special case: the four-part *Thoughts* series of poems, which are integrated into a carefully planned nine-poem sequence at the end of the Dobell manuscript. It seems likely, therefore, that Philip was correct in juxtaposing the two poems belonging to each pair. As long as the poems in each set are printed together, it makes little practical difference whether we regard them as two-part poems, as separate poems that happen to have the same title, or even as innovative 'double poems'. In the present edition, lines and stanzas are numbered consecutively from one part to the next only in *Bells* I and II, where the stanza form – atypically for Traherne – gets repeated, thereby suggesting intended continuity from part to part.

Philip did not number stanzas in *Poems of Felicity*. Since, however, it was Thomas Traherne's habit to do so in almost all the stanzaic verse that we have in his own hand as well as in that found in *Christian Ethics*, which he had prepared for the press, we can safely assume that Philip decided to do without the numbers that are likely to have been present in whatever copy-texts he used. For this reason and also for convenience of reference, I have provided stanza numbers for those poems found only in the Burney manuscript.

While spelling has been modernized in accordance with the editorial policy of the Penguin Selected English Poets series, it must be admitted that Traherne, who (like Blake) is a genuinely eccentric writer, loses some of his distinctiveness as a result. Traherne's reputation for idiosyncrasy, however, may derive in large part from the absence of a seventeenth-century edition of his poems and *Centuries*; as Margoliouth pointed out, no printer of the time would have honoured his singularities in spelling, capitalization, and punctuation as modern scholarly editors have of course done. As for capitalization, I have not found enough consistency in Traherne's use of capitals to support the claims that are sometimes made for its significance or expressive effect; consequently, capitalization is here normalized according to modern usage. Similarly, with respect to punctuation, legibility and freedom from distraction have been my goals. Partly because the two poetry manuscripts are fair copies whereas that of the *Centuries* is not, I have found it possible to re-punctuate the former much more conservatively than the latter.

Anyone who works on Traherne is indebted to the indispensable scholarship of the late H. M. Margoliouth; for much of the content of my notes on the poems I am likewise indebted to the remarkable outpouring of critical studies stimulated by Margoliouth's 1958 edition. I have also consulted the later edition by Anne Ridler as well as the earlier ones by Bertram Dobell, H. I. Bell, and most importantly Gladys Wade. The manuscripts I have used in preparing this edition are Bodleian MSS. Eng. poet. c. 42 (Dobell poems), Eng. th. e. 50 (*Centuries*), and Lat. misc. f. 45 (early notebook); and British Library MS. Burney 392 (*Poems of Felicity*). Printed sources are the 1675 edition of *Christian Ethics* and the 1699 edition of the *Thanksgivings* (*A Serious and Pathetical Contemplation of the Mercies of God*).

I wish to express my gratitude to Connecticut College for financial support; to Westminster College for its hospitality; to the staffs of the British, Bodleian, and Folger Libraries for their assistance; to Dr J. J. Smith of Oxford for kindly sharing Traherne's Bodleian manuscripts with me and for providing me with valuable information, especially on Philip Traherne; and finally to Christopher Ricks for giving me the opportunity to edit Traherne and for his patience and encouragement as time wore on.

TABLE OF DATES

1637	*October* Thomas Traherne born to a shoemaker's family in Hereford.
1652	*1 March* Matriculated as a Commoner at Brasenose College, Oxford.
1656	*13 October* B.A.
1657	*30 December* Appointed Rector of Credenhill (five miles from Hereford) by the Commonwealth Commissioners for the Approbation of Public Preachers, but probably did not take up residency.
1660	*20 October* Ordained deacon and priest under the Restoration.
1661	*6 November* M.A. from Brasenose; reappointed Rector of Credenhill.
1662–5	May have written his *Select Meditations*.
1664	Perhaps took up residence at Credenhill; may have joined Susanna Hopton's religious circle at nearby Kington.
1666–8	Compiles Ficino notebook.
1668–71	Probably wrote his *Centuries of Meditations*.
1669	*11 December* B.D. from Brasenose; appointed chaplain to Sir Orlando Bridgeman, Lord Keeper of the Great Seal; left Credenhill for London but continued to hold Credenhill living.
1670	*April–November* Wrote *The Church's Year-Book* and possibly *Meditations on the Six Days of Creation*.
1670–71	Probably wrote the majority of the *Thanksgivings*; may have collected, arranged, and copied 'Dobell' sequence of poems and entered research notes for *Christian Ethics* and *Commentaries of Heaven* in his commonplace book.

1672	*November* Moved to Bridgeman estate at Teddington after Bridgeman's fall from power; continued to serve as family chaplain and became minister of Teddington Church.
1673	Published *Roman Forgeries*; at work on *Commentaries of Heaven*.
1674	*Early October* Died at Bridgeman villa. *10 October* Buried under the reading-desk at Teddington Church.
1675	*Christian Ethics* published.
1677	*28 June* Philip Traherne carries out his brother's intention to give five tenement houses belonging to Thomas in All Saints parish, Hereford, to the mayor, aldermen, and citizens for use of the poor.
1699	Dr George Hickes publishes anonymously *A Serious and Pathetical Contemplation of the Mercies of God* (Traherne's *Thanksgivings*).
1717	Nathaniel Spinckes publishes Traherne's *Meditations on the Six Days of Creation* in *A Collection of Meditations and Devotions* as the work of Susanna Hopton.
1896	W. T. Brooke discovers and purchases the manuscripts of Traherne's *Centuries of Meditations* and 'Dobell' sequence of poems.
1903	Bertram Dobell publishes the poems contained in the Dobell folio.
1908	Dobell publishes the *Centuries*.
1910	H. I. Bell publishes *Poems of Felicity* (the Burney MS in Philip Traherne's handwriting).
1964	James Osborn discovers the *Select Meditations*.
1967	MS of Traherne's *Commentaries of Heaven* is plucked off a burning rubbish heap in Lancashire.
1982	*Commentaries of Heaven* is identified as Traherne's at the University of Toronto.

FURTHER READING

EDITIONS

Thomas Traherne, *Centuries, Poems, and Thanksgivings*, 2 vols., edited by H. M. Margoliouth, Oxford: Clarendon Press, 1958.

Thomas Traherne, *Christian Ethicks*, edited by Carol L. Marks and George R. Guffey, Ithaca: Cornell University Press, 1968.

Thomas Traherne, *Poems, Centuries and Three Thanksgivings*, edited by Anne Ridler, London: Oxford University Press, 1966.

BIOGRAPHY

Gladys I. Wade, *Thomas Traherne*, Princeton: Princeton University Press, 1944.

CRITICAL STUDIES

A. L. Clements, *The Mystical Poetry of Thomas Traherne*, Cambridge: Harvard University Press, 1969.

Malcolm M. Day, *Thomas Traherne*, Boston: Twayne Publishers, 1982.

Barbara K. Lewalski, *Protestant Poetics and the Seventeenth-Century Religious Lyric*, Princeton: Princeton University Press, 1979.

Louis L. Martz, *The Paradise Within: Studies in Vaughan, Traherne, and Milton*, New Haven: Yale University Press, 1964.

Allan Pritchard, 'Traherne's *Commentaries of Heaven* (With Selections from the Manuscript)', *University of Toronto Quarterly*, vol. 53, 1983, pp. 1–35.

Stanley Stewart, *The Expanded Voice: The Art of Thomas Traherne*, San Marino, Ca.: Huntington Library, 1970.

John M. Wallace, 'Thomas Traherne and the Structure of Meditation', *English Literary History*, vol. 25, 1958, pp. 78–89.

THE DOBELL POEMS

The Salutation

1
These little limbs,
These eyes and hands which here I find,
These rosy cheeks wherewith my life begins,
Where have ye been? Behind
What curtain were ye from me hid so long!
Where was, in what abyss, my speaking tongue?

2
When silent I,
So many thousand thousand years,
Beneath the dust did in a chaos lie,
How could I smiles or tears,
Or lips or hands or eyes or ears perceive?
Welcome, ye treasures which I now receive.

3
I that so long
Was nothing from eternity,
Did little think such joys as ear or tongue,
To celebrate or see:
Such sounds to hear, such hands to feel, such feet,
Beneath the skies, on such a ground to meet.

4
New burnish'd joys!
Which yellow gold and pearl excel!
Such sacred treasures are the limbs in boys,
In which a soul doth dwell;
Their organized joints, and azure veins
More wealth include, than all the world contains.

5
From dust I rise,
And out of nothing now awake,
These brighter regions which salute mine eyes,

  A gift from God I take.
The earth, the seas, the light, the day, the skies,
The sun and stars are mine; if those I prize.   30

6

  Long time before
 I in my mother's womb was born,
A God preparing did this glorious store,
  The world, for me adorn.
Into this Eden so divine and fair,
So wide and bright, I come His son and heir.

7

  A stranger here
Strange things doth meet, strange glories see;
Strange treasures lodg'd in this fair world appear;
  Strange all, and new to me.   40
But that they mine should be, who nothing was,
That strangest is of all, yet brought to pass.

Wonder

1

 How like an angel came I down!
  How bright are all things here!
When first among His works I did appear
 O how their glory me did crown!
The world resembled His eternity,
  In which my soul did walk;
 And every thing that I did see,
  Did with me talk.

2

 The skies in their magnificence,
  The lively, lovely air;   10
Oh how divine, how soft, how sweet, how fair!

The stars did entertain my sense,
And all the works of God so bright and pure,
    So rich and great did seem,
As if they ever must endure,
      In my esteem.

3

A native health and innocence
    Within my bones did grow,
And while my God did all His glories show,
    I felt a vigour in my sense
That was all spirit. I within did flow
    With seas of life, like wine;
I nothing in the world did know,
      But 'twas divine.

4

Harsh ragged objects were conceal'd,
    Oppressions, tears, and cries,
Sins, griefs, complaints, dissensions, weeping eyes,
    Were hid; and only things reveal'd
Which heavenly spirits, and the angels prize.
    The state of innocence
And bliss, not trades and poverties,
      Did fill my sense.

5

The streets were pav'd with golden stones,
    The boys and girls were mine.
Oh how did all their lovely faces shine!
    The sons of men were holy ones.
Joy, beauty, welfare did appear to me,
    And every thing which here I found,
While like an angel I did see,
      Adorn'd the ground.

6

Rich diamond and pearl and gold
    In every place was seen;
Rare splendours, yellow, blue, red, white and green,
    Mine eyes did everywhere behold,
Great wonders cloth'd with glory did appear,
    Amazement was my bliss.
That and my wealth was everywhere:
    No joy to this!

7

Curs'd and devis'd proprieties,
    With envy, avarice
And fraud, those fiends that spoil even Paradise,
    Fled from the splendour of mine eyes.
And so did hedges, ditches, limits, bounds.
    I dream'd not aught of those,
But wander'd over all men's grounds,
    And found repose.

8

Proprieties themselves were mine,
    And hedges ornaments;
Walls, boxes, coffers, and their rich contents
    Did not divide my joys, but shine.
Clothes, ribbons, jewels, laces, I esteem'd
    My joys by others worn;
For me they all to wear them seem'd
    When I was born.

Eden

1

A learned and a happy ignorance
    Divided me
    From all the vanity,
From all the sloth, care, pain, and sorrow that advance

The madness and the misery
Of men. No error, no distraction I
Saw soil the earth, or overcloud the sky.

2

I knew not that there was a serpent's sting,
    Whose poison shed
      On men, did overspread
The world; nor did I dream of such a thing
  As sin: in which mankind lay dead.
They all were brisk and living wights to me,
Yea pure, and full of immortality.

3

Joy, pleasure, beauty, kindness, glory, love,
    Sleep, day, life, light,
      Peace, melody, my sight,
My ears and heart did fill, and freely move.
  All that I saw did me delight.
The universe was then a world of treasure,
To me an universal world of pleasure.

4

Unwelcome penitence was then unknown,
    Vain costly toys,
      Swearing and roaring boys,
Shops, markets, taverns, coaches were unshown;
  So all things were that drown'd my joys.
No thorns chok'd up my path, nor hid the face
Of bliss and beauty, nor eclips'd the place.

5

Only what Adam in his first estate,
    Did I behold;
      Hard silver and dry gold
As yet lay underground; my blessed fate
  Was more acquainted with the old
And innocent delights, which he did see
In his original simplicity.

6

Those things which first his Eden did adorn,
    My infancy
    Did crown. Simplicity
Was my protection when I first was born.
    Mine eyes those treasures first did see, 40
Which God first made. The first effects of love
My first enjoyments upon earth did prove;

7

And were so great, and so divine, so pure,
    So fair and sweet,
    So true; when I did meet
Them here at first, they did my soul allure,
    And drew away my infant feet
Quite from the works of men; that I might see
The glorious wonders of the Deity.

Innocence

1

But that which most I wonder at, which most
I did esteem my bliss, which most I boast,
And ever shall enjoy, is that within
    I felt no stain, nor spot of sin.

    No darkness then did overshade,
    But all within was pure and bright,
    No guilt did crush, nor fear invade
    But all my soul was full of light.

    A joyful sense and purity
        Is all I can remember.
    The very night to me was bright, 10
    'Twas summer in December.

2

A serious meditation did employ
My soul within, which taken up with joy
Did seem no outward thing to note, but fly
    All objects that do feed the eye.

    While it those very objects did
    Admire, and prize, and praise, and love,
    Which in their glory most are hid,
    Which presence only doth remove.

    Their constant daily presence I
        Rejoicing at, did see;
    And that which takes them from the eye
    Of others, offer'd them to me.

3

No inward inclination did I feel
To avarice or pride: my soul did kneel
In admiration all the day. No lust, nor strife,
    Polluted then my infant life.

    No fraud nor anger in me mov'd,
    No malice, jealousy, or spite;
    All that I saw I truly lov'd.
    Contentment only and delight

    Were in my soul. O Heaven! what bliss
        Did I enjoy and feel!
    What powerful delight did this
    Inspire! For this I daily kneel.

4

Whether it be that nature is so pure,
And custom only vicious; or that sure
God did by miracle the guilt remove,
    And make my soul to feel His love,

    So early; or that 'twas one day,
    Wherein this happiness I found:

Whose strength and brightness so do ray,
That still it seemeth to surround.

Whate'er it is, it is a light
    So endless unto me
That I a world of true delight
Did then and to this day do see.

5
That prospect was the gate of Heaven, that day
The ancient light of Eden did convey
Into my soul: I was an Adam there,
    A little Adam in a sphere

Of joys! O there my ravish'd sense
Was entertain'd in Paradise,
And had a sight of innocence.
All was beyond all bound and price.

An antepast of Heaven sure!
    I on the earth did reign.
Within, without me, all was pure.
I must become a child again.

The Preparative

1

My body being dead, my limbs unknown;
    Before I skill'd to prize
    Those living stars mine eyes,
Before my tongue or cheeks were to me shown,
    Before I knew my hands were mine,
Or that my sinews did my members join,
    When neither nostril, foot, nor ear,
As yet was seen, or felt, or did appear;
        I was within
A house I knew not, newly cloth'd with skin.

2

Then was my soul my only all to me,
    A living endless eye,
      Just bounded with the sky,
Whose power, whose act, whose essence was to see.
    I was an inward sphere of light,
Or an interminable orb of sight,
    An endless and a living day,
A vital sun that round about did ray
        All life and sense,
A naked simple pure intelligence.

3

I then no thirst nor hunger did conceive,
    No dull necessity,
      No want was known to me;
Without disturbance then I did receive
    The fair ideas of all things,
And had the honey even without the stings.
    A meditating inward eye
Gazing at quiet did within me lie,
        And every thing
Delighted me that was their heavenly king.

4

For sight inherits beauty, hearing sounds,
    The nostril sweet perfumes,
      All tastes have hidden rooms
Within the tongue; and feeling feeling wounds
    With pleasure and delight, but I
Forgot the rest, and was all sight, or eye.
    Unbodied and devoid of care,
Just as in Heaven the holy angels are.
        For simple sense
Is lord of all created excellence.

5

Being thus prepar'd for all felicity,
    Not prepossess'd with dross,

  Nor stiffly glued to gross
And dull materials that might ruin me,
  Not fetter'd by an iron fate
With vain affections in my earthy state
  To anything that might seduce
My sense, or else bereave it of its use,
    I was as free
As if there were nor sin, nor misery.   50

6

Pure empty powers that did nothing loathe,
  Did like the fairest glass,
  Or spotless polish'd brass,
Themselves soon in their objects' image clothe.
  Divine impressions when they came,
Did quickly enter and my soul inflame.
  'Tis not the object, but the light
That maketh Heaven; 'tis a purer sight.
    Felicity
Appears to none but them that purely see.   60

7

A disentangled and a naked sense,
  A mind that's unpossess'd,
  A disengaged breast,
An empty and a quick intelligence
  Acquainted with the golden mean,
An even spirit pure and serene,
  Is that where beauty, excellence,
And pleasure keep their court of residence.
    My soul, retire,
Get free, and so thou shalt even all admire.   70

The Instruction

1

Spew out thy filth, thy flesh abjure;
Let not contingents thee defile.

For transients only are impure,
And airy things thy soul beguile.

2

Unfelt, unseen let those things be
Which to thy spirit were unknown,
When to thy blessed infancy
The world, thyself, thy God was shown.

3

All that is great and stable stood
Before thy purer eyes at first:
All that in visibles is good
Or pure, or fair, or unaccurst.

4

Whatever else thou now dost see
In custom, action, or desire,
'Tis but a part of misery
In which all men at once conspire.

The Vision

1

Flight is but the preparative: the sight
    Is deep and infinite;
Ah me! 'tis all the glory, love, light, space,
    Joy, beauty, and variety
That doth adorn the Godhead's dwelling place.
    'Tis all that eye can see.
Even trades themselves seen in celestial light,
    And cares and sins and woes are bright.

2

Order the beauty even of beauty is,
    It is the rule of bliss,

The very life and form and cause of pleasure;
    Which if we do not understand,
Ten thousand heaps of vain confused treasure
    Will but oppress the land.
In blessedness itself we that shall miss,
    Being blind, which is the cause of bliss.

3

First then behold the world as thine, and well
    Note that where thou dost dwell.
See all the beauty of the spacious case,
    Lift up thy pleas'd and ravish'd eyes,
Admire the glory of the heavenly place,
    And all its blessings prize.
That sight well seen thy spirit shall prepare;
    The first makes all the other rare.

4

Men's woes shall be but foils unto thy bliss,
    Thou once enjoying this:
Trades shall adorn and beautify the earth,
    Their ignorance shall make thee bright.
Were not their griefs Democritus his mirth?
    Their faults shall keep thee right.
All shall be thine, because they all conspire,
    To feed and make thy glory higher.

5

To see a glorious fountain and an end,
    To see all creatures tend
To thy advancement, and so sweetly close
    In thy repose: to see them shine
In use, in worth, in service, and even foes
    Among the rest made thine.
To see all these unite at once in thee
    Is to behold felicity.

6

To see the fountain is a blessed thing.
    It is to see the King
Of Glory face to face; but yet the end,
    The glorious wondrous end, is more;
And yet the fountain there we comprehend,
    The spring we there adore.
For in the end the fountain best is shown,
    As by effects the cause is known

7

From one, to one, in one to see all things,
    To see the King of Kings
At once in two; to see His endless treasures
    Made all mine own, myself the end
Of all His labours! 'Tis the life of pleasures!
    To see myself His friend!
Who all things finds conjoin'd in him alone,
    Sees and enjoys the Holy One.

The Rapture

1

Sweet infancy!
O fire of Heaven! O sacred light!
    How fair and bright!
    How great am I,
Whom all the world doth magnify!

2

    O heavenly joy!
O great and sacred blessedness,
    Which I possess!
    So great a joy
Who did into my arms convey!

3
From God above
Being sent, the heavens me inflame,
To praise His name.
The stars do move!
The burning sun doth show His love.

4
O how divine
Am I! To all this sacred wealth,
This life and health,
Who rais'd? Who mine
Did make the same? What hand divine!

The Improvement

1
'Tis more to recollect, than make. The one
Is but an accident without the other.
We cannot think the world to be the throne
Of God, unless His wisdom shine as brother
    Unto His power, in the fabric, so
    That we the one may in the other know.

2
His goodness also must in both appear,
And all the children of His love be found,
In the creation of the starry sphere,
And in the forming of the fruitful ground;
    Before we can that happiness descry,
    Which is the daughter of the Deity.

3
His wisdom shines in spreading forth the sky,
His power's great in ordering the sun,
His goodness very marvellous and high
Appears, in every work His hand hath done.

And all His works in their variety,
Even scattered abroad delight the eye.

4

But neither goodness, wisdom, power, nor love,
Nor happiness itself in things could be
Did not they all in one fair order move,
And jointly by their service end in me.
    Had He not made an eye to be the sphere
    Of all things, none of these would e'er appear.

5

His wisdom, goodness, power, as they unite
All things in one, that they may be the treasures
Of one enjoyer, shine in the utmost height
They can attain; and are most glorious pleasures,
    When all the universe conjoin'd in one
    Exalts a creature, as if that alone.

6

To bring the moisture of far distant seas
Into a point, to make them present here,
In virtue, not in bulk; one man to please
With all the powers of the highest sphere,
    From east, from west, from north and south, to bring
    The pleasing influence of everything;

7

Is far more great than to create them there
Where now they stand; His wisdom more doth shine
In that, His might and goodness more appear,
In recollecting; He is more divine
    In making everything a gift to one
    Than in the parts of all His spacious throne.

8

Herein we see a marvellous design,
And apprehending clearly the great skill

Of that great architect, whose love doth shine
In all His works, we find His life and will.
    For lively counsels do the Godhead show,
    And these His love and goodness make us know.

9

By wise contrivance He doth all things guide,
And so dispose them, that while they unite,
For man He endless pleasures doth provide,
And shows that happiness is His delight,
    His creature's happiness as well as His:
    For that in truth He seeks, and 'tis His bliss.

10

O rapture! Wonder! Ecstasy! Delight!
How great must then His glory be, how great
Our blessedness! How vast and infinite
Our pleasure, how transcendent, how complete,
    If we the goodness of our God possess,
    And all His joy be in our blessedness!

11

Almighty power when it is employ'd
For one, that he with glory might be crown'd;
Eternal wisdom when it is enjoy'd
By one, whom all its pleasures do surround,
    Produce a creature that must, all his days,
    Return the sacrifice of endless praise.

12

But Oh! the vigour of mine infant sense
Drives me too far: I had not yet the eye,
The apprehension, or intelligence
Of things so very great, divine, and high.
    But all things were eternal unto me,
    And mine, and pleasing, which mine eye did see.

13

That was enough at first: eternity,
Infinity, and love were silent joys;
Power, wisdom, goodness, and felicity;
All these which now our care and sin destroys,
    By instinct virtually were well discern'd,
    And by their representatives were learn'd.

14

As sponges gather moisture from the earth
(Which seemeth dry) in which they buried are;
As air infecteth salt; so at my birth
All these were unperceiv'd, yet did appear:
    Not by reflection, and distinctly known,
    But, by their efficacy, all mine own.

The Approach

1

    That childish thoughts such joys inspire,
Doth make my wonder and His glory higher,
    His bounty, and my wealth more great;
It shows His kingdom and His work complete;
    In which there is not any thing
Not meet to be the joy of cherubim.

2

    He in our childhood with us walks,
And with our thoughts mysteriously He talks;
    He often visiteth our minds,
But cold acceptance in us ever finds:
    We send Him often griev'd away;
Else would He show us all His kingdom's joy.

3

    O Lord, I wonder at Thy love,
Which did my infancy so early move;

But more at that which did forbear,
And move so long, tho slighted many a year;
   But most of all, at last that Thou
Thyself shouldst me convert I scarce know how.

4

   Thy gracious motions oft in vain
Assaulted me: my heart did hard remain
   Long time: I sent my God away,
Griev'd much that He could not impart His joy.
   I careless was, nor did regard
The end for which He all these thoughts prepar'd.

5

   But now with new and open eyes,
I see beneath as if above the skies;
   And as I backward look again,
See all His thoughts and mine most clear and plain.
   He did approach, He me did woo.
I wonder that my God this thing would do.

6

   From nothing taken first I was.
What wondrous things His glory brought to pass!
   Now in this world I Him behold,
And me enveloped in more than gold;
   In deep abysses of delights,
In present hidden precious benefits.

7

   Those thoughts His goodness long before
Prepar'd as precious and celestial store,
   With curious art in me inlaid,
That childhood might itself alone be said
   My tutor, teacher, guide to be,
Instructed then even by the Deity.

Dumbness

Sure man was born to meditate on things,
And to contemplate the eternal springs
Of God and nature, glory, bliss, and pleasure;
That life and love might be his heavenly treasure:
And therefore speechless made at first, that he
Might in himself profoundly busied be:
And not vent out, before he hath ta'en in
Those antidotes that guard his soul from sin.

    Wise nature made him deaf too, that he might
Not be disturb'd, while he doth take delight   10
In inward things, nor be deprav'd with tongues,
Nor injur'd by the errors and the wrongs
That mortal words convey. For sin and death
Are most infused by accursed breath,
That flowing from corrupted entrails, bear
Those hidden plagues that souls alone may fear.

    This, my dear friends, this was my blessed case;
For nothing spoke to me but the fair face
Of Heaven and earth, before myself could speak.
I then my bliss did, when my silence, break.   20
My non-intelligence of human words
Ten thousand pleasures unto me affords;
For while I knew not what they to me said,
Before their souls were into mine convey'd,
Before that living vehicle of wind
Could breathe into me their infected mind,
Before my thoughts were leaven'd with theirs, before
There any mixture was; the holy door,
Or gate of souls was clos'd, and mine being one
Within itself to me alone was known.   30
Then did I dwell within a world of light,
Distinct and separate from all men's sight,
Where I did feel strange thoughts, and such things see
That were, or seem'd, only reveal'd to me.
There I saw all the world enjoy'd by one;
There I was in the world myself alone;

No business serious seem'd but one; no work
But one was found; and that did in me lurk.

    D'ye ask me what? It was with clearer eyes
To see all creatures full of deities: 40
Especially oneself; and to admire
The satisfaction of all true desire;
'Twas to be pleas'd with all that God hath done;
'Twas to enjoy even all beneath the sun;
'Twas with a steady and immediate sense
To feel and measure all the excellence
Of things; 'twas to inherit endless treasure,
And to be fill'd with everlasting pleasure:
To reign in silence, and to sing alone;
To see, love, covet, have, enjoy, and praise, in one; 50
To prize and to be ravish'd; to be true,
Sincere and single in a blessed view
Of all his gifts. Thus was I pent within
A fort, impregnable to any sin:
Till the avenues being open laid,
Whole legions enter'd, and the forts betray'd.
Before which time a pulpit in my mind,
A temple, and a teacher I did find,
With a large text to comment on. No ear,
But eyes themselves were all the hearers there. 60
And every stone, and every star a tongue,
And every gale of wind a curious song.
The heavens were an oracle, and spake
Divinity: the earth did undertake
The office of a priest; and I being dumb
(Nothing besides was dumb) all things did come
With voices and instructions; but when I
Had gain'd a tongue, their power began to die.
Mine ears let other noises in, not theirs;
A noise disturbing all my songs and prayers. 70
My foes pull'd down the temple to the ground,
They my adoring soul did deeply wound,
And casting that into a swoon, destroy'd
The oracle, and all I there enjoy'd.

And having once inspir'd me with a sense
Of foreign vanities, they march out thence
In troops that cover and despoil my coasts,
Being the invisible, most hurtful hosts.
    Yet the first words mine infancy did hear,
The things which in my dumbness did appear,   80
Preventing all the rest, got such a root
Within my heart, and stick so close unto't
It may be trampl'd on, but still will grow;
And nutriment to soil itself will owe.
The first impressions are immortal all:
And let mine enemies whoop, cry, roar, call,
Yet these will whisper if I will but hear,
And penetrate the heart, if not the ear.

Silence

    A quiet silent person may possess
All that is great or high in blessedness.
The inward work is the supreme: for all
The other were occasion'd by the Fall.
A man, that seemeth idle to the view
Of others, may the greatest business do.
Those acts which Adam in his innocence
Performed, carry all the excellence.
These outward busy acts he knew not, were
But meaner matters, of a lower sphere.   10
Building of churches, giving to the poor,
In dust and ashes lying on the floor,
Administ'ring of justice, preaching peace,
Ploughing and toiling for a forc'd increase,
With visiting the sick, or governing
The rude and ignorant: this was a thing
As then unknown. For neither ignorance
Nor poverty, nor sickness did advance
Their banner in the world, till sin came in:

These therefore were occasion'd all by sin. 20
The first and only work he had to do,
Was in himself to feel his bliss, to view
His sacred treasures, to admire, rejoice,
Sing praises with a sweet and heavenly voice,
See, prize, give thanks within, and love,
Which is the high and only work, above
Them all. And this at first was mine; these were
My exercises of the highest sphere.
To see, approve, take pleasure, and rejoice
Within, is better than an empty voice: 30
No melody in words can equal that;
The sweetest organ, lute, or harp is flat
And dull, compar'd thereto. And O that still
I might admire my Father's love and skill!
This is to honour, worship, and adore,
This is to love Him: nay it is far more.
It is to enjoy Him, and to imitate
The life and glory of His high estate.
'Tis to receive with holy reverence,
To understand His gifts, and with a sense 40
Of pure devotion, and humility,
To prize His works, His love to magnify.
O happy ignorance of other things,
Which made me present with the King of Kings!
And like Him too! All spirit, life, and power,
All love and joy, in His eternal bower.
A world of innocence as then was mine,
In which the joys of Paradise did shine,
And while I was not here I was in Heaven,
Not resting one, but every day in seven. 50
Forever minding with a lively sense
The universe in all its excellence.
No other thoughts did intervene, to cloy,
Divert, extinguish, or eclipse my joy.
No other customs, new-found wants, or dreams
Invented here polluted my pure streams.
No aloes or dregs, no Wormwood star

Was seen to fall into the sea from far.
No rotten soul did, like an apple, near
My soul approach. There's no contagion here. 60
An unperceived donor gave all pleasures,
There nothing was but I, and all my treasures.
In that fair world one only was the friend,
One golden stream, one spring, one only end.
There only one did sacrifice and sing
To only one eternal heavenly King.
The union was so strait between them two,
That all was either's which my soul could view.
His gifts, and my possessions, both our treasures;
He mine, and I the ocean of His pleasures. 70
He was an ocean of delights from whom
The living springs and golden streams did come:
My bosom was an ocean into which
They all did run. And me they did enrich.
A vast and infinite capacity
Did make my bosom like the Deity,
In whose mysterious and celestial mind
All ages and all worlds together shin'd.
Who tho He nothing said did always reign,
And in Himself eternity contain. 80
The world was more in me than I in it.
The King of Glory in my soul did sit.
And to Himself in me He always gave
All that He takes delight to see me have.
For so my spirit was an endless sphere,
Like God Himself, and Heaven and earth was there.

My Spirit

I

My naked simple life was I.
    That act so strongly shin'd
Upon the earth, the sea, the sky,

It was the substance of my mind.
        The sense itself was I.
I felt no dross nor matter in my soul,
No brims nor borders, such as in a bowl
We see, my essence was capacity.
        That felt all things,
            The thought that springs
Therefrom's itself. It hath no other wings
    To spread abroad, nor eyes to see,
        Nor hands distinct to feel,
            Nor knees to kneel:
But being simple like the Deity
    In its own centre is a sphere
    Not shut up here, but everywhere.

2

    It acts not from a centre to
        Its object as remote,
    But present is, when it doth view,
    Being with the being it doth note.
        Whatever it doth do,
It doth not by another engine work,
But by itself: which in the act doth lurk.
Its essence is transform'd into a true
        And perfect act.
        And so exact
Hath God appear'd in this mysterious fact,
    That 'tis all eye, all act, all sight,
        And what it please can be,
            Not only see,
Or do; for 'tis more voluble than light:
    Which can put on ten thousand forms,
    Being cloth'd with what itself adorns.

3

    This made me present evermore
        With whatsoe'er I saw.
    An object, if it were before

My eye, was by Dame Nature's law,
        Within my soul. Her store
Was all at once within me; all her treasures
Were my immediate and internal pleasures,
Substantial joys, which did inform my mind.
        With all she wrought,
        My soul was fraught,
And every object in my heart a thought
    Begot, or was; I could not tell,
        Whether the things did there
            Themselves appear,
Which in my spirit truly seem'd to dwell;
    Or whether my conforming mind
    Were not even all that therein shin'd.

4
    But yet of this I was most sure,
        That at the utmost length
    (So worthy was it to endure),
    My soul could best express its strength.
        It was so quick and pure,
That all my mind was wholly everywhere,
Whate'er it saw, 'twas ever wholly there;
The sun ten thousand legions off, was nigh:
            The utmost star,
            Tho seen from far,
Was present in the apple of my eye.
    There was my sight, my life, my sense,
        My substance and my mind.
        My spirit shin'd
Even there, not by a transeunt influence.
    The act was immanent, yet there.
    The thing remote, yet felt even here.

5
    O joy! O wonder, and delight!
        O sacred mystery!
    My soul a spirit infinite!

An image of the Deity!
A pure substantial light!
That being greatest which doth nothing seem!
Why, 'twas my all, I nothing did esteem
But that alone. A strange mysterious sphere!
A deep abyss
That sees and is
The only proper place of heavenly bliss.
To its Creator 'tis so near   80
In love and excellence,
In life and sense,
In greatness, worth, and nature; and so dear;
In it, without hyperbole,
The son and friend of God we see.

6

A strange extended orb of joy,
Proceeding from within,
Which did on every side convey
Itself, and being nigh of kin
To God did every way   90
Dilate itself even in an instant, and
Like an indivisible centre stand
At once surrounding all eternity.
'Twas not a sphere
Yet did appear
One infinite. 'Twas somewhat everywhere.
And tho it had a power to see
Far more, yet still it shin'd
And was a mind
Exerted for it saw infinity.   100
'Twas not a sphere, but 'twas a power
Invisible, and yet a bower.

7
O wondrous self! O sphere of light,
O sphere of joy most fair;
O act, O power infinite;

O subtle and unbounded air!
O living orb of sight!
Thou which within me art, yet me! Thou eye,
And temple of His whole infinity!
O what a world art thou! A world within!
    All things appear,
    All objects are
Alive in thee! Supersubstantial, rare,
    Above themselves, and nigh of kin
    To those pure things we find
    In His great mind
Who made the world! tho now eclips'd by sin.
    There they are useful and divine,
    Exalted there they ought to shine.

The Apprehension

If this I did not every moment see,
    And if my thoughts did stray
    At any time, or idly play,
    And fix on other objects, yet
    This apprehension set
    In me
Was all my whole felicity.

Fullness

    That light, that sight, that thought,
    Which in my soul at first He wrought,
Is sure the only act to which I may
    Assent today:
    The mirror of an endless life,
    The shadow of a virgin wife,
A spiritual world standing within,
    An universe enclos'd in skin.

    My power exerted, or my perfect being,
If not enjoying, yet an act of seeing.   10
                My bliss
            Consists in this,
            My duty too
            In this I view.
      It is a fountain or a spring,
    Refreshing me in everything.
From whence those living streams I do derive,
By which my thirsty soul is kept alive.
            The centre and the sphere
            Of my delights are here.   20
            It is my David's tower,
            Where all my armour lies,
            The fountain of my power,
            My bliss, my sacrifice:
                A little spark,
            That shining in the dark,
Makes, and encourages my soul to rise.
  The root of hope, the golden chain,
  Whose end is, as the poets feign,
    Fasten'd to the very throne   30
              Of Jove.
       It is a stone,
       On which I sit,
       An endless benefit,
That being made my regal throne,
            Doth prove
An oracle of His eternal love.

Nature

  That custom is a second nature, we
  Most plainly find by nature's purity.
  For nature teacheth nothing but the truth.
  I'm sure mine did in my virgin youth.
  The very day my spirit did inspire,

The world's fair beauty set my soul on fire.
My senses were informers to my heart,
The conduits of His glory, power, and art.
His greatness, wisdom, goodness I did see,
His glorious love, and His eternity,
Almost as soon as born: and every sense
Was in me like to some intelligence.
I was by nature prone and apt to love
All light and beauty, both in Heaven above,
And earth beneath, prone even to admire,
Adore and praise as well as to desire.
My inclinations rais'd me up on high,
And guided me to all infinity.
A secret self I had enclos'd within,
That was not bounded with my clothes or skin,
Or terminated with my sight, the sphere
Of which was bounded with the heavens here:
But that did rather, like the subtle light,
Secur'd from rough and raging storms by night,
Break through the lantern's sides, and freely ray
Dispersing and dilating every way:
Whose steady beams too subtle for the wind,
Are such, that we their bounds can scarcely find.
It did encompass, and possess rare things,
But yet felt more, and on its angel's wings
Pierc'd through the skies immediately, and sought
For all that could beyond all worlds be thought.
It did not move, nor one way go, but stood,
And by dilating of itself, all good
It strove to see, as if 'twere present there,
Even while it present stood conversing here;
And more suggested than I could discern,
Or ever since by any means could learn.
Vast unaffected wonderful desires,
Like inward, native, uncaus'd, hidden fires,
Sprang up with expectations very strange,
Which into new desires did quickly change.
For all I saw beyond the azure round,

Was endless darkness with no beauty crown'd.
Why beauty should not there, as well as here,
Why goodness should not likewise there appear,
Why treasures and delights should bounded be,
Since there is such a wide infinity:
These were the doubts and troubles of my soul,
By which I do perceive without control, 50
A world of endless joys by nature made,
That needs must flourish ever, never fade.
A wide, magnificent, and spacious sky,
So rich 'tis worthy of the Deity,
Clouds here and there like winged chariots flying,
Flowers ever flourishing, yet always dying,
A day of glory where I all things see,
As 'twere enrich'd with beams of light for me,
And drown'd in glorious rays of purer light,
Succeeded with a black, yet glorious night, 60
Stars sweetly shedding to my pleased sense,
On all things their nocturnal influence,
With secret rooms in times and ages more
Past and to come enlarging my great store:
These all in order present unto me
My happy eyes did in a moment see
With wonders thereto, to my soul unknown,
Till they by men and reading first were shown.
All which were made that I might ever be
With some great workman, some great Deity. 70
But yet there were new rooms, and spaces more,
Beyond all these, new regions o'er and o'er,
Into all which my pent-up soul like fire
Did break, surmounting all I here admire.
The spaces fill'd were like a cabinet
Of joys before me most distinctly set:
The empty, like to large and vacant room
For fancy to enlarge in, and presume
A space for more, remov'd, but yet adorning
These near at hand, that pleas'd me every morning. 80
Here I was seated to behold new things,

In the fair fabric of the King of Kings.
All, all was mine. The fountain tho not known,
Yet that there must be one was plainly shown.
Which fountain of delights must needs be Love,
As all the goodness of the things did prove.
It shines upon me from the highest skies,
And all its creatures for my sake doth prize,
Of whose enjoyment I am made the end:
While how the same is so I comprehend. 90

Ease

1

How easily doth Nature teach the soul,
How irresistible is her infusion!
There's nothing found that can her force control,
But sin. How weak and feeble's all delusion!

2

Things false are forc'd, and most elaborate,
Things pure and true are obvious unto sense;
The first impressions, in our earthly state,
Are made by things most great in excellence.

3

How easy is it to believe the sky
Is wide and great and fair? How soon may we 10
Be made to know the sun is bright and high,
And very glorious, when its beams we see?

4

That all the earth is one continued globe,
And that all men thereon are living treasures,
That fields and meadows are a glorious robe,
Adorning it with sweet and heavenly pleasures;

5

That all we see is ours, and everyone
Possessor of the whole; that every man
Is like a god incarnate on the throne,
Even like the first for whom the world began;   20

6

Whom all are taught to honour, serve, and love,
Because he is belov'd of God unknown;
And therefore is on earth itself above
All others, that his wisdom might be shown:

7

That all may happy be, each one most blest,
Both in himself and others; all most high,
While all by each, and each by all possess'd,
Are intermutual joys, beneath the sky.

8

This shows a wise contrivance, and discovers
Some great Creator sitting on the throne,   30
That so disposeth things for all His lovers,
That everyone might reign like God alone.

Speed

1

The liquid pearl in springs,
The useful and the precious things
Are in a moment known.
Their very glory does reveal their worth
(And that doth set their glory forth);
As soon as I was born, they all were shown.

2

True living wealth did flow,
In crystal streams below

    My feet, and trilling down
In pure, transparent, soft, sweet, melting pleasures,
    Like precious and diffusive treasures,
At once my body fed, and soul did crown.

3

    I was as high and great,
    As kings are in their seat.
    All other things were mine.
The world my house, the creatures were my goods,
    Fields, mountains, valleys, woods,
Floods, cities, churches, men, for me did shine.

4

    Great, lofty, endless, stable,
    Various and innumerable,
    Bright, useful, fair, divine,
Immovable and sweet the treasures were,
    The sacred objects did appear
Most rich and beautiful, as well as mine.

5

    New all! New burnish'd joys;
    Tho now by other toys
    Eclips'd: new all and mine.
Great truth so sacred seem'd for this to me,
    Because the things which I did see
Were such, my state I knew to be divine.

6

    Nor did the angels' faces,
    The glories, and the graces,
    The beauty, peace, and joy
Of Heaven itself, more sweetness yield to me.
    Till filthy sin did all destroy,
These were the offspring of the Deity.

The Design

1

When first Eternity stoop'd down to nought,
   And in the earth its likeness sought,
When first it out of nothing fram'd the skies,
     And form'd the moon and sun
   That we might see what it had done,
       It was so wise,
       That it did prize
Things truly greatest, brightest, fairest, best.
   All which it made, and left the rest.

2

Then did it take such care about the Truth,   10
   Its daughter, that even in her youth,
Her face might shine upon us, and be known,
     That by a better fate,
   It other toys might antedate,
       As soon as shown;
       And be our own,
While we were hers; and that a virgin love
   Her best inheritance might prove.

3

Thoughts undefiled, simple, naked, pure;
   Thoughts worthy ever to endure,   20
Our first and disengaged thoughts it loves,
     And therefore made the Truth,
   In infancy and tender youth,
       So obvious to
       Our easy view
That it doth prepossess our soul, and proves
   The cause of what it all ways moves.

4

By merit and desire it doth allure;
   For Truth is so divine and pure,

So rich and acceptable, being seen
    (Not parted, but in whole),
That it doth draw and force the soul,
      As the great queen
      Of bliss, between
Whom and the soul, no one pretender ought
    Thrust in, to captivate a thought.

5

Hence did Eternity contrive to make
    The Truth so fair for all our sake
That being Truth, and fair and easy too,
      While it on all doth shine,
    We might by it become divine
        Being led to woo
        The thing we view,
And as chaste virgins early with it join,
    That with it we might likewise shine.

6

Eternity doth give the richest things
    To every man, and makes all kings.
The best and richest things it doth convey
      To all, and everyone.
    It raised me unto a throne!
        Which I enjoy,
        In such a way,
That Truth her daughter is my only bride,
    Her daughter Truth's my chiefest pride.

7

All mine! And seen so easily! How great, how blest!
    How soon am I of all possess'd!
My infancy no sooner opes its eyes,
      But straight the spacious earth
    Abounds with joy, peace, glory, mirth,
        And being wise,
        The very skies,

And stars do mine become; being all possess'd
    Even in that way that is the best.

The Person

1

Ye sacred limbs,
A richer blazon I will lay
    On you, than first I found:
    That like celestial kings,
Ye might with ornaments of joy
    Be always crown'd.
A deep vermilion on a red,
On that a scarlet I will lay,
    With gold I'll crown your head,
    Which like the sun shall ray.
With robes of glory and delight
    I'll make you bright.
Mistake me not, I do not mean to bring
    New robes, but to display the thing:
Nor paint, nor clothe, nor crown, nor add a ray,
But glorify by taking all away.

2

The naked things
Are most sublime, and brightest show,
    When they alone are seen:
    Men's hands than angels' wings
Are truer wealth even here below:
    For those but seem.
Their worth they then do best reveal,
When we all metaphors remove,
    For metaphors conceal,
    And only vapours prove.
They best are blazon'd when we see
    The anatomy,

Survey the skin, cut up the flesh, the veins
    Unfold: the glory there remains.
The muscles, fibres, arteries, and bones
Are better far than crowns and precious stones.

3
    Shall I not then
Delight in these most sacred treasures
    Which my great Father gave,
    Far more than other men
Delight in gold? Since these are pleasures
    That make us brave!
Far braver than the pearl and gold
That glitter on a lady's neck!
    The rubies we behold,
    The diamonds that deck
The hands of queens, compar'd unto
    The hands we view;
The softer lilies, and the roses are
    Less ornaments to those that wear
The same, than are the hands, and lips, and eyes
Of those who those false ornaments so prize.

4
    Let verity
Be thy delight: let me esteem
    True wealth far more than toys:
    Let sacred riches be,
While falser treasures only seem,
    My real joys.
For golden chains and bracelets are
But gilded manacles, whereby
    Old Satan doth ensnare,
    Allure, bewitch the eye.
Thy gifts O God alone I'll prize,
    My tongue, my eyes,
My cheeks, my lips, my ears, my hands, my feet,
    Their harmony is far more sweet;

Their beauty true. And these in all my ways
Shall themes become, and organs of Thy praise.

The Estate

1

But shall my soul no wealth possess,
    No outward riches have?
Shall hands and eyes alone express
    Thy bounty? Which the grave
Shall straight devour. Shall I become
Within myself a living tomb
Of useless wonders? Shall the fair and brave
And great endowments of my soul lie waste,
Which ought to be a fountain, and a womb
    Of praises unto Thee?
Shall there no outward objects be,
    For these to see and taste?
Not so, my God, for outward joys and pleasures
Are even the things for which my limbs are treasures.

2

My palate ought to be a stone
    To try Thy joys upon;
And every member ought to be
    A tongue, to sing to Thee.
There's not an eye that's fram'd by Thee,
    But ought Thy life and love, to see.
Nor is there, Lord, upon mine head an ear,
But that the music of Thy works should hear.
Each toe, each finger framed by Thy skill,
    Ought ointments to distil.
Ambrosia, nectar, wine should flow
    From every joint I owe,
Or things more rich; while all mine inward powers
Are blessed, joyful, and eternal bowers.

3

They ought, my God, to be the pipes,
    And conduits of Thy praise.
Men's bodies were not made for stripes,
    Nor anything but joys.
They were not made to be alone:
But made to be the very throne
Of blessedness, to be like suns, whose rays,
Dispersed, scatter many thousand ways.
They drink in nectars, and disburse again
    In purer beams, those streams,
Those nectars which are caus'd by joys.
    And as the spacious main
Doth all the rivers, which it drinks, return,
Thy love receiv'd doth make the soul to burn.

4

Elixirs richer are than dross,
    And ends are more divine
Than causes are: material loss
    Materials (tho they shine
Like gold and silver) are, compar'd
To what thy spirit doth regard,
Thy soul desire, thy love embrace, thy mind
Esteem, thy nature most illustrious find.
These are the things wherewith we God reward.
    Our love He more doth prize:
Our gratitude is in His eyes,
    Far richer than the skies.
And those affections which we do return,
Are like the love which in Himself doth burn.

5

We plough the very skies, as well
    As earth, the spacious seas
Are ours; the stars all gems excel.
    The air was made to please
The souls of men: devouring fire

Doth feed and quicken man's desire.
The sun itself doth in its glory shine,
And gold and silver out of very mire,
And pearls and rubies out of earth refine,
   While herbs and flowers aspire
To touch and make our feet divine.
    How glorious is man's fate!
The laws of God, the works He did create,
His ancient ways, are His, and my estate.   70

The Inquiry

1

Men may delighted be with springs,
 While trees and herbs their senses please,
And taste even living nectar in the seas:
  May think their members things
Of earthly worth at least, if not divine,
And sing because the earth for them doth shine.

2

But can the angels take delight,
 To see such faces here beneath?
Or can perfumes indeed from dunghills breathe?
  Or is the world a sight   10
Worthy of them? Then may we mortals be
Surrounded with eternal clarity.

3

Even holy angels may come down
 To walk on earth, and see delights,
That feed and please, even here, their appetites.
  Our joys may make a crown
For them. And in His tabernacle men may be
Like palms we mingled with the cherubs see.

4

Men's senses are indeed the gems,
    Their praises the most sweet perfumes,   20
Their eyes the thrones, their hearts the heavenly rooms,
        Their souls the diadems,
Their tongues the organs which they love to hear,
Their cheeks and faces like to theirs appear.

5

The wonders which our God hath done,
    The glories of His attributes,
Like dangling apples or like golden fruits,
        Angelic joys become.
His wisdom shines, on earth His love doth flow,
Like myrrh or incense even here below.   30

6

And shall not we such joys possess,
    Which God for man did chiefly make?
The angels have them only for our sake!
        And yet they all confess
His glory here on earth to be divine,
And that His Godhead in His works doth shine.

The Circulation

1

    As fair ideas from the sky,
        Or images of things,
    Unto a spotless mirror fly,
        On unperceived wings;
    And lodging there affect the sense,
        As if at first they came from thence;
While being there, they richly beautify
The place they fill, and yet communicate
Themselves, reflecting to the seer's eye,

    Just such is our estate.
  No praise can we return again,
  No glory in ourselves possess,
But what derived from without we gain,
From all the mysteries of blessedness.

2

No man breathes out more vital air
    Than he before suck'd in.
Those joys and praises must repair
    To us, which 'tis a sin
  To bury in a senseless tomb.
  An earthly wight must be the heir
Of all those joys the holy angels prize,
He must a king, before a priest become,
And gifts receive, or ever sacrifice.
    'Tis blindness makes us dumb.
  Had we but those celestial eyes,
  Whereby we could behold the sum
Of all His bounties, we should overflow
With praises, did we but their causes know.

3

  All things to circulations owe
    Themselves; by which alone
  They do exist: they cannot show
    A sigh, a word, a groan,
  A colour, or a glimpse of light,
    The sparkle of a precious stone,
A virtue, or a smell; a lovely sight,
A fruit, a beam, an influence, a tear;
But they another's livery must wear:
    And borrow matter first,
  Before they can communicate.
  Whatever's empty is accurst:
And this doth show that we must some estate
Possess, or never can communicate.

4

    A sponge drinks in that water, which
        Is afterwards express'd.
    A liberal hand must first be rich:
        Who blesseth must be blest.
    The thirsty earth drinks in the rain,
    The trees suck moisture at their roots,
Before the one can lavish herbs again,
Before the other can afford us fruits.
No tenant can raise corn, or pay his rent,
        Nor can even have a lord,
    That has no land. No spring can vent,
        No vessel any wine afford
Wherein no liquor's put. No empty purse
Can pounds or talents of itself disburse.

5

    Flame that ejects its golden beams,
        Sups up the grosser air;
    To seas, that pour out their streams
        In springs, those streams repair;
    Receiv'd ideas make even dreams.
    No fancy painteth foul or fair
But by the ministry of inward light,
That in the spirits cherisheth its sight.
The moon returneth light, and some men say
        The very sun no ray
    Nor influence could have, did it
    No foreign aids, no food admit.
The earth no exhalations would afford,
Were not its spirits by the sun restor'd.

6

    All things do first receive, that give.
        Only 'tis God above,
    That from, and in Himself doth live,
        Whose all-sufficient love
    Without original can flow

       And all the joys and glories show
Which mortal man can take delight to know.
He is the primitive eternal spring,
   The endless ocean of each glorious thing.
       The soul a vessel is,　　　　　　　　　　80
         A spacious bosom to contain
         All the fair treasures of His bliss
Which run like rivers from, into the main,
And all it doth receive returns again.

Amendment

1

       That all things should be mine:
This makes His bounty most divine.
But that they all more rich should be,
         And far more brightly shine,
           As us'd by me:
It ravisheth my soul to see the end,
To which this work so wonderful doth tend.

2

       That we should make the skies
More glorious far before Thine eyes,
Than Thou didst make them, and even Thee　　10
         Far more Thy works to prize,
           As us'd they be,
Than as they're made; is a stupendous work,
Wherein Thy wisdom mightily doth lurk.

3

       Thy greatness and Thy love,
Thy power, in this, my joy doth move,
Thy goodness and felicity,
         In this express'd above
           All praise, I see:

While Thy great Godhead over all doth reign,
And such an end in such a sort attain.

4

What bound may we assign,
O God, to any work of Thine!
Their endlessness discovers Thee
In all to be divine;
A Deity,
That wilt for evermore exceed the end
Of all that creatures' wit can comprehend.

5

Am I a glorious spring
Of joys and riches to my King?
Are men made gods! And may they see
So wonderful a thing
As God in me!
And is my soul a mirror that must shine
Even like the sun, and be far more divine?

6

Thy soul, O God, doth prize
The seas, the earth, our souls, the skies,
As we return the same to Thee;
They more delight Thine eyes,
And sweeter be,
As unto Thee we offer up the same,
Than as to us, from Thee at first they came.

7

O how doth sacred love
His gifts refine, exalt, improve!
Our love to creatures makes them be
In Thine esteem above
Themselves to Thee!
O here His goodness evermore admire:
He made our souls to make His creatures higher.

The Demonstration

1

The highest things are easiest to be shown,
And only capable of being known.
    A mist involves the eye,
     While in the middle it doth lie;
    And till the ends of things are seen,
The way's uncertain that doth stand between.
    As in the air we see the clouds
      Like winding sheets, or shrouds:
    Which tho they nearer are obscure
The sun, which higher far, is far more pure.

2

Its very brightness makes it near the eye,
Tho many thousand leagues beyond the sky.
    Its beams by violence
     Invade, and ravish distant sense.
    Only extremes and heights are known;
No certainty, where no perfection's shown.
    Extremities of blessedness
      Compel us to confess
    A God indeed. Whose excellence,
In all His works, must needs exceed all sense.

3

And for this cause incredibles alone
May be by demonstration to us shown.
    Those things that are most bright
     Sun-like appear in their own light.
    And nothing's truly seen that's mean:
Be it a sand, an acorn, or a bean,
    It must be cloth'd with endless glory,
      Before its perfect story
     (Be the spirit ne'er so clear)
Can in its causes and its ends appear.

4

What can be more incredible than this,
Where may we find a more profound abyss?
    What heavenly height can be
    Transcendent to this summity!
    What more desirable object can
Be offer'd to the soul of hungering man!
    His gifts as they to us come down
        Are infinite, and crown
    The soul with strange fruitions; yet
Returning from us they more value get.   40

5

And what than this can be more plain and clear,
What truth than this more evident appear!
    The Godhead cannot prize
    The sun at all, nor yet the skies,
    Or air, or earth, or trees, or seas,
Or stars, unless the soul of man they please.
    He neither sees with human eyes
        Nor needs Himself seas, skies,
    Or earth, or anything: He draws
No breath, nor eats or drinks by nature's laws.   50

6

The joy and pleasure which His soul doth take
In all His works is for His creatures' sake.
    So great a certainty
    We in this holy doctrine see
    That there could be no worth at all
In anything material, great or small,
    Were not some creature more alive,
        Whence it might worth derive.
    God is the spring whence things came forth,
Souls are the fountains of their real worth.   60

7

The joy and pleasure which His soul doth take
In all His works is for His creatures' sake.
    Yet doth He take delight
  That's altogether infinite
  In them even as they from Him come.
For such His love and goodness is, the sum
    Of all His happiness doth seem,
      At least in His esteem,
    In that delight and joy to lie
Which is His blessed creatures' melody.   70

8

In them He sees, and feels, and smells, and lives,
In them affected is to whom He gives:
    In them ten thousand ways,
  He all his works again enjoys,
  All things from Him to Him proceed
By them; are His in them: as if indeed
    His Godhead did itself exceed.
    To them He all conveys;
  Nay even Himself: He is the end
To whom in them Himself, and all things tend.   80

The Anticipation

1

My contemplation dazzles in the end
    Of all I comprehend.
    And soars above all heights,
Diving into the depths of all delights.
    Can He become the end,
      To whom all creatures tend?
Who is the Father of all infinites!
Then may He benefit receive from things,
And be not parent only of all springs.

2

The end doth want the means, and is the cause,
    Whose sake, by nature's laws,
    Is that for which they are.
Such sands, such dangerous rocks we must beware.
    From all eternity
    A perfect Deity
Most great and blessed He doth still appear.
His essence perfect was in all its features,
He ever blessed in His joys and creatures.

3

From everlasting He these joys did need,
    And all these joys proceed
    From Him eternally.
From everlasting His felicity
    Complete and perfect was:
    Whose bosom is the glass,
Wherein we all things everlasting see.
His name is NOW, His nature is forever.
None can His creatures from their maker sever.

4

The end in Him from everlasting is
    The fountain of all bliss.
    From everlasting it
Efficient was, and influence did emit,
    That caused all. Before
    The world, we do adore
This glorious end: because all benefit
From it proceeds. Both are the very same.
The end and fountain differ but in name.

5

That so the end should be the very spring,
    Of every glorious thing;
    And that which seemeth last,
The fountain and the cause; attain'd so fast,

That it was first; and mov'd
　　　　The efficient, who so lov'd
All worlds and made them for the sake of this,
It shows the end complete before, and is
A perfect token of His perfect bliss.

6

The end complete, the means must needs be so.
　　　　By which we plainly know,
　　　　From all eternity,
The means whereby God is, must perfect be.
　　　　God is Himself the means,
　　　　Whereby He doth exist:
And as the sun by shining's cloth'd with beams,
So from Himself to all His glory streams,
Who is a sun, yet what Himself doth list.

7

His endless wants and His enjoyments be
　　　　From all eternity,
　　　　Immutable in Him:
They are His joys before the cherubim.
　　　　His wants appreciate all,
　　　　And being infinite,
Permit no being to be mean or small
That He enjoys, or is before His sight.
His satisfactions do His wants delight.

8

Wants are the fountains of felicity.
　　　　No joy could ever be
　　　　Were there no want. No bliss,
No sweetness perfect were it not for this.
　　　　Want is the greatest pleasure
　　　　Because it makes all treasure.
O what a wonderful profound abyss
Is God! In whom eternal wants and treasures
Are more delightful 'cause they both are pleasures.

9

He infinitely wanteth all His joys.
    (No want the soul o'ercloys.)
    And all those wanted pleasures
He infinitely hath. What endless measures,
    What heights and depths may we
    In His felicity
Conceive! Whose very wants are endless pleasures.
His life in wants and joys is infinite.   80
And both are felt as His supreme delight.

10

He's not like us; possession doth not cloy,
    Nor sense of want destroy.
    Both always are together:
No force can either from the other sever.
    Yet there's a space between
    That's endless. Both are seen
Distinctly still, and both are seen forever.
As soon as e'er He wanteth all His bliss,
His bliss, tho everlasting, in Him is.   90

11

His essence is all act: He did, that He
    All act might always be.
    His nature burns like fire;
His goodness infinitely doth desire,
    To be by all possess'd;
    His love makes others blest.
It is the glory of His high estate,
And that which I forevermore admire,
He is an act that doth communicate.

12

From all to all eternity He is   100
    That act: an act of bliss:
    Wherein all bliss to all,
That will receive the same, or on Him call,

Is freely given: from whence
'Tis easy even to sense,
To apprehend that all receivers are
In Him, all gifts, all joys, all eyes, even all
At once, that ever will, or shall appear.

13

He is the means of them, they not of Him.
　　The holy cherubim,
　　Souls, angels from Him came
Who is a glorious bright and living flame,
　　That on all things doth shine,
　　And makes their face divine.
And holy, holy, holy, is His name.
He is the means both of Himself and all,
Whom we the fountain, means, and end do call.

14

In whom as in the fountain all things are,
　　In whom all things appear
　　As in the means, and end
From whom they all proceed, to whom they tend.
　　By whom they are made ours
　　Whose souls are spacious bowers
Of all like His. Who ought to have a sense
Of all our wants, of all His excellence,
That while we all, we Him might comprehend.

The Recovery

1

To see us but receive, is such a sight
As makes His treasures infinite!
Because His goodness doth possess
In us, His own, and our own blessedness.
Yea more, His love doth take delight

To make our glory infinite.
    Our blessedness to see
  Is even to the Deity
A beatific vision! He attains
His ends while we enjoy. In us He reigns.

2

  For God enjoy'd is all His end.
  Himself He then doth comprehend.
  When He is blessed, magnified,
Extoll'd, exalted, prais'd and glorified;
  Honour'd, esteem'd, belov'd, enjoy'd,
  Admired, sanctified, obey'd:
    That is receiv'd. For He
  Doth place His whole felicity
In that, who is despised and defied,
Undeified almost if once denied.

3

  In all His works, in all His ways,
  We must His glory see and praise:
  And since our pleasure is the end,
We must His goodness and His love attend.
  If we despise His glorious works,
  Such sin and mischief in it lurks
    That they are all made vain,
  And this is even endless pain
To Him that sees it. Whose diviner grief
Is hereupon (Ah me!) without relief.

4

  We please His goodness that receive:
  Refusers Him of all bereave.
  As bridegrooms know full well that build
A palace for their bride. It will not yield
  Any delight to him at all
  If she for whom he made the hall
    Refuse to dwell in it
  Or plainly scorn the benefit.

Her act that's woo'd, yields more delight and pleasure
If she receives, than all that pile of treasure. 40

5

But we have hands and lips and eyes
And hearts and souls can sacrifice.
And souls themselves are made in vain
If we our evil stubbornness retain.
    Affections, praises, are the things
    For which He gave us all these springs;
        They are the very fruits
    Of all these trees and roots,
The fruits and ends of all His great endeavours,
Which he abolisheth whoever severs. 50

6

'Tis not alone a lively sense,
A clear and quick intelligence,
A free, profound, and full esteem:
Tho these elixirs all and ends too seem;
    But gratitude, thanksgiving, praise,
    A heart return'd for all these joys:
        These are the things admir'd,
    These are the things by Him desir'd.
These are the nectar and the quintessence,
The cream and flower that most affect His sense. 60

7

The voluntary act whereby
These are repaid, is in His eye
More precious than the very sky.
All gold and silver is but empty dross,
    Rubies and sapphires are but loss,
    The very sun and stars and seas
        Far less His spirit please.
    One voluntary act of love
Far more delightful to His soul doth prove
And is above all these as far as Love.

Another

1
He seeks for ours as we do seek for His.
Nay, O my soul, ours is far more His bliss
Than His is ours; at least it so doth seem
    Both in His own and our esteem.

2
His earnest love, His infinite desires,
His living, endless, and devouring fires,
Do rage in thirst, and fervently require
    A love, 'tis strange it should desire.

3
We cold and careless are, and scarcely think
Upon the glorious spring whereat we drink.
Did He not love us, we could be content.
    We wretches are indifferent!

4
He prizes our love with infinite esteem.
And seeks it so that it doth almost seem
Even all His blessedness. His love doth prize
    It as the only sacrifice.

5
'Tis death, my soul, to be indifferent;
Set forth thyself unto thy whole extent,
And all the glory of His passion prize,
    Who for thee lives, who for thee dies.

6
His goodness made thy love so great a pleasure,
His goodness made thy soul so great a treasure
To thee and Him: that thou might'st both inherit.
    Prize it according to its merit.

7

There is no goodness nor desert in thee,
For which thy love so coveted should be;
His goodness is the fountain of thy worth.
    O live to love and set it forth.

8

Thou nothing giv'st to Him, He gave all things
To thee, and made thee like the King of Kings.   30
His love the fountain is of Heaven and earth,
    The cause of all thy joy and mirth.

9

Thy love is nothing but itself, and yet
So infinite is His, that He doth set
A value infinite upon it. Oh!
    This, canst thou careless be, and know!

10

Let that same goodness, which is infinite,
Esteems thy love with infinite delight,
Tho less than His, tho nothing, always be
    An object infinite to thee.   40

11

And as it is the cause of all esteem,
Of all the worth which in thy love doth seem,
So let it be the cause of all thy pleasure
    Causing its being and its measure.

Love

1

O nectar! O delicious stream!
O ravishing and only pleasure! Where
    Shall such another theme

Inspire my tongue with joys, or please mine ear!
    Abridgement of delights!
    And queen of sights!
O mine of rarities! O kingdom wide!
O more! O cause of all! O glorious bride!
    O God! O bride of God! O king!
    O soul and crown of everything!

2

    Did not I covet to behold
Some endless monarch, that did always live
    In palaces of gold,
Willing all kingdoms, realms, and crowns to give
    Unto my soul! Whose love
    A spring might prove
Of endless glories, honours, friendships, pleasures,
Joys, praises, beauties, and celestial treasures!
    Lo, now I see there's such a King,
    The fountainhead of everything!

3

    Did my ambition ever dream
Of such a Lord, of such a love! Did I
    Expect so sweet a stream
As this at any time! Could any eye
    Believe it? Why, all power
    Is used here
Joys down from Heaven on my head to shower,
And Jove beyond the fiction doth appear
    Once more in golden rain to come
    To Danae's pleasing fruitful womb.

4

    His Ganymede! His life! His joy!
Or He comes down to me, or takes me up
    That I might be His boy,
And fill, and taste, and give, and drink the cup.
    But these (tho great) are all

Too short and small,
Too weak and feeble pictures to express
The true mysterious depths of blessedness.
I am His image, and His friend.
His son, bride, glory, temple, end.

Thoughts I

1

Ye brisk divine and living things,
Ye great exemplars, and ye heavenly springs
    Which I within me see;
      Ye machines great,
  Which in my spirit God did seat,
  Ye engines of felicity;
  Ye wondrous fabrics of His hands,
Who all possesseth that He understands;
  That ye are pent within my breast,
  Yet rove at large from east to west,
And are invisible, yet infinite;
Is my transcendent, and my best delight.

2

  By you I do the joys possess
Of yesterday's yet-present blessedness;
    As in a mirror clear,
      Old objects I
  Far distant do even now descry
  Which by your help are present here.
  Ye are yourselves the very pleasures,
The sweetest, last, and most substantial treasures,
  The offsprings and effects of bliss
  By whose return my glory is
Renew'd, and represented to my view:
O ye delights, most pure, divine, and true!

3

    Ye thoughts and apprehensions are
The heavenly streams which fill the soul with rare
        Transcendent perfect pleasures.
        At any time,
    As if ye still were in your prime,
    Ye open all His heavenly treasures.
    His joys accessible are found
To you, and those things enter which surround
    The soul. Ye living things within!
    Where had all joy and glory been
Had ye not made the soul those things to know,
Which seated in it make the fairest show?

4

    I know not by what secret power
Ye flourish so; but ye within your bower,
        More beautiful do seem,
           And better meat
    Ye daily yield my soul to eat,
    Than even the objects I esteem
    Without my soul. What were the sky,
What were the sun, or stars, did ye not lie
    In me! and represent them there
    Where else they never could appear!
Yea what were bliss without such thoughts to me,
What were my life, what were the Deity?

5

    O ye conceptions of delight!
Ye that inform my soul with life and sight!
        Ye representatives, and springs
           Of inward pleasure!
    Ye joys! Ye ends of outward treasure!
    Ye inward, and ye living things!

The thought, or joy conceived is
The inward fabric of my standing bliss.
   It is the substance of my mind
   Transform'd, and with its objects lin'd.
The quintessence, elixir, spirit, cream.
'Tis strange that things unseen should be supreme. 60

6

The eye's confin'd, the body's pent
In narrow room: limbs are of small extent.
      But thoughts are always free.
        And as they're best,
   So can they even in the breast,
   Rove o'er the world with liberty:
   Can enter ages, present be
In any kingdom, into bosoms see.
   Thoughts, thoughts can come to things, and view,
     What bodies can't approach unto. 70
They know no bar, denial, limit, wall:
But have a liberty to look on all.

7

Like bees they fly from flower to flower,
Appear in every closet, temple, bower;
     And suck the sweet from thence,
        No eye can see:
   As tasters to the Deity.
   Incredible's their excellence.
   For evermore they will be seen
Nor ever moulder into less esteem. 80
   They ever show an equal face,
   And are immortal in their place.
Ten thousand ages hence they are as strong,
Ten thousand ages hence they are as young.

Bliss

1

All bliss
Consists in this,
To do as Adam did:
And not to know those superficial toys
    Which in the garden once were hid,
    Those little new invented things.
Cups, saddles, crowns are childish joys.
    So ribbons are and rings.
Which all our happiness destroys.

2

Nor God
In His abode
Nor saints nor little boys
Nor angels made them; only foolish men,
    Grown mad with custom, on those toys
    Which more increase their wants, do dote.
And when they older are do then
    Those baubles chiefly note
With greedier eyes, more boys tho men.

Thoughts II

1

A delicate and tender thought
The quintessence is found of all He wrought.
    It is the fruit of all His works,
        Which we conceive,
        Bring forth, and give,
Yea and in which the greater value lurks.
    It is the fine and curious flower,
Which we return, and offer every hour:
    So tender in our Paradise

    That in a trice 10
  It withers straight, and fades away,
If we but cease its beauty to display.

2

Why things so precious, should be made
So prone, so easy, and so apt to fade
  It is not easy to declare.
    But God would have
    His creatures brave
And that too by their own continual care.
  He gave them power every hour,
Both to erect, and to maintain a tower, 20
  Which He far more in us doth prize
    Than all the skies:
  That we might offer it to Him,
And in our souls be like the seraphim.

3

That temple David did intend,
Was but a thought, and yet it did transcend
  King Solomon's. A thought we know
    Is that for which
    God doth enrich
With joys even Heaven above, and earth below. 30
  For that all objects might be seen
He made the orient azure and the green:
  That we might in His works delight.
    And that the sight
  Of those His treasures might inflame
The soul with love to Him, He made the same.

4

This sight which is the glorious end
Of all His works, and which doth comprehend
  Eternity, and time, and space,
    Is far more dear, 40
    And far more near
To Him, than all His glorious dwelling place.

It is a spiritual world within.
A living world, and nearer far of kin
   To God, than that which first He made.
      While that doth fade
   This therefore ever shall endure,
Within the soul as more divine and pure.

'Ye hidden nectars'

1

Ye hidden nectars, which my God doth drink,
   Ye heavenly streams, ye beams divine,
      On which the angels think,
   How quick, how strongly do ye shine!
Ye images of joy that in me dwell,
      Ye sweet mysterious shades
   That do all substances excel,
      Whose glory never fades;
Ye skies, ye seas, ye stars, or things more fair,
O ever, ever unto me repair.   10

2

Ye pleasant thoughts! O how that sun divine
   Appears today which I did see
      So sweetly then to shine,
   Even in my very infancy!
Ye rich ideas which within me live,
      Ye living pictures here,
   Ye spirits that do bring and give
      All joys; when ye appear,
Even Heaven itself, and God, and all in you,
Come down on earth, and please my blessed view.   20

3

I never glorious, great, and rich am found,
   Am never ravished with joy,
      Till ye my soul surround,
      Till ye my blessedness display.

No soul but stone, no man but clay am I,
    No flesh, but dust; till ye
  Delight, invade to move my eye,
    And do replenish me.
My sweet informers and my living treasures,
My great companions, and my only pleasures!

4

O what incredible delights, what fires,
    What appetites, what joys do ye
      Occasion, what desires,
  What heavenly praises! While we see
What every seraphim above admires!
    Your jubilee and trade,
  Ye are so strangely and divinely made,
    Shall never, never fade.
Ye ravish all my soul, of you I twice
Will speak. For in the dark y'are Paradise.

Thoughts III

Thoughts are the angels which we send abroad,
To visit all the parts of God's abode.
Thoughts are the things wherein we all confess
The quintessence of sin and holiness
Is laid. All wisdom in a thought doth shine,
By thoughts alone the soul is made divine.
Thoughts are the springs of all our actions here
On earth, tho they themselves do not appear.
They are the springs of beauty, order, peace,
The cities' gallantries, the fields' increase.
Rule, government, and kingdoms flow from them,
And so doth all the new Jerusalem.
At least the glory, splendour, and delight,
For 'tis by thoughts that even she is bright.
Thoughts are the things wherewith even God is crown'd,
And as the soul without them's useless found,

So are all other creatures too. A thought
Is even the very cream of all He wrought.
All holy fear, and love, and reverence,
With honour, joy, and praise, as well as sense, 20
Are hidden in our thoughts. Thoughts are the things
That us affect: the honey and the stings
Of all that is, are seated in a thought,
Even while it seemeth weak, and next to nought.
The matter of all pleasure, virtue, worth,
Grief, anger, hate, revenge, which words set forth,
Are thoughts alone. Thoughts are the highest things,
The very offspring of the King of Kings.
Thoughts are a kind of strange celestial creature,
That when they're good, they're such in every feature, 30
They bear the image of their Father's face,
And beautify even all His dwelling place:
So nimble and volatile, unconfin'd,
Illimited, to which no form's assign'd,
So changeable, capacious, easy, free,
That what itself doth please a thought may be.
From nothing to infinity it turns,
Even in a moment: now like fire it burns,
Now's frozen ice: now shapes the glorious sun,
Now darkness in a moment doth become, 40
Now all at once: now crowded in a sand,
Now fills the hemisphere, and sees a land:
Now on a sudden's wider than the sky,
And now runs parile with the Deity.
'Tis such, that it may all or nothing be.
And's made so active, voluble, and free
Because 'tis capable of all that's good,
And is the end of all when understood.
A thought can clothe itself with all the treasures
Of God, and be the greatest of His pleasures. 50
It all His laws, and glorious works, and ways,
And attributes, and counsels; all His praise
It can conceive, and imitate, and give:
It is the only being that doth live.
'Tis capable of all perfection here,

Of all His love and joy and glory there.
It is the only beauty that doth shine,
Most great, transcendent, heavenly, and divine.
The very best or worst of things it is,
The basis of all misery or bliss. 60
Its measures and capacities are such,
Their utmost measure we can never touch.
For ornament on ornament may still
Be laid; beauty on beauty, skill on skill,
Strength still on strength, and life itself on life.
'Tis queen of all things, and its maker's wife.
The best of thoughts is yet a thing unknown,
But when 'tis perfect it is like His own:
Intelligible, endless, yet a sphere
Substantial too: in which all things appear. 70
All worlds, all excellences, senses, graces,
Joys, pleasures, creatures, and the angels' faces.
It shall be married ever unto all:
And all embrace, tho now it seemeth small.
A thought, my soul, may omnipresent be.
For all it toucheth which a thought can see.
Oh that mysterious being! Thoughts are things,
Which rightly used make His creatures kings.

Desire

I

For giving me desire,
An eager thirst, a burning ardent fire,
A virgin infant flame,
A love with which into the world I came,
An inward hidden heavenly love,
Which in my soul did work and move,
And ever ever me inflame,
With restless longing heavenly avarice,
That never could be satisfied,

That did incessantly a Paradise
Unknown suggest, and something undescried
    Discern, and bear me to it; be
    Thy name for ever prais'd by me.

2

    My parch'd and wither'd bones
Burnt up did seem: my soul was full of groans:
    My thoughts extensions were:
Like paces, reaches, steps they did appear:
    They somewhat hotly did pursue,
    Knew that they had not all their due;
    Nor ever quiet were;
But made my flesh like hungry thirsty ground,
    My heart a deep profound abyss,
And every joy and pleasure but a wound,
So long as I my blessedness did miss.
    O happiness! A famine burns,
    And all my life to anguish turns!

3

    Where are the silent streams,
The living waters, and the glorious beams,
    The sweet reviving bowers,
The shady groves, the sweet and curious flowers,
    The springs and trees, the heavenly days,
    The flowery meads, and glorious rays,
    The gold and silver towers?
Alas, all these are poor and empty things:
    Trees, waters, days, and shining beams,
Fruits, flowers, bowers, shady groves and springs,
No joy will yield, no more than silent streams.
    These are but dead material toys,
    And cannot make my heavenly joys.

4

    O love! Ye amities,
And friendships, that appear above the skies!

Ye feasts, and living pleasures!
Ye senses, honours, and imperial treasures!
   Ye bridal joys! Ye high delights,
    That satisfy all appetites!
     Ye sweet affections, and
Ye high respects! Whatever joys there be
   In triumphs, whatsoever stand
In amicable sweet society,
Whatever pleasures are at His right hand,   50
    Ye must, before I am divine,
    In full propriety be mine.

5

This soaring sacred thirst,
Ambassador of bliss, approached first,
    Making a place in me,
That made me apt to prize, and taste, and see;
   For not the objects, but the sense
   Of things, doth bliss to souls dispense,
    And make it, Lord, like Thee.
Sense, feeling, taste, complacency, and sight,   60
   These are the true and real joys,
The living flowing inward melting, bright
And heavenly pleasures; all the rest are toys:
   All which are founded in desire,
   As light in flame, and heat in fire.

Thoughts IV

*In thy presence there is fullness
of joy, and at thy right hand there
are pleasures for evermore.*

Thoughts are the wings on which the soul doth fly,
The messengers which soar above the sky,
Elijah's fiery chariot, that conveys
The soul, even here, to those eternal joys.

Thoughts are the privileged posts that soar
Unto His throne, and there appear before
Ourselves approach. These may at any time
Above the clouds, above the stars may climb.
The soul is present by a thought; and sees
The new Jerusalem, the palaces,
The thrones and feasts, the regions of the sky,
The joys and treasures of the Deity.
His wisdom makes all things so bright and pure,
That they are worthy ever to endure.
His glorious works, His laws and counsels are,
When seen, all like Himself, beyond compare.
All ages with His love and glory shine,
As they are His all kingdoms are divine.
Whole hosts of angels at His throne attend,
And joyful praises from His saints ascend.
Thousands of thousands kneel before His face
And all His benefits with joy embrace.
His goodness makes all creatures for His pleasure,
And makes itself His creatures' chiefest treasure.
Almighty power doth itself employ
In all its works to make itself the joy
Of all His hosts, and to complete the bliss
Which omnipresent and eternal is.
His omnipresence is an endless sphere,
Wherein all worlds as His delights appear.
His bounty is the spring of all delight;
Our blessedness, like His, is infinite.
His glory endless is and doth surround
And fill all worlds, without or end or bound.
What hinders then, but we in Heaven may be
Even here on earth did we but rightly see?
As mountains, chariots, horsemen all on fire,
To guard Elisha did of old conspire,
Which yet his servant could not see, being blind,
Ourselves environ'd with His joys we find.
Eternity itself is that true light,
That doth enclose us being infinite.

The very seas do overflow and swim
With precious nectars as they flow from Him.
The stable earth, which we beneath behold,
Is far more precious than if made of gold.
Fowls, fishes, beasts, trees, herbs, and precious flowers,
Seeds, spices, gums, and aromatic bowers,
Wherewith we are enclos'd and serv'd, each day
By His appointment do their tributes pay, 50
And offer up themselves as gifts of love,
Bestow'd on saints, proceeding from above.
Could we but justly, wisely, truly prize
These blessings, we should be above the skies,
And praises sing with pleasant heart and voice,
Adoring with the angels should rejoice.
The fertile clouds give rain, the purer air
Is warm and wholesome, soft and bright and fair.
The stars are wonders which His wisdom names,
The glorious sun the knowing soul inflames. 60
The very heavens in their sacred worth
At once serve us, and set His glory forth.
Their influences touch the grateful sense,
They please the eye with their magnificence.
While in His temple all His saints do sing,
And for His bounty praise their heavenly King.
All these are in His omnipresence still,
As living waters from His throne they trill.
As tokens of His love they all flow down,
Their beauty, use, and worth the soul do crown. 70
Men are like cherubims on either hand,
Whose flaming love by His divine command
Is made a sacrifice to ours: which streams
Throughout all worlds, and fills them all with beams.
We drink our fill, and take their beauty in,
While Jesus' blood refines the soul from sin.
His grievous cross is a supreme delight,
And of all heavenly ones the greatest sight.
His throne is near, 'tis just before our face,
And all eternity His dwelling place. 80

His dwelling place is full of joys and pleasures,
His throne a fountain of eternal treasures.
His omnipresence is all sight and love,
Which whoso sees, he ever dwells above.
With soft embraces it doth clasp the soul,
And watchfully all enemies control.
It enters in, and doth a temple find,
Or make a living one within the mind.
That while God's omnipresence in us lies,
His treasures might be all before our eyes: 90
For minds and souls intent upon them here,
Do with the seraphims above appear:
And are like spheres of bliss, by love and sight,
By joy, thanksgiving, praise, made infinite.
O give me grace to see Thy face, and be
A constant mirror of eternity.
Let my pure soul, transformed to a thought,
Attend upon Thy throne, and as it ought
Spend all its time in feeding on Thy love,
And never from Thy sacred presence move. 100
So shall my conversation ever be
In Heaven, and I, O Lord my God, with Thee!

Goodness

I

The bliss of other men is my delight
   (When once my principles are right):
     And every soul which mine doth see
       A treasury.
The face of God is goodness unto all,
And while He thousands to His throne doth call,
    While millions bathe in pleasures,
     And do behold His treasures,
       The joys of all
        On mine do fall 10

And even my infinity doth seem
A drop, without them, of a mean esteem.

2

The light which on ten thousand faces shines,
    The beams which crown ten thousand vines
    With glory and delight, appear
        As if they were
Reflected only from them all for me,
That I a greater beauty there might see.
    Thus stars do beautify
    The azure canopy.
        Gilded with rays,
        Ten thousand ways
They serve me, while the sun that on them shines
Adorns those stars, and crowns those bleeding vines.

3

Where goodness is within, the soul doth reign.
    Goodness the only sovereign!
    Goodness delights alone to see
        Felicity.
And while the image of His goodness lives
In me, whatever He to any gives
    Is my delight and ends
    In me in all my friends.
        For goodness is
        The spring of bliss,
And 'tis the end of all it gives away,
And all it gives it ever doth enjoy.

4

His goodness! Lord, it is His highest glory!
    The very grace of all His story!
    What other thing can me delight
        But the blest sight
Of His eternal goodness? While His love,
His burning love the bliss of all doth prove

While it beyond the ends
  Of Heaven and earth extends
    And multiplies
    Above the skies
His glory, love, and goodness in my sight,
Is for my pleasure made more infinite.

5

The soft and swelling grapes that on their vines
  Receive the lively warmth that shines
  Upon them, ripen there for me:
    Or drink they be
Or meat. The stars salute my pleased sense
With a deriv'd and borrow'd influence,
  But better vines do grow,
  Far better wines do flow
    Above, and while
    The sun doth smile
Upon the lilies there, and all things warm,
Their pleasant odours do my spirit charm.

6

Their rich affections me like precious seas
  Of nectar and ambrosia please.
  Their eyes are stars, or more divine:
    And brighter shine.
Their lips are soft and swelling grapes, their tongues
A choir of blessed and harmonious songs.
  Their bosoms fraught with love
  Are heavens all heavens above,
And being images of God, they are
The highest joys His goodness did prepare.

POEMS OF FELICITY:
DIVINE REFLECTIONS ON THE NATIVE OBJECTS OF AN INFANT-EYE

(excluding those contained in the Dobell poems)

The Author to the Critical Peruser

The naked truth in many faces shown,
Whose inward beauties very few have known,
A simple light, transparent words, a strain
That lowly creeps, yet maketh mountains plain,
Brings down the highest mysteries to sense
And keeps them there; that is our excellence:
At that we aim; to th'end thy soul might see
With open eyes thy great felicity,
Its objects view, and trace the glorious way
Whereby thou may'st thy highest bliss enjoy.

   No curling metaphors that gild the sense,
Nor pictures here, nor painted eloquence;
No florid streams of superficial gems,
But real crowns and thrones and diadems!
That gold on gold should hiding shining lie
May well be reckon'd baser heraldry.

   An easy style drawn from a native vein,
A clearer stream than that which poets feign,
Whose bottom may, how deep soe'er, be seen,
Is that which I think fit to win esteem.
Else we could speak Zamzummim words, and tell
A tale in tongues that sound like Babel-hell;
In meteors speak, in blazing prodigies,
Things that amaze, but will not make us wise.

On shining banks we could nigh Tagus walk;
In flowery meads of rich Pactolus talk;
Bring in the druids, and the sybils view;
See what the rites are which the Indians do;
Derive along the channel of our quill
The streams that flow from high Parnassus hill;
Ransack all nature's rooms, and add the things
Which Persian courts enrich: to make us kings.
To make us kings indeed! Not verbal ones,
But real kings, exalted unto thrones;

And more than golden thrones! 'Tis this I do,
Letting poetic strains and shadows go.

   I cannot imitate their vulgar sense
Who clothes admire, not the man they fence
Against the cold; and while they wonder at
His rings, his precious stones, his gold and plate,   40
The middle piece, his body and his mind,
They overlook; no beauty in them find:
God's works they hide, their own they magnify,
His they contemn, or careless pass them by.

Their woven silks and well-made suits they prize,
Value their gems, but not their useful eyes,
Their precious hands, their tongues and lips divine,
Their polished flesh where whitest lilies join
With blushing roses and with sapphire veins,
The bones, the joints, and that which else remains   50
Within that curious fabric, life and strength,
I'th' well-compacted breadth and depth and length
Of various limbs, that living engines be
Of glorious worth; God's work they will not see:
Nor yet the soul, in whose concealed face,
Which comprehendeth all unbounded space,
God may be seen; tho she can understand
The length of ages and the tracts of land
That from the zodiac do extended lie
Unto the poles, and view eternity.   60

Even thus do idle fancies, toys, and words
(Like gilded scabbards hiding rusty swords)
Take vulgar souls, who gaze on rich attire
But God's diviner works do ne'er admire.

An Infant-Eye

I

A simple light from all contagion free,
A beam that's purely spiritual, an eye

That's altogether virgin, things doth see
    Even like unto the Deity:
That is, it shineth in an heavenly sense,
And round about (unmov'd) its light dispense.

2

The visive rays are beams of light indeed,
Refined, subtle, piercing, quick and pure;
And as they do the sprightly winds exceed,
    Are worthy longer to endure: 10
They far out-shoot the reach of grosser air,
Which with such excellence may not compare.

3

But being once debas'd, they soon become
Less active than they were before; and then
After distracting objects out they run,
    Which make us wretched men.
A simple infant's eye is such a treasure
That when 'tis lost, w' enjoy no real pleasure.

4

O that my sight had ever simple been!
And never fall'n into a grosser state! 20
Then might I every object still have seen
    (As now I see a golden plate)
In such an heavenly light, as to descry
In it, or by it, my felicity.

5

As easily might soar aloft as move
On earth; and things remote as well as nigh
My joys should be; and could discern the love
    Of God in my tranquillity.
But streams are heavy which the winds can blow:
Whose grosser body must needs move below. 30

6

The East was once my joy; and so the skies
And stars at first I thought; the West was mine:
Then praises from the mountains did arise
  As well as vapours: every vine
Did bear me fruit; the fields my gardens were;
My larger store-house all the hemisphere.

7

But wantonness and avarice got in
And spoil'd my wealth (I never can complain
Enough, till I am purged from my sin
  And made an infant once again)
So that my feeble and disabled sense
Reach'd only near things with its influence.

8

A house, a woman's hand, a piece of gold,
A feast, a costly suit, a beauteous skin
That vied with ivory, I did behold;
  And all my pleasure was in sin:
Who had at first with simple infant-eyes
Beheld as mine even all eternities.

9

O die! die unto all that draws thine eye
From its first objects: let not fading pleasures
Infect thy mind; but see thou carefully
  Bid them adieu. Return: thy treasures
Abide thee still, and in their places stand
Inviting yet, and waiting thy command.

The Return

1
To infancy, O Lord, again I come,
  That I my manhood may improve:

My early tutor is the womb;
   I still my cradle love.
'Tis strange that I should wisest be,
When least I could an error see.

2

Till I gain strength against temptation, I
   Perceive it safest to abide
An infant still; and therefore fly
   (A lowly state may hide
A man from danger) to the womb,
   That I may yet new-born become.

3

My God, Thy bounty then did ravish me!
   Before I learned to be poor,
I always did Thy riches see,
   And thankfully adore:
Thy glory and Thy goodness were
My sweet companions all the year.

News

1

News from a foreign country came,
As if my treasures and my joys lay there;
So much it did my heart inflame,
'Twas wont to call my soul into mine ear;
   Which thither went to meet
    Th' approaching sweet,
   And on the threshold stood
To entertain the secret good;
   It hover'd there
    As if 'twould leave mine ear,
And was so eager to embrace
Th' expected tidings, as they came,

That it could change its dwelling place
    To meet the voice of fame.

2

    As if new tidings were the things
Which did comprise my wished unknown treasure,
    Or else did bear them on their wings,
With so much joy they came, with so much pleasure,
        My soul stood at the gate
            To recreate
        Itself with bliss, and woo
    Its speedier approach; a fuller view
            It fain would take,
        Yet journeys back would make
    Unto my heart, as if 'twould fain
    Go out to meet, yet stay within,
    Fitting a place to entertain
        And bring the tidings in.

3

    What sacred instinct did inspire
My soul in childhood with an hope so strong?
    What secret force mov'd my desire
T' expect my joys beyond the seas, so young?
        Felicity I knew
            Was out of view;
        And being left alone,
    I thought all happiness was gone
            From earth: for this
        I long'd for absent bliss,
    Deeming that sure beyond the seas,
    Or else in something near at hand
    Which I knew not, since nought did please
        I knew, my bliss did stand.

4

    But little did the infant dream
That all the treasures of the world were by,

And that himself was so the cream
And crown of all which round about did lie.
    Yet thus it was! The gem,
      The diadem,
      The ring enclosing all
    That stood upon this earthen ball;   50
      The heavenly eye,
      Much wider than the sky,
Wherein they all included were;
The love, the soul, that was the king
Made to possess them, did appear
      A very little thing.

Felicity

1

Prompted to seek my bliss above the skies,
    How often did I lift mine eyes
      Beyond the spheres!
Dame Nature told me there was endless space
Within my soul; I spied its very face:
    Sure it not for nought appears.
    What is there which a man may see
      Beyond the spheres?
      Felicity.

2

There in the mind of God, that sphere of love   10
    (In nature, height, extent, above
      All other spheres),
A man may see himself, the world, the bride
Of God His church, which as they there are eyed
    Strangely exalted each appears:
    His mind is higher than the space
      Above the spheres,
      Surmounts all place.

3

No empty space; it is all full of sight,
   All soul and life, an eye most bright,
      All light and love;
Which doth at once all things possess and give,
Heaven and earth, and all that therein live;
   It rests at quiet, and doth move;
   Eternal is, yet time includes;
      A scene above
      All interludes.

Adam

1

   God made man upright at the first;
   Man made himself by sin accurst:
Sin is a deviation from the way
Of God: 'tis that wherein a man doth stray
From the first path wherein he was to walk,
   From the first truth he was to talk.

2

   His talk was to be all of praise,
   Thanksgiving, rapture, holy days;
For nothing else did with his state agree:
Being full of wonder and felicity,
He was in thankful sort to meditate
   Upon the throne in which he sate.

3

   No gold, nor trade, nor silver there,
   Nor clothes, nor coin, nor houses were,
No gaudy coaches, feasts, or palaces,
Nor vain inventions newly made to please;
But native truth, and virgin-purity,
   An uncorrupt simplicity.

4

His faithful heart, his hands, and eyes
    He lifted up unto the skies;
The earth he wondering kneel'd upon; the air,
He was surrounded with; the trees, the fair
And fruitful fields, his needful treasures were;
    And nothing else he wanted there.

5

The world itself was his next theme,
    Whereof himself was made supreme:
He had an angel's eye to see the price
Of every creature; that made Paradise.
He had a tongue, yea more, a cherub's sense
    To feel its worth and excellence.

6

Encompass'd with the fruits of love,
    He crowned was with Heaven above,
Supported with the footstool of God's throne,
A globe more rich than gold or precious stone,
The fertile ground of pleasure and delight,
    Encircled in a sphere of light.

7

The sense of what he did possess
    Fill'd him with joy and thankfulness;
He was transported even here on earth,
As if he then in Heaven had his birth:
The truth is, Heaven did the man surround,
    The earth being in the middle found.

The World

1

When Adam first did from his dust arise,
    He did not see,

Nor could there be
A greater joy before his eyes:
The sun as bright for me doth shine;
　　The spheres above
　　Do show His love,
While they to kiss the earth incline,
The stars as great a service do;
　　The moon as much I view
As Adam did, and all God's works divine
　　Are glorious still, and mine.

2

Sin spoil'd them; but my Saviour's precious blood
　　Sprinkled I see
　　On them to be,
Making them all both safe and good:
With greater rapture I admire
　　That I from hell
　　Redeem'd, do dwell
On earth as yet; and here a fire
Not scorching but refreshing glows,
　　And living water flows,
Which Dives more than silver doth desire,
　　Of crystals far the best.

3

What shall I render unto Thee, my God,
　　For teaching me
　　The wealth to see
Which doth enrich Thy great abode?
My virgin-thoughts in childhood were
　　Full of content,
　　And innocent,
Without disturbance, free and clear,
Even like the streams of crystal springs,
　　Where all the curious things
Do from the bottom of the well appear
　　When no filth or mud is there.

4

For so when first I in the summer-fields
    Saw golden corn
    The earth adorn
(This day that sight its pleasure yields),
No rubies could more take mine eye;
    Nor pearls of price,
    By man's device
Set in enamel'd gold most curiously,
More costly seem to me,
    How rich so e'er they be
By men esteem'd; nor could these more be mine
    That on my finger shine.

5

The skies above so sweetly then did smile,
    Their curtains spread
    Above my head
And with its height mine eye beguile;
So lovely did the distant green
    That fring'd the field
    Appear, and yield
Such pleasant prospects to be seen
From neighbouring hills; no precious stone,
    Or crown, or royal throne,
Which do bedeck the richest Indian lord,
    Could such delight afford.

6

The sun, that gilded all the bordering woods,
    Shone from the sky
    To beautify
My earthly and my heavenly goods;
Exalted in his throne on high,
    He shed his beams
    In golden streams
That did illustrate all the sky;
Those floods of light which he displays,

   Did fill the glittering ways,   70
While that unsufferable piercing eye
   The ground did glorify.

7

The choicest colours, yellow, green, and blue,
    Did on this court
    In comely sort
A mix'd variety bestrew;
Like gold with emeralds between;
    As if my God
    From His abode
By these intended to be seen.   80
And so He was: I Him descried
   In's works, the surest guide
Dame Nature yields; His love, His life doth there
   For evermore appear.

8

No house nor holder in this world did I
    Observe to be;
    What I did see
Seem'd all mine own: wherein did lie
A mine, a garden, of delights;
    Pearls were but stones;   90
    And great kings' thrones,
Compared with such benefits,
But empty chairs; a crown, a toy
   Scarce apt to please a boy.
All other are but petty trifling shows,
   To that which God bestows.

9

A royal crown, inlaid with precious stones,
    Did less surprise
    The infant eyes
Of many other little ones,   100
Than the great beauties of this frame,

Made for my sake,
Mine eyes did take,
Which I divine, and mine, do name.
Surprising joys beyond all price
Compos'd a Paradise,
Which did my soul to love my God inflame,
And ever will the same.

The Apostasy

1

One star
Is better far
Than many precious stones:
One sun, which is above in glory seen,
Is worth ten thousand golden thrones:
A juicy herb, or spire of grass,
In useful virtue, native green,
An emerald doth surpass;
Hath in't more value, tho less seen.

2

No wars,
Nor mortal jars,
Nor bloody feuds, nor coin,
Nor griefs which they occasion, saw I then;
Nor wicked thieves which this purloin;
I had no thoughts that were impure:
Esteeming both women and men
God's work, I was secure,
And reckon'd peace my choicest gem.

3

As Eve
I did believe
Myself in Eden set,

Affecting neither gold, nor ermin'd crowns,
    Nor ought else that I need forget;
    No mud did foul my limpid streams,
    No mist eclips'd my sun with frowns;
      Set off with heavenly beams,
    My joys were meadows, fields, and towns.

4
      Those things
      Which cherubins
    Did not at first behold
Among God's works, which Adam did not see;
    As robes, and stones enchas'd in gold,
    Rich cabinets, and such like fine
    Inventions; could not ravish me:
      I thought not bowls of wine
    Needful for my felicity.

5
      All bliss
      Consists in this,
    To do as Adam did;
And not to know those superficial joys
    Which were from him in Eden hid:
    Those little new-invented things,
    Fine lace and silks, such childish toys
      As ribbons are and rings,
    Or worldly pelf that us destroys.

6
      For God,
      Both great and good,
    The seeds of melancholy
Created not: but only foolish men,
    Grown mad with customary folly
    Which doth increase their wants, so dote
    As when they elder grow they then

Such baubles chiefly note;
More fools at twenty years than ten.

7
But I,
I knew not why,
Did learn among them too
At length; and when I once with blemish'd eyes
Began their pence and toys to view,
Drown'd in their customs, I became
A stranger to the shining skies,
Lost as a dying flame;
And hobby-horses brought to prize.

8
The sun
And moon forgone,
As if unmade, appear
No more to me; to God and Heaven dead
I was, as tho they never were:
Upon some useless gaudy book,
When what I knew of God was fled,
The child being taught to look,
His soul was quickly murdered.

9
'O fine!
O most divine!
O brave!' they cried; and show'd
Some tinsel thing whose glittering did amaze,
And to their cries its beauty owed;
Thus I on riches, by degrees,
Of a new stamp did learn to gaze;
While all the world for these
I lost: my joy turn'd to a blaze.

Solitude

1

How desolate!
Ah! how forlorn, how sadly did I stand
When in the field my woeful state
I felt! Not all the land,
Not all the skies,
Tho Heaven shin'd before mine eyes,
Could comfort yield in any field to me,
Nor could my mind contentment find or see.

2

Remov'd from town,
From people, churches, feasts, and holidays,
The sword of state, the mayor's gown,
And all the neighbouring boys;
As if no kings
On earth there were, or living things,
The silent skies salute mine eyes, the seas
My soul surround; no rest I found, or ease.

3

My roving mind
Search'd every corner of the spacious earth,
From sky to sky, if it could find
(But found not) any mirth:
Not all the coasts,
Nor all the great and glorious hosts,
In Heaven or earth, did comfort me afford;
I pin'd for hunger at a plenteous board.

4

I do believe,
The evening being shady and obscure,
The very silence did me grieve,
And sorrow more procure:
A secret want

Did make me think my fortune scant. 30
I was so blind, I could not find my health,
No joy mine eye could there espy, nor wealth.

5

Nor could I guess
What kind of thing I long'd for: but that I
  Did somewhat lack of blessedness,
    Beside the earth and sky,
      I plainly found;
    It griev'd me much, I felt a wound
Perplex me sore; yet what my store should be
I did not know, nothing would show to me. 40

6

Ye sullen things!
Ye dumb, ye silent creatures, and unkind!
  How can I call you pleasant springs
    Unless ye ease my mind!
      Will ye not speak
    What 'tis I want, nor silence break?
O pity me, at least point out my joy:
Some kindness show to me, altho a boy.

7

They silent stood;
Nor earth, nor woods, nor hills, nor brooks, nor skies, 50
  Would tell me where the hidden good,
    Which I did long for, lies:
      The shady trees,
    The evening dark, the humming bees,
The chirping birds, mute springs and fords, conspire,
To give no answer unto my desire.

8

Bells ringing I
Far off did hear, some country church they spake;
  The noise re-echoing through the sky

> My melancholy brake; 60
> When't reach'd mine ear
> Some tidings thence I hop'd to hear:
> But not a bell me news could tell, or show
> My longing mind, where joys to find, or know.

9

> I griev'd the more,
> 'Cause I thereby somewhat encourag'd was
> That I from those should learn my store;
> For churches are a place
> That nearer stand
> Than any part of all the land 70
> To Heaven; from whence some little sense I might
> To help my mind receive, and find some light.

10

> They louder sound
> Than men do talk, something they should disclose;
> The empty sound did therefore wound
> Because not show repose.
> It did revive
> To think that men were there alive;
> But had my soul, call'd by the toll, gone in,
> I might have found, to ease my wound, a thing. 80

11

> A little ease
> Perhaps, but that might more molest my mind;
> One flattering drop would more disease
> My soul with thirst, and grind
> My heart with grief:
> For people can yield no relief
> In public sort when in that court they shine,
> Except they move my soul with love divine.

12

Th' external rite,
Altho the face be wondrous sweet and fair,
  Will never sate my appetite
    No more than empty air
      Yield solid food.
  Must I the best and highest good
Seek to possess; or blessedness in vain
(Tho 'tis alive in some place) strive to gain?

13

    O! what would I
Diseased, wanting, melancholy, give
  To find what is felicity,
    The place where bliss doth live?
      Those regions fair
  Which are not lodg'd in sea nor air,
Nor woods, nor fields, nor arbour yields, nor springs,
Nor heavens show to us below, nor kings.

14

    I might have gone
Into the city, market, tavern, street,
  Yet only change my station,
    And strove in vain to meet
      That ease of mind
  Which all alone I long'd to find:
A common inn doth no such thing betray,
Nor doth it walk in people's talk, or play.

15

    O Eden fair!
Where shall I seek the soul of holy joy
  Since I to find it here despair;
    Nor in the shining day,
      Nor in the shade,
  Nor in the field, nor in a trade

I can it see? Felicity! O where
Shall I thee find to ease my mind! O where!   120

Poverty

1

As in the house I sate
Alone and desolate,
No creature but the fire and I,
The chimney and the stool, I lift mine eye
Up to the wall,
And in the silent hall
Saw nothing mine
But some few cups and dishes shine;
The table and the wooden stools
Where people us'd to dine.   10
A painted cloth there was
Wherein some ancient story wrought
A little entertain'd my thought
Which light discover'd through the glass.

2

I wonder'd much to see
That all my wealth should be
Confin'd in such a little room,
Yet hope for more I scarcely durst presume.
It griev'd me sore
That such a scanty store   20
Should be my all:
For I forgot my ease and health,
Nor did I think of hands or eyes,
Nor soul nor body prize;
I neither thought the sun,
Nor moon, nor stars, nor people, mine,
Tho they did round about me shine;
And therefore was I quite undone.

3

Some greater things I thought
    Must needs for me be wrought,
Which till my pleased mind could see
I ever should lament my poverty:
    I fain would have
    Whatever bounty gave;
    Nor could there be
Without, or love or Deity:
For, should not He be infinite
    Whose hand created me?
    Ten thousand absent things
Did vex my poor and absent mind,
Which, till I be no longer blind,
Let me not see the King of Kings.

4

His love must surely be
    Rich, infinite, and free;
Nor can He be thought a God
Of grace and power, that fills not his abode,
    His holy court,
    In kind and liberal sort;
    Joys and pleasures,
Plenty of jewels, goods, and treasures
(To enrich the poor, cheer the forlorn),
    His palace must adorn,
    And given all to me:
For till *His* works *my* wealth became,
No love, or peace, did me inflame:
But now I have a DEITY.

Dissatisfaction

1

In clothes confin'd, my weary mind
Pursu'd felicity;
Through every street I ran to meet
My bliss:
But nothing would the same disclose to me.
What is,
O where, the place of holy joy!
Will nothing to my soul some light convey!
In every house I sought for health,
Search'd every cabinet to spy my wealth,
I knock'd at every door,
Ask'd every man I met for bliss,
In every school, and college, sought for this:
But still was destitute and poor.

2

My piercing eyes unto the skies
I lifted up to see;
But no delight my appetite
Would sate;
Nor would that region show felicity:
My fate
Denied the same; above the sky,
Yea all the Heaven of Heavens, I lift mine eye:
But nothing more than empty space
Would there discover to my soul its face.
Then back dissatisfied
To earth I came; among the trees,
In taverns, houses, feasts, and palaces,
I sought it, but was still denied.

3

Panting and faint, full of complaint,
    I it pursu'd again,
In diadems, and eastern gems,
        In bags
Of gold and silver: but got no more gain
        Than rags,
Or empty air, or vanity;
Nor did the temples much more signify:
    Dirt in the streets; in shops I found
Nothing but toil. Walls only me surround
      Of worthless stones or earth;
    Dens full of thieves, glutted with blood,
Complaints and widows' tears: no other good
    Could there descry, no heavenly mirth.

4

Men's customs here but vile appear;
    The oaths of roaring boys,
Their gold that shines, their sparkling wines,
        Their lies,
Their gaudy trifles, are mistaken joys:
        To prize
Such toys I loath'd. My thirst did burn;
But where, O whither should my spirit turn!
    Their games, their bowls, their cheating dice,
Did not complete, but spoil, my Paradise.
      On things that gather rust,
    Or modish clothes, they fix their minds,
Mere outward show their fancy blinds,
    Their eyes being all put out with dust.

5

Sure none of these, senseless as trees,
    Can show me true repose.
Philosophy! canst thou descry
        My bliss?
Will books or sages it to me disclose?

> I miss
> Of this in all: they tell me pleasure,
> Or earthly honour, or a fading treasure,
> Will never with it furnish me.
> But then, where is, what is, felicity?
> Here all men are in doubt,
> And unresolv'd, they cannot speak
> What 'tis; and all or most that silence break
> Discover nothing but their throat. 70

6

> Weary of all that since the Fall
> Mine eyes on earth can find,
> I for a book from Heaven look,
> Since here
> No tidings will salute or ease my mind:
> Mine ear,
> My eye, my hand, my soul, doth long
> For some fair book fill'd with eternal song.
> O that! my soul: for that I burn:
> That is the thing for which my heart did yearn. 80
> Diviner counsels there;
> The joys of God, the angels' songs,
> The secret causes which employ their tongues,
> Will surely please when they appear.

7

> What sacred ways! What heavenly joys!
> Which mortals do not see?
> What hidden springs! What glorious things
> Above!
> What kind of life among them led may be
> In love! 90
> What causes of delight they have!
> What pleasing joyous objects God them gave!
> This mightily I long'd to know;
> Oh, that some angel these would to me show!
> How full, divine, and pure,

Their bliss may be, including all
Things visible or invisible, which shall
    To everlasting firm endure.

8

    O this! In this I hop'd for bliss;
        Of this I dreamt by night:
    For this by day I gasping lay;
        Mine eyes
For this did fail: for this, my great delight
        The skies
    Became, in hopes they would disclose
My sacred joys, and my desir'd repose.
    Oh! that some angel would bring down
The same to me; that book should be my crown.
        I breathe, I long, I seek:
    Fain would I find, but still denied,
I sought in every library and creek
    Until the Bible me supplied.

The Bible

1

    That! That! There I was told
That I the son of God was made,
    His image. O divine! And that fine gold,
        With all the joys that here do fade,
Are but a toy, compared to the bliss
Which heavenly, God-like, and eternal is.

2

    That we on earth are kings;
And, tho we're cloth'd with mortal skin,
Are inward cherubins; have angels' wings;
    Affections, thoughts, and minds within,
Can soar through all the coasts of Heaven and earth;
And shall be sated with celestial mirth.

Christendom

1

When first mine infant-ear
Of *Christendom* did hear,
I much admir'd what kind of place or thing
    It was of which the folk did talk:
    What coast, what region, what therein
    Did move, or might be seen to walk.
        My great desire
        Like ardent fire
Did long to know what things did lie behind
That mystic name, to which mine eye was blind.

2

Some depth it did conceal,
Which, till it did reveal
Itself to me, no quiet, peace, or rest,
    Could I by any means attain;
    My earnest thoughts did me molest
    Till someone should the thing explain:
        I thought it was
        A glorious place,
Where souls might dwell in all delight and bliss;
So thought, yet fear'd lest I the truth might miss:

3

Among ten thousand things,
Gold, silver, cherub's wings,
Pearls, rubies, diamonds, a church with spires,
    Masks, stages, games and plays,
    That then might suit my young desires,
    Fine feathers, farthings, holidays,
        Cards, music, dice,
        So much in price;
A city did before mine eyes present
Itself, wherein there reigned sweet content.

4

A town beyond the seas,
  Whose prospect much did please,
And to my soul so sweetly raise delight
  As if a long expected joy,
  Shut up in that transforming sight,
  Would into me itself convey;
    And blessedness
    I there possess,
As if that city stood on real ground,
And all the profit mine which there was found.   40

5

Whatever force me led,
  My spirit sweetly fed
On these conceits: that 'twas a city strange,
  Wherein I saw no gallant inns,
  No markets, shops or old exchange,
  No childish trifles, useless things;
    No wall, nor bounds
    That town surrounds;
But as if all its streets even endless were,
Without or gate or wall it did appear.   50

6

Things native sweetly grew,
  Which there mine eye did view,
Plain, simple, cheap, on either side the street,
  Which was exceeding fair and wide;
  Sweet mansions there mine eyes did meet;
  Green trees the shaded doors did hide.
    My chiefest joys
    Were girls and boys
That in those streets still up and down did play,
Which crown'd the town with constant holiday.   60

7

A sprightly pleasant time
(Even summer in its prime)
Did gild the trees, the houses, children, skies,
And made the city all divine;
It ravished my wondering eyes
To see the sun so brightly shine:
The heat and light
Seem'd in my sight
With such a dazzling lustre shed on them,
As made me think 'twas th' new Jerusalem.

8

Beneath the lofty trees
I saw, of all degrees,
Folk calmly sitting in their doors; while some
Did standing with them kindly talk,
Some smile, some sing, or what was done
Observe, while others by did walk;
They view'd the boys
And girls, their joys,
The streets adorning with their angel-faces,
Themselves diverting in those pleasant places.

9

The streets like lanes did seem,
Not pav'd with stones, but green,
Which with red clay did partly mix'd appear;
'Twas holy ground of great esteem;
The springs choice liveries did wear
Of verdant grass that grew between
The purling streams,
Which golden beams
Of light did varnish, coming from the sun,
By which to distant realms was service done.

10

In fresh and cooler rooms
Retir'd they dine: perfumes
They wanted not, having the pleasant shade
   And peace to bless their house within,
   By sprinkled waters cooler made,
   For those incarnate cherubin.
        This happy place,
        With all the grace,
The joy and beauty which did it beseem,
Did ravish me and heighten my esteem. 100

11

That here to raise desire
All objects do conspire,
People in years, and young enough to play,
   Their streets of houses, common peace,
   In one continued holy day
   Whose gladsome mirth shall never cease:
        Since these become
        My Christendom,
What learn I more than that Jerusalem
Is mine, as 'tis my Maker's, choicest gem. 110

12

Before I was aware
Truth did to me appear,
And represented to my virgin-eyes
   Th' unthought of joys and treasures
   Wherein my bliss and glory lies;
   My God's delight (which gives me measure),
        His turtledove,
        Is peace and love
In towns: for holy children, maids, and men
Make up the King of Glory's diadem. 120

On Christmas-Day

1

Shall dumpish melancholy spoil my joys
      While angels sing
      And mortals ring
  My Lord and Saviour's praise!
Awake from sloth, for that alone destroys,
'Tis sin defiles, 'tis sloth puts out thy joys.
    See how they run from place to place,
    And seek for ornaments of grace;
    Their houses deck'd with sprightly green,
    In winter makes a summer seen;
      They bays and holly bring
      As if 'twere spring!

2

Shake off thy sloth, my drowsy soul, awake;
      With angels sing
      Unto thy King,
  And pleasant music make;
Thy lute, thy harp, or else thy heart-strings take,
And with thy music let thy sense awake.
    See how each one the other calls
    To fix his ivy on the walls,
    Transplanted there it seems to grow
    As if it rooted were below:
      Thus He, who is thy King,
      Makes winter, spring.

3

Shall houses clad in summer-liveries
      His praises sing
      And laud thy King,
  And wilt not thou arise?
Forsake thy bed, and grow (my soul) more wise,
Attire thyself in cheerful liveries:
    Let pleasant branches still be seen

Adorning thee, both quick and green;
And, which with glory better suits,
Be laden all the year with fruits;
　　Inserted into Him,
　　　　Forever spring.

4

'Tis He that life and spirit doth infuse:
　　Let everything
　　The praises sing
　　Of Christ the King of Jews;
Who makes things green, and with a spring infuse
A season which to see it doth not use:
　　Old Winter's frost and hoary hair,
　　With garland's crowned, bays doth wear;
　　The nipping frost of wrath being gone,
　　To Him the manger made a throne,
　　　　Due praises let us sing,
　　　　　　Winter and spring.

5

See how, their bodies clad with finer clothes,
　　They now begin
　　His praise to sing
　　Who purchas'd their repose:
Whereby their inward joy they do disclose;
Their dress alludes to better works than those:
　　His gayer weeds and finer band,
　　New suit and hat, into his hand
　　The ploughman takes; his neatest shoes,
　　And warmer gloves, he means to use:
　　　　And shall not I, my King,
　　　　　　Thy praises sing?

6

See how their breath doth smoke, and how they haste
　　His praise to sing
　　With cherubim;

>   They scarce a breakfast taste;
> But through the streets, lest precious time should waste,
> When service doth begin, to church they haste.
>   And shall not I, Lord, come to Thee,
>   The beauty of Thy temple see?
>   Thy name with joy I will confess,
>   Clad in my Saviour's righteousness;
>   'Mong all Thy servants sing
>   To Thee my King.

7

> 'Twas Thou that gav'st us cause for fine attires;
>   Even Thou, O King,
>   As in the spring,
>   Dost warm us with Thy fires
> Of love: Thy blood hath bought us new desires;
> Thy righteousness doth clothe with new attires.
>   Made fresh and fine let me appear
>   This day divine, to close the year;
>   Among the rest let me be seen
>   A branch of the true vine and always green,
>   Think it a pleasant thing
>   Thy praise to sing.

8

> At break of day, O how the bells did ring?
>   To Thee, my King,
>   The bells did ring;
>   To Thee the angels sing:
> Thy goodness did produce this other spring,
> For this it is they make the bells to ring:
>   The sounding bells do through the air
>   Proclaim Thy welcome far and near;
>   While I alone with Thee inherit
>   All these joys, beyond my merit.
>   Who would not always sing
>   To such a King?

9

I all these joys, above my merit, see
        By Thee, my King,
        To whom I sing,
    Entire convey'd to me.
My treasure, Lord, Thou mak'st Thy people be
That I with pleasure might Thy servants see.
    Even in their rude external ways
    They do set forth my Saviour's praise,
    And minister a light to me;
    While I by them do hear to Thee
        Praises, my Lord and King,
            Whole churches ring.

10

Hark how remoter parishes do sound!
        Far off they ring
        For Thee, my King,
    Even round about the town:
The churches scatter'd over all the ground
Serve for Thy praise, who art with glory crown'd.
    This city is an engine great
    That makes my pleasure more complete;
    The sword, the mace, the magistrate,
    To honour Thee attend in state;
        The whole assembly sings;
            The minster rings.

Bells

I

1

    Hark! hark, my soul! the bells do ring,
        And with a louder voice
    Call many families to sing
    His public praises, and rejoice:

Their shriller sound doth wound the air,
Their grosser strokes affect the ear,
That we might thither all repair
    And more divine ones hear.
      If lifeless earth
      Can make such mirth,
What then shall souls above the starry sphere!

2

Bells are but clay that men refine
    And raise from duller ore;
Yet now, as if they were divine,
They call whole cities to adore;
Exalted into steeples they
Disperse their sound, and from on high
Chime-in our souls; they every way
    Speak to us through the sky:
      Their iron tongues
      Do utter songs,
And shall our stony hearts make no reply!

3

From darker mines and earthy caves
    At last let souls awake,
And rousing from obscurer graves
From lifeless bells example take;
Lifted above all earthly cares,
Let them (like these) rais'd up on high,
Forsaking all the baser wares
    Of dull mortality,
      His praises sing,
      Tunably ring,
In a less distance from the peaceful sky.

II

4

From clay, and mire, and dirt, my soul,
    From vile and common ore,

Thou must ascend; taught by the toll
In what fit place thou may'st adore;
Refin'd by fire, thou shalt a bell
Of praise become, in metal pure;
In purity thou must excel, 40
    No soil or grit endure,
      Refin'd by love,
      Thou still above
Like them must dwell, and other souls allure.

5

Doth not each trembling sound I hear
    Make all my spirits dance?
Each stroke's a message to my ear
That casts my soul into a trance
Of joy: they're us'd to notify
Religious triumphs, and proclaim 50
The peace of Christianity,
    In Jesus' holy name.
      Authorities
      And victories
Protect, increase, enrich, adorn the same.

6

Kings, O my soul, and princes now
    Do praise His holy name,
Their golden crowns and sceptres bow
In honour of my Lord: His fame
Is gone throughout the world, who died 60
Upon the cross for me: and He
That once was basely crucified
    Is own'd a Deity.
      The higher powers
      Have built these towers
Which here aspiring to the sky we see.

7

Those bells are of a piece, and sound,
    Whose wider mouths declare

>   Our duty to us: being round
>   And smooth and whole, no splinters are
>   In them, no cracks, nor holes, nor flaws
>   That may let out the spirits thence
>   Too soon; that would harsh jarring cause
>   And lose their influence.
>   We must unite
>   If we delight
>   Would yield or feel, or any excellence.

Churches

I

Those stately structures which on earth I view
To God erected, whether old or new;
His sacred temples which the world adorn,
Much more than mines of ore or fields of corn,
My soul delight: how do they please mine eye
When they are fill'd with Christian family!
Upon the face of all the peopl'd earth
There's no such sacred joy or solemn mirth,
To please and satisy my heart's desire,
As that wherewith my Lord is in a choir,
In holy hymns by warbling voices prais'd,
With eyes lift up, and joint affections rais'd.

    The arches built (like Heaven) wide and high
Show His magnificence and majesty
Whose house it is: with so much art and cost,
The pile is fram'd, the curious knobs emboss'd,
Set off with gold, that me it more doth please
Than princes' courts or royal palaces;
Great stones pil'd up by costly labours there
Like mountains carv'd by human skill appear;
Where towers, pillars, pinnacles, and spires
Do all concur to match my great desires,
Whose joy it is to see such structures rais'd
To th' end my God and Father should be prais'd.

II

1

    Were there but one alone
  Wherein we might approach his throne,
One only where we should accepted be,
    As in the days of old
  It was, when Solomon of gold
  His temple made; we then should see
A numerous host approaching it,
Rejoicing in the benefit:
    The Queen of Sheba come
    With all her glorious train,
      The Pope from Rome,
    The kings beyond the main;
The wise men of the East from far,
    As guided by a star,
With reverence would approach unto that ground,
At that sole altar be adoring found.

2

    Great lords would thither throng,
  And none of them without a song
Of praise; rich merchants also would approach
    From every foreign coast;
  Of ladies too a shining host,
  If not on horseback, in a coach;
This single church would crowded be
With men of great and high degree:
    We princes might behold
    With glittering sceptres there
      Inlaid with gold
    And precious stones, draw near.
No room for mean ones there would be,
    Nor place for thee and me:
An endless troop would crowding there appear,
Bringing new presents daily every year.

3

But now we churches have
In every coast, which bounty gave
Most freely to us; now they sprinkled stand
With so much care and love,
In this rich vale, nigh yonder grove
That men might come in every land
To them with greater ease; lo, we
Those blest abodes neglected see:
As if our God were worse
Because His love is more,
And doth disburse
Itself in greater store;
Nor can object with any face
The distance of the place;
Ungrateful we with slower haste do come
Unto His temple, 'cause 'tis nearer home.

Misapprehension

1

Men are not wise in their true interest,
Nor in the worth of what they long possess'd:
They know no more what is their own
Than they the value of 't have known.
They pine in misery,
Complain of poverty,
Reap not where they have sown,
Grieve for felicity,
Blaspheme the Deity;
And all because they are not blest
With eyes to see the worth of things:
For did they know their real interest,
No doubt they'd all be kings.

2

There's not a man but covets and desires
A kingdom, yea a world; nay, he aspires
    To all the regions he can see
    Beyond the heavens' infinity:
        The world too little is
        To be his sphere of bliss;
        Eternity must be
        The object of his view
        And his possession too;
    Or else infinity's a dream
    That quickly fades away; he loves
All treasures; but he hates a failing stream
        That dries up as it moves.

3

Can fancy make a greater king than God?
Can man within his Sovereign's abode
    Be dearer to himself than He
    That is the angels' Deity?
        Man is as well belov'd
        As they, if he improv'd
        His talent as we see
        They do; and may as well
        In blessedness excel.
    But man hath lost the ancient way,
    That road is gone into decay;
Brambles shut up the path, and briars tear
        Those few that pass by there.

4

They think no realms nor kingdoms theirs,
No lands nor houses, that have other heirs.
    But native sense taught me more wit,
    The world did too, I may admit:
        As soon as I was born
        It did my soul adorn,
        And was a benefit

That round about me lay;
　　　And yet without delay
　　'Twas seated quickly in my mind,
　　　Its uses also I yet find 50
Mine own: for God, that all things would impart,
　　　Centre'd it in my heart.

5

The world set in man's heart, and yet not his!
Why, all the compass of this great abyss,
　　Th' united service and delight,
　　Its beauty that attracts the sight,
　　　That goodness which I find,
　　　Doth gratify my mind;
　　　The common air and light
　　　That shines, doth me a pleasure 60
　　　And surely is my treasure:
　　Of it I am th' inclusive sphere,
　　It doth entire in me appear
As well as I in it: it gives me room,
　　　Yet lies within my womb.

The Odour

1

　　These hands are jewels to the eye,
Like wine, or oil, or honey, to the taste:
These feet which here I wear beneath the sky
　　　Are us'd, yet never waste.
My members all do yield a sweet perfume;
They minister delight, yet not consume.

2

　　Ye living gems, how true! how near!
How real, useful, pleasant! O how good!
How valuable! Yea, how sweet! how fair!
　　　Being once well understood! 10

For use ye permanent remain entire,
Sweet scents diffus'd do gratify desire.

3

Can melting sugar sweeten wine?
Can light communicated keep its name?
Can jewels solid be, tho they do shine?
    From fire rise a flame?
Ye solid are, and yet do light dispense;
Abide the same, tho yield an influence.

4

Your uses flow while ye abide:
The services which I from you receive
Like sweet infusions through me daily glide
    Even while they sense deceive,
Being unobserved: for only spirits see
What treasures services and uses be.

5

The services which from you flow
Are such diffusive joys as know no measure;
Which show His boundless love who did bestow
    These gifts to be my treasure.
Your substance is the tree on which it grows;
Your uses are the oil that from it flows.

6

Thus honey flows from rocks of stone;
Thus oil from wood; thus cider, milk, and wine,
From trees and flesh; thus corn from earth; to one
    That's heavenly and divine.
But he that cannot like an angel see,
In Heaven itself shall dwell in misery.

7

If first I learn not what's your price
Which are alive, and are to me so near;

How shall I all the joys of Paradise,
    Which are so great and dear,   40
Esteem? Gifts even at distance are our joys,
But lack of sense the benefit destroys.

8

Live to thyself; thy limbs esteem:
From Heaven they came; with money can't be bought,
They are such works as God Himself beseem,
    May precious well be thought.
Contemplate then the value of this treasure,
By that alone thou feelest all the pleasure.

9

Like amber fair thy fingers grow;
With fragrant honey-sucks thy head is crown'd;   50
Like stars, thine eyes; thy cheeks like roses show:
    All are delights profound.
Talk with thyself; thyself enjoy and see:
At once the mirror and the object be.

10

What's cinnamon, compar'd to thee?
Thy body is than cedars better far:
Those fruits and flowers which in fields I see,
    With thine cannot compare.
Where'er thou movest, there the scent I find
Of fragrant myrrh and aloes left behind.   60

11

But what is myrrh? What cinnamon?
What aloes, cassia, spices, honey, wine?
O sacred uses! You to think upon
    Than these I more incline.
To see, taste, smell, observe, is to no end,
If I the use of each don't apprehend.

Admiration

1

Can human shape so taking be,
    That angels come and sip
Ambrosia from a mortal lip!
Can cherubims descend with joy to see
       God in His works beneath!
         Can mortals breathe
          Felicity!
Can bodies fill the heavenly rooms
With welcome odours and perfumes!
Can earth-bred flowers adorn celestial bowers
Or yield such fruits as please the heavenly powers!

2

Then may the seas with amber flow;
    The earth a star appear;
Things be divine and heavenly here.
The Tree of Life in Paradise may grow
       Among us now: the sun
         Be overcome
         With beams that show
More bright than his: celestial mirth
May yet inhabit all this earth.
It cannot be! Can mortals be so blind?
Have joys so near them, which they never mind?

3

The lily and the rosy-train
    Which, scatter'd on the ground,
Salute the feet which they surround,
Grow for thy sake, O man; that like a chain
       Or garland they may be
         To deck even thee:
         They all remain
Thy gems; and bowing down their head
Their liquid pearl they kindly shed

In tears; as if they meant to wash thy feet,
For joy that they to serve thee are made meet.

4

The sun doth smile, and looking down
    From Heaven doth blush to see
Himself excelled here by thee:
Yet frankly doth disperse his beams that crown
    A creature so divine;
        He loves to shine,
        Nor lets a frown 40
    Eclipse his brow, because he gives
    Light for the use of one that lives
Above himself. Lord! What is man that he
Is thus admired like a deity!

Right Apprehension

1

Give but to things their true esteem,
And those which now so vile and worthless seem
    Will so much fill and please the mind,
That we shall there the only riches find.
        How wise was I
        In infancy!
    I then saw in the clearest light;
But corrupt custom is a second night.

2

Custom: that must a trophy be
When wisdom shall complete her victory; 10
    For trades, opinions, errors, are
False lights, but yet receiv'd to set off ware
        More false: we're sold
        For worthless gold.
    Diana was a goddess made
That silversmiths might have the better trade.

3

But give to things their true esteem,
And then what's magnified most vile will seem:
What commonly's despis'd, will be
The truest and the greatest rarity.
        What men should prize
        They all despise;
The best enjoyments are abus'd;
The only wealth by madmen is refus'd.

4

A globe of earth is better far
Than if it were a globe of gold: a star
   Much brighter than a precious stone:
The sun more glorious than a costly throne;
        His warming beam,
        A living stream
Of liquid pearl, that from a spring
Waters the earth, is a most precious thing.

5

What newness once suggested to,
Now clearer reason doth improve, my view:
   By novelty my soul was taught
At first; but now reality my thought
        Inspires: and I
        With clarity
Both ways instructed am; by sense,
Experience, reason, and intelligence.

6

A globe of gold must barren be,
Untill'd and useless: we should neither see
   Trees, flowers, grass, or corn
Such a metalline massy globe adorn:
        As splendour blinds,
        So hardness binds;

No fruitfulness it can produce;
A golden world can't be of any use.

7

Ah me! This world is more divine: 50
The wisdom of a God in this doth shine.
What ails mankind to be so cross?
The useful earth they count vile dirt and dross:
And neither prize
Its qualities,
Nor donor's love. I fain would know
How or why men God's goodness disallow.

8

The earth's rare ductile soil,
Which duly yields unto the ploughman's toil,
Its fertile nature, gives offence;
And its improvement by the influence 60
Of Heaven; for these
Do not well please,
Because they do upbraid men's harden'd hearts,
And each of them an evidence imparts

9

Against the owner; whose design
It is that nothing be reputed fine,
Nor held for any excellence,
Of which he hath not in himself the sense.
He too well knows
That no fruit grows 70
In his obdurateness, nor yields
Obedience to the heavens like the fields:

10

But being, like his loved gold,
Stiff, barren, hard, impenetrable; tho told
He should be otherwise: he is

Uncapable of any heavenly bliss.
      His gold and he
      Do well agree;
   For he's a formal hypocrite;
Like that unfruitful, yet on th' outside bright.   80

11

   Ah! Happy infant! Wealthy heir!
How blessed did the Heaven and earth appear
    Before thou knew'st there was a thing
Call'd gold! Barren of good; of ill the spring
      Beyond compare!
      Most quiet were
   Those infant-days, when I did see
Wisdom and wealth couch'd in simplicity.

The Image

If I be like my God, my King
   (Tho not a cherubim),
    I will not care,
  Since all my powers derived are
    From none but Him.
The best of images shall I
   Comprised in me see;
    For I can spy
  All angels in the Deity
    Like me to lie.   10

The Evidence

I

  His Word confirms the sale:
  Those sheets enfold my bliss:
Eternity itself's the pale

Wherein my true estate enclosed is:
    Each ancient miracle's a seal:
Apostles, prophets, martyrs, patriarchs are
The witnesses; and what their words reveal,
    Their written records do declare.
All may well wonder such a 'state to see
In such a solemn sort settled on me.

2

    Did not His Word proclaim
    My title to th' estate,
His works themselves affirm the same
By what they do; my wish they antedate.
    Before I was conceiv'd, they were
Allotted for my great inheritance;
As soon as I among them did appear
    They did surround me, to advance
My interest and love. Each creature says,
'God made us thine, that we might show His praise.'

3

    The services they do,
    Aloud proclaim them mine;
  In that they are adapted to
Supply my wants; in which they all combine
    To please and serve me, that I may
God, angels, men, fowls, beasts, and fish enjoy,
Both in a natural and transcendent way;
    And to my soul the sense convey
Of wisdom, goodness, power, and love divine,
Which made them all, and made them to be mine.

Shadows in the Water

1

In unexperienc'd infancy
Many a sweet mistake doth lie:

Mistake tho false, intending true;
A seeming somewhat more than view;
    That doth instruct the mind
    In things that lie behind,
And many secrets to us show
Which afterwards we come to know.

2

Thus did I by the water's brink
Another world beneath me think;
And while the lofty spacious skies
Reversed there abus'd mine eyes,
    I fancied other feet
    Came mine to touch and meet;
As by some puddle I did play
Another world within it lay.

3

Beneath the water people drown'd,
Yet with another Heaven crown'd,
In spacious regions seem'd to go
Freely moving to and fro:
    In bright and open space
    I saw their very face;
Eyes, hands, and feet they had like mine;
Another sun did with them shine.

4

'Twas strange that people there should walk,
And yet I could not hear them talk:
That through a little watery chink,
Which one dry ox or horse might drink,
    We other worlds should see,
    Yet not admitted be;
And other confines there behold
Of light and darkness, heat and cold.

5

I call'd them oft, but call'd in vain;
No speeches we could entertain:
Yet did I there expect to find
Some other world, to please my mind.
    I plainly saw by these
    A new antipodes,
Whom, tho they were so plainly seen,
A film kept off that stood between.   40

6

By walking men's reversed feet
I chanc'd another world to meet;
Tho it did not to view exceed
A phantasm, 'tis a world indeed,
    Where skies beneath us shine,
    And earth by art divine
Another face presents below,
Where people's feet against ours go.

7

Within the regions of the air,
Compass'd about with heavens fair,   50
Great tracts of land there may be found
Enrich'd with fields and fertile ground;
    Where many numerous hosts,
    In those far distant coasts,
For other great and glorious ends,
Inhabit, my yet unknown friends.

8

O ye that stand upon the brink,
Whom I so near me, through the chink,
With wonder see: what faces there,
Whose feet, whose bodies, do ye wear?   60
    I my companions see
    In you, another me.
They seemed others, but are we;
Our second selves those shadows be.

9

Look how far off those lower skies
Extend themselves! Scarce with mine eyes
I can them reach. O ye my friends,
What secret borders on those ends?
    Are lofty heavens hurl'd
    'Bout your inferior world? 70
Are ye the representatives
Of other people's distant lives?

10

Of all the playmates which I knew
That here I do the image view
In other selves; what can it mean?
But that below the purling stream
    Some unknown joys there be
    Laid up in store for me;
To which I shall, when that thin skin
Is broken, be admitted in. 80

On Leaping over the Moon

1

I saw new worlds beneath the water lie,
    New people; and another sky,
        And sun, which seen by day
        Might things more clear display.
        Just such another
        Of late my brother
Did in his travel see, and saw by night
    A much more strange and wondrous sight:
Nor could the world exhibit such another,
    So great a sight, but in a brother. 10

2

Adventure strange! No such in story we
    New or old, true or feigned, see.

On earth he seem'd to move
Yet Heaven went above;
   Up in the skies
   His body flies
In open, visible, yet magic, sort:
  As he along the way did sport,
Like Icarus over the flood he soars
  Without the help of wings or oars.   20

3

As he went tripping o'er the king's highway,
  A little pearly river lay,
    O'er which, without a wing
    Or oar, he dar'd to swim,
      Swim through the air
      On body fair;
He would not use nor trust Icarian wings
  Lest they should prove deceitful things;
For had he fall'n, it had been wondrous high,
  Not from, but from above, the sky: 30

4

He might have dropp'd through that thin element
  Into a fathomless descent;
    Unto the nether sky
    That did beneath him lie,
      And there might tell
      What wonders dwell
On earth above. Yet bold he briskly runs
  And soon the danger overcomes;
Who, as he leapt, with joy related soon
  How happy he o'er-leapt the moon.   40

5

What wondrous things upon the earth are done
  Beneath, and yet above, the sun?
    Deeds all appear again
    In higher spheres; remain

In clouds as yet:
  But there they get
Another light, and in another way
 Themselves to us above display.
The skies themselves this earthly globe surround;
 We're even here within them found.　　　　50

6

On heavenly ground within the skies we walk,
 And in this middle centre talk:
  Did we but wisely move,
  On earth in Heaven above,
   We then should be
   Exalted high
Above the sky: from whence whoever falls,
 Through a long dismal precipice,
Sinks to the deep abyss where Satan crawls
 Where horrid death and despair lies.　　　　60

7

As much as others thought themselves to lie
 Beneath the moon, so much more high
  Himself he thought to fly
  Above the starry sky,
   As that he spied
   Below the tide.
Thus did he yield me in the shady night
 A wondrous and instructive light,
Which taught me that under our feet there is,
 As o'er our heads, a place of bliss.　　　　70

'To the same purpose'

1

To the same purpose: he, not long before
 Brought home from nurse, going to the door

To do some little thing
He must not do within,
    With wonder cries,
    As in the skies
He saw the moon, 'O yonder is the moon
  Newly come after me to town,
That shin'd at Lugwardine but yesternight,
  Where I enjoy'd the selfsame light.'

2

As if it had even twenty thousand faces,
  It shines at once in many places;
    To all the earth so wide
    God doth the stars divide,
    With so much art,
    The moon impart,
They serve us all; serve wholly every one
  As if they served him alone.
While every single person hath such store,
  'Tis want of sense that makes us poor.

Sight

1

    Mine infant-eye,
    Above the sky
  Discerning endless space,
    Did make me see
    Two *sights* in me;
  Three eyes adorn'd my face:
  Two luminaries in my flesh
    Did me refresh;
    But one did lurk within,
    Beneath my skin.
That was of greater worth than both the other;
For those were twins; but this had ne'er a brother.

2

Those eyes of sense
That did dispense
Their beams to natural things,
I quickly found
Of narrow bound
To know but earthly springs.
But *that* which through the heavens went
Was excellent,
And endless; for the ball
Was spiritual:
A visive eye things visible doth see;
But with th' invisible, invisibles agree.

3

One world was not
(Be't ne'er forgot)
Even then enough for me:
My better sight
Was infinite,
New regions I must see.
In distant coasts new glories I
Did long to spy:
What this world did present
Could not content;
But, while I look'd on outward beauties *here*,
Most earnestly expected others *there*.

4

I know not well
What did me tell
Of endless space; but I
Did in my mind
Some such thing find
To be beyond the sky
That had no bound, as certainly
As I can see
That I have foot or hand

To feel or stand:
Which I discern'd by another sight
Than that which grac'd my body much more bright.

5

I own it was
A looking-glass
Of signal worth; wherein,
More than mine eyes
Could see or prize,
Such things as virtues win,
Life, joy, love, peace, appear'd: a light
Which to my sight
Did objects represent
So excellent;
That I no more without the same can see
Than beasts that have no true felicity.

6

This eye alone
(That peer hath none)
Is such, that it can pry
Into the end
To which things tend,
And all the depths descry
That God and nature do include.
By this are view'd
The very ground and cause
Of sacred laws,
All ages too, thoughts, counsels, and designs;
So that no light in Heaven more clearly shines.

Walking

1

To walk abroad is, not with eyes,
But thoughts, the fields to see and prize;

Else may the silent feet,
    Like logs of wood,
Move up and down, and see no good,
    Nor joy nor glory meet.

2

Even carts and wheels their place do change,
But cannot see; tho very strange
    The glory that is by:
        Dead puppets may
Move in the bright and glorious day,
    Yet not behold the sky.

3

And are not men than they more blind,
Who having eyes yet never find
    The bliss in which they move?
        Like statues dead
They up and down are carried,
    Yet neither see nor love.

4

To walk is by a thought to go;
To move in spirit to and fro;
    To mind the good we see;
        To taste the sweet:
Observing all the things we meet
    How choice and rich they be.

5

To note the beauty of the day,
And golden fields of corn survey;
    Admire the pretty flowers
        With their sweet smell;
To celebrate their Maker, and to tell
    The marks of His great powers.

6

To fly abroad like active bees,
Among the hedges and the trees,
   To cull the dew that lies
      On every blade,
From every blossom; till we lade
   Our minds, as they their thighs.

7

Observe those rich and glorious things,
The rivers, meadows, woods, and springs,
   The fructifying sun;
      To note from far
The rising of each twinkling star
   For us his race to run.

8

A little child these well perceives,
Who, tumbling among grass and leaves,
   May rich as kings be thought;
      But there's a sight
Which perfect manhood may delight,
   To which we shall be brought.

9

While in those pleasant paths we talk
'Tis that towards which at last we walk;
   But we may by degrees
      Wisely proceed
Pleasures of love and praise to heed,
   From viewing herbs and trees.

The Dialogue

Q. Why dost thou tell me that the fields are mine?
A. Because for thee the fields so richly shine.

Q. Am I the heir of the works of men?
A. For thee they dress, for thee manure them.

Q. Did I myself by them intended see,
That I the heir of their works should be,
It well would please; but they themselves intend:
I therefore am not of their works the end.
A. The real benefit of all their works,
Wherein such mighty joy and beauty lurks, 10
Derives itself to thee; to thee doth come,
As do the labours of the shining sun;
Which doth not think on *thee* at all, my friend,
Yet all his beams of light on thee do tend:
For thee they shine and do themselves display;
For thee they do both make and gild the day;
For thee doth rise that glorious orb of light;
For thee it sets, and so gives way for night;
That glorious bridegroom daily shows his face,
Adorns the world, and swiftly runs his race, 20
Disperseth clouds, and raiseth vapours too,
Exciteth winds, distils the rain and dew,
Concocteth mines, and makes the liquid seas
Contribute moisture to thy plants and trees,
Doth quicken beasts, revive thy vital powers,
Thrusts forth the grass, and beautifies thy flowers,
By tacit causes animates the trees,
As they do thee so he doth cherish bees,
Digesteth metals, raiseth fruit and corn,
Makes rivers flow, and mountains doth adorn: 30
All these it doth, not by its own design,
But by thy God's, which is far more divine;
Who so disposeth things, that they may be
In Heaven and earth kind ministers to thee:
And tho the men that toil for meat, and drink,
And clothes, or houses, do not on thee think;
Yet all their labours by His heavenly care
To thee, in mind or body, helpful are:
And that God thus intends thy single self,

Should please thee more, than if to heap up wealth 40
All men for thee did work, and sweat, and bleed;
Mean thee alone (my friend) in every deed.

Dreams

1

'Tis strange! I saw the skies;
I saw the hills before mine eyes;
The sparrow fly;
The lands that did about me lie;
The real sun, that heavenly eye!
Can closed eyes even in the darkest night
See through their lids, and be inform'd with sight?

2

The people were to me
As true as those by day I see;
As true the air, 10
The earth as sweet, as fresh, as fair
As that which did by day repair
Unto my waking sense! Can all the sky,
Can all the world, within my brain-pan lie?

3

What sacred secret's this,
Which seems to intimate my bliss?
What is there in
The narrow confines of my skin,
That is alive and feels within
When I am dead? Can magnitude possess 20
An active memory, yet not be less?

4

May all that I can see
Awake, by night within me be?
My childhood knew
No difference, but all was true,

As real all as what I view;
The world itself was there. 'Twas wondrous strange,
That Heaven and earth should so their place exchange.

5

Till that which vulgar sense
Doth falsely call experience,
Distinguish'd things:
The ribbons, and the gaudy wings
Of birds, the virtues, and the sins,
That represented were in dreams by night
As really my senses did delight,

6

Or grieve, as those I saw
By day: things terrible did awe
My soul with fear;
The apparitions seem'd as near
As things could be, and things they were.
Yet were they all by fancy in me wrought,
And all their being founded in a thought.

7

O what a thing is thought!
Which seems a dream; yea, seemeth nought,
Yet doth the mind
Affect as much as what we find
Most near and true! Sure men are blind,
And can't the forcible reality
Of things that secret are within them see.

8

Thought! Surely thoughts are true,
They please as much as things can do:
Nay, things are dead,
And in themselves are severed
From souls; nor can they fill the head
Without our thoughts. Thoughts are the real things
From whence all joy, from whence all sorrow springs.

The Inference

I

1

Well-guided thoughts within possess
The treasures of all blessedness.
Things are indifferent; nor give
    Joy of themselves, nor grieve.
The very Deity of God torments
    The malcontents
Of hell; to th' soul alone it proves
A welcome object, that Him loves.
Things true affect not, while they are unknown:
But thoughts most sensibly, when quite alone.

2

Thoughts are the inward balms or spears;
The living joys, or griefs and fears;
The light, or else the fire; the theme
    On which we pore or dream.
Thoughts are alone by men the objects found
    That heal or wound.
Things are but dead: they can't dispense
Or joy or grief. Thoughts! Thoughts the sense
Affect and touch. Nay, when a thing is near
It can't affect but as it doth appear.

3

Since then by thoughts I only see;
Since thought alone affecteth me;
Since these are real things when shown;
    And since as things are known
Or thought, they please or kill: what care ought I
    (Since thoughts apply
Things to my mind) those thoughts aright to frame,
That heavenly thoughts me heavenly things may gain.

4

Ten thousand thousand things are dead;
Lie round about me; yet are fled,
Are absent, lost, and from me gone;
    And those few things alone,
Or grieve my soul, or gratify my mind,
      Which I do find
    Within. Let then the troubles die,
    The noisome poisons buried lie:
Ye cares and griefs avaunt, that breed distress.
Let only those remain which God will bless.

5

How many thousands see the sky,
The sun and moon, as well as I?
How many more that view the seas,
    Feel neither joy nor ease?
Those things are dead and dry and banished.
      Their life is led
    As if the world were yet unmade:
    A feast, fine clothes, or else a trade,
Take up their thoughts; and, like a grosser screen
Drawn o'er their soul, leave better things unseen.

6

But O! let me the excellence
Of God, in all His works, with sense
Discern: Oh! let me celebrate
    And feel my blest estate:
Let all my thoughts be fix'd upon His throne;
      And Him alone
    For all His gracious gifts admire,
    Him only with my soul desire:
Or grieve for sin. That with due sense, the pleasure
I may possess of His eternal treasure.

II

David a temple in his mind conceiv'd;
And that intention was so well receiv'd
By God, that all the sacred palaces
That ever were did less His glory please.
    If thoughts are such; such valuable things;
Such real goods; such human cherubins;
Material delights; transcendent objects; ends
Of all God's works, which most His eye intends.
O! What are men, who can such things produce,   10
So excellent in nature, value, use?
Which not to angels only grateful seem,
But God, most wise, Himself doth them esteem
Worth more than worlds? How many thousand may
Our hearts conceive and offer every day?
Holy affections, grateful sentiments,
Good resolutions, virtuous intents,
Seed-plots of active piety; He values more
Than the materal world He made before.
By these the blessed Virgin (and no other)
Obtain'd the grace to be the happy mother   20
Of God's own Son; for, of her pious care
To treasure up those truths which she did hear
Concerning Christ, in thoughtful mind, we're told;
But not that e'er with offerings of gold
The temple she enrich'd. This understood,
How glorious, how divine, how great, how good
May we become! How like the Deity
In managing our thoughts aright! A piety
More grateful to our God than building walls   30
Of churches, or the founding hospitals:
Wherein He gives us an almighty power
To please Him so, that could we worlds create,
Or more new visible earths and heavens make,
'Twould be far short of this; which is the flower
And cream of strength. This we might plainly see,
But that we rebels to our reason be.

Shall God such sacred might on us bestow?
And not employ't to pay the thanks we owe?
Such grateful offerings able be to give;
Yet them annihilate, and God's spirit grieve? 40
Consider that for all our Lord hath done,
All that He can receive is this bare sum
Of God-like holy thoughts: these only He
Expects from us, our sacrifice to be.

The City

1

What structures here among God's works appear?
   Such wonders Adam ne'er did see
    In Paradise among the trees,
      No works of art like these,
Nor walls, nor pinnacles, nor houses were.
      All these for me,
     For me these streets and towers,
These stately temples, and these solid bowers,
      My Father rear'd:
   For me I thought they thus appear'd. 10

2

The city, fill'd with people, near me stood;
   A fabric like a court divine,
    Of many mansions bright and fair;
     Wherein I could repair
To blessings that were common, great, and good:
      Yet all did shine
     As burnish'd and as new
As if before none ever did them view:
      They seem'd to me
   Environ'd with eternity. 20

3

As if from everlasting they had there
    Been built, more gallant than if gilt
    With gold, they show'd: nor did I know
        That they to hands did owe
Themselves. Immortal they did all appear
        Till I knew guilt.
    As if the public good
Of all the world for me had ever stood,
        They gratified
Me, while the earth they beautified.

4

The living people that mov'd up and down,
    With ruddy cheeks and sparkling eyes;
    The music in the churches, which
        Were angels' joys (tho pitch
Defil'd me afterwards) did then me crown:
        I then did prize
    These only. I did love
As do the blessed hosts in Heaven above:
        No other pleasure
Had I, nor wish'd for other treasure.

5

The heavens were the richly studded case
    Which did my richer wealth enclose;
    No little private cabinet
        In which my gems to set
Did I contrive: I thought the whole earth's face
        At my dispose:
    No confines did include
What I possess'd, no limits there I view'd;
        On every side
All endless was which then I spied.

6

'Tis art that hath the late invention found
    Of shutting up in little room
    One's boundless expectations: men
        Have in a narrow pen
Confin'd themselves: free souls can know no bound;
           But still presume
        That treasures everywhere
From everlasting hills must still appear,
        And be to them
    Joys in the new Jerusalem.   60

7

We first by nature all things boundless see;
    Feel all illimited; and know
    No terms or periods: but go on
        Throughout the endless throne
Of God, to view His wide eternity;
        Even here below
        His omnipresence we
Do pry into, that copious treasury.
        Tho we are taught
    To limit and to bound our thought.   70

8

Such treasures as are to be valued more
    Than those shut up in chests and tills,
    Which are by citizens esteem'd,
        To me the people seem'd:
The city doth increase my glorious store,
        Which sweetly fills
        With choice variety
The place wherein I see the same to be;
        And strangely is
    A mansion or tower of bliss.   80

9

Nor can the city such a soul as mine
    Confine; nor be my only treasure:
  I must see other things to be
      For my felicity
Concurrent instruments, and all combine
      To do me pleasure.
    And God, to gratify
This inclination, helps me to descry
      Beyond the sky
More wealth provided, and more high.   90

Insatiableness

I

1

No walls confine! Can nothing hold my mind?
Can I no rest nor satisfaction find?
    Must I behold eternity
      And see
  What things above the heavens be?
    Will nothing serve the turn?
    Nor earth, nor seas, nor skies?
      Till I what lies
    In time's beginning find:
Must I till then forever burn?   10

2

Not all the crowns; not all the heaps of gold
On earth; not all the tales that can be told,
    Will satisfaction yield to me:
        Nor tree,
  Nor shade, nor sun, nor Eden, be
    A joy: nor gems in gold
      (Be't pearl or precious stone),
        Nor spring, nor flowers,

>   Answer my craving powers,
>   Nor anything that eyes behold.

3

Till I what was before all time descry,
The world's beginning seems but vanity.
>   My soul doth there long thoughts extend;
>   No end
>   Doth find, or being comprehend:
>   Yet somewhat sees that is
>   The obscure shady face
>   Of endless space,
>   All room within; where I
>   Expect to meet eternal bliss.

II

1

>   This busy, vast, inquiring soul
>   Brooks no control,
>   No limits will endure,
>   Nor any rest: it will all see,
> Not time alone, but even eternity.
>   What is it? Endless sure.

2

>   'Tis mean ambition to desire
>   A single world:
>   To many I aspire,
>   Tho one upon another hurl'd;
> Nor will they all, if they be all confin'd,
>   Delight my mind.

3

>   This busy, vast, inquiring soul
>   Brooks no control:
>   'Tis hugely curious too.
>   Each one of all those worlds must be

Enrich'd with infinite variety
>And worth; or 'twill not do.

4

'Tis nor delight nor perfect pleasure
>To have a purse 20
That hath a bottom of its treasure,
Since I must thence endless expense disburse.
Sure there's a GOD (for else there's no delight),
>One infinite.

Consummation

1

The thoughts of men appear
Freely to move within a sphere
>Of endless reach; and run,
Tho in the soul, beyond the sun.
The ground on which they acted be
Is unobserv'd infinity.

2

Extended through the sky,
Tho here, beyond it far they fly:
>Abiding in the mind
An endless liberty they find: 10
Throughout all spaces can extend,
Nor ever meet or know an end.

3

They, in their native sphere,
At boundless distances appear:
>Eternity can measure;
Its no beginning see with pleasure.
Thus in the mind an endless space
Doth naturally display its face.

4

Wherein because we no
Object distinctly find or know;
    We sundry things invent,
That may our fancy give content;
See points of space beyond the sky,
And in those points see creatures lie.

5

    Spy fishes in the seas,
Conceit them swimming there with ease;
    The dolphins and the whales,
Their very fins, their very scales,
As there within the briny deep
Their tails the flowing waters sweep.

6

    Can see the very skies,
As if the same were in our eyes;
    The sun, tho in the night,
As if it mov'd within our sight;
One space beyond another still
Discovered; think while ye will.

7

    Which, tho we don't descry
(Much like by night an idle eye,
    Not shaded with a lid,
But in a darksome dungeon hid),
At last shall in a glorious day
Be made its objects to display.

8

    And then shall ages be
Within its wide eternity;
    All kingdoms stand,
Howe'er remote, yet nigh at hand;
The skies, and what beyond them lie,
Exposed unto every eye.

9

    Nor shall we then invent
Nor alter things; but with content 50
    All in their places see,
As doth the glorious Deity;
Within the scope of whose great mind,
We all in their true nature find.

Hosanna

1

No more shall walls, no more shall walls confine
That glorious soul which in my flesh doth shine:
    No more shall walls of clay or mud
      Nor ceilings made of wood,
    Nor crystal windows, bound my sight,
But rather shall admit delight.
      The skies that seem to bound
        My joys and treasures,
      Of more endearing pleasures
      Themselves become a ground: 10
While from the centre to the utmost sphere
My goods are multiplied everywhere.

2

The Deity, the Deity to me
Doth all things give, and make me clearly see
    The moon and stars, the air and sun
      Into my chamber come:
    The seas and rivers hither flow,
Yea, here the trees of Eden grow,
      The fowls and fishes stand,
        Kings and their thrones, 20
      As 'twere, at my command;
      God's wealth, His holy ones,
The ages too, and angels all conspire:
While I, that I the centre am, admire.

3

No more, no more shall clouds eclipse my treasures,
Nor viler shades obscure my highest pleasures;
    No more shall earthen husks confine
      My blessings which do shine
    Within the skies, or else above:
    Both worlds one Heaven made by love,   30
      In common happy I
        With angels walk
      And there my joys espy;
      With God Himself I talk;
Wondering with ravishment all things to see
Such real joys, so truly mine, to be.

4

No more shall trunks and dishes be my store,
Nor ropes of pearl, nor chains of golden ore;
    As if such beings yet were not,
      They all shall be forgot.   40
    No such in Eden did appear,
    No such in Heaven: Heaven here
      Would be, were those remov'd;
        The sons of men
      Live in Jerusalem,
      Had they not baubles lov'd.
These clouds dispers'd, the heavens clear I see,
Wealth new invented, mine shall never be.

5

Transcendent objects doth my God provide,   50
In such convenient order all contriv'd,
    That all things in their proper place
      My soul doth best embrace,
    Extends its arms beyond the seas,
    Above the heavens itself can please,
      With God enthron'd may reign:
        Like sprightly streams
      My thoughts on things remain;

> Or else like vital beams
> They reach to, shine on, quicken things, and make
> Them truly useful; while I all partake. 60

6

For me the world created was by Love;
For me the skies, the seas, the sun, do move;
> The earth for me doth stable stand;
> For me each fruitful land,
For me the very angels God made His
And my companions in bliss:
> His laws command all men
> > That they love me,
> Under a penalty
> Severe, in case they miss: 70
His laws require His creatures all to praise
His name, and when they do't be most my joys.

The Review

I

1

> Did I grow, or did I stay?
> Did I prosper or decay?
> > When I so
> From things to thoughts did go?
Did I flourish or diminish,
When I so in thoughts did finish
What I had in things begun;
When from God's works to think upon
The thoughts of men my soul did come?
The thoughts of men, had they been wise, 10
Should more delight me than the skies.
> They mighty creatures are,
> > For these the mind

Affect, afflict, do ease or grind;
   But foolish thoughts ensnare.

2

  Wise ones are a sacred treasure;
  True ones yield substantial pleasure:
    Compar'd to them,
  I things as shades esteem.
False ones are a foolish flourish
(Such as mortals chiefly nourish),
When I them to things compare,
Compar'd to things, they trifles are;
Bad thoughts do hurt, deceive, ensnare.
A good man's thoughts are of such price
That they create a Paradise:
   But he that misemploys
    That faculty,
God, men, and angels doth defy;
   Robs them of all their joys.

II

  My childhood is a sphere
Wherein ten thousand heavenly joys appear:
   Those *thoughts* it doth include,
   And those affections, which review'd,
    Again present to me
In better sort the *things* which I did see.
   Imaginations real are,
   Unto my mind again repair:
Which makes my life a circle of delights;
A hidden sphere of obvious benefits:
An earnest that the actions of the just
Shall still revive, and flourish in the dust.

POEMS FROM CHRISTIAN ETHICS
(1675)

'As in a clock'

As in a clock, 'tis hinder'd-force doth bring
The wheels to order'd motion, by a spring;
Which order'd motion guides a steady hand
In useful sort at figures just to stand;
Which, were it not by counter-balance stay'd,
The fabric quickly would aside be laid
As wholly useless: so a might too great,
But well proportion'd, makes the world complete.
Power well-bounded is more great in might,
Than if let loose 'twere wholly infinite.
He could have made an endless sea by this,
But then it had not been a sea of bliss;
A sea that's bounded in a finite shore,
Is better far because it is no more.
Should waters endlessly exceed the skies,
They'd drown the world, and all whate'er we prize.
Had the bright sun been infinite, its flame
Had burnt the world, and quite consum'd the same.
That flame would yield no splendour to the sight,
'Twould be but darkness though 'twere infinite.
One star made infinite would all exclude,
An earth made infinite could ne'er be view'd.
But all being bounded for each other's sake,
He bounding all did all most useful make.
And which is best, in profit and delight,
Though not in bulk, He made all infinite.
He in His wisdom did their use extend,
By all, to all the world from end to end.
In all things, all things service do to all:
And thus a sand is endless, though most small.
    And every thing is truly infinite,
    In its relation deep and exquisite.

'Mankind is sick'

1

Mankind is sick, the world distemper'd lies,
    Oppress'd with sins and miseries.
Their sins are woes; a long corrupted train
    Of poison, drawn from Adam's vein,
    Stains all his seed, and all his kin
    Are one disease of life within.
        They all torment themselves!
The world's one Bedlam, or a greater cave
    Of madmen, that do always rave.

2

The wise and good like kind physicians are,
    That strive to heal them by their care.
They physic and their learning calmly use,
    Although the patient them abuse.
    For since the sickness is (they find)
    A sad distemper of the mind;
        All railings they impute,
All injuries, unto the sore disease,
    They are expressly come to ease!

3

If we would to the world's distemper'd mind
    Impute the rage which there we find,
We might, even in the midst of all our foes,
    Enjoy and feel a sweet repose.
    Might pity all the griefs we see,
    Anointing every malady
        With precious oil and balm;
And while ourselves are calm, our art improve
    To rescue them, and show our love.

4

But let's not fondly our own selves beguile;
    If we revile 'cause they revile,

Ourselves infected with their sore disease,
>   Need others' helps to give us ease.
> For we more mad than they remain,
>   Need to be cut, and need a chain
>   Far more than they. Our brain
> Is craz'd; and if we put our wit to theirs,
>   We may be justly made their heirs.

5

But while with open eyes we clearly see
>   The brightness of His majesty;
> While all the world, by sin to Satan sold,
>   In daily wickedness grows old,
>   Men in chains of darkness lie,
>   In bondage and iniquity,
>   And pierce and grieve themselves!
> The dismal woes wherein they crawl, enhance
>   The peace of our inheritance.

6

We wonder to behold ourselves so nigh
>   To so much sin and misery,
> And yet to see ourselves so safe from harm!
>   What amulet, what hidden charm
>   Could fortify and raise the soul
>   So far above them; and control
>   Such fierce malignity!
> The brightness and the glory which we see
>   Is made a greater mystery.

7

And while we feel how much our God doth love
>   The peace of sinners, how much move,
> And sue, and thirst, entreat, lament, and grieve,
>   For all the crimes in which they live,
>   And seek and wait, and call again,
>   And long to save them from the pain
>   Of sin, from all their woe!

With greater thirst, as well as grief we try,
    How to relieve their misery.

8

The life and splendour of felicity,
    Whose floods so overflowing be,
The streams of joy which round about His throne,
    Enrich and fill each holy one,
    Are so abundant, that we can
    Spare all, even all to any man!
        And have it all ourselves!   70
Nay have the more! We long to make them see
    The sweetness of felicity.

9

While we contemplate their distresses, how,
    Blind wretches, they in bondage bow,
And tear and wound themselves, and vex and groan,
    And chafe and fret so near His throne,
    And know not what they ail, but lie
    Tormented in their misery
        (Like madmen that are blind)
In works of darkness nigh such full delight: 80
    That they might find and see the sight,

10

What would we give! that they might likewise see
    The glory of His majesty!
The joy and fullness of that high delight,
    Whose blessedness is infinite!
    We would even cease to live, to gain
    Them from their misery and pain,
        And make them with us reign.
For they themselves would be our greatest treasures
    When sav'd, our own most heavenly pleasures.   90

11

O holy Jesus who didst for us die,
    And on the altar bleeding lie,
Bearing all torment, pain, reproach and shame,
    That we by virtue of the same,
      Though enemies to God, might be
      Redeem'd, and set at liberty.
          As Thou didst us forgive,
So meekly let us love to others show,
    And live in Heaven on earth below!

12

Let's prize their souls, and let them be our gems,
    Our temples and our diadems,
Our brides, our friends, our fellow-members, eyes,
    Hands, hearts and souls, our victories,
      And spoils and trophies, our own joys!
      Compar'd to souls all else are toys!
          O Jesus, let them be
Such unto us, as they are unto Thee,
    Vessels of glory and felicity!

13

How will they love us, when they find our care
    Brought them all thither where they are!
When they conceive, what terror 'tis to dwell
    In all the punishments of hell:
      And in a lively manner see,
      O Christ, eternal joys in Thee!
          How will they all delight
In praising Thee for us, with all their might,
    How sweet a grace, how infinite!

'Contentment is a sleepy thing'

Contentment is a sleepy thing!
   If it in death alone must die;
A quiet mind is worse than poverty!
   Unless it from enjoyment spring!
That's blessedness alone that makes a king!
Wherein the joys and treasures are so great,
They all the powers of the soul employ,
   And fill it with a work complete,
     While it doth all enjoy.
True joys alone contentment do inspire,
Enrich content, and make our courage higher.
   Content alone's a dead and silent stone:
     The real life of bliss
   Is glory reigning in a throne,
     Where all enjoyment is.
The soul of man is so inclin'd to see,
Without his treasures no man's soul can be,
   Nor rest content uncrown'd!
     Desire and love
Must in the height of all their rapture move,
   Where there is true felicity.
Employment is the very life and ground
Of life itself; whose pleasant motion is
   The form of bliss:
All blessedness a life with glory crown'd.
Life! Life is all: in its most full extent
Stretch'd out to all things, and with all content!

FROM AN EARLY NOTEBOOK

'Rise, noble soul'

1

Rise, noble soul, and come away;
Let us no longer waste the day.
Come, let us haste to yonder hill,
Where pleasures fresh are growing still.
    The way at first is rough and steep,
    And something hard for to ascend;
    But on the top do pleasures keep,
    And ease and joys do still attend.

2

Come, let us go; and do not fear
The hardest way, while I am near.
My heart with thine shall mingl'd be;
Thy sorrows mine, my joys with thee.
    And all our labours as we go
    True love shall sweeten still,
    And strew our way with flowers too,
    Whilst we ascend the hill.

3

The hill of rest, where angels live:
Where Bliss her palace hath to give;
Where thousands shall thee welcome make,
And joy that thou their joys dost take.
    O come, let's haste to this sweet place,
    I pray thee quickly heal thy mind!
    Sweet, let us go with joyful pace
    And leave the baser world behind.

4

Come, let's unite; and we'll aspire
Like brighter flames of heavenly fire,
That with sweet incense do ascend,
Still purer to their journey's end.

Two rising flames in one we'll be,
And with each other twining play, 30
And how, 'twill be a joy to see,
We'll fold and mingle all the way.

FROM A SERIOUS AND PATHETICAL CONTEMPLATION OF THE MERCIES OF GOD,
in Several Most Devout and Sublime Thanksgivings for the Same
(1699)

Thanksgivings for the Body

Bless the Lord, O my soul: and all that is within me bless His holy name.

    Bless the Lord, O my soul: and forget not all His benefits.

    Who forgiveth all thine iniquities: who healeth all thy diseases:

    Who redeemeth thy life from destruction. Who crowneth thee with loving kindness and tender mercies.

    Who satisfieth thy mouth with good things, so that thy youth is renewed as the eagle's.

    O Lord who art clothed with majesty,
>   My desire is to praise Thee.
>> With the holy angels and archangels
>>> To glorify Thee.

And with all Thy saints in the church triumphant.
>   For the eternal brightness
>> Of Thine infinite bounty,
>   The freedom of Thy love

Wherein Thou excellest the beams of the sun
>   To celebrate Thee.

    I will praise Thee, for I am fearfully and wonderfully made, marvellous are Thy works; and that my soul knoweth right well.

    My substance was not hid from Thee when I was made in secret, and curiously wrought in the lowest parts of the earth.

    Thine eyes did see my substance yet being unperfect; and in Thy book all my members were written; which in continuance were fashioned when as yet there was none of them.

    How precious are Thy thoughts also unto me, O God! How great is the sum of them!

    If I should count them, they are more in number than the sand: When I awake I am still with Thee.
>   Blessed be Thy holy name,
>> O Lord, my God!

Forever blessed be Thy holy name,
>   For that I am made
>> The work of Thy hands,
>   Curiously wrought

>   By Thy divine Wisdom,
> Enriched
>   By Thy Goodness,
> Being more Thine
>   Than I am mine own.   40
>   O Lord!
> Thou hast given me a body,
> Wherein the glory of Thy power shineth,
> Wonderfully composed above the beasts,
> Within distinguished into useful parts,
> Beautified without with many ornaments.
>   Limbs rarely poised,
>   And made for Heaven:
>   Arteries filled
>   With celestial spirits: 50
>   Veins, wherein blood floweth,
>   Refreshing all my flesh,
>   Like rivers.
>   Sinews fraught with the mystery
>   Of wonderful strength,
>   Stability,
>   Feeling.
>   O blessed be Thy glorious name!
> That Thou hast made it,
>   A treasury of wonders,   60
>   Fit for its several ages;
>   For dissections,
>   For sculptures in brass,
>   For drafts in anatomy.
>   For the contemplation of the sages.
>   Whose inward parts,
>   Enshrined in Thy libraries,
>   ⎧ The amazement of the learned,
>   ⎪ The admiration of kings and queens,
> Are ⎨ The joy of angels;   70
>   ⎪ The organs of my soul,
>   ⎩ The wonder of cherubims.
>   Those blinder parts of refined earth,

> Beneath my skin;
> Are full of Thy depths,
> For { Many thousand uses,
>   Hidden operations,
>   Unsearchable offices.
> But for the diviner treasures wherewith Thou hast endowed
> > My brains,   Mine eyes,
> > My heart,   Mine ears,
> > My tongue,   My hands,
> O what praises are due unto Thee,
> > Who hast made me
> > > A living inhabitant
> > > > Of the great world.
> > > And the centre of it!
> > > A sphere of sense,
> > > > And a mine of riches,
> Which when bodies are dissected fly away.
> > The spacious room
> > > Which Thou hast hidden in mine eye,
> > The chambers for sounds
> > > Which Thou hast prepar'd in mine ear,
> > The receptacles for smells
> > > Concealed in my nose;
> > The feeling of my hands,
> > > The taste of my tongue.
> But above all, O Lord, the glory of speech, whereby Thy servant
> is enabled with praise to celebrate Thee.
> > > For
> All the beauties in Heaven and earth,
> The melody of sounds,
> The sweet odours
> > Of Thy dwelling-place.
> The delectable pleasures that gratify my sense,
> > That gratify the feeling of mankind.
> The light of history,
> > Admitted by the ear.
> The light of Heaven,
> > Brought in by the eye.

The volubility and liberty
>   Of my hands and members.
Fitted by Thee for all operations;
>   Which the fancy can imagine,
>   >   Or soul desire:
From the framing of a needle's eye,
>   To the building of a tower:
From the squaring of trees,
>   To the polishing of kings' crowns.   120

For all the mysteries, engines, instruments, wherewith the world is filled, which we are able to frame and use to Thy glory.

For all the trades, variety of operations, cities, temples, streets, bridges, mariner's compass, admirable picture, sculpture, writing, printing, songs and music; wherewith the world is beautified and adorned.

>   Much more for the regent Life,
>   >   And power of perception,
>   >   >   Which rules within.
That secret depth of fathomless consideration   130
>   That receives the information
>   >   Of all our senses,
That makes our centre equal to the heavens,
>   And comprehendeth in itself the magnitude of the world;
>   >   The involved mysteries
>   >   >   Of our common sense;
>   >   The inaccessible secret
>   >   >   Of perceptive fancy;
>   >   The repository and treasury
>   >   >   Of things that are past;   140
>   >   The presentation of things to come;
>   >   >   Thy name be glorified
>   >   >   >   For evermore.
For all the art which Thou hast hidden
>   In this little piece
>   >   Of red clay.
For the workmanship of Thy hand,
>   Who didst Thyself form man
>   >   Of the dust of the ground,

And breathe into his nostrils
> The breath of life.

For the high exaltation whereby Thou hast glorified every body,
> Especially mine,
>> As Thou didst Thy servant
>>> Adam's in Eden.

Thy works themselves speaking to me the same thing that was said unto him in the beginning,
WE ARE ALL THINE.
And why, O Lord, wouldst Thou so delight
To magnify the dust taken from the ground?
> From the dark obscurity of a silent grave

Thou raisest it, O Lord!
>> Herein indeed

Thou raisest the poor out of the dust, and liftest the needy out of the dunghill,

That thou mayst set him with princes; even with the princes of Thy people.

But why would the Lord take pleasure in creating an earthly body? Why at all in making a visible world? Couldst thou not have made us immortal souls, and seated us immediately in the throne of glory?
> O Lord, Thou lover of righteousness,
>> Whose Kingdom is everlasting;

Who lovest to govern thy subjects by laws, and takest delight to distribute rewards and punishments according to right.

Thou hast hidden Thyself
>> By an infinite miracle,

And made this world the chamber of Thy presence; the ground and theatre of Thy righteous Kingdom.

> That putting us at a distance
>> A little from Thee,

> Thou mayest satisfy the capacities
>> Of Thy righteous nature.

Thou wast always fit to reign like a King,
> Able to rule by the best of laws,

To distribute the greatest rewards and punishments.
> That therefore Thou might'st raise up

>> Objects for these,
> Thou hast seated us at a little distance from Thee,
>> Not in respect of Thy ubiquity, but degree of knowledge.
>> In Heaven Thou dwellest
>>> As a bridegroom with Thy bride,
>>>> A Father with Thy children,
>>>> A King with kings, governors and peers,
>>> Showing and manifesting all Thy glory.
>> Unto which Thou wouldst have us first to come,
> As humble and obedient servants:
>> That in us Thou mightst see
>>>> Ingenuity,   Thanksgiving,
>>>> Fidelity,   Wisdom,
>>>>> Love,
>>> Even to an absent benefactor.
>> There is the Kingdom of eternal glory,
> Beyond which can be no rewards,
>> The highest of all being there attained.
> In which can be no trial,
>> Blessedness being seen with open face.
> Beneath which it was necessary that we should be made:
>> To the intent we might be governed
>>> In a righteous Kingdom.
>> But couldst Thou not have remitted our knowledge, and established to Thyself a righteous Kingdom, without composing our bodies, or the world?
>> By the fall of some, we know, O Lord,
>>> That the angels were tried,
>>> Which are invisible spirits,
>>>> Needing not the world,
>>> Nor clothed in bodies,
>>>> Nor endued with senses.
>> For our bodies therefore, O Lord, for our earthly bodies, hast Thou made the world: which Thou so lovest, that Thou hast supremely magnified them by the works of Thy hands:
>> And made them lords of the whole creation.
>>> Higher than the heavens,
>>>> Because served by them:

THANKSGIVINGS

    More glorious than the sun,
        Because it ministreth to them:
  Greater in dignity than the material world.
        Because the end of its creation.
      Revived by the air,
      Served by the seas,
  Fed by the beasts, and fowls, and fishes,
        Our pleasure.
Which fall as sacrifices to
        Thy glory.
Being made to minister and attend upon us.
    O miracle
      Of divine goodness!
O fire! O flame of zeal, and love, and joy!
Even for our earthly bodies, hast Thou created all things.

    All things { Visible. / Material. / Sensible. }

        Animals,
        Vegetables,
        Minerals,
          Bodies celestial,
          Bodies terrestrial,
          The four elements,
          Volatile spirits,
    Trees, herbs, and flowers,
      The influences of Heaven,
  Clouds, vapours, wind,
      Dew, rain, hail, and snow,
Light and darkness, night and day,
      The seasons of the year.
Springs, rivers, fountains, oceans,
    Gold, silver, and precious stones.
      Corn, wine, and oil,
      The sun, moon, and stars,
        Cities, nations, kingdoms.
And the bodies of men, the greatest treasures of all,
        For each other.

What then, O Lord, hast Thou intended for our souls, who givest to our bodies such glorious things!
>Everything in Thy Kingdom, O Lord,
Conspireth to mine exaltation.
>In everything I see Thy wisdom and goodness.
>>And I praise the power by which I see it.

My body is but the cabinet, or case of my soul: 270
>What then, O Lord, shall the jewel be!

Thou makest it the heir of all the profitable trades and occupations in the world.
>And the heavens and the earth
>>More freely mine,
>>More profitably,
>>More gloriously,
>>More comfortably
>Than if no man were alive but I alone.
>>Yea though I am a sinner, Thou lovest me more than if 280

Thou hadst given all things to me alone.
>The sons of men Thou hast made my treasures,
>>Those lords,
>>Incarnate cherubims,
>>Angels of the world,
>>The cream of all things,
>>And the sons of God,

Hast Thou given to me, and made them mine,
>For endless causes ever to be enjoyed.
>>Were I alone, 290

Briars and thorns would devour me;
Wild beasts annoy me;
My guilt terrify me;
The world itself be a desert to me;
The skies a dungeon,
>But mine ignorance more.

The earth a wilderness;
All things desolate:
>And I in solitude,
>Naked and hungry, 300
>Blind and brutish,

Without house or harbour;
Subject unto storms;
Lying upon the ground;
Feeding upon roots;
 But more upon melancholy,
 Because void of Thee.
Therefore Thou providest for me, and for me they build, and get and provide for me

| My Bread, | Drink, |
| Clothes, | Bed, |

My household stuff, { Books, Utensils, Furniture.

The use of meats, fire, fuel, &c.
They teach unto me, provide for me.

While I, O Lord, exalted by Thy hand,
Above the skies in glory seem to stand:
The skies being made to serve me, as they do,
While I Thy glories in Thy goodness view.
To be in glory higher than the skies,
Is greater bliss, than 'tis in place to rise
Above the stars: more blessed and divine,
To live and see, than like the sun to shine.
O what profoundness in my body lies,
For whom the earth was made, the sea, the skies!
So greatly high our human bodies are,
That angels scarcely may with these compare.
In all the heights of glory seated, they,
Above the sun in Thine eternal day,
Are seen to shine; with greater gifts adorn'd
Than gold with light, or flesh with life suborn'd.
Suns are but servants! Skies beneath their feet;
The stars but stones; moons but to serve them meet.
Beyond all heights above the world they reign,
In Thy great throne ordained to remain.
 All tropes are clouds; truth doth itself excel,
 Whatever heights, hyperboles can tell.

O that I were as David, the sweet singer of Israel!
> In meeter Psalms to set forth Thy praises.

Thy raptures ravish me, and turn my soul all into melody.

Whose Kingdom is so glorious, that nothing in it shall at all be unprofitable, mean, or idle.
> So constituted!

That everyone's glory is beneficial unto all; and everyone magnified in his place by service.

What is man, O Lord, that Thou art mindful of him! or the son of man, that Thou visitest him!

Kings in all their glory minister to us, while we repose in peace and safety.

Priests and bishops serve at Thine altar, guiding our bodies to eternal glory.

Physicians heal us.

Courts of judicature stand open for our preservation.

The outgoings of the morning and evening rejoice to do us service.

The holy angels minister unto us.

Architects and masons build us temples.

The sons of harmony fill Thy choirs.

Where even our sensible bodies are entertained by Thee with great magnificence; and solaced with joys.

Jesus Christ hath washed our feet.

He ministered to us by dying for us.
> And now in our human body, sitteth at Thy right hand, in the throne of glory.
>> As our head,
>> For our sakes,

Being there adored by angels and cherubims.
> What is it Lord
>> That Thou so esteemest us!

Thou passed'st by the angels,
> Pure spirits;

And didst send Thy Son to die for us
> That are made of both
>> Soul and body.
> Are we drawn unto Thee?

O why dost Thou make us
So Thy treasures?
Are eyes and hands such jewels unto Thee?
What, O Lord, are tongues and sounds, 380
And nostrils unto Thee?
Strange materials are visible bodies!
Things strange even compared to Thy nature,
Which is wholly spiritual.
For our sakes do the angels enjoy the visible heavens.
The sun and stars,
Thy terrestrial glories,
And all Thy wisdom
In the $\begin{cases} \text{Ordinances of Heaven.} \\ \text{Seasons of the year.} \end{cases}$ 390
Wondering to see Thee by another way,
So highly exalting dust and ashes.
Thou makest us treasures
And joys unto them;
Objects of delight, and spiritual lamps,
Whereby they discern visible things.
They see Thy Paradise among the sons of men.
Thy wine and oil, Thy gold and silver,
By our eyes. 400
They smell Thy perfumes,
And taste Thy honey, milk, and butter,
By our senses.
Thy angels have neither ears nor eyes,
Nor tongues nor hands,
Yet feel the delights of all the world,
And hear the harmonies, not only which earth but Heaven
maketh.
The melody of kingdoms,
The joys of ages, 410
Are objects of their joy.
They sing Thy praises for our sakes;
While we upon earth are highly exalted
By being made Thy gifts,

    And blessings unto them:
Never their contempt;
    More their amazement;
And did they not love us
    Their envy hereafter,
    But now their joy.   420
    When our glory being understood,
We shall shine as the sun
    In Thy heavenly Kingdom.
From whence also we look for the Saviour, the Lord Jesus Christ.
Who shall change our vile body, that it may be fashioned like unto His glorious body; according to the working whereby He is able to subdue all things to Himself.

> *Then shall each limb a spring of joy be found,*
> *And every member with its glory crown'd:*
> *While all the senses, fill'd with all the good*   430
> *That ever ages in them understood,*
> *Transported are: containing worlds of treasure,*
> *At one delight with all their joy and pleasure.*
> *From hence, like rivers, joy shall overflow,*
> *Affect the soul, though in the body grow.*
> *Return again, and make the body shine*
> *Like Jesus Christ, while both in one combine,*
> *Mysterious contacts are between the soul,*
> *Which touch the spirits, and by those its bowl:*
> *The marrow, bowels, spirits, melt and move,*   440
> *Dissolving ravish, teach them how to love.*
> *He that could bring the heavens through the eye,*
> *And make the world within the fancy lie,*
> *By beams of light that closing meet in one,*
> *From all the parts of His celestial throne,*
> *Far more than this in framing bliss can do,*
> *Inflame the body and the spirit too:*
> *Can make the soul by sense to feel and see,*
> *And with her joy the senses rapt to be.*
> *Yea while the flesh or body subject lies*   450
> *To those affections which in souls arise;*

All holy glories from the soul redound,
And in the body by the soul abound,
Are felt within, and ravish every sense,
With all the Godhead's glorious excellence:
Who found the way Himself to dwell within,
As if even flesh were nigh to Him of kin.
His goodness, wisdom, power, love divine,
Make, by the soul convey'd, the body shine.
Not like the sun (that earthly darkness is) 460
But in the strengths and heights of all this bliss.
For God designs thy body, for His sake,
A temple of the Deity to make.

But now, O Lord, how highly great have my transgressions been, who have abused this Thy glorious creature, by surfeiting and excess, by lust and wantonness, by drunkenness, by passion, by immoderate cares, excessive desires, and earthly fears?

Yea, had I been guilty of none of those, had no lies and oaths polluted my tongue, no vain imaginations defiled my heart, no stealing my hands, nor idle speeches profaned mine ears, 470

Yet have I been wholly estranged from Thee, by the sinful courses of this world, by the delusions of vain conversation.

Being unsensible of these things, I have been blind and dead, profane and stupid, seared and ingrateful; and for living beneath such a glorious estate, may justly be excluded Thine everlasting Kingdom.

Enable me to keep Thy temple sacred!
   Which Thou hast prepared for Thyself.
Turn away mine eyes
   From beholding vanity. 480
Enable me to wash my hands in innocency.
That I may compass Thine altar about,
   And lift up my hands
     To Thy holy oracle.
Put a watch over the door of my lips,
That I speak not unadvisedly with my tongue.
   Let my glory awake early in the morning,
     To bring praises unto Thee.

Enter, O Lord, the gates of my heart.
> Bow down the heavens, O Lord, 490
And break open those everlasting doors,
> That the King of Glory may enter in.

Let the ark of Thy presence rest within me.

Let not sin reign in our mortal bodies, that we should obey it in the lusts thereof.

Neither let us yield our members as instruments of unrighteousness unto sin, but let us yield ourselves to God, as those that are alive from the dead: and our members as instruments of righteousness to God.

My beloved put in his hand by the hole of the door, and my 500 bowels were moved for him.

I rose up to open to my beloved, and my hands dropped with myrrh, and my fingers with sweet-smelling myrrh, upon the handles of the lock.

O my beloved be not as a wayfaring man, that turneth aside to tarry but for a night.

Thou hast ravished mine heart with one of thine eyes.

How fair is thy love, my sister, my spouse! How much better is thy love than wine! and the smell of thine ointments than all spices!

Thy lips, O my spouse, drop as an honeycomb; honey and 510 milk are under thy tongue, and the smell of thy garments is as the smell of Lebanon.

Or ever I was aware my soul made me like the chariots of Aminadab.

Return O my love!
> I would lead thee, and bring thee
>> Into my mother's house.
> I would kiss thee, yet should I not be despised.
>> O let me live in thy bosom forever.

O infinite God, centre of my soul, convert me powerfully unto Thee, 520 *that in Thee I may take rest, for Thou didst make me for Thee, and my heart's unquiet till it be united to Thee. And seeing, O eternal Father, Thou didst create me that I might love Thee as a son, give me grace that I may love Thee as my Father. O only begotten Son of God, Redeemer of the world, seeing Thou didst create and redeem me that I might obey and imitate Thee, make me to obey and imitate Thee in all Thy imitable perfection. O Holy Ghost, seeing Thou didst create me to sanctify me, do it, O do it for Thine own glory: that I may acceptably praise and serve the holy and undivided Trinity in unity, and unity in Trinity.   Amen.*

Let all Thy creatures bless Thee O Lord, and my soul praise and bless Thee for them all. I give Thee thanks for the being Thou givest unto the heavens, sun, moon, stars, and elements; to beasts, plants, and all other bodies of the earth; to the fowls of the air, the fishes of the sea. I give Thee thanks for the beauty of colours, for the harmony of sounds, for the pleasantness of odours, for the sweetness of meats, for the warmth and softness of our raiment, and for all my five senses, and all the pores of my body, so curiously made as before recited, and for the preservation as well as use of all my limbs and senses, in keeping me from precipices, fractures, and dislocations in my body, from a distracted, discomposed, confused, discontented spirit. Above all, I praise Thee for manifesting Thyself unto me, whereby I am made capable of praise and magnify Thy name for evermore.

FROM CENTURIES OF MEDITATIONS

From The First Century

1

An empty book is like an infant's soul, in which anything may be written. It is capable of all things, but containeth nothing. I have a mind to fill this with profitable wonders. And since Love made you put it into my hands, I will fill it with those truths you love without knowing them; and with those things which, if it be possible, shall show my love: to you, in communicating most enriching truths; to Truth, in exalting her beauties in such a soul.

2

Do not wonder that I promise to fill it with those truths you love, but know not: for tho it be a maxim in the schools, that there is no love of a thing unknown; yet I have found, that things unknown have a secret influence on the soul: and like the centre of the earth unseen, violently attract it. We love we know not what: and therefore everything allures us. As iron at a distance is drawn by the lodestone, there being some invisible communications between them: so is there in us a world of love to somewhat, tho we know not what in the world that should be. There are invisible ways of conveyance, by which some great thing doth touch our souls, and by which we tend to it. Do you not feel yourself drawn with the expectation and desire of some great thing?

3

I will open my mouth in parables: I will utter things that have been kept secret from the foundations of the world. Things strange, yet common; incredible, yet known; most high, yet plain; infinitely profitable, but not esteemed. Is it not a great thing, that you should be heir of the world? Is it not a very enriching verity? In which the fellowship of the mystery, which from the beginning of the world hath been hid in God, lies concealed! The thing hath been from the creation of the world, but hath not so been explained as that the interior beauty should be understood. It is my design therefore in such a plain manner to unfold it that my friendship may appear, in making you possessor of the whole world.

4

I will not by the noise of bloody wars, and the dethroning of kings, advance you to glory; but by the gentle ways of peace and love. As a deep friendship meditates and intends the deepest designs for the advancement of its objects, so doth it show itself in choosing the sweetest and most delightful methods whereby not to weary, but please the person it desireth to advance. Where Love administers physic, its tenderness is expressed in balms and cordials. It hateth corrosives, and is rich in its administrations. Even so God, designing to show His love in exalting you, hath chosen the ways of ease and repose, by which you should ascend. And I after His similitude will lead you into paths plain and familiar. Where all envy, rapine, bloodshed, complaint, and malice shall be far removed; and nothing appear but contentment and thanksgiving. Yet shall the end be so glorious that angels durst not hope for so great a one till they had seen it.

5

The fellowship of the mystery that hath been hid in God since the Creation, is not only the contemplation of His love in the work of redemption, tho that is wonderful: but the end for which we are redeemed: a communion with Him in all His glory. For which cause, St Peter saith, 'The God of all grace hath called us unto His eternal glory by Jesus Christ.' His eternal glory by the methods of His divine wisdom being made ours; and our fruition of it, the end for which our Saviour suffered.

6

True Love, as it intendeth the greatest gifts, intendeth also the greatest benefits. It contenteth not itself in showing great things unless it can make them greatly useful. For Love greatly delighteth in seeing its object continually seated in the highest happiness. Unless therefore I could advance you higher by the uses of what I give, my love could not be satisfied in giving you the whole world. But because when you enjoy it, you are advanced to the throne of God and may see His love, I rest well pleased in bestowing it. It will make you to see your own greatness, the truth of the Scriptures, the amiableness of virtue, and the beauty of religion. It will enable you also to contemn the world, and to overflow with praises.

7

To contemn the world, and to enjoy the world, are things contrary to each other. How then can we contemn the world which we are born to enjoy? Truly there are two worlds. One was made by God, the other by men. That made by God was great and beautiful. Before the Fall, it was Adam's joy, and the temple of His glory. That made by men is a Babel of confusions: invented riches, pomps, and vanities, brought in by sin. Give all (saith Thomas a Kempis) for all. Leave the one that you may enjoy the other.

8

What is more easy and sweet than meditation? Yet in this hath God commended His love, that by meditation it is enjoyed. As nothing is more easy than to think, so nothing is more difficult than to think well. The easiness of thinking we received from God, the difficulty of thinking well proceedeth from ourselves. Yet in truth, it is far more easy to think well than ill, because good thoughts be sweet and delightful; evil thoughts are full of discontent and trouble. So that an evil habit, and custom, have made it difficult to think well, not nature. For by nature, nothing is so difficult as to think amiss.

9

Is it not easy to conceive the world in your mind? To think the heavens fair? The sun glorious? The earth fruitful? The air pleasant? The sea profitable? And the Giver bountiful? Yet these are the things which it is difficult to retain. For could we always be sensible of their use and value, we should be always delighted with their wealth and glory.

10

To think well is to serve God in the interior court: to have a mind composed of divine thoughts, and set in frame, to be like Him within. To conceive aright and to enjoy the world, is to conceive the Holy Ghost, and to see His love; which is the mind of the Father. And this more pleaseth Him than many worlds, could we create as fair and great as this. For when you are once acquainted with the world, you will find the goodness and wisdom of God so manifest therein, that it was impossible another or better should be made.

Which being made to be enjoyed, nothing can please or serve Him more than the soul that enjoys it. For that soul doth accomplish the end of His desire in creating it.

11

Love is deeper than at first it can be thought. It never ceaseth but in endless things. It ever multiplies. Its benefits and its designs are always infinite. Were you not holy, divine, and blessed in enjoying the world, I should not care so much to bestow it. But now in this you accomplish the end of your creation, and serve God best, and please Him most: I rejoice in giving it. For to enable you to please God, is the highest service a man can do you. It is to make you pleasing to the King of Heaven, that you may be the darling of His bosom.

12

Can you be holy without accomplishing the end for which you are created? Can you be divine unless you be holy? Can you accomplish the end for which you were created, unless you be righteous? Can you then be righteous, unless you be just in rendering to things their due esteem? All things were made to be yours. And you were made to prize them according to their value: which is your office and duty, the end for which you were created, and the means whereby you enjoy. *The end for which you were created is that by prizing all that God hath done, you may enjoy yourself and Him in blessedness.*

13

To be holy is so zealously to desire, so vastly to esteem, and so earnestly to endeavour it, that we would not for millions of gold and silver, decline, nor fail, nor mistake in a tittle. For then we please God when we are most like Him. We are like Him when our minds are in frame. Our minds are in frame when our thoughts are like His. And our thoughts are then like His when we have such conceptions of all objects as God hath, and prize all things according to their value. For God doth prize all things rightly. Which is a key that opens into the very thoughts of His bosom. It seemeth arrogance to pretend to the knowledge of His secret thoughts. But how shall we have the mind of God, unless we know His thoughts? Or how shall we be led by His divine spirit, till we have His mind? His thoughts are hidden: but He hath revealed unto us the hidden things of darkness. By His works and by His attributes we know His thoughts. And by thinking the same are divine and blessed.

14

When things are ours in their proper places, nothing is needful but prizing, to enjoy them. God therefore hath made it infinitely easy to enjoy, by making every thing ours, and us able so easily to prize them. Every thing is ours that serves us in its place. The sun serves us as much as is possible, and more than we could imagine. The clouds and stars minister unto us, the world surrounds us with beauty, the air refresheth us, the sea revives the earth and us. The earth itself is better than gold because it produceth fruits and flowers. And therefore in the beginning, was it made manifest to be mine, because Adam alone was made to enjoy it. By making one, and not a multitude, God evidently showed one alone to be the end of the world, and everyone its enjoyer; for everyone may enjoy it as much as he.

15

Such endless depths lie in the divinity and the wisdom of God, that as He maketh one, so He maketh everyone the end of the world: the supernumerary persons being enrichers of his inheritance. Adam and the world are both mine. And the posterity of Adam enrich it infinitely. Souls are God's jewels. Every one of which is worth many worlds. They are His riches because His image, and mine for that reason. So that I alone am the end of the world. Angels and men being all mine. And if others are so, they are made to enjoy it for my further advancement. God only being the giver, and I the receiver. So that Seneca philosophized rightly, when he said, *Deus me dedit solum toti mundo, et totum mundum mihi soli.* God gave me alone to all the world, and all the world to me alone.

16

That all the world is yours, your very senses and the inclinations of your mind declare. The works of God manifest, His laws testify, and His Word doth prove it. His attributes most sweetly make it evident.

The powers of your soul confirm it. So that in the midst of such rich demonstrations, you may infinitely delight in God as your Father, friend, and benefactor; in yourself as His heir, child, and bride; in the whole world, as the gift and token of His love. Neither can anything but ignorance destroy your joys; for if you know yourself, or God, or the world, you must of necessity enjoy it.

17

To know God is life eternal. There must therefore some exceeding great thing be always attained in the knowledge of Him. To know God is to know goodness; it is to see the beauty of infinite love: to see it attended with almighty power and eternal wisdom; and using both those in the magnifying of its object. It is to see the King of Heaven and earth take infinite delight in giving. Whatever knowledge else you have of God, it is but superstition. Which Plutarch rightly defineth to be 'an ignorant dread of His divine power, without any joy in His goodness'. He is not an object of terror, but delight. To know Him therefore as He is, is to frame the most beautiful Idea in all worlds. He delighteth in our happiness more than we; and is of all other the most lovely object. An infinite Lord, who having all riches, honours, and pleasures in His own hand, is infinitely willing to give them unto me. Which is the fairest Idea that can be devised.

18

The world is not this little cottage of Heaven and earth. Tho this be fair, it is too small a gift. When God made the world, He made the heavens and the heavens of heavens, and the angels and the celestial powers. These also are parts of the world; so are all those infinite and eternal treasures that are to abide forever, after the Day of Judgement. Neither are these, some here, and some there, but all everywhere, and at once to be enjoyed. The world is unknown, till the value and glory of it is seen: till the beauty and the serviceableness of its parts is considered. When you enter into it, it is an illimited field of variety and beauty: where you may lose yourself in the multitude of wonders and delights. But it is an happy loss to lose oneself in admiration at one's own felicity; and to find GOD in exchange for oneself. Which we then do when we see Him in His gifts, and adore His glory.

19

You never know yourself, till you know more than your body. The image of God was not seated in the features of your face, but in the lineaments of your soul. In the knowledge of your powers, inclinations, and principles, the knowledge of yourself chiefly consisteth. Which are so great that even to the most learned of men their greatness is incredible; and so divine, that they are infinite in value. Alas, the world is but a little centre in comparison of you. Suppose it millions of miles from the earth to the heavens, and millions of millions above the stars, both here and over the heads of our antipodes: it is surrounded with infinite and eternal space; and like a gentleman's house to one that is travelling, it is a long time before you come unto it, you pass it in an instant, and leave it forever. The omnipresence and eternity of God are your fellows and companions. And all that is in them ought to be made your familiar treasures. Your understanding comprehends the world like the dust of a balance, measures Heaven with a span, and esteems a thousand years but as one day. So that great endless eternal delights are only fit to be its enjoyments.

20

The laws of God, which are the commentaries of His works, show them to be yours: because they teach you to love God with all your soul, and with all your might. Whom if you love with all the endless powers of your soul, you will love Him in Himself, in His attributes, in His counsels, in all His works, in all His ways; and in every kind of thing wherein He appeareth, you will prize Him, you will honour Him, you will delight in Him, you will ever desire to be with Him and to please Him. For to love Him includeth all this. You will feed with pleasure upon everything that is His. So that the world shall be a grand jewel of delight unto you: a very Paradise; and the gate of Heaven. It is indeed the beautiful frontispiece of eternity, the temple of God, the palace of His children. The laws of God discover all that is therein to be created for your sake. For they command you to love all that is good, and when you see well, you enjoy what you love. They apply the endless powers of your soul to all their objects, and by ten thousand methods make everything to serve you. They command you to love all angels and men, they command all angels and men to love you. When you love them, they are your treasures; when they love you, to your great advantage you are theirs. All things serve you for serving them whom you love, and of whom you are beloved. The entrance of His words giveth light to the simple. You are magnified among angels and men: enriched by them, and happy in them.

21

By the very right of your senses you enjoy the world. Is not the beauty of the hemisphere present to your eye? Doth not the glory of the sun pay tribute to your sight? Is not the vision of the world an amiable thing? Do not the stars shed influences to perfect the air? Is not that a marvellous body to breathe in? To visit the lungs: repair the spirits: revive the senses: cool the blood: fill the empty spaces between the earth and heavens; and yet give liberty to all objects? Prize these first: and you shall enjoy the residue. Glory, dominion, power, wisdom, honour, angels, souls, kingdoms, ages. Be faithful in a little, and you shall be master over much. If you be not faithful in esteeming these, who shall put into your hands the true treasures? If you be negligent in prizing these, you will be negligent in prizing all. There is a disease in him who despiseth present mercies, which till it be cured, he can never be happy. He esteemeth nothing that he hath, but is ever gaping after more: which when he hath he despiseth in like manner. Insatiableness is good, but not ingratitude.

22

It is of the nobility of man's soul that he is insatiable, for he hath a benefactor so prone to give, that He delighteth in us for asking. Do not your inclinations tell you that the world is yours? Do you not covet all? Do you not long to have it; to enjoy it; to overcome it? To what end do men gather riches, but to multiply more? Do they not like Pyrrhus the king of Epire, add house to house and lands to lands, that they may get it all? It is storied of that prince, that having conceived a purpose to invade Italy, he sent for Cineas, a philosopher and the king's friend: to whom he communicated his design, and desired his counsel. Cineas asked him to what purpose he invaded Italy? He said, 'To conquer it.' 'And what will you do when you have conquered it?' 'Go into France,' said the king, 'and conquer that.' 'And what will you do when you have conquered France?' 'Conquer Germany.' 'And what then?' said the philosopher. 'Conquer Spain.' 'I perceive,' said Cineas, 'you mean to conquer all the world. What will you do when you have conquered all?' 'Why then,' said the king, 'we will return, and enjoy ourselves at quiet in our own land.' 'So you may now,' said the philosopher, 'without all this ado.' Yet could he not divert him till he was ruined by the Romans. Thus men get one hundred pound a year that they may get another; and having two covet eight, and there is no end of all their labour, because the desire of their soul is insatiable. Like Alexander the Great, they must have all: and when they have got it all be quiet. And may they not do all this before they begin? Nay, it would be well if they could be quiet. But if after all, they shall be like the stars, that are seated on high, but have no rest, what gain they more, but labour for their trouble? It was wittily feigned that that young man sate down and cried for more worlds. So insatiable is man that millions will not please him. They are no more than so many tennis balls, in comparison of the greatness and highness of his soul.

23

The noble inclination whereby man thirsteth after riches and dominion is his highest virtue, when rightly guided; and carries him as in a triumphant chariot to his sovereign happiness. Men are made miserable only by abusing it. Taking a false way to satisfy it, they pursue the wind: nay labour in the very fire, and after all reap but vanity. Whereas, as God's love, which is the fountain of all, did cost us nothing: so were all other things prepared by it, to satisfy our inclinations in the best of manners, freely, without any cost of ours. Being therefore all satisfactions are near at hand, by going further we do but leave them: and wearying ourselves in a long way round about, like a blind man, forsake them. They are immediately near to the very gates of our senses. It becometh the bounty of God to prepare them freely: to make them glorious, and their enjoyment easy. For because His love is free, so are His treasures. He therefore that will despise them because he hath them, is marvellously irrational. The way to possess them is to esteem them. And the true way of reigning over them, is to break the world all into parts, to examine them asunder. And if we find them so excellent that better could not possibly be made, and so made that they could not be more ours, to rejoice in all with pleasure answerable to the merit of their goodness. We being then kings over the whole world, when we restore the pieces to their proper places, being perfectly pleased with the whole composure. This shall give you a thorough grounded contentment, far beyond what troublesome wars or conquests can acquire.

24

Is it not a sweet thing to have all covetousness and ambition satisfied, suspicion and infidelity removed, courage and joy infused? Yet is all this in the fruition of the world attained; for thereby God is seen in all His wisdom, power, goodness, and glory.

25

Your enjoyment of the world is never right, till you so esteem it that everything in it is more your treasure than a king's exchequer full of gold and silver. And that exchequer yours also in its place and service. Can you take too much joy in your Father's works? He is Himself in everything. Some things are little on the outside, and rough and common. But I remember the time, when the dust of the streets were as precious as gold to my infant eyes, and now they are more precious to the eye of reason.

26

The services of things, and their excellencies are spiritual: being objects not of the eye, but of the mind; and you more spiritual by how much more you esteem them. Pigs eat acorns, but neither consider the sun that gave them life, nor the influences of the heavens by which they were nourished, nor the very root of the tree from whence they came. This being the work of angels, who in a wide and clear light see even the sea that gave them moisture. And feed upon that acorn spiritually, while they know the ends for which it was created and feast upon all these, as upon the world of joys within it; while to ignorant swine that eat the shell, it is an empty husk of no taste nor delightful savour.

27

You never enjoy the world aright, till you see how a sand exhibiteth the wisdom and power of God; and prize in everything the service which they do you, by manifesting His glory and goodness to your soul, far more than the visible beauty of their surface, or the material services they can do your body. Wine by its moisture quencheth my thirst, whether I consider it or no; but to see it flowing from His love who gave it unto man, quencheth the thirst even of the holy angels. To consider it is to drink it spiritually. To rejoice in its diffusion is to be of a public mind. And to take pleasure in all the benefits it doth to all is heavenly. For so they do in Heaven. To do so is to be divine and good and to imitate our infinite and eternal Father.

28

Your enjoyment of the world is never right, till every morning you awake in Heaven: see yourself in your Father's palace; and look upon the skies and the earth and the air, as celestial joys: having such a reverend esteem of all, as if you were among the angels. The bride of a monarch, in her husband's chamber, hath no such causes of delight as you.

29

You never enjoy the world aright, till the sea itself floweth in your veins, till you are clothed with the heavens, and crowned with the stars; and perceive yourself to be the sole heir of the whole world: and more than so, because men are in it who are every one sole heirs, as well as you. Till you can sing and rejoice and delight in God, as misers do in gold, and kings in sceptres, you never enjoy the world.

30

Till your spirit filleth the whole world, and the stars are your jewels; till you are as familiar with the ways of God in all ages as with your walk and table; till you are intimately acquainted with that shady nothing out of which the world was made; till you love men so as to desire their happiness, with a thirst equal to the zeal of your own; till you delight in God for being good to all: you never enjoy the world. Till you more feel it than your private estate, and are more present in the hemisphere, considering the glories and the beauties there, than in your own house. Till you remember how lately you were made, and how wonderful it was when you came into it; and more rejoice in the palace of your glory than if it had been made but today morning.

31

Yet further, you never enjoy the world aright, till you so love the beauty of enjoying it, that you are covetous and earnest to persuade others to enjoy it. And so perfectly hate the abominable corruption of men in despising it, that you had rather suffer the flames of hell than willingly be guilty of their error. There is so much blindness, and ingratitude, and damned folly in it. The world is a mirror of infinite beauty, yet no man sees it. It is a temple of majesty, yet no man regards it. It is a region of light and peace, did not men disquiet it. It is the Paradise of God. It is more to man since he is fallen than it was before. It is the place of angels, and the gate of Heaven. When Jacob waked out of his dream, he said, 'God is here and I wist it not. How dreadful is this place! This is none other than the house of God, and the gate of Heaven.'

32

Can any ingratitude be more damned than that which is fed by benefits? Or folly greater than that which bereaveth us of infinite treasures? They despise them merely because they have them; and invent ways to make themselves miserable in the presence of riches. They study a thousand newfangled treasures, which God never made; and then grieve and repine that they be not happy. They dote on their own works, and neglect God's. Which are full of majesty, riches, and wisdom. And having fled away from them because they are solid, divine, and true, greedily pursuing tinselled vanities, they walk on in darkness, and will not understand. They do the works of darkness, and delight in the riches of the Prince of Darkness, and follow them till they come into eternal darkness. According to that of the Psalmist, 'All the foundations of the earth are out of course.'

33

The riches of darkness are those which men have made during their ignorance of God Almighty's treasures: that lead us from the love of all, to labour and contention, discontentment and vanity. The works of darkness are repining, envy, malice, covetousness, fraud, oppression, discontent, and violence: all which proceed from the corruption of men, and their mistake in the choice of riches: for having refused those which God made, and taken to themselves treasures of their own, they invented scarce and rare, insufficient, hard to be gotten, little, movable, and useless treasures. Yet as violently pursue them as if they were the most necessary and excellent things in the whole world. And tho they are all mad, yet having made a combination they seem wise; and it is a hard matter to persuade them either to truth or reason. There seemeth to be no way but theirs; whereas God knoweth they are as far out of the way of happiness as the East is from the West. For by this means, they have let in broils and dissatisfactions into the world, and are ready to eat and devour one another: particular and feeble interests, false proprieties, insatiable longings, fraud, emulation, murmuring, and dissension being everywhere seen; theft and pride and danger and cozenage, envy and contention drowning the peace and beauty of nature as waters cover the sea. O how they are ready to sink always under the burden and cumber of devised wants! Verily, the prospect of their ugly errors is able to turn one's stomach: they are so hideous and deformed.

34

Would one think it possible for a man to delight in gauderies like a butterfly, and neglect the heavens? Did we not daily see it, it would be incredible. They rejoice in a piece of gold more than in the sun; and get a few little glittering stones and call them jewels. And admire them because they be resplendent like the stars, and transparent like the air, and pellucid like the sea. But the stars themselves which are ten thousand times more useful, great, and glorious, they disregard. Nor shall the air itself be counted anything, tho it be worth all the pearls and diamonds in ten thousand worlds, a work so divine by reason of its precious and pure transparency, that all worlds would be worth nothing without such a treasure.

35

The riches of the light are the works of God, which are the portion and inheritance of His sons, to be seen and enjoyed in Heaven and earth, the sea and all that is therein, the light and the day. Great and fathomless in use and excellency, true, necessary. Freely given, proceeding wholly from His infinite love, as worthy as they are easy to be enjoyed. Obliging us to love Him, and to delight in Him, filling us with gratitude, and making us to overflow with praises and thanksgivings. The works of contentment and pleasure are of the day. So are the works which flow from the understanding of our mutual serviceableness to each other: arising from the sufficiency and excellency of our treasures, contentment, joy, peace, unity, charity &c. Whereby we are all knit together and delight in each other's happiness. For while everyone is heir of all the world, and all the rest his superadded treasures, all the world serves him in himself, and in them, as his superadded treasures.

36

The common error which makes it difficult to believe all the world to be wholly ours, is to be shunned as a rock of shipwreck or a dangerous quicksand. For the poison which they drank hath infatuated their fancies and now they know not, neither will they understand, they walk on in darkness. *All the foundations of the earth are out of course.* It is safety not to be with them. And a great part of happiness to be freed from their seducing and enslaving errors. That while others live in a Golgotha or prison, we should be in Eden, is a very great mystery. And a mercy it is that we should be rejoicing in the temple of Heaven, while they are toiling and lamenting in hell, for the world is both a Paradise and a prison to different persons.

37

The brightness and magnificence of this world, which by reason of its height and greatness is hidden from men, is divine and wonderful. It addeth much to the glory of that temple in which we live. Yet it is the cause why men understand it not. They think it too great and wide to be enjoyed. But since it is all filled with the majesty of His glory who dwelleth in it; and the goodness of the Lord filleth the world, and His wisdom shineth everywhere within it and about it; and it aboundeth in an infinite variety of services, we need nothing but open eyes to be ravished like the cherubims. Well may we bear the greatness of the world, since it is our storehouse and treasury. That our treasures should be endless is an happy inconvenience: that all regions should be full of joys; and the room infinite wherein they are seated.

38

You never enjoy the world aright, till you see all things in it so perfectly yours, that you cannot desire them any other way: and till you are convinced that all things serve you best in their proper places. For can you desire to enjoy anything a better way than in God's image? It is the height of God's perfection that hideth His bounty: and the lowness of your base and sneaking spirit, that make you ignorant of His perfection. (Everyone hath in him a spirit, with which he may be angry.) God's bounty is so perfect that He giveth all things in the best of manners: making those to whom He giveth so noble, divine, and glorious, that they shall enjoy in His similitude. Nor can they be fit to enjoy in His presence, or in communion with Him, that are not truly divine and noble. So that you must have glorious principles implanted in your nature; a clear eye able to see afar off; a great and generous heart, apt to enjoy at any distance; a good and liberal soul prone to delight in the felicity of all; and an infinite delight to be their treasure. Neither is it any prejudice to you that this is required. For there is great difference between a worm and a cherubim. And it more concerneth you to be an illustrious creature than to have the possession of the whole world.

39

Your enjoyment is never right, till you esteem every soul so great a treasure as our Saviour doth; and that the laws of God are sweeter than the honey and honeycomb because they command you to love them all in such perfect manner. For how are they God's treasures? Are they not the riches of His love? Is it not His goodness that maketh Him glorious to them? Can the sun or stars serve Him any other way than by serving them? And how will you be the son of God, but by having a great soul like unto your Father's? The laws of God command you to live in His image, and to do so is to live in Heaven. God commandeth you to love all like Him, because He would have you to be His son, all them to be your riches, you to be glorious before them, and all the creatures in serving them to be your treasures, while you are His delight, like Him in beauty, and the darling of His bosom.

40

Socrates was wont to say, they are most happy and nearest the gods that needed nothing. And coming once up into the exchange at Athens, where they that traded asked him, 'What will you buy; what do you lack?' After he had gravely walked up into the middle, spreading forth his hands and turning about, 'Good gods,' saith he, 'who would have thought there were so many things in the world which I do not want!' And so left the place under the reproach of nature. He was wont to say, that happiness consisted not in having many, but in needing the fewest things: for the gods needed nothing at all, and they were most like them that least needed. We needed Heaven and earth, our senses, such souls and such bodies, with infinite riches in the image of God to be enjoyed: which God of His mercy having freely prepared, they are most happy that so live in the enjoyment of those, as to need no accidental trivial thing. No splendours, pomps, and vanities. Socrates perhaps, being an heathen, knew not that all things proceeded from God to man, and by man returned to God; but we that know it must need all things as God doth that we may receive them with joy, and live in His image.

41

As pictures are made curious by lights and shades, which without shades could not be: so is felicity composed of wants and supplies, without which mixture there could be no felicity. Were there no needs, wants would be wanting themselves, and supplies superfluous: want being the parent of celestial treasure. It is very strange; want itself is a treasure in Heaven: and so great an one, that without it there could be no treasure. God did infinitely for us when He made us to want like Gods, that like Gods we might be satisfied. The heathen deities wanted nothing, and were therefore unhappy; for they had no being. But the Lord God of Israel, the living and true God, was from all eternity, and from all eternity wanted like a God. He wanted the communication of His divine essence, and persons to enjoy it. He wanted worlds, He wanted spectators, He wanted joys, He wanted treasures. He wanted, yet He wanted not, for He had them.

42

This is very strange that God should want, for in Him is the fullness of all blessedness: He overfloweth eternally. His wants are as glorious as infinite. Perfective needs that are in His nature, and ever blessed, because always satisfied. He is from eternity full of want; or else He would not be full of treasure. Infinite want is the very ground and cause of infinite treasure. It is incredible, yet very plain: want is the fountain of all His fullness. Want in God is a treasure to us. For had there been no need He would not have created the world, nor made us, nor manifested His wisdom, nor exercised His power, nor beautified eternity, nor prepared the joys of Heaven. But He wanted angels and men, images, companions. And these He had from all eternity.

43

Infinite wants satisfied produce infinite joys; and, in the possession of those joys, are infinite joys themselves. The desire satisfied is a tree of life. Desire imports something absent: and a need of what is absent. God was never without this tree of life. He did desire infinitely, yet He was never without the fruits of this tree, which are the joys it produced. I must lead you out of this, into another world, to learn your wants. For till you find them you will never be happy. Wants themselves being sacred occasions and means of felicity.

From The Second Century

22

His power is evident by upholding it all. But how shall His life appear in that which is dead? Life is the root of activity and motion. Did I see a man sitting in a chair, as long as he was quiet, I could not tell but his body was inanimate; but if he stirred, if he moved his lips, or stretched forth his arms, if he breathed or twinkled with his eyes: I could easily tell he had a soul within him. Motion being a far greater evidence of life than all lineaments whatsoever. Colours and features may be in a dead picture, but motion is always attended with life. What shall I think therefore when the winds blow, the seas roar, the waters flow, the vapours ascend, the clouds fly, the drops of rain fall, the stars march forth in armies, the sun runneth swiftly round about the world? Can all these things move so without a life, or spring of motion? But the wheels in watches move, and so doth the hand that pointeth out the figures. This being a motion of dead things. Therefore hath God created living ones: that by lively motions and sensible desires, we might be sensible of a Deity. They breathe, they see, they feel, they grow, they flourish, they know, they love. O what a world of evidences! We are lost in abysses, we now are absorbed in wonders and swallowed up of demonstrations. Beasts, fowls, and fishes teaching and evidencing the glory of their Creator. But these by an endless generation might succeed each other from everlasting. Let us therefore survey their order, and see by that whether we cannot discern their Governor. The sun and moon and stars shine, and by shining minister influences to herbs and flowers. These grow and feed the cattle; the seas also and springs minister unto them, as they do unto fowls and fishes. All which are subservient unto man, a more noble creature, endued with understanding to admire his Creator, who being king and lord of this world, is able to prize all in a reflexive manner, and render praises for all with joy, living blessedly in the fruition of them. None can question the being of a Deity, but one that is ignorant of man's excellencies and the glory of his dominion over all the creatures.

40

In all love there is a love begetting, a love begotten, and a love proceeding. Which tho they are one in essence, subsist nevertheless in three several manners. For love is benevolent affection to another. Which is of itself, and by itself relateth to its object. It floweth from itself, and resteth in its object. Love proceedeth of necessity from itself, for unless it be of itself it is not love. Constraint is destructive and opposite to its nature. The love from which it floweth, is the fountain of love; the love which streameth from it is the communication of love, or love communicated; and the love which resteth in the object is the love which streameth to it. So that in all love the Trinity is clear. By secret passages without stirring it proceedeth to its object, and is as powerfully present as if it did not proceed at all. The love that lieth in the bosom of the lover, being the love that is perceived in the spirit of the beloved: that is, the same in substance, tho in the manner of substance, or subsistence, different. Love in the bosom is the parent of love, love in the stream is the effect of love, love seen, or dwelling in the object, proceedeth from both. Yet are all three one and the selfsame love: tho three loves.

41

Love in the fountain and love in the stream are both the same. And therefore are they both equal in time and glory. For love communicateth itself; and therefore love in the fountain is the very love communicated to its object. Love in the fountain is love in the stream, and love in the stream equally glorious with love in the fountain. Tho it streameth to its object, it abideth in the lover and is the love of the lover.

42

Where love is the lover, love streaming from the lover is the lover; the lover streaming from himself, and existing in another person.

43

This person is the Son of God: who as He is the wisdom of the Father, so is He the love of the Father. For the love of the Father is the wisdom of the Father. And this person did God by loving us beget, that He might be the means of all our glory.

44

This person differs in nothing from the Father but only in this: that He is begotten of Him. He is eternal with the Father, as glorious and as intelligent. He is of the same mind in everything in all worlds, loveth the same objects in as infinite a measure. Is the means by which the Father loveth, acteth, createth, redeemeth, governeth, and perfecteth all things. And the means also by which we see and love the Father: our strength and our eternity. He is the mediator between

God and His creatures. God therefore being willing to redeem us by His own blood (Acts 20) by Him redeemed us, and in His person died for us.

45

How wonderful is it, that God by being love should prepare a Redeemer to die for us? But how much more wonderful, that by this means Himself should be: and be *God* by being *Love*! By this means also He refineth our nature and enableth us to purge out the poison and the filthy plague of sin, for love is so amiable and desirable to the soul that it cannot be resisted. Love is the spirit of God. In Himself it is the Father, or else the Son, for the Father is in the Son, and the Son is in the Father; in us it is the Holy Ghost: the love of God being seen, being God in us. Purifying, illuminating, strengthening, and comforting the soul of the seer. For God by showing communicateth Himself to men and angels. And when He dwelleth in the soul, dwelleth in the sight. And when He dwelleth in the sight achieving all that love can do for such a soul. And thus the world serveth you as it is a mirror wherein you contemplate the blessed Trinity. For it plainly showeth that God is love, and in His being love you see the unity of the blessed Trinity, and a glorious Trinity in the blessed unity.

46

In all love there is some producer, some means, and some end: all these being internal in the thing itself. Love loving is the producer, and that is the Father; love produced is the means, and that is the Son: for love is the means by which a lover loveth. The end of these means is love: for it is love, by loving; and that is the Holy Ghost. The end and the producer being both the same, by the means attained; for by loving love attaineth its self and being. The producer is attained by loving, and is the end of himself. That love is the end of itself, and that God loveth than He might be love, is as evident to him that considers spiritual things, as the sun. Because it is impossible there should be a higher end, or a better proposed. What can be more desirable than the most delightful operation; what more eligible than the most glorious being; what further can be proposed than the most blessed and perfect life? Since God therefore chooseth the most perfect, what can be more perfect than that life and that being which is at once the fountain and the end of all things? There being in it the perpetual joy of giving and receiving infinite treasures. To be the fountain of joys and blessings is delightful. And by being love God is the fountain of all worlds. To receive all and to be the end of all is equally delightful, and by being love God receiveth, and is the end of all. For all the benefits that are done unto all, by loving all, Himself receiveth. What good could Heaven and earth do Him, were it not for His love to the children of men? By being what He is, which is love unto all, He enjoyeth all.

47

What life can be more pleasant than that which is delighted in itself, and in all objects; in which also all objects infinitely delight? What life can be more pleasant than that which is blessed in all and glorious before all? Now this life is the life of love. For this end therefore did He desire to love, that He might be *Love*. Infinitely delightful to all objects, infinitely delighted in all, and infinitely pleased in Himself, for being infinitely delightful to all, and delighted in all. All this He attaineth by love. For love is the most delightful of all employments: all the objects of love are delightful to it, and love is delightful to all its objects. Well then may love be the end of loving, which is so complete. It being a thing so delightful, that God infinitely rejoiceth in Himself for being love. And thus you see how God is the end of Himself. He doth what He doth, that He may be what He is: wise and glorious and bountiful and blessed in being perfect love.

48

Love is so divine and perfect a thing, that it is worthy to be the very end and being of the Deity. It is His goodness, and it is His glory. We therefore so vastly delight in love, because all these excellencies and all other whatsoever lie within it. By loving a soul does propagate and beget itself. By loving it does dilate and magnify itself. By loving it does enlarge and delight itself. By loving also it delighteth others, as by loving it doth honour and enrich itself. But above all by loving it does attain itself. Love also being the end of souls, which are never perfect till they are in act, what they are in power. They were made to love and are dark and vain and comfortless till they do it. Till they love they are idle, or misemployed. Till they love they are desolate: without their objects, and narrow and little and dishonourable; but when they shine by love upon all objects, they are accompanied with them and enlightened by them. Till we become therefore all act as God is, we can never rest, nor ever be satisfied.

49

Love is so noble that it enjoyeth others' enjoyments. Delighteth in giving all unto its object, and in seeing all given to its object. So that whosoever loveth all mankind, he enjoyeth all the goodness of God to the whole world, and endeavoureth the benefit of kingdoms and ages. With all whom he is present by love, which is the best manner of presence that is possible.

50

God is present by love alone. By love alone He is great and glorious. By love alone He liveth and feeleth in other persons. By love alone He enjoyeth all the creatures, by love alone He is pleasing to Himself. By love alone He is rich and blessed. O why dost not thou by love alone seek to achieve all these! By love alone attain another self. By love alone live in others. By love attain thy glory. The soul is shrivelled up and buried in a grave that does not love. But that which does love wisely and truly is the joy and end of all the world, the king of Heaven and the friend of God, the shining light and temple of eternity: the brother of Christ Jesus, and one spirit with the Holy Ghost.

51

Love is a far more glorious being than flesh and bones. If thou wilt, it is endless and infinitely more sweet than thy body can be to thee and others. Thy body is confined and is a dull lump of heavy clay, by which thou art retarded, rather than doest move; it was given thee to be a lantern only to the candle of love that shineth in thy soul. By it thou dost see and feel and eat and drink; but the end of all is that thou mightst be as God is: a joy and blessing by being love. Thy love is illimited. Thy love can extend to all objects. Thy love can see God and accompany His love throughout all eternity.

Thy love is infinitely profitable to thyself and others: to thyself, for thereby mayst thou receive infinite good things: to others, for thereby thou art prone to do infinite good to all. Thy body can receive but few pleasures. Thy love can feed upon all: take into itself all worlds, and all eternities above all worlds and all the joys of God before and after. Thy flesh and bones can do but little good: nor that little unless as by love it is inspired and directed. A poor carcass thy body is; but love is delightful and profitable to thousands. O live therefore by the more noble part. Be like Him who baptizeth with fire: feel thy spirit, awaken thy soul, be an enlarged seraphim – an infinite good, or like unto Him.

52

The true way we may go unto His throne, and can never exceed, nor be too high. All hyperboles are but little pygmies, and diminutive expressions, in comparison of the truth. All that Adam could propose to himself or hope for was laid up in store for him, in a better way than he could ask or think; but in seeking for it a false way, he lost all: what he had in hope, and what he had in fruition. To be as Gods, we are prompted to desire by the instinct of nature. And that we shall be by loving all as He doth. But by loving Him? What, O what shall we be? By loving Him according to the greatness of His love unto us, according to His amiableness, as we ought, and according to the obligations that lie upon us; we shall be no man can devise what. We shall love Him infinitely more than ourselves, and therefore live infinitely more in Him than in ourselves: and be infinitely more delighted with His eternal blessedness than our own. We shall infinitely more delight Him than ourselves. All worlds, all angels, all men, all kingdoms, all creatures will be more ours in Him than in ourselves: so will His essence and eternal Godhead. Oh Love, what hast thou done!

53

And He will so love us, when all this beauty of love is within us, that tho we by our love to Him seem more blessed in His blessedness than He, He is infinitely more blessed than we even in our blessedness. We being so united to each other that nothing can divide us forevermore.

54

Love is infinitely delightful to its object, and the more violent the more glorious. It is infinitely high, nothing can hurt it. And infinitely great in all extremes: of beauty and excellency. Excess is its true moderation; activity its rest; and burning fervency its only refreshment. Nothing is more glorious, yet nothing more humble; nothing more precious, yet nothing more cheap: nothing more familiar, yet nothing so inaccessible; nothing more nice, yet nothing more laborious; nothing more liberal, yet nothing more covetous; it doth all things for its object's sake, yet it is the most self-ended thing in the whole world: for of all things in nature it can least endure to be displeased. Since therefore it containeth so many miracles, it may well contain this one more: that it maketh everyone greatest, and among lovers everyone is supreme and sovereign.

55

God by love wholly ministereth to others, and yet wholly ministereth to Himself. Love having this wonder in it also, that among innumerable millions, it maketh every one the sole and single end of all things. It attaineth all unattainables and achieveth impossibles, that is seeming impossibles to our inexperience, and real impossibles to any other means or endeavours; for indeed it maketh every one more than the end of all things: and infinitely more than the sole supreme and sovereign of all for it maketh him so first in himself, and then in all. For while all things in Heaven and earth fall out after my desire, I am the end and sovereign of all: which conspiring always to crown my friends with glory and happiness, and pleasing all in the same manner whom I love as myself, I am in every one of them the end of all things again: being as much concerned in their happiness as my own.

56

By loving a soul does propagate and beget itself, because before it loved it lived only in itself; after it loved, and while it loveth, it liveth in its object. Nay, it did not so much as live in itself before it loved, for as the sun would be unseen did it not scatter and spread abroad its beams, by which alone it becometh glorious; so the soul without extending, and living in its object, is dead within itself. An idle chaos of blind and confused powers, for which when it loveth, it gaineth three subsistences in itself by the act of loving: a glorious spirit that abideth within; a glorious spirit that floweth in the stream; a glorious spirit that resideth in the object. Insomuch that now it can enjoy a sweet communion with itself: in contemplating what it is in itself and to its object.

57

Love is so vastly delightful in the lover because it is the communication of his goodness; for the natural end of goodness is to be enjoyed: it desireth to be another's happiness. Which goodness of God is so deeply implanted in our natures, that we never enjoy ourselves but when we are the joy of others: of all our desires the strongest is to be good to others. We delight in receiving, more in giving. We love to be rich, but then it is that we thereby might be more greatly delightful; thus we see the seeds of eternity sparkling in our natures.

61

How happy we are that we may live in all, as well as one; and how all-sufficient love is, we may see by this: the more we live in all, the more we live in one. For while He seeth us to live in all, we are a more great and glorious object unto Him; the more we are beloved of all, the more we are admired by Him; the more we are the joy of all, the more blessed we are to Him. The more blessed we are to Him, the greater is our blessedness. We are all naturally ambitious of being magnified in others, and of seeming great in others. Which inclination was implanted in us that our happiness might be enlarged by the multitude of spectators.

62

Love is the true means by which the world is enjoyed. Our love to others, and others' love to us. We ought therefore above all things to get acquainted with the nature of love, for love is the root and foundation of nature; love is the soul of life, and crown of rewards. If we cannot be satisfied in the nature of love, we can never be satisfied at all. The very end for which God made the world was that He might manifest His love. Unless therefore we can be satisfied with His love manifested we can never be satisfied. There are many glorious excellencies in the material world, but without love they are all abortive. We might spend ages in contemplating the nature of the sun, and entertain ourselves many years with the beauty of the stars, and services of the sea; but the soul of man is above all these, it comprehendeth all ages in a moment; and unless it perceive something more excellent, is very desolate. All worlds being but a silent wilderness, without some living thing more sweet and blessed after which it aspireth. Love in the fountain, and love in the end is the glory of the world, and the soul of joy. Which it infinitely preferreth above all worlds, and delighteth in, and loveth to contemplate, more than all visible beings that are possible. So that you must be sure to see causes wherefore infinitely to be delighted with the love of God, if ever you would be happy.

63

See causes also wherefore to be delighted in your love to men, and love of men to you. For the world serves you to this end, that you might love them and be beloved of them. And unless you are pleased with the end for which the world serves you, you can never be pleased with the means leading to that end. Above all things therefore contemplate the glory of loving men, and of being beloved of them. For this end our Saviour died, and for this end He came into the world, that you might be restored from hatred, which is the greatest misery. From the hatred of God and men which was due for sin, and from the misery of hating God and men; for to hate and be hated is the greatest misery. The necessity of hating God and men being the greatest bondage that hell can impose.

64

When you love men, the world quickly becometh yours: and yourself become a greater treasure than the world is. For all their persons are your treasures, and all the things in Heaven and earth that serve them are yours. For those are the riches of love, which minister to its object.

65

You are as prone to love as the sun is to shine. It being the most delightful and natural employment of the soul of man: without which you are dark and miserable. Consider therefore the extent of love, its vigour and excellency. For certainly he that delights not in love makes vain the universe, and is of necessity to himself the greatest burden. The whole world ministers to you as the theatre of your love. It sustains you and all objects that you may continue to love them. Without which it were better for you to have no being. Life without objects is sensible emptiness. Objects without love are the delusion of life. The objects of love are its greatest treasures, and without love it is impossible they should be treasures. For the objects which we love are the pleasing objects, and delightful things. And whatsoever is not pleasing and delightful to us can be no treasure. Nay, it is distasteful, and worse than nothing, since we had rather it should have no being.

66

That violence wherewith sometimes a man doteth upon one creature, is but a little spark of that love, even towards all, which lurketh in his nature. We are made to love: both to satisfy the necessity of our active nature, and to answer the beauties in every creature. By love our souls are married and soldered to the creatures, and it is our duty like God to be united to them all. We must love them infinitely, but in God and for God, and God in them: namely all His excellencies manifested in them. When we dote upon the perfections and beauties of some one creature, we do not love that too much, but other things too little. Never was anything in this world loved too much, but many things have been loved in a false way; and all in too short a measure.

67

Suppose a river or a drop of water, an apple or a sand, an ear of corn, or an herb: God knoweth infinite excellencies in it more than we; He seeth how it relateth to angels and men; how it proceedeth from the most perfect lover to the most perfectly beloved; how it representeth all His attributes; how it conduceth in its place, by the best of means, to the best of ends: and for this cause it cannot be beloved too much. God the author and God the end is to be beloved in it; angels and men are to be beloved in it; and it is highly to be esteemed for all their sakes. O what a treasure is every sand when truly understood! Who can love anything that God made too much? His infinite goodness and wisdom and power and glory are in it. What a world would this be, were every thing beloved as it ought to be!

68

Suppose a curious and fair woman. Some have seen the beauties of Heaven in such a person. It is a vain thing to say they loved too much. I dare say there are 10,000 beauties in that creature which they have not seen. They loved it not too much but upon false causes. Nor so much upon false ones, as only upon some little ones. They love a creature for sparkling eyes and curled hair, lily breasts and ruddy cheeks: which they should love moreover for being God's image, queen of the universe, beloved by angels, redeemed by Jesus Christ, an heiress of Heaven, and temple of the Holy Ghost: a mine and fountain of all virtues, a treasury of graces, and a child of God. But these excellencies are unknown. They love her perhaps, but do not love God more: nor men as much: nor Heaven and earth at all. And so being defective to other things, perish by a seeming excess to that. We should be all life and mettle and vigour and love to everything. And that would poise us. I dare confidently say that every person in the whole world ought to be beloved as much as this; and she if there be any cause of difference more than she is. But God being beloved infinitely more will be infinitely more our joy, and our heart will be more with Him. So that no man can be in danger by loving others too much, that loveth God as he ought.

69

The sun and stars please me in ministering to you. They please me in ministering to a thousand others as well as you. And you please me because you can live and love in the image of God: not in a blind and brutish manner, as beasts do, by a mere appetite and rude propensity, but with a regulated well-ordered love upon clear causes, and with a rational affection, guided to divine and celestial ends. Which is to love with a divine and holy love, glorious and blessed. We are all prone to love, but the art lies in managing our love: to make it truly amiable and proportionable. To love for God's sake, and to this end, that we may be well pleasing unto Him; to love with a design to imitate Him, and to satisfy the principles of intelligent nature and to become honourable, is to love in a blessed and holy manner.

70

In one soul we may be entertained and taken up with innumerable beauties. But in the soul of man there are innumerable infinities. One soul in the immensity of its intelligence is greater and more excellent than the whole world. The ocean is but the drop of a bucket to it, the heavens but a centre, the sun obscurity, and all ages but as one day. It being by its understanding a temple of eternity, and God's omnipresence, between which and the whole world there is no proportion. Its love is a dominion greater than that which Adam had in Paradise, and yet the fruition of it is but solitary. We need spectators, and other diversities of friends and lovers, in whose souls we might likewise dwell, and with whose beauties we might be crowned and entertained. In all whom we can dwell exactly, and be present with them fully. Lest therefore the other depths and faculties of our souls should be desolate and idle, they also are created to entertain us. And as in many mirrors we are so many other selves, so are we spiritually multiplied when we meet ourselves more sweetly, and live again in other persons.

71

Creatures are multiplied that our treasures may be multiplied, their places enlarged that the territories of our joys might be enlarged. With all which our souls may be present in immediate manner. For since the sun, which is a poor little dead thing, can at once shine upon many kingdoms, and be wholly present, not only in many cities and realms upon earth, but in all the stars in the firmament of Heaven: surely the soul which is a far more perfect sun, nearer unto God in excellency and nature, can do far more. But that which of all wonders is the most deep is that a soul, whereas one would think it could measure but one soul, which is as large as it, can exceed that and measure all souls, wholly and fully. This is an infinite wonder indeed. For admit that the powers of one soul were fathomless and infinite: are not the powers so also of another? One would think therefore that one soul should be lost in another, and that two souls should be exactly adequate. Yet my soul can examine and search all the chambers and endless operations of another: being prepared to see innumerable millions.

72

Here is a glorious creature! But that which maketh the wonder infinitely infinite is this. That one soul which is the object of mine can see all souls, and all the secret chambers, and endless perfections, in every soul; yea and all souls with all their objects in every soul. Yet mine can accompany all these in one soul; and without deficiency exceed that soul, and accompany all these in every other soul. Which shows the work of God to be deep and infinite.

73

Here upon earth perhaps where our estate is imperfect this is impossible: but in Heaven where the soul is all act it is necessary. For the soul is there all that it can be; here it is to rejoice in what it may be. Till therefore the mists of error and clouds of ignorance that confine this sun be removed, it must be present in all kingdoms and ages virtually, as the sun is by night. If not by clear sight and love, at least by its desire. Which are its influences and its beams. Working in a latent and obscure manner on earth, above in a strong and clear.

74

The world serveth you, therefore, in maintaining all people in all kingdoms: which are your Father's treasures, and your as yet invisible joys, that their multitudes at last may come to Heaven, and make those innumerable thousands, whose hosts and employments will be your joy. Whose order, beauty, melody, and glory will be your eternal delights. And of whom you have many a sweet description in the Revelation. These are they of whom it is said, 'After this I beheld, and a great multitude which no man could number of all nations and kindred and people and tongues stood before the throne and before the Lamb, clothed with white robes and palms in their hands, and they cried with a loud voice, saying "Salvation to our God which sitteth upon the throne and to the Lamb"': of which it is said, 'They fell down before the Lamb, having every one of them harps and golden vials full of odours which are the prayers of the saints, and they sung a new song, saying "Thou art worthy to take the book and to open the seals thereof; for Thou wast slain, and hast redeemed us to God by Thy blood, out of every kindred and tongue and people and nation, and hast made us unto our God kings and priests"': of whom it is said, 'I saw a sea of glass, and they that had gotten the victory over the beast standing on it, and they sing the song of Moses the servant of God, and the song of the Lamb, saying "Great and marvellous are Thy works, Lord God Almighty; just and true are Thy ways, Thou King of saints. Who shall not fear Thee O Lord and glorify Thy name, for Thou only art holy; for all nations shall come and worship before Thee, because Thy judgements are made manifest."'

75

That all the powers of your soul shall be turned into act in the Kingdom of Heaven is manifest by what St John writeth, in the isle Patmos. 'And I beheld and I heard the voice of many angels round about the throne: and the beasts and the elders, and the number of them was ten thousand times ten thousand, and thousands of thousands: saying, with a loud voice, "Worthy is the Lamb that was slain, to receive power and riches and wisdom, and strength and honour and glory and blessing." And every creature which is in Heaven and on earth, and under the earth, and such as are in the sea, and all that are in them, heard I saying, "Blessing and honour and glory and power, be unto Him that sitteth upon the throne and unto the Lamb forever and ever."'

76

These things shall never be seen with your bodily eyes, but in a more perfect manner. You shall be present with them in your understanding. You shall be in them to the very centre and they in you. As light is in a piece of crystal, so shall you be with every part and excellency of them. An act of the understanding is the presence of the soul, which being no body but a living act, is a pure spirit, and mysteriously fathomless in its true dimensions. By an act of the understanding therefore be present now with all the creatures among which you live: and hear them in their beings and operations praising God in an heavenly manner. Some of them vocally, others in their ministry, all of them naturally and continually. We infinitely wrong ourselves by laziness and confinement. All creatures in all nations and tongues and people praise God infinitely; and the more, for being your sole and perfect treasures. You are never what you ought till you go out of yourself and walk among them.

77

Were all your riches here in some little place, all other places would be empty. It is necessary therefore for your contentment, and true satisfaction, that your riches be dispersed everywhere. Whether is more delightful: to have some few private riches in one, and all other places void, or to have all places everywhere filled with our proper treasures? Certainly to have treasures in all places, for by that means we are entertained everywhere with pleasures, are everywhere at home honoured and delighted, everywhere enlarged, and in our own possessions. But to have a few riches in some narrow bounds, tho we should suppose a kingdom full, would be to have our delights limited, and infinite spaces dark and empty, wherein we might wander without satisfaction. So that God must of necessity to satisfy His love give us infinite treasures. And we of necessity seek for our riches in all places.

78

The heavens and the earth serve you, not only in showing unto you your Father's glory, as all things without you are your riches and enjoyments. But as within you also, they magnify and beautify and illuminate your soul. For as the sunbeams illuminate the air and all objects, yet are themselves also illuminated by them, so fareth it with the powers of your soul. The rays of the sun carry light in them as they pass through the air, but go on in vain till they meet an object: and there they are expressed. They illuminate a mirror, and are illuminated by it. For a looking glass without them would be in the dark, and they without the glass unperceived. There they revive and overtake themselves, and represent the effigies from whence they came; both of the sun and heavens and trees and mountains, if the glass be seated conveniently to receive them. Which were it not that the glass were present there one would have thought even the ideas of them absent from the place. Even so your soul in its rays and powers is unknown; and no man would believe it present everywhere, were there no objects there to be discerned. Your thoughts and inclinations pass on and are unperceived, but by their objects are discerned to be present: being illuminated by them, for they are present with them and active about them. They recover and feel themselves, and by those objects live in employment. Being turned into the figure and idea of them. For as light varieth upon all objects whither it cometh, and returneth with the form and figure of them: so is the soul transformed into the being of its object. Like light from the sun, its first effigies is simple life, the pure resemblance of its primitive fountain, but on the object which it meeteth it is quickly changed, and by understanding becometh all things.

79

Objective treasures are always delightful, and tho we travail endlessly, to see them all our own is infinitely pleasant: and the further we go the more delightful. If they are all ours wholly and solely, and yet nevertheless everyone's too, it is the most delightful accident that is imaginable for thereby two contrary humours are at once delighted, and two inclinations, that are both in our natures, yet seem contradictory are at once satisfied. The one is the avaricious humour and love of propriety: whereby we refer all unto ourselves and naturally desire to have all alone in our private possession, and to be the alone and single end in all things. This we perceive ourselves because all universally and everywhere is ours. The other is the communicative humour that is in us, whereby we desire to have companions in our enjoyments to tell our joys, and to spread abroad our delights, and to be ourselves the joy and delight of other persons. For thousands enjoy all as well as we, and are the end of all, and God communicateth all to them as well as us. And yet to us alone, because He communicateth them to us, and maketh them our rich and glorious companions: to whom we may tell our joys and be blessed again. How much ought we to praise God, for satisfying two such insatiable humours that are contrary to each other. One would think it impossible that both should be pleased, and yet His divine wisdom hath made them helpful and perfective to each other.

80

Infinite love cannot be expressed in finite room, but must have infinite places wherein to utter and show itself. It must therefore fill all eternity and the omnipresence of God with joys and treasures for my fruition. And yet it must be expressed in a finite room: by making me able in a centre to enjoy them. It must be infinitely expressed in the smallest moment by making me able in every moment to see them all. It is both ways infinite, for my soul is an infinite sphere in a centre. By this may you know that you are infinitely beloved: God hath made your spirit a centre in eternity comprehending all; and filled all about you in an endless manner with infinite riches, which shine before you and surround you with divine and heavenly enjoyments.

81

Few will believe the soul to be infinite, yet infinite is the first thing which is naturally known. Bounds and limits are discerned only in a secondary manner. Suppose a man were born deaf and blind. By the very feeling of his soul he apprehends infinite about him, infinite space, infinite darkness. He thinks not of wall and limits till he feels them and is stopped by them. That things are finite therefore we learn by our senses but infinity we know and feel by our souls: and feel it so naturally, as if it were the very essence and being of the soul. The truth of it is, it is individually in the soul; for God is there, and more near to us than we are to ourselves. So that we cannot feel our souls, but we must feel Him, in that first of properties, infinite space. And this we know so naturally, that it is the only *primo et necessario cognitum in rerum natura*: of all things the only first and most necessarily known. For we can unsuppose Heaven and earth, and annihilate the world in our imagination, but the place where they stood will remain behind, and we cannot unsuppose or annihilate that, do what we can. Which without us is the chamber of our infinite treasures, and within us the repository and recipient of them.

84

Your soul being naturally very dark and deformed and empty when extended through infinite but empty space, the world serves you in beautifying and filling it with amiable ideas for the perfecting of its stature in the eye of God: for the thorough understanding of which, you must know that God is a being whose power from all eternity was prevented with act. And that He is one infinite act of knowledge and wisdom, which is infinitely beautified with many consequences of love &c. Being one act of eternal knowledge, He knows all which He is able to know. All objects in all worlds being seen in His understanding. His greatness is the presence of His soul with all objects in infinite spaces, and His brightness the light of eternal wisdom. His essence also is the sight of things. For He is all eye and all ear. Being therefore perfect, and the mirror of all perfection, He hath commanded us to be perfect as He is perfect; and we are to grow up into Him till we are filled with the fullness of His Godhead. We are to be conformed to the image of His glory, till we become the resemblance of His great exemplar. Which we then are, when our power is converted into act and covered with it, we being an act of knowledge and wisdom as He is. When our souls are present with all objects, and beautified with the ideas and figures of them all. For then shall we be *mentes* as He is *Mens*: we being of the same mind with Him who is an infinite eternal mind. As both Plato and Cato with the Apostle term Him:

> *Si Deus est animus sit pura mente colendus.*
> If God as verses say a spirit be,
> We must in spirit like the Deity
> Become. We must the image of His mind
> And union with it in our spirit find.

Heaven and earth, angels and men, God and all things must be contained in our souls, that we may become glorious personages, and like unto Him in all our actions.

85

You know that love receives a grandeur of value and esteem from the greatness of the person from whom it doth proceed. The love of a king is naturally more delightful than the love of a beggar. The love of God more excellent than the love of a king. The love of a beautiful person is more pleasing than that of one deformed. The love of a wise man is far more precious than the love of a fool. When you are so great a creature as to fill ages and kingdoms with the beauty of your soul, and to reign over them like the wisdom of the Father filling eternity with light and glory, your love shall be acceptable and sweet and precious. The world therefore serveth you, not only in furnishing you with riches and making you beautiful and great and wise, when it is rightly used; but in doing that which doth infinitely concern you, in making your love precious. For above all things in all worlds you naturally desire most violently that your love should be prized; and the reason is, because that being the best thing you can do or give, all is worthless that you can do besides; and you have no more power left to be good, or to please, or to do anything, when once your love is despised.

86

Since therefore love does all it is able, to make itself accepted both in increasing its own vehemence and in adorning the person of the lover, as well as in offering up the most choice and perfect gifts, with what care ought [you] to express your love in beautifying yourself with this wisdom, and in making your person acceptable? Especially since your person is the greatest gift your love can offer up to God Almighty. Clothe yourself with light as with a garment, when you come before Him; put on the greatness of Heaven and earth, adorn yourself with the excellencies of God Himself; when you prepare yourself to speak to Him, be all the knowledge and light you are able, as great, as clear, and as perfect as is possible. So at length shall you appear before God in Sion: and as God converse with God forevermore.

87

God hath made it easy to convert our soul into a thought containing Heaven and earth, not that it should be contemptible because it is easy: but done, because it is divine. Which thought is as easily abolished, that by a perpetual influx of life it may be maintained. If He would but suspend His power, no doubt but Heaven and earth would straight be abolished, which He upholds in Himself as easily and as continually, as we do the idea of them in our own mind. Since therefore all things depending so continually upon His care and love, the perpetual influx of His almighty power is infinitely precious and His life exercised incessantly in the manifestation of eternal love, in that every moment throughout all generations He continueth without failing to uphold all things for us. We likewise ought to show our infinite love by upholding Heaven and earth, time and eternity, God and all things in our souls, without wavering or intermission: by the perpetual influx of our life. To which we are by the goodness of all things infinitely obliged. Once to cease is to draw upon ourselves infinite darkness, after we have begun to be so illuminated; for it shows a forgetfulness and defect in love, and it is an infinite wonder that we are afterward restored.

89

Being that we are here upon earth turmoiled with cares and often shaken with winds and by disturbances distracted, it is the infinite mercy of God that we are permitted to breathe and be diverted. For all the things in Heaven and earth attend upon us, while we ought to answer and observe them by upholding their beauty within; but we are spared and God winketh at our defect, all the world attending us while we are about some little trifling business. But in the estate of glory the least intermission would be an eternal apostasy. But there by reason of our infinite union with God it is impossible.

90

We could easily show that the idea of Heaven and earth in the soul of man is more precious with God than the things themselves, and more excellent in nature. Which because it will surprise you a little, I will. What would Heaven and earth be worth, were there no spectator, no enjoyer? As much therefore as the end is better than the means, the thought of the world whereby it is enjoyed is better than the world. So is the idea of it in the soul of man better than the world in the esteem of God: it being the end of the world, without which Heaven and earth would be in vain. It is better to you, because by it you receive the world, and it is the tribute you pay. It more immediately beautifies and perfects your nature. How deformed would you be should all the world stand about you and you be idle? Were you able to create other worlds, God had rather you should think on this; for thereby you are united to Him. The sun in your eye is as much to you as the sun in the Heavens, for by this the other is enjoyed. It would shine on all rivers, trees, and beasts in vain to you, could you not think upon it. The sun in your understanding illuminates your soul, the sun in the heavens enlightens the hemisphere. The world within you is an offering returned. Which is infinitely more acceptable to God Almighty, since it came from Him that it might return unto Him. Wherein the mystery is great. For God hath made you able to create worlds in your own mind, which are more precious unto Him than those which He created: and to give and offer up the world unto Him, which is very delightful in flowing from Him, but much more in returning to Him. Besides all which, in its own nature also a thought of the world, or the world in a thought, is more excellent than the world, because it is spiritual and nearer unto God. The material world is dead and feeleth nothing. But this spiritual world tho it be invisible hath all dimensions, and is a divine and living being, the voluntary act of an obedient soul.

91

Once more, that I might close up this point with an infinite wonder: as among divines it is said that every moment's preservation is a new creation; and therefore blessings continued must not be despised, but be more and more esteemed, because every moment's preservation is another obligation, even so in the continual series of thoughts whereby we continue to uphold the frame of Heaven and earth in the soul towards God, every thought is another world to the Deity as acceptable as the first. Yea, the continuance puts an infinite worth and lustre on them. For to be desultory and inconstant is the part of a fickle and careless soul, and makes the imagination of it worthless and despised. But to continue serious in upholding these thoughts for God's sake, is the part of a faithful and loving soul: which as it thereby continues great and honourable with God, so is it thereby divine and holy; and every act of it of infinite importance; and the continuance of its life transcendently esteemed. So that tho you can build or demolish such worlds as often as you please, yet it infinitely concerneth you faithfully to continue them and wisely to repair them. For tho to make them suddenly be to a wise man very easy, yet to uphold them always is very difficult, a work of unspeakable diligence, and an argument of infinite love.

94

As the world serves you by showing the greatness of God's love to you, so doth it serve you as fuel to foment and increase your praises.

Men's lips are closed because their eyes are blinded; their tongues are dumb because their ears are deaf; and there is no life in their mouths because death is in their hearts. But did they all see their Creator's glory, which appeareth chiefly in the greatness of His bounty; did they all know the blessedness of their estate, O what a place full of joys, what an amiable region and territory of praises would the world become; yea, what a sphere of light and glory! As no man can breathe out more air than he draweth in, so no man can offer up more praises than he receiveth benefits, to return in praises. For praises are transformed and returning benefits. And therefore doth God so greatly desire the knowledge of Him, because God when He is known is all love; and the praises which He desires are the reflection of His beams, which will not return till they are apprehended. The world therefore is not only the temple of these praises, and the altar whereon they are offered, but the fuel also that enkindles them, and the very matter that composeth them. Which so much the more serves you, because it enkindles a desire in you that God should be praised, and moves you to take delight in all that praise Him. So that as it incites yours, it gives you an interest in others' praises; and is a valley of vision, wherein you see the blessed sight of all men's praises ascending and of all God's blessings coming down upon them.

The Third Century

I

Will you see the infancy of this sublime and celestial greatness? Those pure and virgin apprehensions I had from the womb, and that divine light wherewith I was born, are the best unto this day, wherein I can see the universe. By the gift of God they attended me into the world, and by His special favour I remember them till now. Verily they seem the greatest gifts His wisdom could bestow for without them all other gifts had been dead and vain. They are unattainable by book, and therefore I will teach them by experience. Pray for them earnestly: for they will make you angelical, and wholly celestial. Certainly Adam in Paradise had not more sweet and curious apprehensions of the world, than I when I was a child.

2

All appeared new, and strange at the first, inexpressibly rare, and delightful, and beautiful. I was a little stranger which at my entrance into the world was saluted and surrounded with innumerable joys. My knowledge was divine: I knew by intuition those things which since my apostasy, I collected again, by the highest reason. My very ignorance was advantageous. I seemed as one brought into the estate of innocence. All things were spotless and pure and glorious: yea, and infinitely mine, and joyful and precious. I knew not that there were any sins, or complaints, or laws. I dreamed not of poverties, contentions, or vices. All tears and quarrels were hidden from mine eyes. Everything was at rest, free, and immortal. I knew nothing of sickness or death or exaction; in the absence of these I was entertained like an angel with the works of God in their splendour and glory; I saw all in the peace of Eden; Heaven and earth did sing my Creator's praises, and could not make more melody to Adam, than to me. All time was eternity, and a perpetual Sabbath. Is it not strange, that an infant should be heir of the world, and see those mysteries which the books of the learned never unfold?

3

The corn was orient and immortal wheat, which never should be reaped, nor was ever sown. I thought it had stood from everlasting to everlasting. The dust and stones of the street were as precious as gold. The gates were at first the end of the world, the green trees when I saw them first through one of the gates transported and ravished me; their sweetness and unusual beauty made my heart to leap, and almost mad with ecstasy, they were such strange and wonderful things. The men! O what venerable and reverend creatures did the aged seem! Immortal cherubims! And young men glittering and sparkling angels and maids strange seraphic pieces of life and beauty! Boys and girls tumbling in the street, and playing, were moving jewels. I knew not that they were born or should die. But all things abided eternally as they were in their proper places. Eternity was manifest in the light of the day, and something infinite behind everything appeared: which talked with my expectation and moved my desire. The city seemed to stand in Eden, or to be built in Heaven. The streets were mine, the temple was mine, the people were mine, their clothes and gold and silver was mine, as much as their sparkling eyes, fair skins, and ruddy faces. The skies were mine, and so were the sun and moon and stars, and all the world was mine, and I the only spectator and enjoyer of it. I knew no churlish proprieties, nor bounds nor divisions; but all proprieties and divisions were mine: all treasures and the possessors of them. So that with much ado I was corrupted; and made to learn the dirty devices of this world. Which now I unlearn, and become as it were a little child again, that I may enter into the Kingdom of God.

4

Upon those pure and virgin apprehensions which I had in my infancy, I made this poem.

1

That childish thoughts such joys inspire,
Doth make my wonder, and His glory higher;
   His bounty, and my wealth more great:
It shows His kingdom, and His work complete.
   In which there is not anything,
Not meet to be the joy of cherubim.

2

He in our childhood with us walks,
And with our thoughts mysteriously He talks;
   He often visiteth our minds,
But cold acceptance in us ever finds.
   We send Him often griev'd away,
Who else would show us all His kingdom's joy.

3

O Lord, I wonder at Thy love,
Which did my infancy so early move:
   But more at that which did forbear
And move so long, tho slighted many a year:

> But most of all, at last that Thou
> Thyself shouldst me convert, I scarce know how.

4

> Thy gracious motions oft in vain
> Assaulted me: my heart did hard remain
>   Long time! I sent my God away
> Griev'd much, that He could not give me His joy.
>   I careless was, nor did regard
> The end for which He all those thoughts prepar'd.

5

> But now, with new and open eyes,
> I see beneath, as if I were above the skies:
>   And as I backward look again
> See all His thoughts and mine most clear and plain.
>   He did approach, He me did woo.
> I wonder that my God this thing would do.

6

> From nothing taken first I was;
> What wondrous things His glory brought to pass!
>   Now in the world I Him behold,
> And me, enveloped in precious gold;
>   In deep abysses of delights,
> In present hidden glorious benefits.

7

> Those thoughts His goodness long before
> Prepar'd as precious and celestial store:
>   With curious art in me inlaid,
> That childhood might itself alone be said
>   My tutor, teacher, guide to be,
> Instructed then even by the Deity.

5

Our Saviour's meaning, when He said, he must be born again and become a little child that will enter into the Kingdom of Heaven, is deeper far than is generally believed. It is not only in a careless reliance upon divine providence, that we are to become little children, or in the feebleness and shortness of our anger and simplicity of our passions: but in the peace and purity of all our soul. Which purity also is a deeper thing than is commonly apprehended, for we must disrobe ourselves of all false colours, and unclothe our souls of evil habits; all our thoughts must be infant-like and clear: the powers of our soul free from the leaven of this world, and disentangled from men's conceits and customs. Grit in the eye or the yellow jaundice will not let a man see those objects truly that are before it. And therefore it is requisite that we should be as very strangers to the thoughts, customs, and opinions of men in this world as if we were but little children. So those things would appear to us only which do to children when they are first born. Ambitions, trades, luxuries, inordinate affections, casual and accidental riches invented since the Fall would be gone, and only those things appear, which did to Adam in Paradise, in the same light, and in the same colours. God in His works, glory in the light, love in our parents, men, ourselves, and the face of Heaven. Every man naturally seeing those things, to the enjoyment of which he is naturally born.

6

Everyone provideth objects, but few prepare senses whereby, and light wherein to see them. Since therefore we are born to be a burning and shining light, and whatever men learn of others, they see in the light of others' souls: I will in the light of my soul show you the universe. Perhaps it is celestial, and will teach you how beneficial we may be to each other. I am sure it is a sweet and curious light to me: which had I wanted, I would have given all the gold and silver in all worlds to have purchased. But it was the gift of God and could not be bought with money. And by what steps and degrees I proceeded to that enjoyment of all eternity which now I possess I will likewise show you. A clear and familiar light it may prove unto you.

7

The first light which shined in my infancy in its primitive and innocent clarity was totally eclipsed: insomuch that I was fain to learn all again. If you ask me how it was eclipsed? Truly by the customs and manners of men, which like contrary winds blew it out; by an innumerable company of other objects: rude, vulgar, and worthless things that like so many loads of earth and dung did overwhelm and bury it; by the impetuous torrent of wrong desires in all others whom I saw or knew that carried me away and alienated me from it; by a whole sea of other matters and concernments that covered and drowned it; finally by the evil influence of a bad education that did not foster and cherish it. All men's thoughts and words were about other matters; they all prized new things which I did not dream of. I was a stranger and unacquainted with them; I was little and reverenced their authority; I was weak, and easily guided by their example; ambitious also, and desirous to approve myself unto them. And finding no one syllable in any man's mouth of those things, by degrees they vanished, my thoughts (as indeed what is more fleeting than a thought?) were blotted out. And at last all the celestial, great, and stable treasures to which I was born, as wholly forgotten as if they had never been.

8

Had any man spoken of it, it had been the most easy thing in the world to have taught me, and to have made me believe, that Heaven and earth was God's house, and that He gave it me. That the sun was mine and that men were mine, and that cities and kingdoms were mine also; that earth was better than gold, and that water was, every drop of it, a precious jewel. And that these were great and living treasures; and that all riches whatsoever else was dross in comparison. From whence I clearly find how docible our nature is, in natural things, were it rightly entreated. And that our misery proceedeth ten thousand times more from the outward bondage of opinion and custom, than from any inward corruption or depravation of nature; and that it is not our parents' loins, so much as our parents' lives, that enthrals and blinds us. Yet is all our corruption derived from Adam: inasmuch as all the evil examples and inclinations of the world arise from his sin. But I speak it in the presence of God and of our Lord Jesus Christ, in my pure primitive virgin light, while my apprehensions were natural, and unmixed, I cannot remember, but that I was ten thousand times more prone to good and excellent things, than evil. But I was quickly tainted and fell by others.

9

It was a difficult matter to persuade me that the tinselled ware upon a hobbyhorse was a fine thing. They did impose upon me, and obtrude their gifts that made me believe a ribbon or a feather curious. I could not see where the curiousness or fineness. And to teach me that a purse of gold was of any value seemed impossible, the art by which it becomes so, and the reasons for which it is accounted so were so deep and hidden to my inexperience. So that nature is still nearest to natural things, and farthest off from preternatural, and to esteem that the reproach of nature, is an error in them only who are unacquainted with it. Natural things are glorious, and to know them glorious; but to call things preternatural, natural, monstrous. Yet all they do it, who esteem gold, silver, houses, lands, clothes &c. the riches of nature, which are indeed the riches of invention. Nature knows no such riches, but art and error makes them. Not the God of nature, but sin only was the parent of them. The riches of nature are our souls and bodies, with all their faculties, senses, and endowments. And it had been the easiest thing in the whole world, that all felicity consisted in the enjoyment of all the world, that it was prepared for me before I was born, and that nothing was more divine and beautiful.

10

Thoughts are the most present things to thoughts, and of the most powerful influence. My soul was only apt and disposed to great things; but souls to souls are like apples to apples, one being rotten rots another. When I began to speak and go nothing began to be present to me, but what was present in their thoughts. Nor was anything present to me any other way, than it was so to them. The glass of imagination was the only mirror wherein anything was represented or appeared to me. All things were absent which they talked not of. So I began among my playfellows to prize a drum, a fine coat, a penny, a gilded book &c. who before never dreamed of any such wealth. Goodly objects to drown all the knowledge of Heaven and earth! As for the heavens and the sun and stars, they disappeared and were no more unto me than the bare walls. So that the strange riches of man's invention quite overcame the riches of nature – being learned more laboriously and in the second place.

11

By this let nurses, and those parents that desire holy children, learn to make them possessors of Heaven and earth betimes, to remove silly objects from before them, to magnify nothing but what is great indeed, and to talk of God to them and of His works and ways before they can either speak or go. For nothing is so easy as to teach the truth because the nature of the thing confirms the doctrine. As when we say the sun is glorious, a man is a beautiful creature, sovereign over beasts and fowls and fishes, the stars minister unto us, the world was made for you, &c. But to say this house is yours, and these lands are another man's, and this bauble is a jewel and this gewgaw a fine thing, this rattle makes music &c. is deadly, barbarous, and uncouth to a little child; and makes him suspect all you say, because the nature of the thing contradicts your words. Yet doth that blot out all noble and divine ideas, dis-settle his foundation, render him uncertain in all things, and divide him from God. To teach him those objects are little vanities, and that tho God made them by the ministry of man, yet better and more glorious things are more to be esteemed, is natural and easy.

12

By this you may see who are the rude and barbarous Indians. For verily there is no savage nation under the cope of Heaven, that is more absurdly barbarous than the Christian world. They that go naked and drink water and live upon roots are like Adam or angels in comparison of us. But they indeed that call beads and glass buttons jewels, and dress themselves with feather, and buy pieces of brass and broken hafts of knives of our merchants are somewhat like us. But we pass them in barbarous opinions and monstrous apprehensions: which we nickname civility, and the mode, amongst us. I am sure those barbarous people that go naked come nearer to Adam, God, and angels: in the simplicity of their wealth, tho not in knowledge.

13

You would not think how these barbarous inventions spoil your knowledge. They put grubs and worms in men's heads: that are enemies to all pure and true apprehensions, and eat out all their happiness. They make it impossible for them in whom they reign to believe there is any excellency in the works of God, or to taste any sweetness in the nobility of nature, or to prize any common, tho never so great a blessing. They alienate men from the life of God, and at last make them to live without God in the world. To live the life of God is to live to all the works of God, and to enjoy them in His image, from which they are wholly diverted that follow fashions. Their fancies are corrupted with other jingles.

14

Being swallowed up therefore in the miserable gulf of idle talk and worthless vanities, thenceforth I lived among shadows, like a prodigal son feeding upon husks with swine. A comfortless wilderness full of thorns and troubles the world was, or worse: a waste place covered with idleness and play, and shops and markets and taverns. As for churches, they were things I did not understand. And schools were a burden: so that there was nothing in the world worth the having, or enjoying, but my game and sport, which also was a dream and, being passed, wholly forgotten. So that I had utterly forgotten all goodness, bounty, comfort, and glory: which things are the very brightness of the glory of God, for lack of which therefore He was unknown.

15

Yet sometimes in the midst of these dreams, I should come a little to myself so far as to feel I wanted something, secretly to expostulate with God for not giving me riches, to long after an unknown happiness, to grieve that the world was so empty, and to be dissatisfied with my present state because it was vain and forlorn. I had heard of angels, and much admired that here upon earth nothing should be but dirt and streets and gutters, for as for the pleasures that were in great men's houses I had not seen them; and it was my real happiness they were unknown, for because nothing deluded me, I was the more inquisitive.

16

Once I remember (I think I was about four years old) when I thus reasoned with myself, sitting in a little obscure room in my father's poor house. If there be a God, certainly He must be infinite in goodness. And that I was prompted to by a real whispering instinct of nature. And if He be infinite in goodness, and a perfect being in wisdom and love, certainly He must do most glorious things, and give us infinite riches; how comes it to pass therefore that I am so poor? Of so scanty and narrow a fortune, enjoying few and obscure comforts? I thought I could not believe Him a God to me, unless all His power were employed to glorify me. I knew not then my soul, or body; nor did I think of the heavens and the earth, the rivers and the stars, the sun or the seas: all those were lost, and absent from me. But when I found them made out of nothing for me, then I had a God indeed, whom I could praise, and rejoice in.

17

Sometimes I should be alone, and without employment, when suddenly my soul would return to itself, and forgetting all things in the whole world which mine eyes had seen, would be carried away to the ends of the earth; and my thoughts would be deeply engaged with inquiries: How the earth did end? Whether walls did bound it, or sudden precipices, or whether the heavens by degrees did come to touch it; so that the face of the earth and Heaven were so near, that a man with difficulty could creep under? Whatever I could imagine was inconvenient, and my reason being posed was quickly wearied. What also upheld the earth (because it was heavy) and kept it from falling; whether pillars, or dark waters? And if any of these, what then upheld those, and what again those, of which I saw there would be no end? Little did I think that the earth was round, and the world so full of beauty, light, and wisdom. When I saw that, I knew by the perfection of the work there was a God, and was satisfied, and rejoiced. People underneath and fields and flowers with another sun and another day pleased me mightily: but more when I knew it was the same sun that served them by night, that served us by day.

18

Sometimes I should soar above the stars and inquire how the heavens ended, and what was beyond them: concerning which by no means could I receive satisfaction. Sometimes my thoughts would carry me to the creation, for I had heard now, that the world which at first I thought was eternal, had a beginning: how therefore that beginning was, and why it was; why it was no sooner, and what was before; I mightily desired to know. By all which I easily perceive that my soul was made to live in communion with God, in all places of His dominion, and to be satisfied with the highest reason in all things. After which it so eagerly aspired, that I thought all the gold and silver in the world but dirt, in comparison of satisfaction in any of these. Sometimes I wondered why men were made no bigger? I would have had a man as big as a giant, a giant as big as a castle, and a castle as big as the heavens. Which yet would not serve: for there was infinite space beyond the heavens, and all was defective and but little in comparison; and for him to be made infinite, I thought it would be to no purpose, and it would be inconvenient. Why also there was not a better sun, and better stars, a better sea and better creatures I much admired. Which thoughts produced that poem upon moderation, which afterwards was written. Some part of the verses are these:

19
In making bodies Love could not express
Itself, or Art; unless it made them less.
O what a monster had in man been seen,
Had every thumb or toe a mountain been!
What worlds must he devour when he did eat?
What oceans drink! yet could not all his meat,
Or stature, make him like an angel shine;
Or make his soul in glory more divine.
A soul it is that makes us truly great,
Whose little bodies make us more complete.   10
An understanding that is infinite,
An endless, wide, and everlasting sight,
That can enjoy all things and nought exclude,
Is the most sacred greatness may be view'd.
'Twas inconvenient that his bulk should be
An endless hill; he nothing then could see.
No figure have, no motion, beauty, place,
No colour, feature, member, light, or grace.

>   A body like a mountain is but cumber.
>   An endless body is but idle lumber.
>   It spoils converse, and time itself devours,
>   While meat in vain, in feeding idle powers.
>   Excessive bulk being most injurious found,
>   To those conveniences which men have crown'd.
>   His wisdom did His power here repress,
>   God made man greater while He made him less.

20

The excellencies of the sun I found to be of another kind than that splendour after which I sought, even in unknown and invisible services; and that God by moderation wisely bounding His almighty power, had to my eternal amazement and wonder, made all bodies far greater than if they were infinite: there not being a sand nor mote in the air that is not more excellent than if it were infinite. How rich and admirable then is the Kingdom of God: where the smallest is greater than an infinite treasure! Is not this incredible? Certainly to the placets and doctrines of the schools: till we all consider, that infinite worth shut up in the limits of a material being, is the only way to a real infinity. God made nothing infinite in bulk, but everything there where it ought to be. Which, because moderation is a virtue observing the golden mean, in some other parts of the former poem, is thus expressed:

21

>   His power bounded, greater is in might,
>   Than if let loose, 'twere wholly infinite.
>   He could have made an endless sea by this.
>   But then it had not been a sea of bliss.
>   Did waters from the centre to the skies
>   Ascend, 'twould drown whatever else we prize.
>   The ocean bounded in a finite shore,
>   Is better far because it is no more.
>   No use nor glory would in that be seen;
>   His power made it endless in esteem.
>   Had not the sun been bounded in its sphere,

> Did all the world in one fair flame appear,
> And were that flame a real infinite,
> 'Twould yield no profit, splendour, nor delight.
> Its corpse confin'd, and beams extended be
> Effects of wisdom in the Deity.
> One star made infinite would all exclude.
> An earth made infinite could ne'er be view'd.
> But one being fashioned for the other's sake,
> He bounding all, did all most useful make;   20
> And which is best, in profit and delight
> Tho not in bulk, they all are infinite.

22

These liquid clear satisfactions were the emanations of the highest reason, but not achieved till a long time afterwards. In the meantime I was sometimes tho seldom visited and inspired with new and more vigorous desires after that bliss which nature whispered and suggested to me. Every new thing quickened my curiosity and raised my expectation. I remember once, the first time I came into a magnificent or noble dining room, and was left there alone, I rejoiced to see the gold and state and carved imagery, but when all was dead, and there was no motion, I was weary of it and departed dissatisfied. But afterwards, when I saw it full of lords and ladies and music and dancing, the place which once seemed not to differ from a solitary den, had now entertainment and nothing of tediousness but pleasure in it. By which I perceived (upon a reflection made long after) that men and women are when well understood a principal part of our true felicity. By this I found also that nothing that stood still, could by doing so be a part of happiness; and that affection, tho it were invisible, was the best of motions. But the august and glorious exercise of virtue, was more solemn and divine, which yet I saw not. And that all men and angels should appear in Heaven.

23

Another time, in a lowering and sad evening, being alone in the field, when all things were dead and quiet, a certain want and horror fell upon me, beyond imagination. The unprofitableness and silence of the place dissatisfied me, its wideness terrified me, from the utmost ends of the earth fears surrounded me. How did I know but dangers might suddenly arise from the East, and invade me from the unknown regions beyond the seas? I was a weak and little child, and had forgotten there was a man alive in the earth. Yet something also of hope and expectation comforted me from every border. This taught me that I was concerned in all the world; and that in the remotest borders the causes of peace delight me, and the beauties of the earth when seen were made to entertain me; that I was made to hold a communion with the secrets of divine providence in all the world; that a remembrance of all the joys I had from my birth ought always to be with me; that the presence of cities, temples, and kingdoms ought to sustain me; and that to be alone in the world was to be desolate and miserable. The comfort of houses and friends, and the clear assurance of treasures everywhere, God's care and love, His goodness, wisdom, and power, His presence and watchfulness in all the ends of the earth, were my strength and assurance forever; and that these things, being absent to my eye, were my joys and consolations: as present to my understanding as the wideness and emptiness of the universe which I saw before me.

24

When I heard of any new kingdom beyond the seas, the light and glory of it pleased me immediately, entered into me, it rose up within me and I was enlarged wonderfully. I entered into it, I saw its commodities, rarities, springs, meadows, riches, inhabitants, and became possessor of that new room, as it if had been prepared for me, so much was I magnified and delighted in it. When the Bible was read my spirit was present in other ages. I saw the light and splendour of them: the land of Canaan, the Israelites entering into it, the ancient glory of the Amorites, their peace and riches, their cities, houses, vines, and fig trees, the long prosperity of their kings, their milk and honey, their slaughter and destruction, with the joys and triumphs of God's people, all which entered into me, and God among them. I saw all and felt all in such a lively manner, as if there had been no other way to those places, but in spirit only. This showed me the liveliness of interior presence, and that all ages were for most glorious ends, accessible to my understanding, yea with it, yea within it, for without changing place in myself I could behold and enjoy all those. Anything when it was proposed, tho it was 10000 ages ago, being always before me.

25

When I heard any news I received it with greediness and delight, because my expectation was awakened with some hope that my happiness and the thing I wanted was concealed in it. Glad tidings you know from a far country brings us our salvation, and I was not deceived. In Jewry was Jesus killed, and from Jerusalem the Gospel came. Which when I once knew I was very confident that every kingdom contained like wonders and causes of joy, tho that was the fountain of them. As it was the first fruits so was it the pledge of what I shall receive in other countries. Thus also when any curious cabinet, or secret in chemistry, geometry, or physic was offered to me, I diligently looked in it, but when I saw it to the bottom and not my happiness I despised it. These imaginations and this thirst of news occasioned these reflections.

26

On News

1

News from a foreign country came,
As if my treasure and my wealth lay there:
So much it did my heart inflame!
'Twas wont to call my soul into mine ear.
 Which thither went to meet
  The approaching sweet;
 And on the threshold stood,
To entertain the unknown good.
 It hover'd there,
  As if 'twould leave mine ear.
And was so eager to embrace
The joyful tidings as they came,
'Twould almost leave its dwelling place,
 To entertain the same.

2

    As if the tidings were the things,
My very joys themselves, my foreign treasure,
    Or else did bear them on their wings:
With so much joy they came, with so much pleasure.
        My soul stood at the gate
            To recreate
        Itself with bliss; and to
        Be pleas'd with speed. A fuller view
            It fain would take
        Yet journeys back would make
        Unto my heart: as if 'twould fain
        Go out to meet, yet stay within
        To fit a place, to entertain,
            And bring the tidings in.

3

    What sacred instinct did inspire
My soul in childhood with a hope so strong?
    What secret force mov'd my desire,
To expect my joys beyond the seas, so young?
        Felicity I knew
            Was out of view:
        And being here alone,
        I saw that happiness was gone
            From me! for this,
        I thirsted absent bliss,
        And thought that sure beyond the seas,
        Or else in something near at hand
        I knew not yet (since nought did please
            I knew) my bliss did stand.

4

    But little did the infant dream
That all the treasures of the world were by:
    And that himself was so the cream
And crown of all, which round about did lie.
        Yet thus it was. The gem,

>   The diadem,
>   The ring enclosing all
>   That stood upon this earthy ball;   50
>   The heavenly eye,
>   Much wider than the sky,
>   Wherein they all included were,
>   The glorious soul that was the king
>   Made to possess them, did appear
>   A small and little thing!

27

Among other things, there befell me a most infinite desire of a book from Heaven, for observing all things to be rude and superfluous here upon earth I thought the ways of felicity to be known only among the holy angels; and that unless I could receive information from them, I could never be happy. This thirst hung upon me a long time; till at last I perceived that the God of angels had taken care of me, and prevented my desires. For He had sent the book I wanted before I was born; and prepared it for me, and also commended, and sent it unto me, in a far better manner than I was able to imagine. Had some angel brought it to me, which was the best way wherein I could then desire it, it would have been a peculiar favour, and I should have thought myself therein honoured above all mankind. It would have been the soul of this world, the light of my soul, the spring of life, and a fountain of happiness. You cannot think what riches and delights I promised myself therein. It would have been a mine of rarities, curiosities and wonders, to have entertained the powers of my soul, to have directed me in the way of life, and to have fed me with pleasures unknown to the whole world.

28

Had some angel brought it miraculously from Heaven, and left it at my foot, it had been a present meet for seraphims. Yet had it been a dream in comparison of the glorious way wherein God prepared it. I must have spent time in studying it, and with great diligence, have read it daily to drink in the precepts and instructions it contained. It had in a narrow obscure manner come unto me, and all the world had been ignorant of felicity, but I. Whereas now there are thousands in the world, of whom I being a poor child was ignorant, that in temples, universities and secret closets enjoy felicity, whom I saw not in shops, or schools, or trades; whom I found not in streets, or at feasts, or taverns: and therefore thought not to be in the world: who enjoy communion with God, and have fellowship with the angels every day. And these I discerned to be a great help unto me.

29

This put me upon two things: upon inquiring into the matter contained in the Bible, and into the manner wherein it came unto me. In the matter I found all the glad tidings my soul longed after, in its desire of news; in the manner, that the wisdom of God was infinitely greater than mine and that He had appeared in His wisdom, exceeding my desires. Above all things I desired some great lord or mighty king, that having power in his hand, to give me all kingdoms, riches, and honours, was willing to do it. And by that book I found that there was an eternal God, who loved me infinitely, that I was His son, that I was to overcome Death, and to live forever, that He created the world for me, that I was to reign in His throne, and to inherit all things. Who would have believed this had not that book told me? It told me also that I was to live in communion with Him, in the image of His life and glory, that I was to enjoy all His treasures and pleasures, in a more perfect manner than I could devise, and that all the truly amiable and glorious persons in the world were to be my friends and companions.

30

Upon this I had enough. I desired no more the honours and pleasures of this world, but gave myself to the illimited and clear fruition of that: and to this day see nothing wanting to my felicity but mine own perfection. All other things are well; I only, and the sons of men about me are disordered. Nevertheless could I be what I ought, their very disorders would be my enjoyments, for all things shall work together for good to them that love God. And if the disorders then certainly the troubles, and if the troubles, much more the vanities of men would be mine. Not only their enjoyments, but their very errors and distractions increasing my felicity. So that being heir of the whole world alone, I was to walk in it, as in a strange, marvellous, and amiable possession, and alone to render praises unto God for its enjoyment.

31

This taught me that those fashions and tinselled vanities, which you and I despised erewhile, fetching a little course about, became ours. And that the wisdom of God in them also was very conspicuous. For it becometh His goodness to make all things treasures: and His power is able to bring light out of darkness, and good out of evil. Nor would His love endure, but that I also should have a wisdom, whereby I could draw order out of confusion. So that it is my admiration and joy, that while so many thousand wander in darkness, I am in the light; and that while so many dote upon false treasures and pierce themselves through with many sorrows; I live in peace, and enjoy the delights of God and Heaven.

32

In respect of the matter, I was very sure that angels and cherubims could not bring unto me better tidings than were in the scriptures contained, could I but believe them to be true; but I was dissatisfied about the manner, and that was the ground of my unbelief. For I could not think that God being Love would neglect His son, and therefore surely I was not His son, nor He Love: because He had not ascertained me more carefully, that the Bible was His book from Heaven. Yet I was encouraged to hope well, because the matter was so excellent, above my expectation. And when I searched into it, I found the way infinitely better than if all the angels in Heaven had brought it to me.

33

Had the angels brought it to me alone, these several inconveniences had attended the vision: 1. It had been out one sudden act wherein it was sent me, whereas now God hath been all ages in preparing it. 2. It had been done by inferior ministers, whereas now it is done by God Himself. 3. Being Satan is able to transform himself into an angel of light, I had been still dubious, till having recourse to the excellency of the matter, by it I was informed and satisfied. 4. Being corrupted, that one miracle would have been but like a single spark upon green wood, it would have gone out immediately; whereas I needed 10000 miracles to seal it, yea and to awaken me to the meditation of the matter that was revealed to me. 5. Had it been revealed no other way, all the world had been dark and empty round about me; whereas now it is my joy and my delight and treasure, being full of knowledge, light, and glory. 6. Had it been revealed at no other time, God had now only been good unto me, whereas He hath manifested His love in all ages, and been carefully and most wisely revealing it from the beginning of the world. 7. Had He revealed it to no other person, I had been weak in faith being solitary, and sitting alone like a sparrow upon the housetop, who now have the concurrent and joint affections of kingdoms and ages. Yea notwithstanding the disadvantage of this weakness, I must have gone abroad, and published this faith to others, both in love to God, and love to men. For I must have done my duty, or the book would have done me no good, and love to God and men must have been my duty, for without that I could never be happy. Yea finally had not the book been revealed before, neither had God been glorious, nor I blessed, for He had been negligent of other persons, His goodness had been defective to all ages, whom now I know to be God by the universality of His love unto mankind; and the perfection of His wisdom to every person.

34

To talk now of the necessity of bearing all calamities and persecutions in preaching, is little: to consider the reproaches, mockings and derisions I must have endured of all the world, while they scoffed at me, for pretending to be the only man, that had a book from Heaven, is nothing; nor is it much to mention the impossibility of convincing others, all the world having been full of darkness, and God always silent before. All ages had been void of treasure had not the Bible been revealed till the other day, wherein now I can expatiate with perfect liberty, and everywhere see the love of God to all mankind love to me alone. All the world being adorned with miracles, prophets, patriarchs, apostles, martyrs, revelations from Heaven, lively examples, holy souls, divine affairs, for my enjoyment. The glory of God and the light of Heaven appearing everywhere, as much as it would have done in that seeming instant, had the book I desired come unto me any other way.

35

You will not believe what a world of joy this one satisfaction and pleasure brought me. Thenceforth I thought the light of Heaven was in this world: I saw it possible, and very probable, that I was infinitely beloved of almighty God, the delights of Paradise were round about me, Heaven and earth were open to me, all riches were little things, this one pleasure being so great that it exceeded all the joys of Eden. So great a thing it was to me, to be satisfied in the manner of God's revealing Himself unto mankind. Many other inquiries I had concerning the manner of His revealing Himself, in all which I am infinitely satisfied.

36

Having been at the university, and received there the taste and tincture of another education, I saw that there were things in this world of which I never dreamed, glorious secrets, and glorious persons past imagination. There I saw that logic, ethics, physics, metaphysics, geometry, astronomy, poesy, medicine, grammar, music, rhetoric, all kind of arts, trades, and mechanicisms that adorned the world pertained to felicity. At least there I saw those things, which afterwards I knew to pertain unto it; and was delighted in it. There I saw into the nature of the sea, the heavens, the sun, the moon and stars, the elements, minerals and vegetables. All which appeared like the king's daughter, all glorious within, and those things which my nurses and parents should have talked of, there were taught unto me.

37

Nevertheless some things were defective too. There was never a tutor that did professly teach felicity, tho that be the mistress of all other sciences. Nor did any of us study these things but as *aliena*, which we ought to have studied as our own enjoyments. We studied to inform our knowledge, but knew not for what end we so studied. And for lack of aiming at a certain end, we erred in the manner.

Howbeit there we received all those seeds of knowledge that were afterwards improved; and our souls were awakened to a discerning of their faculties, and exercise of their powers.

38

The manner is in everything of greatest concernment. Whatever good thing we do, neither can we please God, unless we do it well; nor can He please us, whatever good He does, unless He do it well. Should He give us the most perfect things in Heaven and earth to make us happy, and not give them to us in the best of all possible manners, He would but displease us, and it were impossible for Him to make us happy. It is not sufficient therefore for us to study the most excellent things unless we do it in the most excellent of manners. And what that is it is impossible to find till we are guided thereunto by the most excellent end, with a desire of which I flagrantly burned.

39

The best of all possible ends is the glory of God, but happiness was that I thirsted after. And yet I did not err, for the glory of God is to make us happy. Which can never be done but by giving us most excellent natures and satisfying those natures: by creating all treasures of infinite value, and giving them to us in an infinite manner, to wit both in the best that to omnipotence was possible. This led me to inquire, whether all things were excellent and of perfect value, and whether they were mine in propriety?

40

It is the glory of God to give all things to us in the best of all possible manners. To study things therefore under the double notion of interest and treasure, is to study all things in the best of all possible manners. Because in studying so we inquire after God's glory and our own happiness. And indeed enter into the way that leadeth to all contentments, joys, and satisfactions, to all praises, triumphs, and thanksgivings, to all virtues, beauties, adorations, and graces, to all dominion, exaltation, wisdom, and glory, to all holiness, union, and communion with God, to all patience and courage and blessedness, which it is impossible to meet any other way. So that to study object for ostentation, vain knowledge, or curiosity is fruitless impertinence tho God Himself, and angels, be the object. But to study that which will oblige us to love Him, and feed us with nobility and goodness toward men, that is blessed. And so is it to study that which will lead us to the temple of wisdom, and seat us in the throne of glory.

41

Many men study the same things, which have not the taste of, nor delight in them. And their palates vary according to the ends at which they aim. He that studies polity, men, and manners, merely that he may know how to behave himself and get honour in this world, has not that delight in his studies, as he that contemplates these things that he might see the ways of God among them, and walk in communion with Him. The attainments of the one are narrow, the other grows a celestial king of all kingdoms. Kings minister unto him, temples are his own, thrones are his peculiar treasure. Governments, officers, magistrates, and courts of judicature are his delights in a way ineffable, and a manner unconceivable to the other's imagination. He that knows the secrets of nature with Albertus Magnus, or the motions of the heavens with Galileo, or the cosmography of the moon with Hevelius, or the body of man with Galen, or the nature of diseases with Hippocrates, or the harmonies in melody with Orpheus, or of poesy with Homer, or of grammar with Lilly, or of whatever else with the greatest artist; he is nothing, if he knows them merely for talk or idle speculation, or transient and external use. But he that knows them for value, and knows them for his own, shall profit infinitely. And therefore of all kind of learnings, humanity and divinity are the most excellent.

42

By humanity we search into the powers and faculties of the soul, inquire into the excellencies of human nature, consider its wants, survey its inclinations, propensities, and desires, ponder its principles, proposals, and ends, examine the causes and fitness of all, the worth of all, the excellency of all. Whereby we come to know what man is in this world, what his sovereign end and happiness, and what is the best means by which he may attain it. And by this we come to see what wisdom is: which namely is a knowledge exercised in finding out the way to perfect happiness, by discerning man's real wants and sovereign desires. We come moreover to know God's goodness, in seeing into the causes, wherefore He implanted such faculties and inclinations in us, and the objects and ends prepared for them. This leadeth us to divinity. For God gave man an endless intellect to see all things, and a proneness to covet them, because they are his treasures; and an infinite variety of apprehensions and affections, that he might have an all-sufficiency in himself to enjoy them; a curiosity profound and unsatiable to stir him up to look into them; an ambition great and everlasting to carry him to the highest honours, thrones, and dignities. An emulation whereby he might be animated and quickened by all examples, a tenderness and compassion whereby he may be united to all persons; a sympathy and love to virtue, a tenderness of his credit in every soul, that he might delight to be honoured in all persons; an eye to behold eternity and the omnipresence of God, that he might see eternity and dwell within it: a power of admiring, loving, and prizing, that seeing the goodness and beauty of God, he might be united to it forevermore.

43

In divinity we are entertained with all objects from everlasting to everlasting, because with Him whose outgoings from everlasting: being to contemplate God, and to walk with Him in all His ways; and therefore to be entertained with all objects, as He is the fountain, governor, and end of them. We are to contemplate God in the unity of His essence, in the Trinity of Persons, in His manifold attributes, in all His works, internal and external, in His counsels and decrees, in the work of creation, and in His work of providence. And man, as he is a creature of God, capable of celestial blessedness, and a subject in His kingdom: in his fourfold estate of innocency, misery, grace, and glory. In this estate of innocency we are to contemplate the nature and manner of his happiness, the laws under which he was governed, the joys of Paradise, and the immaculate powers of his immortal soul. In the estate of misery we have his Fall, the nature of sin original and actual, his manifold punishments, calamity, sickness, death &c. In the estate of grace: the tenor of the New Covenant, the manner of its exhibition under the various dispensations of the Old and New Testament, the mediator of the Covenant, the conditions of it, faith and repentance, the sacraments or seals of it, the scriptures, ministers, and Sabbaths, the nature and government of the church, its histories and successions from the beginning to the end of the world &c. In the state of glory: the nature of separate souls, their advantages, excellencies, and privileges, the resurrection of the body, the day of judgement and life everlasting. Wherein further we are to see and understand the communion of saints, heavenly joys, and our society with angels. To all which I was naturally born, to the fruition of all which I was by grace redeemed, and in the enjoyment of all which I am to live eternally.

44

Natural philosophy teaches us the causes and effects of all bodies simply and in themselves. But if you extend it a little further, to that indeed which its name imports, signifying the love of nature, it leads us into a diligent inquisition into all natures, their qualities, affections, relations, causes, and ends, so far forth as by nature and reason they may be known. And this noble science as such is most sublime and perfect, it includes all humanity and divinity together: God, angels, men, affections, habits, actions, virtues; everything as it is a solid entire object singly proposed, being a subject of it, as well as material and visible things. But taking it as it is usually bounded in its terms, it treateth only of corporeal things, as Heaven, earth, air, water, fire, the sun and stars, trees, herbs, flowers, influences, winds, fowls, beasts, fishes, minerals and precious stones; with all other beings of that kind. And as thus it is taken it is nobly subservient to the highest ends: for it openeth the riches of God's kingdom, and the nature of His territories, works, and creatures in a wonderful manner, clearing and preparing the eye of the enjoyer.

45

Ethics teach us the mysteries of morality, and the nature of affections, virtues, and manners, as by them we may be guided to our highest happiness. The former for speculation, this for practice. The former furnisheth us with riches, this with honours and delights, the former feasteth us, and this instructeth us. For by this we are taught to live honourably among men, and to make ourselves noble and useful among them. It teacheth us how to manage our passions, to exercise virtues, and to form our manners, so as to live happily in this world. And all these put together discover the materials of religion to be so great, that it plainly manifesteth the revelation of God to be deep and infinite. For it is impossible for language, miracles, or apparitions to teach us the infallibility of God's word or to show us the certainty of true religion, without a clear sight into truth itself, that is into the truth of things. Which will themselves when truly seen, by the very beauty and glory of them, best discover and prove religion.

46

When I came into the country, and being seated among silent trees, had all my time in mine own hands, I resolved to spend it all, whatever it cost me, in search of happiness, and to satiate that burning thirst which nature had enkindled in me from my youth. In which I was so resolute, that I chose rather to live upon ten pounds a year, and to go in leather clothes, and feed upon bread and water, so that I might have all my time clearly to myself: than to keep many thousands per annum in an estate of life where my time would be devoured in care and labour. And God was so pleased to accept of that desire, that from that time to this I have had all things plentifully provided for me, without any care at all, my very study of felicity making me more to prosper, than all the care in the whole world. So that through His blessing I live a free and a kingly life, as if the world were turned again into Eden, or much more, as it is at this day.

47

I

A life of Sabbaths here beneath!
Continual jubilees and joys!
The days of Heaven, while we breathe
On earth! Where sin all bliss destroys.
This is a triumph of delights!
That doth exceed all appetites.
No joy can be compar'd to this,
It is a life of perfect bliss.

2

Of perfect bliss! How can it be?
To conquer Satan, and to reign
In such a vale of misery,
Where vipers, stings, and tears remain;
Is to be crown'd with victory.
To be content, divine and free,
Even here beneath is great delight
And next the beatific sight.

3

But inward lusts do oft assail,
Temptations work us much annoy.
We'll therefore weep, and to prevail
Shall be a more celestial joy.
To have no other enemy,
But one; and to that one to die:
To fight with that and conquer it,
Is better than in peace to sit.

4

'Tis better for a little time:
For he that all his lusts doth quell,
Shall find this life to be his prime,
And vanquish sin and conquer hell.
The next shall be his double joy:
And that which here seem'd to destroy,
Shall in the other life appear
A root of bliss; a pearl each tear.

48

Thus you see I can make merry with calamities, and while I grieve at sins, and war against them, abhorring the world, and myself more; descend into the abysses of humility, and there admire a new offspring and torrent of joys, God's mercies. Which accepteth of our fidelity in bloody battles, tho every wound defile and poison; and when we slip or fall, turneth our true penitent tears into solid pearl, that shall abide with Him for evermore. But oh let us take heed that we never willingly commit a sin against so gracious a Redeemer, and so great a Father.

49

1
Sin!
O only fatal woe,
That mak'st me sad and mourning go!
That all my joys dost spoil,
His kingdom and my soul defile!
I never can agree
With thee!

2
Thou!
Only thou! O thou alone
(And my obdurate heart of stone)
The poison and the foes
Of my enjoyments and repose,
The only bitter ill:
Dost kill!

3
Oh!
I cannot meet with thee,
Nor once approach thy memory,
But all my joys are dead,
And all my sacred treasures fled;
As if I now did dwell
In hell.

4
Lord!
O hear how short I breathe!
See how I tremble here beneath!
A sin! Its ugly face
More terror than its dwelling place

Contains (O dreadful Sin),
Within!

50

The Recovery

Sin! wilt thou vanquish me!
And shall I yield the victory?
Shall all my joys be spoil'd,
And pleasures soil'd
By thee!
Shall I remain
As one that's slain
And never more lift up the head?
Is not my Saviour dead!
His blood, thy bane; my balsam, bliss, joy, wine; 10
Shall thee destroy; heal, feed, make me divine.

51

I cannot meet with sin, but it kills me, and 'tis only by Jesus Christ that I can kill it, and escape. Would you blame me to be confounded, when I have offended my eternal Father, who gave me all the things in Heaven and earth? One sin is a dreadful stumbling block in the way to Heaven. It breeds a long parenthesis in the fruition of our joys. Do you not see, my friend, how it disorders and disturbs my proceeding? There is no calamity but sin alone.

52

When I came into the country, and saw that I had all time in my own hands, having devoted it wholly to the study of felicity, I knew not where to begin or end; nor what objects to choose, upon which most profitably I might fix my contemplation. I saw myself like some traveller, that had destined his life to journeys, and was resolved to spend his days in visiting strange places: who might wander in vain, unless his undertakings were guided by some certain rule; and that innumerable millions of objects were presented before me, unto any of which I might take my journey. Fain I would have visited them all, but that was impossible. What then should I do? Even imitate a traveller, who because he cannot visit all coasts, wildernesses, sandy deserts, seas, hills, springs, and mountains, chooseth the most populous and flourishing cities, where he might see the fairest prospects, wonders, and rarities, and be entertained with greatest courtesy; and where indeed he might most benefit himself with knowledge, profit, and delight: leaving the rest, even the naked and empty places unseen. For which cause I made it my prayer to God Almighty, that He, whose eyes are open upon all things, would guide me to the fairest and divinest.

53

And what rule do you think I walked by? Truly a strange one, but the best in the whole world. I was guided by an implicit faith in God's goodness: and therefore led to the study of the most obvious and common things. For thus I thought within myself: God being, as we generally believe, infinite in goodness, it is most consonant and agreeable with His nature, that the best things should be most common, for nothing is more natural to infinite goodness than to make the best things most frequent; and only things worthless, scarce. Then I began to inquire what things were most common: air, light, Heaven and earth, water, the sun, trees, men and women, cities, temples &c. These I found common and obvious to all: rubies, pearls, diamonds, gold and silver, these I found scarce, and to the most denied. Then began I to consider and compare the value of them, which I measured by their serviceableness, and by the excellencies which would be found in them, should they be taken away. And in conclusion I saw clearly, that there was a real valuableness in all the common things; in the scarce, a feigned.

54

Beside these common things I have named, there were others as common, but invisible. The laws of God, the soul of man, Jesus Christ and His Passion on the cross, with the ways of God in all ages. And these by the general credit they had obtained in the world confirmed me more. For the ways of God were transient things, they were past and gone; our Saviour's sufferings were in one particular obscure place, the laws of God were no object of the eye, but only found in the minds of men; these therefore which were so secret in their own nature, and made common only by the esteem men had of them, must of necessity include unspeakable worth for which they were celebrated, of all, and so generally remembered. As yet I did not see the wisdom and depths of knowledge, the clear principles, and certain evidences whereby the wise and holy, the ancients and the learned that were abroad in the world knew these things, but was led to them only by the fame which they had vulgarly received. Howbeit I believed that there were unspeakable mysteries contained in them, and tho they were generally talked of their value was unknown. These therefore I resolved to study, and no other. But to my unspeakable wonder, they brought me to all the things in Heaven and in earth, in time and eternity, possible and impossible, great and little, common and scarce, and discovered them all to be infinite treasures.

55

That anything may be found to be an infinite treasure, its place must be found in eternity, and in God's esteem. For as there is a time, so there is a place for all things. Everything in its place is admirable, deep, and glorious; out of its place like a wandering bird, is desolate and good for nothing. How therefore it relateth to God and all creatures must be seen before it can be enjoyed. And this I found by many instances. The sun is good, only as it relateth to the stars, to the seas, to your eye, to the fields, &c. As it relateth to the stars it raiseth their influences; as to the seas it melteth them and maketh the waters flow; as to your eye, it bringeth in the beauty of the world; as to the fields; it clotheth them with fruits and flowers. Did it not relate to others it would not be good. Divest it of these operations and divide it from these objects, it is useless and good for nothing. And therefore worthless, because worthless and useless go together. A piece of gold cannot be valued, unless we know how it relates to clothes, to wine, to victuals, to the esteem of men, and to the owner. Some little piece in a kingly monument severed from the rest hath no beauty at all. It enjoys its value in its place, by the ornament it gives to, and receives from all the parts. By this I discerned, that even a little knowledge could not be had in the mystery of felicity, without a great deal. And that that was the reason why so many were ignorant of its nature, and why so few did attain it, for by the labour required to much knowledge they were discouraged, and for lack of much did not see any glorious motives to allure them.

56

Therefore of necessity they must at first believe that felicity is a glorious tho an unknown thing. And certainly it was the infinite wisdom of God, that did implant by instinct so strong a desire of felicity in the soul, that we might be excited to labour after it, tho we know it not, the very force wherewith we covet it supplying the place of understanding. That there is a felicity we all know by the desires after, that there is a most glorious felicity we know by the strength and vehemence of those desires; and that nothing but felicity is worthy of our labour, because all other things are the means only which conduce unto it. I was very much animated by the desires of philosophers, which I saw in heathen books aspiring after it. But the misery is it was unknown. An altar was erected to it like that in Athens with this inscription TO THE UNKNOWN GOD.

57

Two things in perfect felicity I saw to be requisite; and that felicity must be perfect, or not felicity. The first was the perfection of its objects, in nature, serviceableness, number, and excellency. The second was the perfection of the manner wherein they are enjoyed, for sweetness, measure, and duration. And unless in these I could be satisfied I should never be contented. Especially about the latter for the manner is always more excellent than the thing. And it far more concerneth us that the manner wherein we enjoy be complete and perfect than that the matter which we enjoy be complete and perfect. For the manner as we contemplate its excellency is itself a great part of the matter of our enjoyment.

58

In discovering the matter or objects to be enjoyed, I was greatly aided by remembering that we were made in God's image. For thereupon it must of necessity follow that God's treasures be our treasures, and His joys our joys. So that by inquiring what were God's, I found the objects of our felicity God's treasures being ours, for we were made in His image that we might live in His similitude. And herein I was mightily confirmed by the apostles blaming the Gentiles, and charging it upon them as a very great fault that they were alienated from the life of God, for hereby I perceived that we were to live the life of God: when we lived the true life of nature according to knowledge; and that by blindness and corruption we had strayed from it. Now God's treasures are His own perfections, and all His creatures.

59

The image of God implanted in us, guided me to the manner wherein we were to enjoy, for since we were made in the similitude of God, we were made to enjoy after His similitude. Now to enjoy the treasures of God in the similitude of God, is the most perfect blessedness God could devise. For the treasures of God are the most perfect treasures and the manner of God is the most perfect manner. To enjoy therefore the treasures of God after the similitude of God is to enjoy the most perfect treasures in the most perfect manner. Upon which I was infinitely satisfied in God, and knew there was a Deity, because I was satisfied. For exerting Himself wholly in achieving thus an infinite felicity, He was infinitely delightful, great, and glorious, and my desires so august and insatiable that nothing less than a Deity could satisfy them.

60

This spectacle, once seen, will never be forgotten. It is a great part of the beatific vision. A sight of happiness is happiness. It transforms the soul and makes it heavenly, it powerfully calls us to communion with God, and weans us from the customs of this world. It puts a lustre upon God and all His creatures, and makes us to see them in a divine and eternal light. I no sooner discerned this but I was (as Plato saith, *In summa rationis arce quies habitat*) seated in a throne of repose and perfect rest. All things were well in their proper places, I alone was out of frame and had need to be mended, for all things were God's treasures in their proper places, and I was to be restored to God's image. Whereupon you will not believe how I was withdrawn from all endeavours of altering and mending outward things. They lay so well, methoughts, they could not be mended; but I must be mended to enjoy them.

61

The image of God is the most perfect creature. Since there cannot be two Gods, the utmost endeavour of almighty power is the image of God. It is no blasphemy to say that God cannot make a God: the greatest thing that He can make is His image: a most perfect creature, to enjoy the most perfect treasures, in the most perfect manner. A creature endued with the most divine and perfect powers, for measure, kind, number, duration, excellency, is the most perfect creature: able to see all eternity with all its objects, and as a mirror to contain all it seeth: able to love all it contains, and as a sun to shine upon its loves. Able by shining to communicate itself in beams of affection, and to illustrate all it illuminates with beauty and glory: able to be wise, holy, glorious, blessed in itself as God is, being adorned inwardly with the same kind of beauty, and outwardly superior to all creatures.

62

Upon this I began to believe that all other creatures were such that God was Himself in their creation, that is *almighty power wholly exerted*; and that every creature is indeed as it seemed in my infancy: not as it is commonly apprehended, everything being sublimely rich and great and glorious, every spire of grass is the work of His hand; and I in a world where everything is mine, and far better than the greater sort of children esteem diamonds and pearls. Gold and silver being the very refuse of nature, and the worst things in God's kingdom. Howbeit truly good in their proper places.

63

To be satisfied in God is the highest difficulty in the whole world. And yet most easy to be done. To make it possible that we should be satisfied in God was an achievement of infinite weight, before it was attempted, and the most difficult thing in all worlds before it was achieved. For we naturally expect infinite things of God, and can be satisfied only with the highest reason. So that the best of all possible things must be wrought in God, or else we shall remain dissatisfied. But it is most easy at present, because God is. For God is not a being compounded of body and soul, or substance and accident, or power and act but is all act, pure act, a simple being. Whose essence is to be, whose being is to be perfect, so that He is most perfect towards all and in all. He is most perfect for all and by all. He is in nothing imperfect because His being is to be perfect. It is impossible for Him to be God, and imperfect: and therefore do we so ardently and infinitely desire His absolute perfection.

64

Neither is it possible to be otherwise. All His power being turned into act, it is all exerted: infinitely and wholly. Neither is there any power in Him which He is not able and willing to use; or which He cannot wisely guide to most excellent ends. So that we may expect most angelical and heavenly rarities in all the creatures. Were there any power in God unemployed He would be compounded of power and act. Being therefore God is all act, He is a God in this, that Himself is power exerted. An infinite act because infinite power infinitely exerted, an eternal act because infinite power eternally exerted. Wherein consisteth the generation of His Son, the perfection of His love, and the immutability of God. For God by exerting Himself begot His son, and doing [it] wholly for the sake of His creatures, is perfect love; and doing it wholly from all eternity, is an eternal act and therefore unchangeable.

65

With this we are delighted because it is absolutely impossible that any power dwelling with love should continue idle. Since God therefore was infinitely and eternally communicative, all things were contained in Him from all eternity. As Nazianzen in his 38th oration admirably expresseth it, in these words, 'Because it was by no means sufficient for *goodness* to move only in the contemplation of itself but it became what was *good* to be diffused and propagated, that more might be affected with the benefit (for this was the part of the highest goodness) first He thought upon angelical and celestial virtues, and that thought was the work, which He wrought by the *Word*, and fulfilled by the spirit. *Atque ita secundi splendores procreati sunt primi splendoris administri.*' And so were there second splendours created, and made to minister to the first splendour, so that all motions, successions, creatures, and operations with their beginnings and ends were in Him from everlasting. To whom nothing can be added, because from all eternity He was, whatsoever to all eternity He can be. All things being now to be seen and contemplated in His bosom: and advanced therefore into a diviner light, being infinitely older and more precious than we were aware. Time itself being in God eternally.

66

Little did I imagine that while I was thinking these things I was conversing with God. I was so ignorant that I did not think any man in the world had had such thoughts before. Seeing them therefore so amiable, I wondered not a little, that nothing was spoken of them in former ages. But as I read the Bible I was here and there surprised with such thoughts, and found by degrees that these things had been written of before, not only in the Scriptures but in many of the fathers, and that this was the way of communion with God in all saints, as I saw clearly in the person of David. Methoughts a new light darted in into all his Psalms, and finally spread abroad over the whole Bible. So that things which for their obscurity I thought not in being were there contained; things which for their greatness were incredible, were made evident and things obscure, plain. God by this means bringing me into the very heart of His kingdom.

67

There I saw Moses blessing the Lord for the precious things of Heaven, for the dew and for the deep that coucheth beneath; and for the precious fruits brought forth by the sun, and for the precious things put forth by the moon; and for the chief things of the ancient mountains and for the precious things of the lasting hills; and for the precious things of the earth, and fullness thereof. There I saw Jacob, with awful apprehensions admiring the glory of the world, when awaking out of his dream he said, 'How dreadful is this place! This is none other than the house of God, and the gate of Heaven.' There

I saw God leading forth Abraham, and showing him the stars of Heaven, and all the countries round about him, and saying, 'All these will I give thee, and thy seed after thee.' There I saw Adam in Paradise, surrounded with the beauty of Heaven and earth, void of all earthly comforts: to wit such as were devised, gorgeous apparel, palaces, gold and silver, coaches, musical instruments &c., and entertained only with celestial joys. The sun and moon and stars, beasts and fowls and fishes, trees and fruits and flowers, with the other naked and simple delights of nature. By which I evidently saw that the way to become rich and blessed was not by heaping accidental and devised riches to make ourselves great in the vulgar manner; but to approach more near, and to see more clearly with the eye of our understanding, the beauties and glories of the whole world; and to have communion with the Deity in the riches of God and nature.

68

I saw moreover that it did not so much concern us what objects were before us, as with what eyes we beheld them; with what affections we esteemed them, and what apprehensions we had about them. All men see the same objects, but do not equally understand them. Intelligence is the tongue that discerns and tastes them, knowledge is the light of Heaven. Love is the wisdom and glory of God. Life extended to all objects is the sense that enjoys them. So that knowledge, life, and love are the very means of all enjoyment, which above all things we must seek for and labour after. All objects are in God eternal: which we by perfecting our faculties are made to enjoy. Which then are turned into act when they are exercised about their objects, but without them are desolate and idle; or discontented and forlorn. Whereby I perceived the meaning of that definition wherein Aristotle describeth felicity, when he saith felicity is the perfect exercise of perfect virtue in a perfect life. For life is perfect when it is perfectly extended to all objects, and perfectly sees them and perfectly loves them: which is done by a perfect exercise of virtue about them.

69

I

In Salem dwelt a glorious king,
Rais'd from a shepherd's lowly state,

That did His praises like an angel sing
    Who did the world create.
  By many great and bloody wars,
  He was advanced unto thrones;
  But more delighted in the stars
Than in the splendour of his precious stones.
Nor gold nor silver did his eye regard:
The works of God were his sublime reward.

2

  A warlike champion he had been
  And many feats of chivalry
Had done; in kingly courts his eye had seen
    A vast variety
  Of earthly joys; yet he despis'd
  Those fading honours and false pleasures
  Which are by mortals so much priz'd;
And plac'd his happiness in other treasures.
No state of life which in this world we find
Could yield contentment to his greater mind.

3

  His fingers touch'd his trembling lyre,
  And every quavering string did yield
A sound that filled all the Jewish choir
    And echo'd in the field.
  No pleasure was so great to him
  As in a silent night to see
  The moon and stars: a cherubim
Above them even here he seem'd to be.
Inflam'd with love, it was his great desire
To sing, contemplate, ponder, and admire.

4

  He was a prophet, and foresaw
  Things extant in the world to come;
He was a judge, and ruled by a law
    That than the honeycomb

>   Was sweeter far; he was a sage,
>   And all his people could advise;
>   An oracle, whose every page
>   Contain'd in verse the greatest mysteries.
>   But most he then enjoy'd himself, when he
>   Did as a poet praise the Deity. 40

5

>   A shepherd, soldier, and divine,
>   A judge, a courtier, and a king,
>   Priest, angel, prophet, oracle did shine
>   At once; when he did sing.
>   Philosopher and poet too
>   Did in his melody appear;
>   All these in him did please the view
>   Of those that did his heavenly music hear.
>   And every drop that from his flowing quill
>   Came down, did all the world with nectar fill. 50

6

>   He had a deep and perfect sense
>   Of all the glories and the pleasures
>   That in God's works are hid, the excellence
>   Of such transcendent treasures
>   Made him on earth an heavenly king,
>   And fill'd his solitudes with joy;
>   He never did more sweetly sing
>   Than when alone, tho that doth mirth destroy.
>   Sense did his soul with heavenly life inspire
>   And made him seem in God's celestial choir. 60

7

>   Rich, sacred, deep, and precious things
>   Did here on earth the man surround.
>   With all the glory of the King of Kings
>   He was most strangely crown'd.
>   His clear soul and open sight

> Among the sons of God did see
> Things filling angels with delight;
> His ear did hear their heavenly melody.
> And when he was alone he all became,
> That bliss implied, or did increase his fame. 70
>
> 8
> All arts he then did exercise,
> And as his God he did adore,
> By secret ravishments above the skies
> He carried was, before
> He died. His soul did see and feel
> What others know not; and became
> While he before his God did kneel
> A constant heavenly pure seraphic flame.
> Oh that I might unto his throne aspire;
> And all his joys above the stars admire! 80

70

When I saw those objects celebrated in his Psalms which God and nature had proposed to me, and which I thought chance only presented to my view, you cannot imagine how unspeakably I was delighted: to see so glorious a person, so great a prince, so divine a sage, that was a man after God's own heart by the testimony of God Himself, rejoicing in the same things, meditating on the same and praising God for the same. For by this I perceived we were led by one spirit; and that following the clew of nature into this labyrinth I was brought into the midst of celestial joys; and that to be retired from earthly cares and fears and distractions that we might in sweet and heavenly peace contemplate all the works of God, was to live in Heaven and the only way to become what David was: a man after God's own heart. There we might be inflamed with those causes for which we ought to love Him; there we might see those viands which feed the soul with angels' food; there we might bathe in those streams of pleasure that flow at His right hand forevermore.

71

That hymn of David in the eighth Psalm was supposed to be made by night, wherein he celebrateth the works of God; because he mentioneth the moon and stars, but not the sun in his meditation. When I consider the heavens which Thou hast made, the moon and stars which are the works of Thy fingers, what is man that Thou art mindful of him, or the son of man that Thou visitest him? Thou hast made him a little lower than the angels, and hast crowned him with glory and honour. Thou hast given him dominion over the works of Thy hands, Thou hast put all things in subjection under his feet: all sheep and oxen, yea and the beasts of the field; the fowls of the air and the fishes of the sea, and whatsoever passeth through the paths of the sea. This glory and honour wherewith man is crowned ought to affect every person that is grateful with celestial joy: and so much the rather, because it is every man's proper and sole inheritance.

72

His joyful meditation in the nineteenth Psalm directeth every man to consider the glory of Heaven and earth. The heavens declare the glory of God, and the firmament showeth His handiwork. Day unto day uttereth speech, and night unto night showeth knowledge. There is no speech nor language where their voice is not heard. Their line is gone throughout all the earth, and their voice to the end of the world. In them hath He set a tabernacle for the sun, which is as a bridegroom coming out of his chamber, and rejoiceth as a strong man to run his race. His going forth is from the end of the heaven, and his circuit to the ends of it, and nothing is hid from the heat thereof. From thence he proceedeth to the laws of God, as things more excellent in their nature than His works. The law of the Lord is perfect, converting the soul; the testimony of the Lord is sure, making wise the simple. The statutes of the Lord are right, rejoicing the heart; the commandment of the Lord is pure, enlightening the eyes. The fear of the Lord is clean, enduring forever; the judgements of the Lord are true and righteous altogether. More to be desired are they than gold, yea than much fine gold; sweeter also than honey and the honeycomb. Whereby he plainly showeth that divine and kingly delights are in the laws and works of God to be taken, by all those that would be angelical and celestial creatures. For that in the Kingdom of Heaven everyone being disentangled from particular relations and private riches, as if he were newly taken out of nothing to the fruition of all eternity, was in these alone to solace himself as his peculiar treasures.

73

Ye that fear the Lord, praise Him; all ye seed of Jacob, glorify Him; and fear Him, all ye seed of Israel. For He hath not despised nor abhorred the affliction of the afflicted, neither hath He hid His face from him, but when he cried unto Him, He heard. My praise shall be of Thee in the great congregation; I will pay my vows before them that fear Him. The meek shall eat and be satisfied. They shall praise the Lord that seek Him; your heart shall live forever. All the ends of the world shall remember and turn unto the Lord, all the kindreds of the nations shall worship before Thee. For the kingdom is the Lord's, and He is the governor among the nations. All they that be fat upon earth shall eat and worship; all they that go down to the dust shall bow before Him, and none can keep alive his own soul. A seed shall serve Him; it shall be counted to the Lord for a generation. They shall come and declare His righteousness to a people that shall be born, that He hath done this. Here he showeth that it was his desire and delight to have all nations praising God; and that the condescension of the Almighty in stooping down to the poor and needy was the joy of his soul. He prophesieth also of the conversion of the Gentiles to the knowledge of Jesus Christ, which to see was to him an exceeding pleasure.

74

The earth is the Lord's and the fullness thereof, the round world and they that dwell therein. He observeth here that God by a comprehensive possession and by way of eminence, enjoyeth the whole world; all mankind and all the earth, with all that is therein, being His peculiar treasures. Since therefore we are made in the image of God, to live in His similitude, as they are His, they must be our treasures. We being wise and righteous over all as He is. Because they regard not the works of the Lord, nor the operation of His hands, therefore shall He destroy them and not build them up.

75

By the word of the Lord were the heavens made, and all the host of them by the breath of His mouth. He gathereth the waters of the sea together, He layeth up the depth in storehouses. Let all the earth fear the Lord, let all the inhabitants of the world stand in awe of Him. For He spake, and it was done, He commanded and it stood fast. He frequently meditateth upon the works of God, and affirmeth the contemplation of them to beget His fear in our hearts for that He being great in strength, not one faileth.

76

All my bones shall say, Lord, who is like unto Thee, who deliverest the poor from him that is too strong for him; yea, the poor and the needy from him that spoileth him! Thy mercy, O Lord, is above the heavens and Thy faithfulness reacheth to the clouds. Thy righteousness is like the great mountains, Thy judgements are a great deep: O Lord, Thou preservest man and beast. How excellent is Thy loving kindness, O God! Therefore the children of men put their trust under the shadow of Thy wings. They shall be abundantly satisfied with the fatness of Thy house; and Thou shalt make them drink of the river of Thy pleasures. For with Thee is the fountain of life. In Thy light we shall see light. The judgements of God, and His loving kindness, His mercy and faithfulness, are the fatness of His house, and His righteousness being seen in the light of glory is the torrent of pleasure at His right hand forevermore.

77

Hearken, O daughter, and consider, and incline thine ear; forget also thine own people and thy father's house. So shall the King greatly desire thy beauty, for He is thy Lord and worship thou Him. The King's daughter is all glorious within, her clothing is of wrought gold. She shall be brought unto the King in raiment of needlework; the virgins her companions that follow her, shall be brought unto Thee. With gladness and rejoicing shall they be brought, they shall enter into the King's palace. Instead of thy fathers shall be thy children whom thou mayest make princes in all the earth. The Psalmist here singeth an epithalamium upon the marriage between Christ and His church: whom He persuadeth to forsake her country and her father's house, together with all the customs and vanities of this world, and to dedicate herself wholly to our Saviour's service since she is in exchange to enter into His palace and become a bride to so glorious a person. The bridegroom and the bride, the palace (which is all the world) with all that is therein, being David's joy and his true possession. Nay, every child of this bride is, if a male, a prince over all the earth; if a female, bride to the King of Heaven. And every soul that is a spouse of Jesus Christ esteemeth all the saints her own children and her own bowels.

78

There is a river the streams whereof shall make glad the city of God: the holy place of the tabernacle of the most High. He praiseth the means of grace, which in the midst of this world are great consolations and in all distresses refresh our souls. Come behold the works of the Lord, what desolations He hath made in the earth. He exhorteth us to contemplate God's works, which are so perfect, that when His secret and just judgements are seen, the very destruction of nations, and laying waste of cities, shall be sweet and delightful.

79

O clap your hands, all ye people, shout unto God with the voice of triumph. For the Lord most high is terrible, He is a great King over all the earth. He shall choose our inheritance for us, the excellency of Jacob whom He loved. Beautiful for situation, the joy of the whole earth is Mount Sion, on the sides of the north the city of the great King. God is known in her palaces for a refuge. Walk about Sion and go round about her, tell the towers thereof; mark ye well her bulwarks, consider her palaces, that ye may tell it to the generation following. For this God is our God forever and ever. He will be our guide even unto death.

80

As in the former Psalms, he proposeth true and celestial joys, so in this following he discovereth the vanity of false imaginations. They that trust in their wealth, and boast themselves in the multitude of their riches, none of them can by any means redeem his brother, or give unto God a ransom for him. For the redemption of their soul is precious and it ceaseth forever. For he seeth that wise men die; likewise the fool and the brutish person perish, and leave their wealth to others. Their inward thought is that their houses shall continue forever, and their dwelling places to all generations; they call their lands after their own names. This their way is their folly, yet their posterity approve their sayings. Like sheep they are laid in the grave, death shall feed sweetly on them, and the upright shall have dominion over them in the morning; and their beauty shall consume in the grave from their dwelling. Man that is in honour and understandeth not, is like the beast that perisheth.

81

Hear, O my people, and I will speak: O Israel, and I will testify against thee. I am God, even thy God. I will not reprove thee for thy sacrifices or thy burnt offerings to have been continually before me. I will take no bullock out of thy house, nor he-goats out of thy folds. For every beast of the forest is mine and the cattle upon a thousand hills. I know all the fowls of the mountains, and the wild beasts of the field are mine. If I were hungry, I would not tell thee: for the world is mine, and the fullness thereof. Will I eat the flesh of bulls or drink the blood of goats? Offer unto God thanksgiving and pay thy vows to the most High. And call upon me in the day of trouble; I will deliver thee, and thou shalt glorify me. When I was a little child, I thought that everyone that lifted up his eyes to behold the sun, did me in looking on it wonderful service. And certainly being moved thereby to praise my Creator, it was in itself a service wonderfully delightful. For since God so much esteemeth praises that He preferreth them above thousands of rams and tens of thousands of rivers of oil: if I love Him with that inflamed ardour and zeal I ought, His praises must needs be delightful to me above all services and riches whatsoever. That which hinders us from seeing the glory and discerning the sweetness of praises, hinders us also from knowing the manner how we are concerned in them, but God knoweth infinite reasons for which He preferreth them. If I should tell you what they are, you would be apt to despise them. Divine and heavenly mysteries being thirsted after till they are known, but by corrupted nature undervalued. Howbeit since grace correcteth the perverseness of nature, and tasteth in a better manner, it shall not be long, till somewhere we disclose them.

82

Are not praises the very end for which the world was created? Do they not consist as it were of knowledge, complacency, and thanksgiving? Are they not better than all the fowls and beasts and fishes in the world? What are the cattle upon a thousand hills but carcasses, without creatures that can rejoice in God, and enjoy them? It is evident that praises are infinitely more excellent than all the creatures because they proceed from men and angels, for as streams do they derive an excellency from their fountains, and are the last tribute that can possibly be paid to the Creator. Praises are the breathings of interior love, the marks and symptoms of an happy life, overflowing gratitude, returning benefits, an oblation of the soul, and the heart ascending upon the wings of divine affection to the throne of God. God is a spirit and cannot feed on carcasses; but He can be delighted with thanksgivings, and is infinitely pleased with the emanations of our joy, because His works are esteemed and Himself is admired. What can be more acceptable to love than that it should be prized and magnified? Because therefore God is love and His measure infinite, He infinitely desires to be admired and beloved: and so our praises enter into the very secret of His eternal bosom, and mingle with Him who dwelleth in that light which is inaccessible. What strengths are there even in flattery to please a great affection? Are not your bowels moved, and your affections melted with delight and pleasure, when your soul is precious in the eye of those you love? When your affection is pleased, your love prized, and they satisfied? To prize love is the highest service in the whole world that can be done unto it. But there are a thousand causes moving God to esteem our praises, more than we can well apprehend. However let these inflame you, and move you to praise Him night and day forever.

83

Of our Saviour it is said, sacrifice and offering Thou wouldst not but a body hast Thou prepared me, all sacrifices being but types and figures of Himself, and Himself infinitely more excellent than they all. Of a broken heart also it is said, Thou desirest not sacrifice; else I would give it. Thou delightest not in burnt offering. The sacrifices of God are a broken spirit: a broken and a contrite heart, O God, Thou wilt not despise. One deep and serious groan is more acceptable to God than the creation of a world. In spiritual things we find the greatest excellency. As praises because they are the pledges of our mutual affection, so groans because they are the pledges of a due contrition are the greatest sacrifices. Both proceed from love. And in both we manifest and exercise our friendship. In contrition we show our penitence for having offended, and by that are fitted to rehearse His praises. All the desire wherewith He longs after a returning sinner, makes Him to esteem a broken heart. What can more melt and dissolve a lover than the tears of an offending and returning friend? Here also is the saying verified. The falling out of lovers is the beginning of love: the renewing, the repairing, and the strengthening of it.

84

An enlarged soul that seeth all the world praising God, or penitent by bewailing their offences and converting to Him, hath his eye fixed upon the joy of angels. It needeth nothing but the sense of God, to inherit all things. We must borrow and derive it from Him by seeing His and aspiring after it. Do but clothe yourself with divine resentments and the world shall be to you the valley of vision, and all the nations and kingdoms of the world shall appear in splendour and celestial glory.

85

The righteous shall rejoice when he seeth the vengeance, he shall wash his feet in the blood of the wicked. But I will sing of Thy power, yea I will sing aloud of Thy mercy in the morning, for Thou hast been my defence in the day of my trouble. The deliverances of your former life are objects of your felicity, and so is the vengeance of the wicked, with both which in all times and places you are ever to be present in your memory and understanding. For lack of considering its objects the soul is desolate.

86

My soul thirsteth for Thee, my flesh longeth for Thee in a dry and thirsty land where no water is. To see Thy power and Thy glory so as I have seen Thee in the sanctuary. Because Thy loving kindness is better than life my lips shall praise Thee. Thus will I bless Thee while I live, I will lift up my hands in Thy name. My soul shall be satisfied as with marrow and fatness, and my mouth shall praise Thee with joyful lips. O Thou that hearest prayer, unto Thee shall all flesh come. Blessed is the man whom Thou choosest and causest to approach unto Thee, that he may dwell in Thy courts. We shall be satisfied with the goodness of Thy house, even of Thy holy temple. See how in the 65th Psalm he introduceth the meditation of God's visible works sweetly into the tabernacle and maketh them to be the fatness of His house, even of His holy temple. God is seen when His love is manifested. God is enjoyed when His love is prized. When we see the glory of His wisdom and goodness, and His power exerted, then we see His glory. And these we cannot see till we see their works. When therefore we see His works, in them as in a mirror we see His glory.

87

Make a joyful noise unto God, all ye lands, sing forth the honour of His name, make His praise glorious. Say unto God, How terrible art Thou in thy works! Through the greatness of Thy power shall Thine enemies submit themselves unto Thee. All the earth shall worship Thee and sing unto Thee, they shall sing to Thy name. Come and see the works of God; He is terrible in His doing towards the children of men. The prospect of all nations praising Him is far sweeter than the prospect of the fields or silent heavens serving them, tho you see the skies adorned with stars and the fields covered with corn and flocks of sheep and cattle. When the eye of your understanding shineth upon them, they are yours in Him, and all your joys.

88

God is my King of old working salvation in the midst of the earth. He divided the sea by His strength. He brake the heads of Leviathan in pieces. His heart is always abroad in the midst of the earth: seeing and rejoicing in His wonders there. His soul is busied in the ancient works of God for his people Israel. The day is Thine, the night also is Thine, Thou hast prepared the light and the sun. Thou hast set all the borders of the earth, Thou hast made summer and winter. He proposeth more objects of our felicity in which we ought to meet the goodness of God, that we might rejoice before Him. The day and night, the light and the sun are God's treasures, and ours also.

89

In the 78th Psalm, he commandeth all ages to record the ancient ways of God, and recommendeth them to our meditation, showing the ordinance of God, that fathers should teach their children, and they another generation. Which certainly since they are not to be seen in the visible world, but only in the memory and minds of men. The memory and mind are a strange region of celestial light, and a wonderful place as well as a large and sublime one in which they may be seen. What is contained in the souls of men being as visible to us as the very heavens.

90

In the 84th Psalm he longeth earnestly after the tabernacles of God, and preferreth a day in His courts above a thousand. Because there, as Deborah speaketh in her song, was the place of drawing waters, that is of repentance; and of rehearsing the righteous acts of the Lord. Which it is more blessed to do than to inherit the palaces of wicked men.

91

Among the gods there is none like unto Thee. Neither are there any works like unto Thy works. All nations whom Thou hast made shall come and worship before Thee, O Lord, and shall glorify Thy name. For Thou art great, and doest wondrous things. Thou art God alone. This is a glorious meditation, wherein the Psalmist gives himself liberty to examine the excellency of God's works, and finding them infinitely great and above all that can be besides, rejoiceth, and admireth the goodness of God, and resteth satisfied with complacency in them. That they were all his he knew well, being the gifts of God made unto him, and that he was to have communion with God in the enjoyment of them. But their excellency was a thing unsearchable, and their incomparableness above all imagination, which he found by much study to his infinite delectation.

92

In his other Psalms he proceedeth to speak of the works of God over and over again: sometimes stirring up all creatures to praise God for the very delight he took in their admirable perfection, sometimes showing God's goodness and mercy by them, and sometimes rejoicing himself and triumphing in them. By all this teaching us what we ought to do, that we might become divine and heavenly. In the 103 Psalm he openeth the nature of God's present mercies, both towards himself in particular and towards all in general, turning emergencies in this world into celestial joys. In the 104 Psalm he insisteth wholly upon the beauty of God's works in the creation, making all things in Heaven and earth and in the Heaven of heavens, in the wilderness and the sea his private and personal delights. In the 105 and 106 Psalms he celebrateth the ways of God in former ages with as much vehemency, zeal, and pleasure as if they were new things, and as if he were present with them, seeing their beauty and tasting their delight that very moment. In the 107 Psalm he contemplates the ways of God in the dispensations of His providence, over travellers, sick men, seamen &c. showing that the way to be much in Heaven is to be much employed here upon earth in the meditation of divine and celestial things, for such are these tho they seem terrestrial. All which he concludeth thus: Whoso considereth these things, even he shall understand the loving kindness of the Lord. In the 119th Psalm, like an enamoured person and a man ravished in spirit with joy and pleasure, he treateth upon divine laws, and over and over again maketh mention of their beauty and perfection. By all which we may see what inward life we ought to lead with God in the temple. And that to be much in the meditation of God's works and ways and laws, to see their excellency, to taste their sweetness, to behold their glory, to admire and rejoice and overflow with praises, is to live in Heaven. But unless we have a communion with David in a rational knowledge of their nature and excellency, we can never understand the grounds of his complacency or the depth of his resentments.

93

In our outward life towards men the Psalmist also is an admirable precedent. In weeping for those that forget God's law, in publishing his praises in the congregation of the righteous, in speaking of his testimonies without cowardice or shame even before princes, in delighting in the saints, in keeping promises tho made to his hurt, in tendering the life of his enemies and clothing himself with sackcloth when they were sick, in showing mercy to the poor, in enduring the songs and mockings of the drunkards, in taking care to glorify the Author of all bounty with a splendid temple and musical instruments in this world, in putting his trust and confidence in God among all his enemies, evermore promoting His honour and glory, instructing others in the excellency of His ways, and endeavouring to establish His worship in Israel. Thus ought we to the best of our power to express our gratitude and friendship to so great a Benefactor in all the effects of love and fidelity. Doing His pleasure with all our might, and promoting His honour with all our power.

94

There are Psalms more clear wherein he expresseth the joy he taketh in God's works and the glory of them, wherein he teacheth us at divers times and in divers manners to ponder on them. Among which the 145 Psalm (and so onward to the last) are very eminent. In which he openeth the nature of God's kingdom, and so vigorously and vehemently exciteth all creatures to praise Him, and all men to do it with all kind of musical instruments by all expressions, in all nations for all things as if 10000 vents were not sufficient to ease his fullness, as if all the world were but one celestial temple in which he was delighted, as if all nations were present before him and he saw God face to face in this earthly tabernacle, as if his soul like an infinite ocean were full of joys, and all these but springs and channels overflowing. So purely, so joyfully, so powerfully he walked with God, all creatures, as they brought a confluence of joys unto him, being pipes to ease him.

95

His soul recovered its pristine liberty and saw through the mud walls of flesh and blood. Being alive, he was in the spirit all his days; while his body therefore was enclosed in this world his soul was in the temple of eternity and clearly beholds the infinite life and omnipresence of God, having conversation with invisible, spiritual, and immaterial things which were its companions: itself being invisible, spiritual, and immaterial. Kingdoms and ages did surround him, as clearly as the hills and mountains; and therefore the kingdom of God was ever round about him. Everything was one way or other his sovereign delight and transcendent pleasure, as in Heaven everything will be everyone's peculiar treasure.

96

He saw these things only in the light of faith, and yet rejoiced as if he had seen them in the light of Heaven, which argued the strength and glory of his faith. And whereas he so rejoiced in all the nations of the earth for praising God, he saw them doing it in the light of prophecy, not of history. Much more therefore should we rejoice, who see these prophecies fulfilled, since the fulfilling of them is so blessed, divine, and glorious that the very prevision of their accomplishment transported and ravished this glorious person. But we wither, and for lack of sense shrivel up into nothing, who should be filled with the delights of ages.

97

By this we understand what it is to be the sons of God and what it is to live in communion with Him, what it is to be advanced to His throne, and to reign in His kingdom with all those other glorious and marvellous expressions that are applied to men in the holy Scriptures. To be the sons of God is not only to enjoy the privileges and the freedom of His house, and to bear the relation of children to so great a Father, but it is to be like Him and to share with Him in all His glory and in all His treasures. To be like Him in spirit and understanding; to be exalted above all creatures as the end of them; to be present as He is by sight and love, without limit and so without bound, with all His works; to be holy towards all and wise towards all as He is. Prizing all His goodness in all with infinite ardour, that as glorious and eternal kings being pleased in all we might reign over all forevermore.

98

This greatness both of God towards us, and of ourselves towards Him, we ought always as much as possible to retain in our understanding. And when we cannot effectually keep it alive in our senses, to cherish the memory of it in the centre of our hearts, and do all things in the power of it; for the angels, when they come to us, so fulfil their outward ministry that within they nevertheless maintain the beatific vision: ministering before the throne of God, and among the sons of men at the same time. The reason whereof S. Gregory saith is this: tho the spirit of an angel be limited and circumscribed in itself, yet the supreme spirit, which is God, is uncircumscribed. He is everywhere and wholly everywhere: which makes their knowledge to be dilated everywhere, for being wholly everywhere they are immediately present with His omnipresence in every place and wholly. It filleth them forever.

99

This sense that God is so great in goodness, and we so great in glory as to be His sons, and so rich as to live in communion with Him, and so individually united to Him that He is in us and we in Him, will make us do all our duties not only with incomparable joy, but courage also. It will fill us with zeal and fidelity and make us to overflow with praises, for which one cause alone the knowledge of it ought infinitely to be esteemed; for to be ignorant of this is to sit in darkness, and to be a child of darkness: it maketh us to be without God in the world, exceeding weak, timorous and feeble, comfortless and barren, dead and unfruitful, lukewarm, indifferent, dumb, unfaithful. To which I may add that it makes us uncertain, for so glorious is the face of God and true religion, that it is impossible to see it but in transcendent splendour. Nor can we know that God is, till we see Him infinite in goodness. Nothing therefore will make us certain of His being but His glory.

100

To enjoy communion with God is to abide with Him in the fruition of His divine and eternal glory, in all His attributes, in all His thoughts, in all His creatures; in His eternity, infinity, almighty power, sovereignty &c. In all those works which from all eternity He wrought in Himself: as the generation of His Son, the proceeding of the Holy Ghost, the eternal union and communion of the blessed Trinity, the councils of His bosom, the attainment of the end of all His endeavours wherein we shall see ourselves exalted and beloved from all eternity. We are to enjoy communion with Him in the creation of the world, in the government of angels, in the redemption of mankind, in the dispensations of His providence, in the Incarnation of His Son, in His passion, resurrection, and ascension, in His shedding abroad the Holy Ghost, in His government of the church, in His judgement of the world, in the punishment of His enemies, in the rewarding of His friends, in eternal glory. All these therefore particularly ought to be near us, and to be esteemed by us as our riches: being those delectable things that adorn the house of God, which is eternity; and those living fountains from whence we suck forth the streams of joy, that everlastingly overflow to refresh our souls.

From The Fourth Century

16

Of what vast importance right principles are, we may see by this: *Things prized are enjoyed.* All things are ours; all things serve us and minister to us, could we find the way; nay they are ours, and serve us so perfectly that they are best enjoyed in their proper places: even from the sun to a sand, from a cherubim to a worm. I will not except gold and silver and crowns and precious stones, nor any delights or secret treasures in closets and palaces. For if otherwise God would not be perfect in bounty. But suppose the world were all yours. If this principle be rooted in you, to prize nothing that is yours, it blots out all at one dash and bereaves you of a whole world in a moment.

17

Tho God be yours, and all the joys and inhabitants in Heaven, if you be resolved to prize nothing great and excellent, nothing sublime and eternal, you lay waste your possessions and make vain your enjoyment of all permanent and glorious things. So that you must be sure to inure yourself frequently to these principles and to impress them deeply: *I will prize all I have, and nothing shall with me be less esteemed because it is excellent. A daily joy shall be more my joy because it is continual. A common joy is more my delight because it is common. For all mankind are my friends. And everything is enriched in serving them.* A little grit in the eye destroyeth the sight of the very heavens, and a little malice or envy a world of joys. One wry principle in the mind is of infinite consequence. *I will ever prize what I have, and so much the more because I have it.* To prize a thing when it is gone breedeth torment and repining; to prize it while we have it joy and thanksgiving.

18

All these relate to enjoyment, but those principles that relate to communication are more excellent. These are principles of retirement and solitude; but the principles that aid us in conversation are far better and help us, tho not so immediately, to enjoyment in a far more blessed and diviner manner. For it is more blessed to give than to receive, and we are more happy in communication than enjoyment; but only that communication is enjoyment, as indeed what we give we best receive, for the joy of communicating and the joy of receiving maketh perfect happiness. And therefore are the sons of men our greatest treasures, because they can give and receive: treasures perhaps infinite as well as affections. But this I am sure: they are our treasures. And therefore is conversation so delightful because they are the greatest.

19

The world is best enjoyed and most immediately while we converse wisely and blessedly with men. I am sure it were desirable that they could give and receive infinite treasures. And perhaps they can, for whomsoever I love as myself, to him I give myself and all my happiness, which I think is infinite; and I receive him and all his happiness. Yea in him I receive God, for God delighteth me for being his blessedness. So that a man obligeth me infinitely that maketh himself happy, and by making himself happy giveth me himself and all his happiness. Besides this he loveth me infinitely, as God doth; and he dare do no less for God's sake. Nay he loveth God for loving me, and delighteth in Him for being good unto me. So that I am magnified in his affections, represented in his understanding tenderly beloved, caressed, and honoured; and this maketh society delightful. But here upon earth it is subject to changes. And therefore this principle is always to be firm, as the foundation of bliss: *God only is my sovereign happiness and friend in the world.* Conversation is full of dangers, and friendships are mortal among the sons of men. But communion with God is infinitely secure, and He my happiness.

20

He from whom I received these things always thought that to be happy in the midst of a generation of vipers was become his duty, for men and he are fallen into sin. Were all men wise and innocent, it were easy to be happy; for no man would injure and molest another. But he that would be happy now must be happy among ingrateful and injurious persons. That knowledge which would make a man happy among just and holy persons, is unuseful now; and those principles only profitable that will make a man happy not only in peace, but blood. On every side we are environed with enemies, surrounded with reproaches, encompassed with wrongs, besieged with offences, receiving evil for good, being disturbed by fools, and invaded with malice. This is the true estate of this world. Which lying in wickedness, as our saviour witnesseth, yieldeth no better fruits than the bitter clusters of folly and perverseness: the grapes of Sodom and the seeds of Gomorrah. Blind wretches that wound themselves, offend me. I need therefore the oil of pity and the balm of love to remedy and heal them. Did they see the beauty of holiness or the face of happiness, they would not do so. To think the world therefore a general bedlam, or place of madmen, and oneself a physician, is the most necessary point of present wisdom: an important imagination, and the way to happiness.

21

He thought within himself that this world was far better than Paradise, had men eyes to see its glory and their advantages; for the very miseries and sins and offences that are in it, are the materials of his joy and triumph and glory. So that he is to learn a diviner art that will now be happy: and that is like a royal chemist to reign among poisons, to turn scorpions into fishes, weeds into flowers, bruises into ornaments, poisons into cordials. And he that cannot this art, of extracting good out of evil, is to be accounted nothing. Heretofore, to enjoy beauties and be grateful for benefits was all the art that was required to felicity, but now a man must like a God bring light out of darkness, and order out of confusion. Which we are taught to do by His wisdom, that ruleth in the midst of storms and tempests.

22

He generally held, that whosoever would enjoy the happiness of Paradise must put on the charity of Paradise. And that nothing was his felicity but his duty. He called his house the house of Paradise: not only because it was the place wherein he enjoyed the whole world, but because it was everyone's house in the whole world. For observing the methods, and studying the nature of charity in Paradise, he found that all men would be brothers and sisters throughout the whole world and evermore love one another as their own selves, tho they had never seen each other before. From whence it would proceed that every man approaching him would be as welcome as an angel, and the coming of a stranger as delightful as the sun, all things in his house being as much the foreigner's as they were his own. Especially if he could infuse any knowledge or grace into him.

25

But order and charity, in the midst of these, is like a bright star in an obscure night, like a summer's day in the depth of winter, like a sun shining among the clouds, like a giant among his enemies, that receiveth strength from their numbers, like a king sitting in the midst of an army. By how much the more scarce it is, by so much the more glorious; by how much the more assaulted, by so much the more invincible; by how much the more lonely, by so much the more pitied of God and Heaven. And surely He, who being perfect love, designed the felicity of the world with so much care, in the beginning, will now be more tender of a soul that is like Him, in its de-ordination.

26

He thought that men were more to be beloved now than before. And which is a strange paradox, the worse they are the more they were to be beloved. The worse they are the more they were to be pitied and tendered and desired, because they had more need and were more miserable tho the better they are, they are more to be delighted in. But his true meaning in that saying was this: comparing them with what they were before they were fallen, they are more to be beloved. They are now worse yet more to be beloved. For Jesus Christ hath been crucified for them. God loved them more, and He gave His Son to die for them, and for me also: which are strong obligations, leading us to greater charity. So that men's unworthiness and our virtue are alike increased.

27

He conceived it his duty and much delighted in the obligation: that he was to treat every man in the whole world as the representative of mankind, and that he was to meet in him, and to pay unto him all the love of God, angels, and men.

28

He thought that he was to treat every man in the person of Christ. That is, both as if himself were Christ in the greatness of his love, and also as if the man were Christ he was to use him, having respect to all others. For the love of Christ is to dwell within him, and every man is the object of it. God and he are to become one spirit: that is, one in will and one in desire. Christ must live within him. He must be filled with the Holy Ghost, which is the God of love; he must be of the same mind with Christ Jesus, and led by His spirit. For on the other side he was well acquainted with this mystery: that every man, being the object of our Saviour's love, was to be treated as our Saviour. Who hath said, 'Inasmuch as ye have done it to the least of these my brethren, ye have done it unto me.' And thus he is to live upon earth among sinners.

29

He had another saying, 'He lives most like an angel that lives upon least himself, and doth most good to others.' For the angels neither eat nor drink, and yet do good to the whole world. Now a man is an incarnate angel. And he that lives in the midst of riches as a poor man himself, enjoying God and Paradise, or Christendom which is better, conversing with the poor, and seeing the value of their souls through their bodies, and prizing all things clearly with a due esteem, is arrived here to the estate of immortality. He cares little for the delicacies either of food or raiment himself, and delighteth in others.

God, angels, and men are his treasures. He seeth through all the mists and veils of invention, and possesseth here beneath the true riches. And he that doth this always, is a rare phoenix; but he confessed that he had often cause to bewail his infirmities.

30

I speak not his practices but his principles. I should too much praise your friend did I speak his practices, but it is no shame for any man to declare his principles, tho they are the most glorious in the world. Rather they are to be shamed that have no glorious principles, or that are ashamed of them. This he desired me to tell you because of modesty. But with all, that indeed his practices are so short of these glorious principles, that to relate them would be to his shame; and that therefore you would never look upon him but as clothed in the righteousness of Jesus Christ. Nevertheless I have heard him often say, that he never allowed himself in swerving from any of these. And that he repented deeply of every miscarriage, and moreover firmly resolved as much as was possible never to err or wander from them again.

31

I heard him often say that holiness and happiness were the same, and he quoted a mighty place of scripture: 'All her ways are pleasantness and her paths are peace.' But he delighted in giving the reason of scripture, and therefore said, that holiness and wisdom in effect were one for no man could be wise that knew excellent things, without doing them. Now to do them is holiness, and to do them wisdom. No man therefore can be further miserable than he swerveth from the ways of holiness and wisdom.

32

If he might have had but one request of God Almighty it should have been above all other, that he might be a blessing to mankind. That was his daily prayer above all his petitions. He wisely knew that it included all petitions, for he that is a blessing to mankind must be blessed, that he may be so, and must inherit all their affections and in that their treasures. He could not help it. But he so desired to love them, and to be a joy unto them, that he protested often, that he could never enjoy himself, but as he was enjoyed of others, and that above all delights in all worlds, he desired to be a joy and blessing to others. Tho for this he was not to be commended, for he did but right to God and nature, who had implanted in all that inclination.

33

The desire of riches was removed from himself pretty early. He often protested, if he had a palace of gold and a Paradise of delights, besides that he enjoyed, he could not understand a farthing worth of benefit that he should receive thereby, unless in giving it away. But for others he sometimes could desire riches till at last perceiving that root of covetousness in him, and that it would grow as long as it was shrouded under that mould, he rooted it quite up with this principle. *Sometimes it may so happen, that to contemn the world in the whole lump, was as acceptable to God, as first to get it with solicitude and care, and then to retail it out in particular charities.*

34

After this he could say with Luther, that covetousness could never fasten the least hold upon him. And concerning his friends even to the very desire of seeing them rich, he could say as Phocion the poor Athenian did of his children: 'Either they will be like me or not. If they are like me they will not need riches; if they are not they will be but needless and hurtful superfluities.'

35

He desired no other riches for his friends, but those which cannot be abused: to wit the true treasures, God and Heaven and earth and angels and men, &c., with the riches of wisdom and grace to enjoy them. And it was his principle that all the treasures in the whole world would not make a miser happy. A miser is not only a covetous man but a fool. Any needy man that wanteth the world, is miserable. He wanteth God and all things.

36

He thought also that no poverty could befall him that enjoyed Paradise, for when all the things are gone which men can give, a man is still as rich as Adam was in Eden: who was naked there. A naked man is the richest creature in all worlds and can never be happy till he sees the riches of his nakedness. He is very poor in knowledge that thinks Adam poor in Eden. See here how one principle helps another. All our disadvantages contracted by the Fall are made up and recompensed by the love of God.

37

'Tis not change of place, but glorious principles well practised that establish Heaven in the life and soul. An angel will be happy anywhere; and a devil miserable, because the principles of the one are always good, of the other bad. From the centre to the utmost bounds of the everlasting hills, all is Heaven before God, and full of treasure. And he that walks like God in the midst of them, blessed.

38

Love God, angels, and men, triumph in God's works, delight in God's laws, take pleasure in God's ways in all ages, correct sins, bring good out of evil, subdue your lusts, order your senses, conquer the customs and opinions of men, and render good for evil: you are in Heaven everywhere. Above the stars earthly things will be celestial joys, and here beneath will things delight you that are above the heavens. All things being infinitely beautiful in their places: and wholly yours in all their places. Your riches will be as infinite in value and excellency as they are in beauty and glory, and that is, as they are in extent.

39

Thus he was possessor of the whole world, and held it his treasure, not only as the gift of God, but as the theatre of virtues. Esteeming it principally his, because it upheld and ministered to many objects of his love and goodness. Towards whom, before whom, among whom he might do the work of fidelity and wisdom, exercise his courage and prudence, show his temperance, and bring forth the fruits of faith and repentance. For all those are the objects of our joy that are the objects of our care; they are our true treasures about whom we are wisely employed.

40

He had one maxim of notable concernment, and that was, that God having reserved all other things in His own disposal, had left his heart to him. Those things that were in God's care he would commit to God, those things that were committed to his, he would take care about. He said therefore that he had but one thing to do, and that was to order and keep his heart, which alone being well guided, would order all other things blessedly and successfully. The things about him were innumerable and out of his power, but they were in God's power. And if he pleased God within in that which was committed to him, God would be sure to please him in things without committed unto God. For He was faithful that had promised; in all that belonged unto Him God was perfect, all the danger being, lest we should be imperfect in ours, and unfaithful in those things that pertain unto us.

41

Having these principles, nothing was more easy than to enjoy the world, which being enjoyed, he had nothing more to do than to spend his life in praises and thanksgivings. All his care being to be sensible of God's mercies, and to behave himself as the friend of God in the universe. If anything were amiss, he still would have recourse to his own heart, and found nothing but that out of frame, by restoring which all things were rectified and made delightful. As much as that had swerved from the rule of justice, equity, and right, so far was he miserable, and no more so that by experience he found the words of the wise man true, and worthy of all acceptation: 'In all thy keeping keep thy heart, for out of it are the issues of life and death.'

42

One thing he saw, which is not commonly discerned: and that is, that God made man a free agent for his own advantage; and left him in the hand of his own counsel, that he might be the more glorious. It is hard to conceive how much this tended to his satisfaction, for all the things in Heaven and earth being so beautiful, and made as it were on purpose for his own enjoyment, he infinitely admired God's wisdom in that it salved his and all men's exigencies, in which it fully answered his desires; for his desire was that all men should be happy as well as he. And he admired His goodness, which had enjoined no other duty than what pertained to the more convenient fruition of the world which He had given: and at the marvellous excellency of His love, in committing that duty to the sons of men, to be performed freely. For thereby He adventured such a power into the hands of His creatures, which angels and cherubims wonder at, and which when it is understood all eternity will admire the bounty of giving. For He thereby committed to their hands a power to do that which He infinitely hated. Which nothing certainly could move Him to entrust them with, but some infinite benefit which might be attained thereby. What that was if you desire to know, it was the excellency, dignity, and exaltation of His creature.

43

O adorable and eternal God! Hast Thou made me a free agent! And enabled me if I please to offend Thee infinitely! What other end couldst Thou intend by this, but that I might please Thee infinitely! That having the power of pleasing or displeasing I might be the friend of God! Of all exaltations in all worlds this is the greatest. To make a world for me was much, to command angels and men to love me was much, to prepare eternal joys for me was more. But to give me a power to displease Thee, or to set a sin before Thy face, which Thou infinitely hatest, to profane eternity, or to defile Thy works, is more stupendous than all these. What other couldst Thou intend by it, but that I might infinitely please Thee? And having the power of pleasing or displeasing, might please Thee and myself infinitely, in being pleasing! Hereby Thou hast prepared a new fountain and torrent of joys, greater than all that went before, seated us in the throne of God, made us Thy companions, endued us with a power most dreadful to ourselves, that we might live in sublime and incomprehensible blessedness for evermore. For the satisfaction of our goodness is the most sovereign delight of which we are capable. And that by our own actions we should be well pleasing to Thee, is the greatest felicity nature can contain. O Thou who art infinitely delightful to the sons of men, make me, and the sons of men, infinitely delightful unto Thee. Replenish our actions with amiableness and beauty, that they may be answerable to Thine, and like unto Thine in sweetness and value. That as Thou in all Thy works art pleasing to us, we in all our works may be so to Thee; our own actions as they are pleasing to Thee being an offspring of pleasures sweeter than all.

44

This he thought a principle at the bottom of nature, that whatsoever satisfied the goodness of nature was the greatest treasure. Certainly men therefore err because they know not this principle, for all inclinations and desires in the soul flow from, and tend to the satisfaction of goodness. 'Tis strange that an excess of goodness should be the fountain of all evil. An ambition to please, a desire to gratify, a great desire to delight others being the greatest snare in the world. Hence is it that all hypocrisies and honours arise; I mean esteem of honours. Hence all imitations of human customs, hence all compliances and submissions to the vanities and errors of this world. For men being mistaken in the nature of felicity, and we by a strong inclination prone to please them, follow a multitude to do evil. We naturally desire to approve ourselves to them, and above all other things covet to be excellent, to be greatly beloved, to be esteemed, and magnified, and therefore endeavour what they endeavour, prize what they prize, magnify what they desire, desire what they magnify: ever doing that which will render us accepted to them; and coveting that which they admire and praise, that so we might be delightful. And the more there are that delight in us, the more great and happy we account ourselves.

45

This principle of nature, when you remove the rust it hath contracted by corruption, is pure gold; and the most orient jewel that shines in man. Few consider it either in itself, or in the design of the implanter. No man doubts but it is blessed to receive. To be made a glorious creature, and to have worlds given to one is excellent. But to be a glorious creature and to give, is a blessedness unknown. It is a kind of paradox in our Saviour, and not (as we read of) revealed upon earth, but to S. Paul from Heaven: *It is more blessed to give than to receive.* It is a blessedness too high to be understood. To give is the happiness of God; to receive, of man. But O the mystery of His loving kindness, even that also hath He imparted to us. Will you that I ascend higher? In giving us Himself, in giving us the world, in giving us our souls and bodies He hath done much; but all this had been nothing, unless He had given us a power to have given Him ourselves, in which is contained the greatest pleasure and honour that is. We love ourselves earnestly, and therefore rejoice to have palaces and kingdoms. But when we have these, yea Heaven and earth, unless we can be delightful and joyous to others, they will be of no value. One soul to whom we may be pleasing is of greater worth than all dead things. Some unsearchable good lieth in this, without which the other is but a vile and desolate estate. So that to have all worlds, with a certain sense that they are infinitely beautiful and rich and glorious, is miserable vanity, and leaves us forlorn, if all things are dead, or if ourselves are not divine and illustrious creatures.

46

O the superlative bounty of God! Where all power seemeth to cease, He proceedeth in goodness; and is wholly infinite, unsearchable, and endless. He seemeth to have made as many things depend upon man's liberty, as His own. When all that could be wrought by the use of His own liberty were attained, by man's liberty He attained more. This is incredible, but experience will make it plain. By His own liberty He could but create worlds and give Himself to creatures, make images and endow them with faculties, or seat them in glory. But to see them obedient, or to enjoy the pleasure of their amity and praises, to make them fountains of actions like His own (without which indeed they could not be glorious), or to enjoy the beauty of their free imitation, this could by no means be, without the liberty of His creatures intervening. Nor indeed could the world be glorious, or they blessed without this attainment. For can the world be glorious unless it be useful? And to what use could the world serve Him, if it served not those that in this were supremely glorious, that they could obey and admire and love and praise and imitate their Creator? Would it not be wholly useless without such creatures? In creating liberty therefore and giving it to His creatures He glorified all things: Himself, His works, and the subjects of His kingdom.

47

You may feel in yourself how conducive this is to your highest happiness. For that you should be exalted to the fruition of worlds, and in the midst of innumerable most glorious creatures be vile and ingrateful, injurious and dishonourable, hateful and evil, is the greatest misery and dissatisfaction imaginable. But to be the joy and delight of innumerable thousands, to be admired as the similitude of God, to be amiable and honourable, to be an illustrious and beautiful creature, to be a blessing: O the good we perceive in this! O the suavity! O the contentation! O the infinite and unspeakable pleasure! Then indeed we reign and triumph when we are delighted in. Then are we blessed when we are a blessing. When all the world is at peace with us and takes pleasure in us, when our actions are delightful, and our persons lovely, when our spirits amiable, and our affections inestimable, then are we exalted to the throne of glory. For things when they are useful are most glorious, and it is impossible for you or me to be useful, but as we are delightful to God and His attendants. And that the head of the world or the end for which all worlds were made should be useless, as it is improportioned to the glory of the means and methods of his exaltation, so is it the reproach of his nature, and the utter undoing of all his glory. It is improportionable to the beauty of His ways who made the world, and to the expectation of His creatures.

48

By this you may see, that the works or actions flowing from your own liberty are of greater concernment to you than all that could possibly happen besides. And that it is more to your happiness what you are, than what you enjoy. Should God give Himself and all worlds to you, and you refuse them, it would be to no purpose. Should He love you and magnify you, should He give his Son to die for you and command all angels and men to love you, should He exalt you in His throne and give you dominion over all His works, and you neglect them, it would be to no purpose. Should He make you in His image, and employ all His wisdom and power to fill eternity with treasures, and you despise them, it would be in vain. In all these things you have to do; and therefore your actions are great and magnificent, being of infinite importance in all eyes, while all creatures stand in expectation what will be the result of your liberty. Your exterior works are little in comparison of these. And God infinitely desires you should demean yourself wisely in these affairs: that is, rightly. Esteeming and receiving what He gives, with veneration and joy and infinite thanksgiving. Many other works there are, but this is the great work of all works to be performed. Consider whether more depends upon God's love to you, or your love to Him. From His love all the things in Heaven and earth flow unto you; but if you love neither Him nor them, you bereave yourself of all, and make them infinitely evil and hurtful to you and yourself abominable. So that upon your love naturally depends your own excellency and the enjoyment of His. It is by your love that you enjoy all His delights, and are delightful to Him.

49

It is very observable by what small principles infusing them in the beginning God attaineth infinite ends. By infusing the principle of self-love He hath made a creature capable of enjoying all worlds: to whom, did he not love himself, nothing could be given. By infusing grateful principles and inclinations to thanksgiving, He hath made that creature capable of more than all worlds, yea of more than enjoying the Deity in a simple way: tho we should suppose it to be infinite. For to enjoy God as the fountain of infinite treasures, and as the giver of all, is infinite pleasure; but He by His wisdom infusing grateful principles, hath made us upon the very account of self-love to love Him more than ourselves. And us, who without self-love could not be pleased at all, even as we love ourselves He hath so infinitely pleased, that we are able to rejoice in Him and to love Him more than ourselves. And by loving Him more than ourselves, in very gratitude and honour, to take more pleasure in His felicity than in our own, by which way we best enjoy Him. To see His wisdom, goodness, and power employed in creating all worlds for our enjoyment, and infinitely magnified in beautifying them for us, and governing them for us, satisfies our self-love; but withal it so obligeth us, that in love to Him, which it createth in us, it maketh us more to delight in those attributes as they are His than as they are our own. And the truth is, without this we could not fully delight in them, for the most excellent and glorious effect of all had been unachieved.

But now there is an infinite union between Him and us, He being infinitely delightful to us and we to Him. For He infinitely delighteth to see creatures act upon such illustrious and eternal principles, in a manner so divine, heroic, and most truly blessed; and we delight in seeing Him giving us the power.

50

That I am to receive all the things in Heaven and earth is a principle not to be slighted. That in receiving I am to behave myself in a divine and illustrious manner, is equally glorious. That God and all eternity are mine is surely considerable: that I am His, is more. How ought I to adorn myself, who am made for His enjoyment? If man's heart be a rock of stone, these things ought to be engraven in it with a pen of a diamond; and every letter to be filled up with gold that it might eternally shine in him and before him; wherever we are living, whatever we are doing, these things ought always to be felt within him. Above all trades, above all occupations this is most sublime, this is the greatest of all affairs. Whatever else we do, it is only in order to this end that we may live conveniently to enjoy the world, and God within it; which is the sovereign employment including and crowning all the celestial life of a glorious creature, without which all other estates are servile and impertinent.

51

Man being to live in the image of God, and thus of necessity to become productive of glorious actions, was made good, that he might rejoice in the fruits which himself did yield. That goodness, which by error and corruption becomes a snare, being in the clear and pure estate of innocency the fountain and the channel of all his joys.

52

Thus you see how God has perfectly pleased me; it ought also to be my care perfectly to please Him. He has given me freedom, and adventured the power of sinning into my hands; it ought to be a principle engraven in me, to use it nobly to be illustrious and faithful, to please Him in the use of it, to consult His honour, and having all the creatures in all worlds by His gift ministering unto me, to behave myself as a faithful friend to so great a majesty, so bountiful a Lord, so divine a benefactor. Nothing is so easy as to yield one's assent to glorious principles, nothing so clear in upright nature, nothing so obscure to find in perverted, nothing so difficult to practise at all. In the rubbish of depraved nature they are lost, tho when they are found by any one, and shown, like jewels they shine by their native splendour.

53

If you ask what is become of us since the Fall, because all these things now lately named seem to pertain to the estate of innocency; truly now we have superadded treasures: Jesus Christ. And are restored to the exercise of the same principles, upon higher obligations. I will not say with more advantage, tho perhaps obligations themselves are to us advantage. For what enabled Adam to love God? Was it not that God loved him? What constrained him to be averse from God? Was it not that God was averse from him? When he was fallen, he thought God would hate him and be his enemy eternally. And this was the miserable bondage that enslaved him. But when he was restored: O the infinite and eternal change! His very love to himself made him to prize His eternal love. I mean his Redeemer's. Do we not all love ourselves? Self-love maketh us to love those that love us, and to hate all those that hate us. So that obligations themselves are to us advantage. How we come to lose those advantages I will not stand here to relate. In a clear light it is certain no man can perish. For God is more delightful than He was in Eden. Then He was as delightful as was possible, but He had not that occasion, as by sin was offered, to superadd many more delights than before. Being more delightful and more amiable, He is more desirable, and may now be more easily yea strongly beloved. For the amiableness of the object enables us to love it.

54

It was your friend's delight to meditate the principles of upright nature, and to see how things stood in Paradise before they were muddied and blended and confounded; for now they are lost and buried in ruins. Nothing appearing but fragments, that are worthless shreds and parcels of them. To see the entire piece ravisheth the angels. It was his desire to recover them and to exhibit them again to the eyes of men. Above all things he desired to see those principles which a stranger in this world would covet to behold upon his first appearance. And that is what principles those were, by which the inhabitants of this world are to live blessedly and to enjoy the same. He found them very easy, and infinitely noble: very noble, and productive of unspeakable good, were they well pursued. We have named them, and they are such as these: a man should know the blessings he enjoyeth. A man should prize the blessings which he knoweth. A man should be thankful for the benefits which he prizeth. A man should rejoice in that for which he is thankful. These are easy things, and so are those also which are drowned in a deluge of errors and customs: that blessings the more they are, are the sweeter; the longer they continue, the more to be esteemed; the more they serve, if lovers and friends, the more delightful. Yet these are the hard lessons, in a perverse and retrograde world, to be practised and almost the only lessons necessary to its enjoyment.

55

He was a strict and severe applier of all things to himself. And would first have his self-love satisfied, and then his love of all others. It is true that self-love is dishonourable, but then it is when it is alone. And self-endedness is mercenary, but then it is when it endeth in oneself. It is more glorious to love others, and more desirable, but by natural means to be attained. That pool must first be filled, that shall be made to overflow. He was ten years studying before he could satisfy his self-love. And now finds nothing more easy than to love others better than oneself and that to love mankind so is the comprehensive method to all felicity. For it makes a man delightful to God and men, to himself and spectators, and God and men delightful to him, and all creatures infinitely in them. But as not to love oneself at all is brutish – or rather absurd and stonish (for beasts do love themselves) – so hath God by rational methods enabled us to love others better than ourselves, and thereby made us the most glorious creatures. Had we not loved ourselves at all, we could never have been obliged to love anything. So that self-love is the basis of all love. But when we do love ourselves, and self-love is satisfied infinitely in all its desires and possible demands, then it is easily led to regard the benefactor more than itself, and for his sake overflows abundantly to all others. So that God, by satisfying my self-love, hath enabled and engaged me to love others.

56

No man loves, but he loves another more than himself. In mean instances this is apparent. If you come into an orchard with a person you love, and there be but one ripe cherry, you prefer it to the other. If two lovers delight in the same piece of meat, either takes pleasure in the other, and more esteems the beloved's satisfaction. What ails men, that they do not see it? In greater cases this is evident. A mother runs upon a sword to save her beloved. A father leaps into the fire to fetch out his beloved. Love brought Christ from Heaven to die for His beloved. It is in the nature of love to despise itself: and to think only of its beloved's welfare. Look to it, it is not right love that is otherwise. Moses and S. Paul were no fools. God make me one of their number. I am sure nothing is more acceptable to Him than to love others so as to be willing to impart even one's own soul for their benefit and welfare.

57

Nevertheless it is infinitely rewarded, tho it seemeth difficult; for by this love do we become heirs of all men's joys, and co-heirs with Christ. For what is the reason of your own joys, when you are blessed with benefits? Is it not self-love? Did you love others as you love yourself, you would be as much affected with their joys. Did you love them more, more. For according to the measure of your love to others will you be happy in them, for according thereto you will be delightful to them, and delighted in your felicity. The more you love men, the more delightful you will be to God, and the more delight you will take in God, and the more you will enjoy Him. So that the more like you are to Him in goodness, the more abundantly you will enjoy His goodness. By loving others you live in others to receive it.

58

Shall I not love him infinitely for whom God made the world and gave His Son? Shall I not love Him infinitely who loveth me infinitely? Examine yourself well, and you will find it a difficult matter to love God so as to die for Him, and not to love your brother, so as to die for him in like manner. Shall I not love him infinitely whom God loveth infinitely, and commendeth to my love, as the representative of Himself, with such a saying, 'What ye do to him is done unto Me'? And if I love him so, can I forbear to help him? Verily had I but one crown in the world, being in an open field, where both he and I were ready to perish, and 'twere necessary that one of us must have it all or be destroyed, tho I knew not where to have relief, he should have it, and I would die with comfort. I will not say, how small a comfort so small a succour is did I keep it: but how great a joy, to be the occasion of another's life! Love knows not how to be timorous, because it receives what it gives away. And is unavoidably the end of its own afflictions and another's happiness. Let him that pleases keep his money. I am more rich in this noble charity to all the world, and more enjoy myself in it, than he can be in both the Indies.

59

Is it unnatural to do what Jesus Christ hath done? He that would not in the same cases do the same things can never be saved, for unless we are led by the spirit of Christ we are none of His. Love in him that in the same cases would do the same things, will be an oracle always inspiring and teaching him what to do: how far to adventure upon all occasions. And certainly he whose love is like his Saviour's will be far greater than any that is now alive, in goodness and love to God and men. This is a sure rule. Love studies not to be scanty in its measures, but how to abound and overflow with benefits. He that pincheth and studieth to spare is a pitiful lover: unless it be for others' sakes. Love studieth to be pleasing, magnificent, and noble, and would in all things be glorious and divine unto its object. Its whole being is to its object, and its whole felicity in its object. And it hath no other thing to take care for. It doth good to its own soul while it doth good to another.

60

Here upon earth, it is under many disadvantages and impediments that maim it in its exercise. But in Heaven it is most glorious. And it is my happiness that I can see it on both sides the veil or screen.

There it appeareth in all its advantages, for every soul being full, and fully satisfied, at ease, in rest, and wanting nothing, easily overflows and shines upon all. It is its perfect interest so to do, and nothing hinders it. Self-love there being swallowed up and made perfect in the love of others. But here it is pinched and straitened by wants: here it is awakened and put in mind of itself: here it is divided and distracted between two. It has a body to provide for, necessities to relieve, and a person to supply. Therefore is it in this world the more glorious, if in the midst of these disadvantages it exert itself in its operations. In the other world it swimmeth down the stream and acteth with its interest. Here therefore is the place of its trial where its operations and its interest are divided. And if our Lord Jesus Christ, as some think, knew the glory to which He should ascend by dying for others, and that all was safe which He undertook, because in humbling Himself to the death of the cross He did not forsake but attain His glory: the like fate shall follow us; only let us expect it after death as He did. And remember that this and the other life are made of a piece: but this is the time of trial, that of rewards. The greatest disadvantages of love are its highest advantages. In the greatest hazards it achieveth to itself the greatest glory. It is seldom considered; but a love to others stronger than what we bear to ourselves, is the mother of all the heroic actions that have made histories pleasant and beautified the world.

61

Since love will thrust in itself as the greatest of all principles, let us at last willingly allow it room. I was once a stranger to it, now I am familiar with it as a daily acquaintance. 'Tis the only heir and benefactor of the world. It seems it will break in everywhere, as that without which the world could not be enjoyed. Nay as that without which it would not be worthy to be enjoyed, for it was beautified by love, and commandeth the love of a donor to us. Love is a phoenix that will revive in its own ashes, inherit death, and smell sweetly in the grave.

62

These two properties are in it: that it can attempt all, and suffer all. And the more it suffers the more it is delighted, and the more it attempteth the more it is enriched; for it seems that all love is so mysterious, that there is something in it which needs expression, and can never be understood by any manifestation (of itself, in itself): but only by mighty doings and sufferings. This moved God the Father to create the world and God the Son to die for it. Nor is this all. There are many other ways whereby it manifests itself as well as these, there being still something infinite in it behind. In its laws, in its tenderness, in its provisions, in its caresses, in its joys as well as in its hazards, in its honours as well as in its cares, nor does it ever cease till it has poured out itself in all its communications. In all which it ever rights and satisfies itself. For above all things in all worlds it desires to be magnified, and taketh pleasure in being glorified before its object. For which cause also it does all those things which magnify its object and increase its happiness.

63

Whether love principally intends its own glory, or its object's happiness is a great question: and of the more importance, because the right ordering of our own affections depends much upon the solution of it. For on the one side, to be self-ended is mercenary, and base and slavish, and to do all things for one's own glory, is servile, and vain glory. On the other God doth all things for Himself, and seeketh His glory as His last end, and is Himself the end whom He seeks and attains in all His ways. How shall we reconcile this riddle? Or untie this knot? For some men have taken occasion hereby seeing this in love, to affirm that there is no true love in the world. But it is all self-love whatsoever a man doth. Implying also that it was self-love in our Saviour, that made Him to undertake for us. Whereupon we might justly question, whether it were more for His own ends, or more for ours? As also whether it were for His own end that God created the world or more for ours? For extraordinary much of our duty and felicity hangeth upon this point; and whatsoever sword untieth this Gordian knot, will open a world of benefit and instruction to us.

64

God doth desire glory as His sovereign end, but true glory. From whence it followeth that He doth sovereignly and supremely desire both His own glory and man's happiness. Tho that be miraculous, yet it's very plain. For true glory is to love another for his own sake, and to prefer his welfare and to seek his happiness. Which God doth because it is true glory. So that He seeks the happiness of angels and men as His last end, and in that His glory: to wit His true glory. False and vain glory is inconsistent with His nature, but true glory is the very essence of His being. Which is love unto His beloved, love unto Himself, love unto His creatures.

65

How can God be love unto Himself, without the imputation of self-love? Did He love Himself under any other notion than as He is the lover of His beloved, there might be some danger. But the reason why He loves Himself being because He is love, nothing is more glorious than His self-love. For He loves Himself because He is infinite and eternal love to others. Because He loves Himself He cannot endure that His love should be displeased. And loving others vehemently and infinitely, all the love He bears to Himself is tenderness towards them. All that wherein He pleaseth Himself is delightful to them: He magnifieth Himself in magnifying them. And in fine, His love unto Himself is His love unto them. And His love unto them is love unto Himself. They are individually one, which it is very amiable and beautiful to behold. Because therein the simplicity of God doth evidently appear. The more He loveth them the greater He is and the more glorious. The more He loveth them the more precious and dear they are to Him. The more He loveth them the more joys and treasures He possesseth. The more He loveth them the more He delighteth in their felicity. The more He loveth them, the more He delighteth in Himself for being their felicity. The more He loveth them, the more He rejoiceth in all His works for serving them: and in all His Kingdom for delighting them. And being love to them, the more He loveth Himself and the more jealous He is lest Himself should be displeased, the more He loveth them and tendereth them and secureth their welfare. And the more He desires His own glory the more good He doth for them, in the more divine and genuine manner. You must love after His similitude.

66

He from whom I derived these things delighted always that I should be acquainted with principles that would make me fit for all ages. And truly in love there are enough of them. For since Nature never created anything in vain, and love of all other is the most glorious, there is not any relic or parcel of that that shall be unused. It is not like gold made to be buried and concealed in darkness. But like the sun to communicate itself wholly in its beams unto all. It is more excellent and more communicative. It is hid in a centre, and nowhere at all, if we respect its body. But if you regard its soul, it is an interminable sphere, which as some say of the sun, is infinities infinite, in the extension of its beams, being equally vigorous in all places, equally near to all objects, equally acceptable to all persons, and equally abundant in all its overflowings: infinitely everywhere. This of naked and divested love in its true perfection. Its own age is too little to contain it, its greatness is spiritual, like the Deity's. It filleth the world, and exceeds what it filleth. It is present with all objects, and tastes all excellencies, and meeteth the infiniteness of God in everything. So that in length it is infinite as well as in breadth, being equally vigorous at the utmost bound to which it can extend as here, and as wholly there as here and wholly everywhere. Thence also it can see into further spaces, things present and things to come, height and depth being open before it, and all things in Heaven, eternity, and time equally near.

67

Were not love the darling of God, this would be a rash and a bold sally. But since it is His image, and the love of God, I may almost say the God of God, because His beloved: all this happeneth unto love. And this love is your true self when you are in act what you are in power: the great Daemon of the world, the end of all things, the desire of angels and of all nations. A creature so glorious, that having seen it, it puts an end to all curiosity and swallows up all admiration. Holy, wise, and just towards all things, blessed in all things, the bride of God, glorious before all, His offspring and firstborn, and so like Him that being described, one would think it He. I should be afraid to say all this of it, but that I know Him, how He delighteth to have it magnified. And how He hath magnified it infinitely before because it is His bride and firstborn. I will speak only a little of its violence and vigour afar off. It can love an act of virtue in the utmost Indies, and hate a vice in the highest heavens, it can see into hell and adore the justice of God among the damned, it can behold and admire His love from everlasting. It can be present with His infinite and eternal love, it can rejoice in the joys which it foreseeth, can love Adam in Eden, Moses in the wilderness, Aaron in the tabernacle, David before the ark, S. Paul among the nations, and Jesus either in the manger or on the cross. All these it can love with violence. And when it is restored from all that is terrene and sensual, to its true spiritual being, it can love these and any of these as violently as any person in the living age.

68

Shall it not love violently what God loveth, what Jesus Christ loveth, what all saints and angels love? Moses glorified God in a wonderful manner, he prophesied of Christ, he plagued the Egyptians, he brought the Israelites out of the land of Egypt, he guided them in the wilderness, he gave us the law, he loved the people more than his own life: yea than his own self and all the possible glory that might have accrued to him. Shall not he be beloved? And what shall we think of Christ Himself? Shall not all our love be where His is? Shall it not wholly follow and attend Him? Yet shall it not forsake other objects, but love them all in Him, and Him in them, and them the more because of Him, and Him the more because of them. For by Him it is redeemed to them. So that as God is omnipresent our love shall be at once with all: that is we: having these strengths to animate and quicken our affection.

69

To love one person with a private love, is poor and miserable: to love all is glorious. To love all persons in all ages, all angels, all worlds is divine and heavenly. To love all cities and all kingdoms, all kings and all peasants, and every person in all worlds with a natural intimate familiar love, as if him alone, is blessed. This makes a man effectually blessed in all worlds, a delightful lord of all things, a glorious friend to all persons, a concerned person in all transactions, and ever present with all affairs. So that he must ever be filled with company, ever in the midst of all nations, ever joyful, and ever blessed. The greatness of this man's love no man can measure, it is stable like the sun, it endureth forever as the moon, it is a faithful witness in Heaven. It is stronger and more great than all private affections. It representeth every person in the light of eternity, and loveth him with the love of all worlds. With a love conformable to God's, guided to the same ends and founded upon the same causes. Which however lofty and divine it is, is ready to humble itself into the dust to serve the person beloved. And by how much the more glorious and sublime it is, is so much the more sweet and truly delightful: majesty and pleasure concurring together.

70

Now you may see what it is to be a son of God more clearly. Love in its glory is the friend of the Most High. It was begotten of Him and is to sit in His throne, and to reign in communion with Him. It is to please Him, and to be pleased by Him, in all His works, ways, and operations. It is ordained to hold an eternal correspondence with Him in the highest heavens. It is here in its infancy, there in its manhood and perfect stature. He wills and commands that it should be reverenced of all, and takes pleasure to see it admired in its excellencies. If love thus displayed be so glorious a being, how much more glorious and great is He that is sovereign Lord of all lords, and the heavenly King of all these? So many monarchs under one supreme, mightily set forth the glory of his kingdom. If you ask by what certainty, or by what rules we discover this? As by the seed we conjecture what plant will arise, and know by the acorn what tree will grow forth, or by the eagle's egg what kind of bird; so do we by the powers of the soul upon earth, know what kind of being, person, and glory it will be in the heavens. Its blind and latent powers shall be turned into act, its inclinations shall be completed, and its capacities filled, for by this means is it made perfect. A spiritual king is an eternal spirit. Love in the abstract is a soul exerted. Neither do you esteem yourself to be any other than love alone. God is love. And you are never like Him, till you are so: love unto all objects in like manner.

71

To sit in the throne of God is the most supreme estate that can befall a creature. It is promised in the Revelations. But few understand what is promised there, and but few believe it.

72

To sit in the throne of God is to inhabit eternity. To reign there is to be pleased with all things in Heaven and earth from everlasting to everlasting, as if we had the sovereign disposal of them. For He is to dwell in us, and we in Him, because He liveth in our knowledge and we in His. His will is to be in our will, and our will is to be in His will, so that both being joined and becoming one, we are pleased in all His works as He is; and herein the image of God perfectly consisteth. No artist maketh a throne too wide for the person. God is the greatest and divinest artist. Thrones proper and fit for the persons are always prepared by the wisest kings: for little bodies bodily thrones; for spirits invisible. God's throne is His omnipresence, and that is infinite: who dwelleth in Himself, or in that light which is inaccessible. The omnipresence therefore and the eternity of God are our throne, wherein we are to reign for evermore. His infinite and eternal love are the borders of it, which everywhere we are to meet, and everywhere to see for evermore. In this throne our Saviour sitteth, who is the Alpha and Omega, the first and the last, the Amen, and the faithful witness, who said, 'The glory which Thou hast given me, I have given them, that they may be one as we are one.' In Him the fullness of the Godhead dwelleth bodily. If that be too great to be applied to men, remember what follows, His church is the fullness of Him that filleth all in all. The fullness of the Godhead dwelleth in Him for our sakes. And if yet it seemeth too great to be enjoyed: by the surpassing excellency of His eternal power, it is made more than ours, for in Him we shall more enjoy it than if it were infinitely, and wholly, all in ourselves.

73

If anything yet remaineth that is dreadful, or terrible or doubtful, that seemeth to startle us, there is more behind that will more amaze us; for God is infinite in the expression of His love, as we shall all find to our eternal comfort. Objects are so far from diminishing, that they magnify the faculties of the soul beholding them. A sand in your conception conformeth your soul, and reduceth it to the size and similitude of a sand. A tree apprehended is a tree in your mind, the whole hemisphere and the heavens magnify your soul to the wideness of the heavens. All the spaces above the heavens enlarge it wider to their own dimensions. And what is without limit maketh your conception illimited and endless. The infinity of God is infinitely profitable as well as great: as glorious as incomprehensible: so far from straitening that it magnifieth all things. And must be seen in you, or God will be absent. Nothing less than infinite is God, and as finite He cannot be enjoyed.

74

But what is there more that will more amaze us? Can anything be behind such glorious mysteries? Is God more sovereign in other excellencies? Hath He showed Himself glorious in anything besides? Verily there is no end of all His greatness, His understanding is infinite, and His ways innumerable. 'How precious,' saith the Psalmist, 'are Thy thoughts to me, O God, when I would count them they are more than can be numbered. There is no man that reckoneth them up in order unto Thee.' O my Lord, I will endeavour it: and I will glorify Thee for evermore. The most perfect laws are agreeable only to the most perfect creatures. Since therefore Thy laws are the most perfect of all that are possible, so are Thy creatures. And if infinite power be wholly expressed, O Lord what creatures! what creatures shall we become! What divine, what illustrious beings! Souls worthy of so great a love, blessed forever. Made worthy, tho not found, for love either findeth, or maketh an object worthy of itself. For which cause Picus Mirandula admirably saith, in his tract *De Dignitate Hominis*, 'I have read in the monuments of Arabia, that Abdala the Saracen, being asked . . . what in this world was most admirable, answered, "Man," than whom he saw nothing more to be admired. Which sentence of his is seconded by that of Mercurius Trismegistus, *Magnum, O Asclepi, miraculum, Homo.* "Man is a great and wonderful miracle." Ruminating upon the reason of these sayings, those things did not satisfy me, which many have spoken concerning the excellency of human nature. As that man was . . . a messenger between the creatures, lord of inferior things, and familiar to those above; by the keenness of his senses, the piercing of his reason, and the light of knowledge, the interpreter of nature, a seeming interval between time and eternity and the inhabitant of both, the golden link or tie of the world, yea the Hymenaeus marrying the Creator and his creatures together; made as David witnesseth a little lower than the angels. All these things are great, but they are not the principal: that is, they are not those which rightly challenge the name and title of most admirable.' And so he goeth on, admiring and exceeding all that had been spoken before concerning the excellency of man: 'Why do we not rather admire the angels and the choirs above the heavens? At length I seemed to understand why man was the most happy, and therefore the most worthy to be admired of all the creatures; and to know that estate which in the order of things he doth enjoy, not only above the beasts but above the stars, and that might be envied even of the supra-celestial spirits,' which he styleth, *ultra-mundanis mentibus invidiosám.*

75

'The supreme Architect and our everlasting Father, having made the world, this most glorious house, and magnificent temple of His divinity, by the secret laws of His hidden wisdom; He adorned the regions above the heavens with most glorious spirits, the spheres He enlivened with eternal souls, the dreggy parts of the inferior world He filled with all kind of herds of living creatures. *Sed opere consummato*, but His work being completed, He desired someone that might weigh and reason, love the beauty, and admire the vastness of so great a work. All things therefore being (as Moses and Timaeus witness) already finished, at last He thought of creating man. But there was not in all the platforms before conceived any being after whom He might form this new offspring: nor in all His treasures what He might give this new son by way of inheritance: nor yet a place in all the regions of the world, wherein this contemplator of the universe might be seated. All things were already full, all things were already distributed into their various orders of supreme, middle, and inferior. But it was not the part of infinite Power, to fail as defective in the last production; it was not the part of infinite Wisdom, for want of counsel to fluctuate in so necessary an affair; it was not the part of infinite Goodness, or sovereign Love, that he who should be raised up to praise the divine bounty in other things, should condemn it in himself.... The wisest and best of workmen appointed therefore, that he to whom nothing proper to himself could be added, should have something of all that was peculiar to everything. And therefore He took man, the image of all His work, and placing him in the middle of the world, spake thus unto him.

76

'"O Adam, we have given thee neither a certain seat, nor a private face, nor a peculiar office, that whatsoever seat or face or office thou dost desire, thou mayst enjoy. All other things have a nature bounded within certain laws, thou only art loose from all, and according to thy own counsel in the hand of which I have put thee, mayst choose and prescribe what nature thou wilt to thyself. I have placed thee in the middle of the world, that from thence thou mayst behold on every side more commodiously everything in the whole world. We have made thee neither heavenly nor earthly, neither mortal nor immortal, that being the honoured former and framer of thyself, thou mayst shape thyself into what nature thyself pleaseth."

77

'O infinite liberality of God the Father! O admirable and supreme felicity of man! to whom it is given to have what he desires and to be what he wisheth. The brutes when they are brought forth bring into the world with them what they are to possess continually. The spirits that are above were, either from the beginning or a little after, that which they are about to be to all eternities. *Nascenti homini omnigena vitae germina indidit Pater*, God infused the seeds of every kind of life into man; whatever seeds every one chooseth those spring up with him, and the fruits of those shall he bear and enjoy. If sensual things are chosen by him he shall become a beast, if reasonable a celestial creature; if intellectual an angel and a son of God; and if being content with the lot of no creatures, he withdraws himself into the centre of his own unity, he shall be one spirit with God, and dwell above all in the solitary darkness of his eternal Father.'

78

This Picus Mirandula spake in an oration made before a most learned assembly in a famous university. Any man may perceive, that he permitteth his fancy to wander a little wantonly after the manner of a poet; but most deep and serious things are secretly hidden under his free and luxuriant language. The changeable power he ascribeth to man is not to be referred to his body; for as he wisely saith, 'Neither doth the bark make a plant, but its stupid and nothing-perceiving nature; neither doth the skin make a beast, but his brutish and sensual nature; neither doth separation from a body make an angel, but his spiritual intelligence.' So neither doth his rind or coat or skin or body make a man to be this or that, but the interior stupidness, or sensuality, or angelical intelligence of his soul, make him accordingly a plant, a beast, or an angel. The deformity or excellency is within.

79

Neither is it to be believed, that God filled all the world with creatures before He thought of man: but by that little fable he teacheth us the excellency of man. Man is the end, and therefore the perfection of all the creatures; but as Eusebius Pamphilus saith (in the Nicene Council) he was first in the intention, tho last in the execution. All angels were spectators as well as he, all angels were free agents as well as he: as we see by their trial, and the fall of some; all angels were seated in as convenient a place as he. But this is true, that he was the end of all, and the last of all. And the comprehensive head and the bond of all, and in that more excellent than all the angels: as for whom the visible and invisible worlds were made, and to whom all creatures ministered; as one also, that contained more species in his nature than the angels, which is not as some have thought derogatory, but perfective to his being. It is true also that God hath prevented him, and satisfied all wishes, in giving him such a being as he now enjoyeth. And that for infinite reasons it was best that he should be in a changeable estate, and have power to choose what himself listed; for he may so choose as to become one spirit with God Almighty.

80

By choosing a man may be turned and converted into love. Which as it is an universal sun filling and shining in the eternity of God, so is it infinitely more glorious than the sun is, not only shedding abroad more amiable and delightful beams, illuminating and comforting all objects: yea glorifying them in the supreme and sovereign manner, but is of all sensibles the most quick and tender; being able to feel like the long-legged spider, at the utmost end of its divaricated feet: and to be wholly present in every place where any beam of itself extends. The sweetness of its healing influences is inexpressible. And of all beings such a being would I choose to be forever. One that might inherit all in the most exquisite manner, and be the joy of all in the most perfect measure.

81

Nazianzen professed himself to be a lover of right reason and by it did undertake even to speak oracles. Even so may we by right reason discover all the mysteries of Heaven. And what our author here observeth, is very considerable, that man by retiring from all externals and withdrawing into himself, in the centre of his own unity becometh most like unto God. What Mercurius said in the dialogue is most true, man is of all other the greatest miracle. Yea verily. Should all the miracles that ever were done be drawn together, man is a miracle greater than they. And as much may be written of him alone as of the whole world. The dividing of the sea, the commanding of the sun, the making of the world is nothing to the single creation of one soul: there is so much wisdom and power expressed in its faculties and inclinations. Yet is this greatest of all miracles unknown because men are addicted only to sensible and visible things. So great a world in the explication of its parts is easy; but here the dimensions of innumerable worlds are shut up in a centre. Where it should lodge such innumerable objects as it doth by knowing, whence it should derive such infinite streams as flow from it by loving, how it should be a mirror of all eternity, being made of nothing, how it should be a fountain or a sun of eternity out of which such abundant rivers of affection flow, it is impossible to declare. But above all, how having no material or bodily existence, its substance tho invisible should be so rich and precious. The consideration of one soul is sufficient to convince all the atheists in the whole world.

82

The abundance of its beams, the reality of its beams, the freedom of its beams, the excellency and value of its beams are all transcendent. They shine upon all the things in Heaven and earth and cover them all with celestial waters: waters of refreshment, beams of comfort. They flow freely from a mind desiring to be obedient, pleasing, and good. The soul communicates itself wholly by them: and is richer in its communications than all odours and spices whatsoever. It containeth in its nature the influences of the stars by way of eminence, the splendour of the sun, the verdure of trees, the value of gold, the lustre of precious stones, the sense of beasts, and the life of angels: the fatness of feasts, the magnificence of palaces, the melody of music, the sweetness of wine, the beauty of the excellent, the excellency of virtue, and the glory of cherubims. The harmony and the joys of Heaven appear in love; for all these were made for her, and all these are to be enjoyed in her.

83

Whether it be the soul itself, or God in the soul, that shines by love, or both, it is difficult to tell; but certainly the love of the soul is the sweetest thing in the world. I have often admired what should make it so excellent. If it be God that loves, it is the shining of His essence; if it be the soul, it is His image; if it be both, it is a double benefit.

84

That God should love in the soul is most easy to believe, because it is most easy to conceive. But it is a greater mystery that the soul should love in itself. If God loveth in the soul, it is the more precious; if the soul loveth, it is the more marvellous. If you ask how a soul that was made of nothing can return so many flames of love, where it should have them or out of what ocean it should communicate them, it is impossible to declare (for it can return those flames upon all eternity, and upon all the creatures and objects in it). Unless we say, as a mirror returneth the very self-same beams it receiveth from the sun, so the soul returneth those beams of love that shine upon it from God. For as a looking-glass is nothing in comparison of the world, yet containeth all the world in it, and seems a real fountain of those beams which flow from it, so the soul is nothing in respect of God, yet all eternity is contained in it, and it is the real fountain of that love that proceedeth from it. They are the sunbeams which the glass returneth; yet they flow from the glass and from the sun within it. The mirror is the well-spring of them, because they shine from the sun within the mirror. Which is as deep within the glass as it is high within the heavens. And this showeth the exceeding richness and preciousness of love: it is the love of God shining upon, and dwelling in the soul, for the beams that shine upon it reflect upon others and shine from it.

The Fifth Century

1

The objects of felicity, and the way of enjoying them, are two material themes wherein to be instructed is infinitely desirable, because as necessary as profitable. Whether of the two, the object or the way be more glorious, it is difficult to determine. God is the object, and God is the way of enjoying. God in all His excellencies, laws, and works, in all His ways and counsels is the sovereign object of all felicity. Eternity and time, Heaven and earth, kingdoms and ages, angels and men, are in Him to be enjoyed. In Him the fountain, in Him the end; in Him the light, the life, the way; in Him the glory and crown of all. Yet for distinction sake, we will speak of several eminent particulars. Beginning with His attributes.

2

The infinity of God is our enjoyment, because it is the region and extent of His dominion. Barely as it comprehends infinite space, it is infinitely delightful; because it is the room and the place of our treasures, the repository of our joys, and the dwelling place, yea the sea and throne and kingdom of our souls. But as it is the light wherein we see, the life that inspires us, the violence of His love, and the strength of our enjoyments, the greatness and perfection of every creature, the amplitude that enlargeth us, and the field wherein our thoughts expatiate without limit or restraint, the ground and foundation of all our satisfactions, the operative energy and power of the Deity, the measure of our delights, and the grandeur of our souls, it is more our treasure, and ought more abundantly to be delighted in. It surroundeth us continually on every side, it fills us, and inspires us. It is so mysterious, that it is wholly within us, and even then it wholly seems, and is, without us. It is more inevitably and constantly, more nearly and immediately our dwelling place, than our cities and kingdoms and houses. Our bodies themselves are not so much ours, or within us, as that is. The immensity of God is an eternal tabernacle. Why then we should not be sensible of that as much as of our dwellings, I cannot tell, unless our corruption and sensuality destroy us. We ought always to feel, admire, and walk in it. It is more clearly objected to the eye of the soul than our castles and palaces to the eye of the body. Those accidental buildings may be thrown down, or we may be taken from them, but this can never be removed, it abideth forever. It is impossible not to [be] within it; nay to be so surrounded as evermore to be in the centre and midst of it, wherever we can possibly remove, is inevitably fatal to every being.

3

Creatures that are able to dart their thoughts into all spaces, can brook no limit or restraint, they are infinitely indebted to this illimited extent, because were there no such infinity, there would be no room for their imaginations; their desires and affections would be cooped up, and their souls imprisoned. We see the heavens with our eyes, and know the world with our senses. But had we no eyes, nor senses, we should see infinity like the holy angels. The place wherein the world standeth, were it all annihilated, would still remain, the endless extent of which we feel so really and palpably, that we do not more certainly know the distinctions and figures, and bounds and distances of what we see, than the everlasting expansion of what we feel and behold within us. It is an object infinitely great and ravishing: as full of treasures as full of room, and as fraught with joy as capacity. To blind men it seemeth dark, but is all glorious within, as infinite in light and beauty as extent and treasure. Nothing is in vain, much less infinity. Every man is alone the centre and circumference of it. It is all his own, and so glorious, that it is the eternal and incomprehensible essence of the Deity. A cabinet of infinite value equal in beauty, lustre, and perfection to all its treasures. It is the bosom of God, the soul and security of every creature.

4

Were it not for this infinity, God's bounty would of necessity be limited. His goodness would want a receptacle for its effusions. His gifts would be confined into narrow room, and His almighty power for lack of a theatre magnificent enough, a storehouse large enough, be straitened. But almighty power includes infinity in its own existence. For because God is infinitely able to do all things, there must of necessity be an infinite capacity to answer that power, because nothing itself is an obedient subject to work upon; and the eternal privation of infinite perfections is to almighty power a being capable of all. As sure as there is a space infinite, there is a power, a bounty, a goodness, a wisdom infinite, a treasure, a blessedness, a glory.

5

Infinity of space is like a painter's table, prepared for the ground and field of those colours that are to be laid thereon. Look how great he intends the picture, so great doth he make the table. It would be an absurdity to leave it unfinished, or not to fill it. To leave any part of it naked and bare, and void of beauty, would render the whole ungrateful to the eye, and argue a defect of time, or materials, or wit in the limner. As the table is infinite so are the pictures. God's wisdom is the art, His goodness the will, His word the pencil, His beauty and power the colours, His pictures are all His works and creatures: infinitely more real and more glorious, as well as more great and manifold than the shadows of a landscape. But the life of all is, they are the spectator's own. He is in them as in his territories, and in all these, views his own possessions.

6

One would think that besides infinite space there could be no more room for any treasure. Yet to show that God is infinitely infinite, there is infinite room besides, and perhaps a more wonderful region making this to be infinitely infinite. No man will believe that besides the space from the centre of the earth to the utmost bounds of the everlasting hills, there should be any more. Beyond those bounds perhaps there may, but besides all that space that is illimited and present before us, and absolutely endless every way, where can there be any room for more? This is the space that is at this moment only present before our eye, the only space that was, or that will be, from everlasting to everlasting. This moment exhibits infinite space, but there is a space also wherein all moments are infinitely exhibited, and the everlasting duration of infinite space is another region and room of joys. Wherein all ages appear together, all occurrences stand up at once, and the innumerable and endless myriads of years that were before the creation, and will be after the world is ended are objected as a clear and stable object, whose several parts extended out at length, give an inward infinity to this moment, and compose an eternity that is so seen by all comprehensors and enjoyers.

7

Eternity is a mysterious absence of times and ages: an endless length of ages always present, and forever perfect. For as there is an immovable space wherein all finite spaces are enclosed, and all motions carried on and performed, so is there an immovable duration that contains and measures all moving durations. Without which first the last could not be; no more than finite places, and bodies moving without infinite space. All ages being but successions correspondent to those parts of that eternity wherein they abide, and filling no more of it than ages can do. Whether they are commensurate with it or no, is difficult to determine. But the infinite immovable duration is eternity, the place and duration of all things, even of infinite space itself: the cause and end, the author and beautifier, the life and perfection of all.

8

Eternity magnifies our joys exceedingly. For whereas things in themselves began, and quickly end; before they came, were never in being; do service but for few moments; and after they are gone, pass away and leave us forever, eternity retains the moments of their beginning and ending within itself: and from everlasting to everlasting those things were in their times and places before God, and in all their circumstances eternally will be, serving Him in those moments wherein they existed, to those intents and purposes for which they were created. The swiftest thought is present with Him eternally: the creation and the day of judgement, His first consultation, choice, and determination, the result and end of all just now in full perfection, ever beginning, ever passing, ever ending: with all the intervals of space between things and things. As if those objects that arise many thousand years one after the other were all together. We also were ourselves before God eternally: and have the joy of seeing ourselves eternally beloved, and eternally blessed, and infinitely enjoying all the parts of our blessedness, in all the durations of eternity appearing at once before ourselves, when perfectly consummate in the kingdom of light and glory. The smallest thing, by the influence of eternity, is made infinite and eternal. We pass through a standing continent or region of ages, that are already before us, glorious and perfect while we come to them. Like men in a ship we pass forward, the shores and marks seeming to go backward, tho we move and they stand still. We are not with them in our progressive motion, but prevent the swiftness of our course, and are present with them in our understandings. Like the sun, we dart our rays before us, and occupy those spaces with light and contemplation, which we move towards, but possess not with our bodies. And seeing all things in the light of divine knowledge eternally serving God, rejoice unspeakably in that service, and enjoy it all.

9

His omnipresence is an ample territory or field of joys, a transparent temple of infinite lustre, a strong tower of defence, a castle of repose, a bulwark of security, a palace of delights, an immediate help, and a present refuge in the needful time of trouble, a broad and a vast extent of fame and glory, a theatre of infinite excellency, an infinite ocean by means whereof every action, word, and thought, is immediately diffused like a drop of wine in a pail of water, and everywhere present, everywhere seen and known, infinitely delighted in, as well as filling infinite spaces. It is the spirit that pervades all His works, the life and soul of the universe, that in every point of space from the centre to the heavens, in every kingdom in the world, in every city, in every wilderness, in every house, every soul, every creature, in all the parts of His infinity and eternity sees our persons, loves our virtues, inspires us with itself, and crowns our actions with praise and glory. It makes our honour infinite in extent, our glory immense, and our happiness eternal. The rays of our light are by this means darted from everlasting to everlasting. This spiritual region makes us infinitely present with God, angels, and men in all places from the utmost bounds of the everlasting hills, throughout all the unwearied durations of His endless infinity, and gives us the sense and feeling of all the delights and praises we occasion, as well as of all the beauties and powers, and pleasures and glories which God enjoyeth or createth.

10

Our bridegroom and our King being everywhere, our lover and defender watchfully governing all worlds, no danger or enemy can arise to hurt us, but is immediately prevented and suppressed, in all the spaces beyond the utmost borders of those unknown habitations which He possesseth. Delights of inestimable value are there preparing. For everything is present by its own existence. The essence of God therefore being all light and knowledge, love and goodness, care and providence, felicity and glory, a pure and simple act, it is present in its operations, and by those acts which it eternally exerteth, is wholly busied in all parts and places of His dominion, perfecting and completing our bliss and happiness.

NOTES

The Dobell Poems

THE SALUTATION

This mimetic poem, in which Traherne uses an adult vocabulary to express the infant's earliest awareness of himself and his surroundings, introduces a self-contained sequence of four poems celebrating childhood's vision of the world and the need to perpetuate that vision, in so far as possible, into later life. The tone of joyful amazement and the questioning mode resemble Adam's account of his own emergent consciousness in *Paradise Lost* (1667): 'Myself I then perus'd, and limb by limb / Survey'd. ... how came I thus, how here? / Not of myself; by some great Maker then' (VIII. 267–78). The repetitions of 'strange' in stanza 7 link this poem to the next one by intensifying the sense of wonderment.

WONDER

The opening phrase, 'How like an angel', may come from Hamlet's 'What a piece of work is a man ... how like an angel in apprehension, how like a god!' (*Hamlet* II.ii). Most readers, however, will rightly be reminded of the opening lines of Henry Vaughan's *The Retreat*, from *Silex Scintillans* (1650): 'Happy those early days, when I / Shined in my angel infancy.' These two poems reward close comparison, which highlights the differences between Traherne and Vaughan, to whom Traherne's work was once mistakenly attributed. Although the soul in *Wonder* is imagined as having descended from Heaven, pre-existence plays little part in this poem, which is more concerned with recapturing the young child's earliest experience of the world. In contrast to *The Salutation*, the point of view is that of the adult looking back: sometimes, as in line 2, re-enacting the child's intuitive response to his surroundings; but elsewhere, as in stanzas 4 and 7, applying the mature speaker's perspective with mention of everything that was 'conceal'd' (l. 25) or that 'fled'

(l. 52) from childhood vision: sins, griefs, 'proprieties' (private property), limits, etc. The last line, 'When I was born', emphatically places the poem's raptures in time past. This interplay between the wide-eyed, innocent vision of childhood and the disillusioned adult point of view recalls another Shakespearean context: Miranda's 'O wonder! / How many goodly creatures are there here! / How beauteous mankind is! O brave new world / That has such people in't!' and Prospero's reply, ''Tis new to thee' (*The Tempest* V.i). Much of *Wonder* is a versified version of meditations 2 and 3 from the Third Century, with which it should be compared.

EDEN

In line 1 the speaker's ignorance of sin in his childhood is called 'learned' because the child was paradoxically in possession of truths later obscured by experience, as in *Shadows in the Water* where the child's belief that he has discovered 'another world' in a puddle is a 'Mistake though false, intending true' – i.e., pointing towards the real truth of the existence of an immaterial world beyond the phenomenal one. Cf. also *Centuries* 3.2: 'My knowledge was divine: I knew by intuition those things which since my apostasy, I collected again, by the highest reason. My very ignorance was advantageous.' The phrase 'learned . . . ignorance' may allude, moreover, to Nicholas of Cusa's treatise *De Docta Ignorantia* (1440), whose title is explained by the wisdom of Socrates in knowing only that he knew nothing – though Traherne's child of course has no such knowledge. In stanza 2 the metaphor of 'a serpent's sting' that causes venom to 'overspread / The world' acknowledges original sin while separating it altogether from the child's consciousness. The poem is based on an analogy between Adam's condition of 'original simplicity' in the Garden of Eden (stanza 5) and the protective simplicity of infancy (stanza 6, ll. 38-9) which shielded the speaker from the vanities and distractions of the adult world. Oblivious to the artificial, corrupt 'works of men', the child was able to respond wholeheartedly to the 'glorious wonders of the Deity' (ll. 48-9).

INNOCENCE

This completes the opening sequence of four poems on childhood in the Dobell MS. Along with *Centuries* 3.7-8, *Innocence* is a key text for assessing Traherne's allegedly heretical or 'Pelagian' stance on original sin. Although most non-Augustinian views on this topic were labelled Pelagian (after the British monk Pelagius, who opposed his contemporary St Augustine on this and other doctrinal matters), Traherne's own position may have been closer to that of St Irenaeus, a pre-Nicene father who held the view that Adam was created as a child rather than as a mature and therefore fully responsible adult. The fourth stanza suggests three possible explanations for the fact that the speaker as a child felt 'within . . . no stain, nor spot of sin' (ll. 3–4) and settles on the third. If 'nature is . . . pure', then original sin does not exist; the eventual and inevitable corruption of the child is a cultural process (as described in *Centuries* 3.7). If, on the other hand, the child must be regarded as guilty of innate depravity, then – Traherne boldly suggests – God may have miraculously exempted Traherne's own soul from such guilt. (Both the denial of original sin and the suggestion of a miracle were repudiated by Philip, who substituted for Traherne's lines 38–40, 'or to cure / Its [i.e., nature's] depravation, God did guilt remove / To fix in me a sense of's love'.) The third possibility is that the child may have received on one particular occasion (l. 41) a vision in which his 'ravish'd sense . . . had a sight of innocence' (ll. 53–5). This experience or 'prospect' conveyed 'the ancient light of Eden' into his soul (ll. 49–51). An 'antepast' (l. 57) is an appetizer or a foretaste. The last line alludes to Matthew 18:3 or Mark 10:15, texts that are central to much of Traherne's writing. For Traherne's own gloss on Jesus' statement that one must 'become a little child' in order to enter the Kingdom of Heaven, see *Centuries* 3.5; he regarded its meaning as 'deeper far than is generally believed'.

THE PREPARATIVE

For the title, cf. line 1 of *The Vision*: 'Flight is but the preparative'. (Traherne originally wrote 'The Vision' as the title of this poem and replaced it with 'The Preparative'.) Although this title has not been satisfactorily explained, it does clearly point forward to later poems and perhaps indicates a new stage in the meditative sequence which some think determines the organization of material in the Dobell MS. In particular, this poem is preparatory to *The Vision*, and the flight referred to there is hinted at in its concluding lines, where the poet urges his soul to 'retire' (from the world) and 'Get free' from the entanglements of multiple senses in order to be 'unpossess'd', 'disengaged', and 'empty' (stanza 7) like the 'naked simple pure intelligence' (l. 20) that defined his being when he first entered the world. 'Dead' in line 1 means inert or inactive; the 'house' referred to in line 10 is the body, in which the soul has just taken up residence. The soul is depicted as not yet having learned to motivate the body or activate its various members and their functions. The speaker, in stanza 2, remembers his soul as having been, at that time, 'an inward sphere of light, / Or an interminable orb of sight' (ll. 15–16), two metaphors that operate throughout the poem and, indeed, throughout much of Traherne's work. For the human soul as an internal sun, cf. Sir Thomas Browne's *Hydriotaphia, or Urn Burial* (1658): 'Life is a pure flame, and we live by an invisible sun within us.' This image of the soul as light-emitting is complemented by an emblematic representation of it as light-receiving and percipient: an indefinitely extended eyeball. As a 'meditating inward eye / Gazing at quiet' (ll. 27–8), the speaker's soul was capable of receiving 'the fair ideas' – that is, the Platonic archetypes – 'of all things' (l. 25). Consequently, it was neither 'glued' (l. 43) to matter nor 'fetter'd' by the 'iron fate' (l. 45) of fallen man's condition. Like a mirror, the soul's own powers are said to have 'clothed' themselves 'in their objects' image' (ll. 51–4); that is, they became identified with the Platonic forms or 'divine impressions' (l. 55) that they reflected. (Cf. *Centuries* 2.78: 'For as light varieth upon all objects whither it cometh, and returneth with the form and figure of them: so is the soul transformed into the being of its object'.) In stanza 4, the senses, differentiated by their respective stimuli, come into play but are dismissed by the speaker in favour of the unity and simplicity of the infantile soul as a disembodied eye: a concept to which Traherne will return in the 'Infant-Eye' sequence of the Burney MS. The syntax of lines 34–5 is difficult because 'feeling' doubles as subject and object of the verb 'wounds'; Philip, perhaps puzzled, substituted 'the touching feeleth wounds / Of pain or pleasure'.

In lines 12–13 Traherne originally wrote, 'A living endless eye, / Far wider than the sky', but changed the second of these lines to 'Just bounded with the sky', as given here.

THE INSTRUCTION

As its title indicates, this is a straightforwardly didactic poem – though addressed as much to the speaker's self as to the reader. It harks back to the hortatory conclusion of *The Preparative* and once again calls for a return to the radical innocence of early childhood and to the singleness and purity of the child's vision (l. 10), focused on essential things and undistracted by 'contingents' and 'transients' (ll. 2–3): the accidental and the mutable. As always in Traherne, *custom* (l. 14) is the medium by which the corruption and false values of the adult world are transmitted to the child. In the last line 'all men on earth' was corrected by Traherne to 'all men at once', as given here.

THE VISION

Moving beyond *The Preparative* (l. 1) and continuing the rarefied visual imagery of previous poems, this poem argues in effect that the beatific vision can be attained here and now, that it need not be postponed until the afterlife. In the 'celestial light' (l. 7) of that vision, even the negative aspects of human life – labour, sin, and suffering (ll. 7–8) – are illuminated: a paradox explained in stanza 4 where the speaker predicts that 'Men's woes shall be but foils' to offset and thereby enhance the bliss of the enlightened visionary. The impression of egocentric hedonism that this stanza gives is misleading since Traherne elsewhere insists that the soul's quest for felicity involves a sense of connectedness with other human beings. Traherne's *I* (or *eye*) is at once unique and universal: autobiographical yet impersonal. His often-reiterated belief that the world exists for the enjoyment of the individual self is paradoxical in that all such selves, collectively, are thus privileged. Democritus (l. 29) was proverbially known as the 'laughing philosopher' (as opposed to Heraclitus, the 'weeping philosopher'), and there may be an allusion here to Robert Burton's persona in *The Anatomy of Melancholy* (six editions, 1621–51): 'Democritus Junior'.

There are several difficulties in stanza 3. In line 18 (given here as revised by Traherne; originally 'Upon the object dwell') 'that' must refer to the special way of seeing the world advocated in the preceding line: 'as thine'. The 'spacious case' of line 19 (cf. Shakespeare's 'the casing air' [*Macbeth* III.iv]) is apparently the atmosphere or surface of the earth and not necessarily its cosmic setting (*but* cf. *The City* l. 41: 'The heavens were the richly studded case'); thus 'the heavenly place' of line 21 is the earth itself (cf. Philip's revision 'this heavenly place') *as truly beheld*. Line 24 means that the first sight, the original vision of the infant-eye, makes common things precious by enabling us to 'prize' them (l. 22) at their true value. The last three stanzas clarify the content of the vision. God is the fountain or spring and man the end – the receptacle into which the fountain's water flows. To see all of creation consummated in man is to see God 'At once in two' (l. 51), the fountain in the end – tantamount to the beatific vision (l. 56).

THE RAPTURE

This poem, as characterized by its title, is in Traherne's most ecstatic vein. While its lyric intensity contrasts with the expository mode of *The Vision*, it is closely linked, thematically, to that poem in its celebration of the self's greatness, as magnified (l. 5) by the world that the self was created to possess (l. 8). Line 14 does not simply state the fact of the stars' motion but plays on the word 'move' (as a transitive verb) to assert that the stars *impel* the speaker to praise God.

THE IMPROVEMENT

This tightly organized poem looks behind the rapture of its predecessor to find a logical explanation for the feelings expressed there. It argues the proposition that each human being actually improves on God's act of creation by 'recollecting' (in the obsolete sense of gathering or collecting) in his own person the Deity's 'scattered' works (ll. 17–18). The first two stanzas employ a conceit based on the family to express the interrelationship of God's attributes: wisdom, power, goodness, love, and happiness. But these divine attributes become the properties of created things (l. 20) only by virtue of human perception (ll. 23–4): the eye becomes 'the sphere / Of all things' by comprehending and unifying – 'recollecting' – the diverse works of creation. In the last three stanzas the poet returns to the current meditative topic of the sequence as a whole – his 'infant sense' (l. 67): evidence for the unity of the Dobell MS since this topic has not been mentioned previously in the present poem.

THE APPROACH

This poem reappears as meditation four of the Third Century and is equally at home in both of its contexts. The joys inspired by 'childish thoughts' (l. 1) were listed in stanza 13 of *The Improvement* and are called 'those pure and virgin apprehensions which I had in my infancy' in *Centuries* 3.4. Traherne's God is more personalized, less of a philosophical abstraction here than is normally the case. He 'walks' and 'talks' with children (ll. 7–8), is 'griev'd' when rebuffed by adults (ll. 9–11, 21–2), but continues to 'assault' the hardened human heart with the motions of grace (ll. 19–21). 'Thoughts' (ll. 1, 8, 24, 28, 37) is a key word in this poem because the infant's thoughts (not even recognized as such at the time) are discovered by the converted (l. 18) adult to be divine – i.e., identical to those of the Deity (l. 28) – since they were 'inlaid' (l. 39) in the child's mind at the time of his creation 'from nothing' (l. 31). God in His glory inspires man's wonder (ll. 2, 13, 30, 32) by initiating the 'approach' (l. 29) that gives the poem its title and by persisting in His attentions until the fallen adult recovers, through conversion, the lost childhood vision that enables him to achieve Traherne's goal of seeing 'beneath as if above the skies' (l. 26).

The reader who wishes to compare the two extant versions of the poem will discover that (as Margoliouth noted) this one is the later, thus proving that Traherne made the fair copy of the Dobell poems after having composed the *Centuries*.

DUMBNESS

The dumbness celebrated here is the pre-verbal, pre-linguistic stage of infancy – disrupted by the onset of language but recoverable through meditation; and the deafness of line 9 is the infant's unreceptiveness to verbal communication, a state that safeguards the 'learned ignorance' into which he is born (cf. *Eden*). As a poet, Traherne cannot have considered the acquisition of language an unmitigated disaster; nevertheless, it serves him here as a metaphor for the child's inevitable fall from his private 'world of light' (l. 31) into the confusion of adult experience where 'foreign vanities' (l. 76) prevail amid the general uproar (l. 86). The 'mortal words' of line 13 are, literally, the very words *sin* and *death*; figuratively, they are all words because words as such bring about the child's downfall – just as the 'mortal taste' of the forbidden fruit caused 'all our woe' (*Paradise Lost* I.1–3). In contrast to mortal words (likened to plague-laden breath in lines 14–16), the earliest impressions taken by the child's receptive sensibility are immortal (l. 85). The phrase 'the first words mine infancy did hear' (l. 79) refers not to the literal words spoken by adults, but to these impressions – detailed in lines 59–67 – gleaned from nature. (Like Duke Senior in *As You Like It* II.i, the child is so attuned to his natural surroundings that he 'Finds tongues in trees, books in the running brooks, / Sermons in stones, and good in every thing.') By a paradox highly characteristic of Traherne, eyes rather than ears are the 'hearers' (l. 60) of these divine messages transmitted via nature. Lines 39–53, which describe the 'work' (l. 37) performed by the 'busy' (l. 6) child, define Traherne's central concept of *felicity* as fully as any passage in his poetry. *Avenue* was originally a military term meaning an invading army's route of access to a fortress or other objective, such as a city. The 'avenues' of line 55 are the child's ears and tongue, which, by participating in verbal communication with the adult world, betray the once-'impregnable' (l. 54) fortress of the speaker's infant soul. Lines 53–78 develop both religious and military imagery: an assault on a fortress which is also a temple. Traherne may have had in mind the fall of Jerusalem and the destruction of its temple, first by the Chaldeans and later by the Romans.

Traherne first wrote 'secrets see' in line 33 but, perhaps deciding to sacrifice assonance to sense, changed this to 'such things see', as given here. These things, that is, only *seemed* (l. 34) to be revealed to the child alone and thus were not secrets at all but were available to anyone with eyes to see.

SILENCE

Silence is a companion poem to *Dumbness*. Just as that poem praised the infant's incapacity for speech and consequent freedom from distraction, so this one argues that an adult can simulate that infantile state by retreating at will into contemplative silence in order to resume the spiritual work (ll. 3, 6) interrupted by the fall into speech. An uncommunicative or seemingly idle (l. 5) person should not be misjudged, for he may be as active as Adam, who had only 'to feel his bliss', 'prize' his 'treasures' rightly, and above all to love (ll. 21–6: a passage that closely parallels lines 39–53 in *Dumbness*). These inward activities are 'exercises of the highest sphere' (l. 28), in contrast to 'outward busy acts', which belong to 'a lower sphere' (ll. 9–10). (The latter include even acts of charity and piety, which were unnecessary in an unfallen world.) This imagery of spheres derives from the Ptolemaic system and is reminiscent of Donne's *A Valediction: Forbidding Mourning*, where 'dull sublunary lovers' depend on physical contact and thus require outward displays of emotion at parting whereas the silent separation of lovers who are spiritually united is like 'trepidation of the spheres'. Like Donne, Traherne is contrasting the realm of corruption and mutability within the sphere of the moon with the crystalline purity of the outermost reaches of the Ptolemaic cosmos. Lines 57–8 – 'No aloes or dregs, no Wormwood star / Was seen to fall into the sea from far' – are among the most difficult passages in Traherne, but in context the idea seems reasonably clear: sin, which is represented simultaneously as a bitter substance and a falling star (cf. Revelation 8:10–11: ' . . . and there fell a great star from heaven . . . upon the fountains of waters; And the name of the star is called Wormwood: and the third part of the waters became wormwood; and many men died of the waters, because they were made bitter'), never contaminated the 'pure streams' (l. 56) of the speaker's infant-soul while he was isolated from verbal contact with others. The streams of lines 56, 64, and 72 are currents in the sea (e.g., the Gulf Stream); this entire passage (ll. 55–74) is dominated by the image of the ocean, which represents both God (l. 71) and the speaker's soul (ll. 70, 73). The oceanic 'capacity' of both 'Did make my bosom like the Deity' (ll. 75–6). Traherne thus ends with an analogy between God and the human soul. The speechless infant and the silent meditator are like the Creator prior to His utterance of *Fiat lux* – i.e., when 'He nothing said' but nevertheless contained eternity (ll. 79–80). Similarly, the child contains the world that he inhabits (l. 81) until language begins the process of separating world and self.

MY SPIRIT

This poem, called by Margoliouth 'Traherne's most comprehensive poem', seems to arise spontaneously from the conclusion of *Silence*: 'For so my spirit was an endless sphere, / Like God Himself, and Heaven and earth was there.' As if to prove the thesis about language argued in the two previous poems, *My Spirit* resorts to elaborate verbal paradoxes and ingenious conceits to describe and define an entity that, being 'simple like the Deity' (l. 15), resists description or definition. (Notice that the poet, though representing the soul as a sphere throughout the poem, twice repudiates his own metaphor [ll. 94, 101] – thus making the poem's figurative language, in effect, self-subversive.) Much discussion of the poem has centred on its third stanza, which has been taken to show that Traherne's view of the relation between the mind and the world anticipated the metaphysics of George Berkeley. Traherne, however, does not deny (as Berkeley did) that matter exists independently of the perceiving mind. (For Berkeley, the fabric of the created universe was sustained by the continuous perception of it in the mind of God.) Traherne's anti-materialism is posited tentatively and ambiguously: 'I could not tell ... truly seem'd' (ll. 46–9). The point is that the child does not know whether the world exists outside his consciousness or not, but what truly seems to him the case really is the case, for all practical purposes. The child naturally internalizes the world, but the adult in failing to do so no longer possesses it rightly: 'You never enjoy the world aright, till the sea itself floweth in your veins' (*Centuries* 1.29). 'Is it not easy to conceive the world in your mind?' (*Centuries* 1.9) – easy for the child, yes, but harder for the adult who has lost the habit. This internalization, or spiritualization, of the world does not reduce objective reality to an illusion; nevertheless, Traherne insists, 'The material world is dead' (*Centuries* 2.90) unless the human spirit acts on it by illuminating and animating it. The recurrent image of the soul as shining (ll. 2, 65, 98, 119) and the references to it as light (ll. 73, 103) echo Matthew 5:14: 'Ye are the light of the world.' For the child (or redeemed adult) as creator, cf. *Centuries* 2.91: '... every moment's preservation is a new creation.... So that though you can build or demolish such worlds as often as you please, yet it infinitely concerneth you faithfully to continue them and wisely to repair them.' The 'conforming mind' (l. 50) of the child is his shaping mind, which fashions reality after an internal pattern. This creative participation in his environment is presumably the *act* repeatedly attributed to – and indeed identified with – the child's spirit throughout the poem (ll. 2, 18, 24, 26, 29, 67, 105). In this sense, the spiritual activity of the child is analogous to the expression of God's power in the act of creation; hence Traherne's application to the child's spirit of the traditional definition of God as a circle or sphere whose centre is everywhere and whose circumference is nowhere (stanza 6): the basis of his claim that the human mind is 'nigh of kin' (l. 89) to the Deity and its conceptions closely related to the contents of the Creator's mind (ll. 114–17). Traherne, however, stops short of identifying the soul with God but treats it rather as 'An image of the Deity' (l. 72).

'Voluble' (l. 32) means not only 'protean' but also 'turning easily', like an eyeball. 'Legions' (l. 59) fuses the meanings of 'multitudes' and 'leagues'. 'Transeunt' (l. 66) is here opposed to 'immanent' (rather than 'permanent') and means 'passing outward or operating beyond itself'; I have retained Traherne's spelling, which seems to be used mainly to denote this specialized meaning. 'Supersubstantial' (l. 113) means 'transcending material substance' and was normally applied to the eucharistic bread. The notion that 'All objects' exist 'above themselves' in the mind (ll. 112–14) recalls Marvell's famous stanza 6 from *The Garden*: 'The mind, that ocean where each kind / Does straight its own resemblance find' – which includes the sense of finding a straightened or idealized image of itself. In context, Marvell's lines are another great tribute to the mind's creative power: 'Yet it creates, transcending these, / Far other worlds, and other seas.' But Traherne's infant, instead of 'annihilating all that's made' to a thought, enhances the Creator's work by illuminating it with the light of his own spirit.

Line 79 at first read 'The only proper place or Bower of Bliss', apparently an allusion to Book Two of Spenser's *Faerie Queene*, a work to which Traherne refers at least once in his recently discovered *Commentaries of Heaven*.

THE APPREHENSION

This fragment is given the stanza number one in the manuscript and is presumably a stanza from a longer poem excerpted to form a bridge between *My Spirit* and *Fullness*. The word 'this' in line 1 would therefore refer, collectively, to the affirmations made in the last stanza of the former. The 'apprehension set / In me' (ll. 5–6) is the speaker's grasp of those truths even at moments when he cannot 'see' (l. 1) them; it would be 'that thought' as opposed to that 'light' or 'sight' in line 1 of *Fullness*.

FULLNESS

The exceptional multiplicity and variety of images and allusions in this poem express its theme of plenitude, the sense of divine love filling the soul. The method is *amplificatio*, the rhetorical elaboration of a topic or idea by means of sequentially deployed imagery, and the model may be Herbert's *Prayer* [1]. Many of Traherne's favourite metaphors – light, mirror, fountain, and sphere – appear throughout the poem. Line 6 is difficult, but it seems to anticipate consummation. 'Shadow' probably means image or reflection, in conjunction with 'mirror' in line 5. Just as the light within the soul reflects eternity (l. 5), so it foreshadows ultimate union with Christ the bridegroom. (There may be an allusion to the parable of the ten virgins in Matthew 25:1–13, especially to the five wise ones who kept their lamps burning in anticipation of the bridegroom's triumphant arrival.) In lines 9–10 the speaker claims that this inward light enables him to envision, without yet 'enjoying' (i.e., experiencing directly), the perfection of his being: an idea consistent with *The Vision* – though there the vision itself was so powerful as to constitute enjoyment. 'David's tower' (l. 21) comes from the Song of Solomon 4:4: 'Thy neck is like the tower of David builded for an armoury, whereon there hang a thousand bucklers, all shields of mighty men' (a reference to Psalms 18:2 and 144:2). The golden chain (l. 28) was a Renaissance commonplace which derived ultimately from Homer's *Iliad* (VIII.18–27) by way of Plato's *Theaetetus*. Its most striking recent appearance was at the end of *Paradise Lost* II: 'And fast by hanging in a golden chain / This pendant world, in bigness as a star / Of smallest magnitude close by the moon' (ll. 1051–3). Such a classical allusion is very rare for Traherne, who is careful to attribute this image to the feigning of poets (l. 29). Finally, the stone (l. 32) that is also 'a regal throne' (l. 35) alludes to the Stone of Scone, placed under the coronation chair at Westminster Abbey; that it is oracular (l. 37) or prophetic is in keeping with the anticipatory nature of much of the poem's previous imagery.

NATURE

The title refers both to the natural world surrounding the child and to the nature of childhood itself, which is overlaid by custom (l. 1) in later life to the detriment of the 'secret self' or spiritual being 'enclos'd within' the child's body but not bounded by it (ll. 19–20). As always in Traherne, childhood experience serves as the model for redemption in maturity. Natural beauty ignites the child's soul (l. 6), generating the metaphor of fire that dominates the poem's figurative language and signifies *desire*, which – among the various impulses inspired by nature (ll. 13–16) – becomes the focus of this poem. Lines 23–32 develop the conceit of a ship's lantern to express the way the child's spirit, though immobile, 'dilates' (ll. 26, 34) itself, here as in *My Spirit*, in order to 'encompass ... rare things' (l. 29). The child's imagination 'suggests' more to him than he is able to 'discern' (l. 37), but his curiosity, driven by boundless desire, finds itself frustrated when it tries to transcend the limits of the created universe and envision 'wide infinity' (ll. 43–8). Nature, though finite, offers 'endless joys' (l. 51) and perpetually renews itself. Lines 55–6, reminiscent of 'Time's winged chariot' from Marvell's *To His Coy Mistress*, were inserted marginally, apparently as an afterthought: perhaps to acknowledge mutability within a framework of cyclical order in nature. Finally, the child overcomes the frustration mentioned earlier as his 'pent-up soul' erupts 'like fire' into the vacant spaces of infinity as yet unused by created nature and finds 'new rooms' there (ll. 71–4). Imagination or 'fancy' (l. 78) rescues his soul from the 'doubts and troubles' (l. 49) it felt before by 'enlarging' (ll. 64, 78) its vision (*enlarge* here means both 'increase in scope' and 'set free'). Lines 67–8 contradict the negative view taken of language in *Dumbness* and *Silence* and corroborate *Centuries* 3.36 on the benefits Traherne received from formal education as an aid to the 'enlargement' of the soul's imaginative capacity.

EASE

Having dealt with specific lessons taught by Nature, the poet marvels at the ease (ll. 1, 9) with which the soul absorbs these teachings (subsequently untaught by custom, although that issue does not arise here). The core of the poem and the sum total of Nature's doctrine is in stanza 5, where Traherne reaffirms his favourite paradox that each individual person is 'possessor of the whole' – the unique beneficiary of creation, just as Adam was (l. 20) before other human beings existed: a circumstance that makes each of us godlike (l. 19) and worthy of veneration (l. 21). 'Whom' (l. 21) refers to 'every man'

(l. 18), who is loved by God even before God is known to him (l. 22). 'All others' (l. 24) probably means other creatures on earth, over which man was given dominion (Genesis 1:26). In contrast, the 'others' of line 26 are our fellow human beings, who – no less than ourselves – are 'each one most blest' (l. 25) and whose joys are 'intermutual' (l. 28) with our own. The understanding of these truths communicated by Nature 'discovers' (l. 29) to each of us the God who was at first 'unknown' (l. 22).

SPEED

The sensuously detailed imagery of the opening stanzas amplifies the theme of *Ease*, while the euphonious writing reinforces the impression of speed: everything truly worthwhile on earth was 'in a moment known' (l. 3) to the speaker 'as soon as [he] was born' (l. 6). This poem is comparable to *Wonder* in the way it registers the young child's sensations and impressions while using the adult speaker's vantage point to provide glimpses of the distorted values that eventually 'eclips'd' his 'new burnish'd joys' (ll. 25–7) and of 'filthy sin', which 'did all destroy' (l. 35): references that make this a much darker poem than *Ease* even though both affirm 'how docible our nature is, in natural things, were it rightly entreated' (*Centuries* 3.8). The phrase 'other toys' in line 26 is an ellipsis for other things, which were toys in comparison to the 'sacred objects' (l. 23) with which the child perceived himself to be surrounded as enumerated in stanzas 1–3.

THE DESIGN

Retitled *The Choice* by Philip in both the Dobell MS and *Poems of Felicity*, this poem perhaps derives its original title from the concept of an 'inner design' or *disegno interno* as found in Mannerist art theory. (See Federico Zuccaro, *L'Idea de' Pittori, Scultori e Architetti* [1607].) Just as an artificer creates artifacts by working from an idea or *disegno* conceived in his mind, so the Creator (here personified as Eternity) sought and found in the visible creation His 'likeness' (l. 2) – a concrete projection of the divine, immaterial Idea – where previously there was nothing (ll. 1, 3). (Cf. Ben Jonson's *Masque of Beauty* [1608]: 'the great Artificer, in love with his own *Idea*, did therefore frame the world.') Traherne works with personified abstractions throughout the poem. Proverbially, Truth was the daughter of Time, but Traherne makes her the daughter of Eternity: the essential, immutable Platonic idea of Truth, exempt from the relativity of time-begotten 'truths'. For 'other toys' (l. 14), cf. the note on line 26 of *Speed* above. Truth 'antedates' such toys (i.e., falsely prized artificial wealth as opposed to 'Things truly greatest, brightest, fairest, best' [l. 8]) by pre-empting our affections in childhood. Truth is the 'virgin love' of line 17 and 'the great queen of bliss' of lines 33–4, and rival claimants that try to allure or 'captivate' our thoughts are pretenders (ll. 35–6). The natural kingship of every person's soul (ll. 47, 50) is confirmed by the fact that Eternity 'contrived' (l. 37) – i.e., designed – to make Truth so attractive to the infant soul that a royal marriage would be the inevitable outcome. In the manner of *Ease* and *Speed*, *The Design* stresses (ll. 39, 55–9) how easily and quickly the soul recognizes and embraces Truth, in sharp contrast to Donne's *Satire III*, where, 'On a huge hill, / Cragged and steep, Truth stands, and he that will / Reach her, about must, and about must go; / And what the hill's suddenness resists, win so' (ll. 79–82).

In line 53, Traherne wrote 'chiefest bride', which Philip corrected to 'only bride'. This is the only instance where the present edition adopts one of Philip's revisions of a Dobell poem – on the assumption that (as Margoliouth guessed) Thomas mistakenly transcribed 'chiefest' from the next line; the implication of polygamy makes no sense whatever in the context of the poem.

THE PERSON

The title refers to the human body, which is celebrated in this poem. (Cf. *Thanksgivings for the Body*.) The speaker begins in the vein of the Elizabethan lyric type known as the *blazon* (l. 2) – a lover's catalogue, often in elaborately metaphorical terms, of his mistress's physical beauties – and, indeed, addresses his own limbs (l. 1) as though he were addressing a mistress. (The phrase 'than first I found' in line 3 seems to refer back to the speaker's first ecstatic but bewildered response to his own body as expressed at the beginning of *The Salutation*.) But in a sudden reversal the conclusion of the opening stanza sabotages the poem's generic prototype: the promised adornment will be a radically reductive process of 'taking all away' (l. 16) in order 'to display the thing' (l. 14). As in *King Lear* III.iv, 'the thing itself' is revealed by the removal of 'sophisticated' man's 'lendings'. The attitude towards metaphor expressed in stanza 2 is consistent with Traherne's aesthetic manifesto, *The Author to the Critical Peruser*. Here, as there, metaphorical images are rejected as illusory. Human hands are 'truer wealth' than angels' wings (ll. 20–21) because the latter, being immaterial, can be envisioned only in figurative terms which merely 'seem' (l. 22), as opposed to the literal physicality of the body (an apparent departure from the Neoplatonism of *The Preparative*). In an original development of the 'blazon' motif (ll. 27–32) the speaker calls not just for disrobing but for dissection as the flesh itself becomes (like metaphor) an ornamental covering that conceals the glory of the internal anatomy. Unlike Marvell's *Dialogue between the Soul and Body*, there is no sense here of the soul's being 'hung up ... in chains / Of nerves and arteries and veins'. For Traherne, body and soul co-exist harmoniously (l. 62). 'Brave' in lines 38–9 means splendid. The lilies and roses of line 45, though conventional, may derive immediately from the second of Herbert's two early sonnets to his mother quoted in Izaak Walton's *Lives* (1670): 'Roses and lilies speak Thee; and to make / A pair of cheeks of them is Thy abuse.' Although both poets attack the premises of the erotic blazon, the thrusts of their respective attacks are different. The conclusion of Traherne's second stanza sharply contradicts Herbert's 'Open the bones, and you shall nothing find / In the best face but filth.'

THE ESTATE

'But' at the beginning makes this poem a response to *The Person*; its opening stanza addresses questions raised by that poem and not fully resolved until the end of this one. What is the soul's estate – its inherited property and possessions (not its condition)? The body, though wonderful, is destined to be 'straight' (l. 5) – i.e., immediately – devoured by the grave and is thus an insufficient estate for a soul endowed (l. 8) by a divine Creator. As in Shakespeare's Sonnet 146 – which asks, 'Shall worms, inheritors of this excess, / Eat up thy charge? Is this thy body's end?' – the speaker recognizes that he is only a tenant and not a possessor of his body; for a true estate, consisting of spiritual wealth (l. 1), he must look elsewhere. 'Outward' (ll. 2, 11, 13) means beyond the limits of the self, as opposed to 'within myself' (l. 6). The 'stone' of line 15 is a touchstone (as Philip's revision makes clear) for 'trying' or testing the quality of precious metals. 'They' in line 29 refers back to the parts of the body listed in stanza 2, which are seen as 'conduits' (l. 30) communicating between the soul within and God as manifested in His 'outward' creation. Mortification of the flesh (l. 31) is rejected as unworthy of the body's divine purpose (ll. 34–5), which is fulfilled in the manner described in stanzas 3 and 4. 'Disburse' in line 37 echoes and plays on 'dispersed' (l. 36). Bodies are 'like suns' (l. 35) because they transmit in all directions the beams of God's love with which the soul has been inflamed (l. 42) in a way analogous to the circulation of water between rivers and the ocean (ll. 40–41). This idea is amplified in stanza 4, where the 'elixirs' of line 43 are human love, gratitude, and affections returned to God (ll. 52–5). Using the imagery of the four elements – earth, air, fire, and water – the last stanza triumphantly answers the questions that troubled the speaker in the first stanza. The image of ploughing the skies (l. 57), by depicting the universe as a working farm (cf. *Shadows in the Water*, ll. 49–52: 'Within the regions of the air, / Compass'd about with heavens fair, / Great tracts of land there may be found / Enrich'd with fields and fertile ground'), reflects the dominant metaphor of the estate, explicitly mentioned for the first time at the end of the poem. In *Poems of Felicity* Philip's extensive alterations of this stanza, which he must have considered too fanciful, exemplify his heavy-handed editorial procedure:

> For this the heavens were made as well
>   As earth, the spacious seas
> Are ours: the stars that gems excel,
>   And air, design'd to please
> Our earthly part; the very fire
> For uses which our needs require:
> The orb of light in its wide circuit moves;
> Corn for our food springs out of very mire;
> Fences and fuel grow in woods and groves;
>   Choice herbs and flowers aspire
> To kiss our feet; beasts court our loves.
>   How glorious is man's fate!

The laws of God, the works He did create,
His ancient ways, are His and my estate.

THE INQUIRY

The title refers to the questions asked in stanza 2 – which are all variants of the same query: Can the angels, from their intermediate position between man and God, take any delight in the varied sensory pleasures the earth offers its inhabitants? It may be that men only think their bodies admirable (ll. 4–5), and that to the more refined senses of superior beings 'perfumes' are only the stench of 'dunghills' (l. 9). But the poem gives a positive answer to the question it poses. Apropos of stanzas 3–5, cf. *Paradise Lost* V.397–433. Adam, too, fears that the meal of paradisal fruits he offers the archangel Raphael will be 'unsavoury food perhaps / To spiritual natures', but Raphael assures him that 'pure / Intelligential substances ... contain / Within them every lower faculty / Of sense, whereby they hear, see, smell, touch, taste' and that 'God hath here / Varied His bounty so with new delights, / As may compare with Heaven'. Similarly, in *The Immortality of the Soul* (1659) the Cambridge Platonist Henry More had argued that angels 'have ... something analogical to smell and taste'. When Traherne's speaker renews his interrogation in stanza 6, the question is strictly rhetorical (ll. 31–2). Man's glory is that although earthly delights are capable of gratifying even angelic tastes, they were created for *us*. Apropos of line 18, see 1 Kings 6:29, where cherubim and palm trees figure in the iconography of Solomon's temple.

THE CIRCULATION

This is the first of the poems in the Dobell sequence not to be found also in the manuscript of *Poems of Felicity* prepared by Philip Traherne. None of the remaining Dobell poems appears in Philip's manuscript; consequently, all exist only in the author's autograph version. *The Circulation* reaffirms the answer given to *The Inquiry* (ll. 20–21) and defines more precisely the conditions under which we possess our human *Estate* (ll. 10, 41–2). The poem uses many examples (especially in stanzas 4 and 5) to illustrate its theme, which is explicitly stated in lines 29–31 and again in line 71. There are, nevertheless, difficulties. The 'fair ideas' of line 1 are more Platonic than Cartesian because they come 'from the sky' (i.e., Heaven) rather than being products of our own intellectual activity. They are archetypal forms or patterns, which when they 'borrow matter' (l. 38) in order to 'communicate' (ll. 8, 39, 42) take on the 'livery' (l. 37) of *things* (ll. 2, 29). The opening stanza compares these ideas to mirror-images abstracted from the bodies they represent. Just as such images somehow 'fly' (ll. 3–4) from objects to the mirror and, when reflected, appear to emanate from it (ll. 5–6), so the ideas when embodied in matter (to which they also 'fly', from above) fool our senses by appearing to originate there. Both phenomena (reflections and the materialization of forms) by 'communicating' with our senses illustrate the principle of circulation – of giving what has been received. For Traherne the soul itself is a mirror (cf. stanza 6 of *The Preparative*) – and before the onset of sin, just such a 'spotless' one as in line 3 of this poem, capable of receiving from Heaven 'The fair ideas of all things' (*The Preparative*, l. 25).

Imagination ('fancy', l. 62) concocts 'even dreams' from 'receiv'd ideas' (l. 61) rather than innate ones, which explains the presence of evil in Eve's dream that so puzzled Adam: 'Yet evil whence? in thee can harbour none, / Created pure' (*Paradise Lost* V.99–100). In order to produce Eve's dream, Satan disturbed her 'animal spirits' (*Paradise Lost* IV.805); these are the same 'spirits' in which sight is 'cherished' or nurtured in *The Circulation* (l. 64). According to the ancient Galenic physiology, blood was heated in the heart (a furnace rather than a pump), vaporized, and further refined at the base of the brain into animal spirits, which played a role in sense perception; Marsilio Ficino, in his *Commentary on Plato's Symposium*, calls them 'the chariots or vehicles of the soul'. That Traherne has based this part of his argument on the old, pre-Harveian physiology explains his omission of one example of circulation that we might have expected to find: that of the blood. Even the 'inward light' that ministers to the imagination's creative activity (ll. 62–3) is more derivative – that is, directed inward from outside – than was the 'inner light' of such illuminists as George Fox of the Quakers. Like the moon (l. 65) with which it is implicitly compared, the soul reflects light from an external source and is fed by 'foreign aids' as is the sun (ll. 66–8) or fire (ll. 57–8). (The context forces this interpretation of 'inward light' even though Traherne in *My Spirit* comes very close to claiming that the soul generates its own light.) Stanza 5 gains in meaning, as does *The Inquiry*, from a recollection of Raphael's lecture to Adam in *Paradise Lost* V.404-33: 'For know, whatever was created, needs / To be sustain'd and fed; of elements/ The grosser feeds the purer, earth the sea, / Earth and the sea feed air, the air those fires / Ethereal.... The sun that light imparts to all, receives / From all his alimental recompense / In humid exhalations, and at even / Sups with the ocean.' 'Exhalations' (l. 69), here as in Milton, are hot and dry evaporations believed to be drawn up by the sun; mixed with cold and moist 'vapours' in varying proportions, they accounted for a variety of atmospheric phenomena according to Aristotle's *Meteorologica*. The earth is said to have 'spirits' (l. 70) by analogy with the microcosm of the human body.

For Traherne, this universal reciprocity means that people, if they still had the 'celestial' (l. 25) vision of infancy or of unfallen human nature, would spontaneously 'overflow' (l. 27) with praises for the blessings they would then be able to perceive. But because blinded by sin, we are struck dumb (l. 24), thus interrupting the circulatory flow of love from God to man and back to God. Apropos of stanza 2, cf. *Centuries* 2.94: 'Men's lips are closed because their eyes are blinded.... As no man can breathe out more air than he draweth in, so no man can offer up more praises than he receiveth benefits, to return in praises.... and the praises which He desires are the reflection of His beams, which will not return till they are apprehended.' The poem ends on a positive note by expressing the right relationship in terms of the interchange of water between rivers and the sea (as in *The Estate*, ll. 40-42; cf. also Ecclesiastes 1:7: 'All the rivers run into the sea; yet the sea is not full; unto the place from whence the rivers come, thither they return again').

AMENDMENT

In theme as well as title *The Improvement* is here recalled: 'O how doth sacred love / His gifts refine, exalt, improve!' (ll. 43-4). As in *The Circulation* and elsewhere, the human soul is a *mirror* (l. 34) reflecting love and praise back to the Deity, who takes more delight in His creation as 'amended' by the human response to it than in the act of bringing it into being (stanza 6). Similarly, the poem itself 'amends' the last stanza of *The Circulation*, where it was suggested that God alone is 'all-sufficient', living 'from and in Himself' and thus immune to the principle of reciprocity that governs everything else: a conclusion now shown to be untenable.

THE DEMONSTRATION

The title refers to the argument that reaches its paradoxical conclusion in stanza 3: 'And for this cause incredibles alone / May be by demonstration to us shown.' The idea developed in terms of the sun-image in the first three stanzas is similar to that expressed in Donne's *Satire III*, lines 87-8: 'mysteries / Are like the sun, dazzling, yet plain to all eyes.' The 'incredible' truth made 'plain and clear' (l. 41) to the eye of intellect in this poem is stated in lines 37-40 and elaborated throughout the poem as a whole: 'Returning from us', God's gifts 'more value get' (l. 40). Every created thing – even 'a sand, an acorn, or a bean' – is enhanced by being 'truly seen' (ll. 25-30), for which purpose human senses are required. Consequently, the Deity depends on us for enjoyment of His works: 'In them [His creatures] He sees, and feels, and smells, and lives' (l. 71).

THE ANTICIPATION

Well might the speaker's contemplation 'dazzle' in the *end* (which is God) of his own comprehension (ll. 1-2). The poems in this group, the analytical portion of Traherne's meditative sequence (i.e., from *Amendment* through *Another*) attempt to define the nature of the Deity in conceptual terms. This poem's enigmatic title could be intended to suggest that God's wants anticipate their own satisfaction and are, in fact, satisfied by virtue of their very existence. Anticipation and fulfilment are thus simultaneous because 'His endless wants and His enjoyments be / From all eternity, / Immutable in Him' (ll. 55-7). Previous poems – especially *The Demonstration* – have argued that the creatures are the means by which the Deity enjoys His works. But such an argument is shown to be full of 'sands' and 'dangerous rocks' (l. 13) because it tends to separate the means (creatures) from the cause and end (God): 'None can His creatures from their maker sever' (l. 27). God is eternally creative: 'His essence is all act' (l. 91). Cf. *Centuries* 3.64: 'Were there any power in God unemployed He would be compounded of power and act. Being therefore God is all act, He is a God in this, that Himself is power exerted. An infinite act because infinite power infinitely exerted, an eternal act because infinite power eternally exerted'. Cf. also *Centuries* 2.84: 'God is a being whose power from all eternity was prevented with act'. (*Prevented*, as used here, is synonymous with *anticipated*, as when Hamlet tells Rosencrantz and Guildenstern, 'So shall my anticipation prevent your discovery' [*Hamlet* II.ii].) This means that God's creatures, the means by which His glory is expressed, are eternally part of God ('in Him', l. 107) because His power to create them is eternally exerted in response to His need for them. On God's wants and needs, see *Centuries* 1.41–3: 'This is very strange that God should want, for in Him is the fullness of all blessedness: He overfloweth eternally. His wants are as glorious as infinite. Perfective needs that are in His nature, and ever blessed, because always satisfied. ... He wanted angels and men, images, companions. And these He had from all eternity.' Similarly, according to the poem, what God 'infinitely wanteth ... He infinitely hath' (ll. 73–6); nevertheless, 'Possession doth not cloy' or eliminate the sense of want: 'Both always are together' (ll. 82–4). The poem's conclusion is to reverse the premise of earlier poems in the sequence: 'He is the means of them [His creatures], they not of Him' (l. 109). His threefold holiness is affirmed, echoing Isaiah 6:3 and Revelation 4:8, as the union of 'fountain, means, and end' (ll. 115–17) – Aristotle's first, efficient, and final causes – thereby revealing 'the unity of the blessed Trinity, and a glorious Trinity in the blessed unity' (*Centuries* 2.45, where the Father is the fountain, the Son the means [as mediator between God and His creatures], and the Holy Ghost the end).

THE RECOVERY

The speaker *recovers* from the dazzling effect of the truths about the Deity that his contemplation led him to comprehend in *The Anticipation* and is thus able to review the theme of *Amendment* and *The Demonstration* in the light of those truths. That theme is God's *recovery* of the benefits showered upon mankind in the form of 'A heart return'd for all these joys' (l. 56) by a single 'voluntary act of love' (l. 68). The most concrete expression of this idea occurs in the fourth stanza, with the traditional image of God as the bridegroom – derived from such texts as Isaiah 62:5: ' ... as the bridegroom rejoiceth over the bride, so shall thy God rejoice over thee.' A distinctive device used in this poem is the pairing of contrasted verb-clusters in stanza 2. All the participles in the first part of the stanza contribute to the definition of 'receiv'd' (l. 17), thus clarifying the poem's opening line. The opposite of 'receiv'd' is 'denied' (l. 20), which culminates an alliterative series including 'undeified': human indifference deprives the Deity of the very end of His being, which is 'God enjoy'd' (l. 11).

ANOTHER

In an angrier version of *The Recovery*, the poet castigates coldness, carelessness, and indifference (stanza 3) in himself as well as in others. The message to his own soul is 'Set forth thyself unto thy whole extent' (l. 18): live to the height of the soul's capacity by fully experiencing divine love, unlike those who could be content (l. 11) without it. Human love in itself would be nothing, were it not infinitely valued by the Deity (stanza 9). *Another* thus looks forward to *Love* as much as it looks backwards to *The Recovery*.

LOVE

This is Traherne's most ecstatic account of mystical union with the Deity. Its daring sexual imagery perhaps recalls some of Donne's *Holy Sonnets*, such as 'Batter my heart' or 'Show me, dear Christ', but in sensuous expressiveness it is more comparable to Richard Crashaw's St Teresa poems. Moreover, *Love* is exceptional among Traherne's works in that it contains two of his extremely rare mythological allusions, both of which refer to amatory exploits by the king of the gods. *Danae* (l. 30) became the mother of Perseus when Jupiter, as a shower of gold falling into her lap, impregnated her. Smitten with the beauty of the young boy *Ganymede* (l. 31), whom he had seen bathing, Jupiter as an eagle carried him up to Mount Olympus, where he became cup-bearer to the gods. Traherne finds in the latter myth an analogy to his own vocation as bearer of the Communion chalice. There is precedent for his allusion to Ganymede in George Wither's *A Collection of Emblems* III.22 (1635), where the boy on the eagle's back illustrates the motto 'Take wing, my soul, and mount up higher; / For earth fulfils not my desire.' (Ganymede's bath is baptism, the eagle contemplation, and the cup of nectar delight in Heaven over reclaimed sinners.) In a similar way, Traherne finds truths 'beyond the fiction' (l. 28) in these myths. Nevertheless, finding them in the end 'Too weak and feeble pictures to express' the poem's real subject – 'The true mysterious depths of blessedness' (ll. 37–8) – he abandons them in favour of the less vivid but more direct and perhaps more profound metaphors (ll. 39–40) used in various passages of the Bible to represent the relationship between the human and the divine.

Abridgement (l. 5) means 'epitome'. For lines 11–15, .cf. *Centuries* 3.29: 'Above all things I desired some great lord or mighty king, that having power in his hand, to give me all kingdoms, riches, and honours, was willing to do it.'

THOUGHTS I

Stylistically, the first of the *Thoughts* poems bears a close resemblance to *Love*. As in that poem, an exclamatory outburst of apostrophes characterizes the speaker's attitude towards his subject matter. Thematically, *Thoughts I* is linked with both *Love* and *The Recovery* because the speaker's absorption of the created world into his mind, which thereby becomes 'lin'd' (l. 58) with the physical objects that his thoughts inwardly 'represent' (l. 45), is the 'voluntary act of love' that enables him to 'receive' (*The Recovery*, ll. 68 and 1) the gift of creation in such a way as to delight his benefactor. This idea, which underlies all of the *Thoughts* poems, is explained in *Centuries* 2.90: 'the thought of the world whereby it is enjoyed is better than the world. So is the idea of it in the soul of man better than the world in the esteem of God: it being the end of the world, without which Heaven and earth would be in vain. It is better to you, because by it you receive the world, and it is the tribute you pay.... The world within you is an offering returned.' This explains the speaker's unqualified assertion that his own thoughts yield 'better meat' for his 'soul to eat' than even such natural objects as sky, sun, and stars (ll. 40–46). The bees of stanza 7 (cf. stanza 6 of *Walking*) are an especially apt metaphor to depict these thoughts that range throughout the world 'And suck the sweet from thence', thus acting 'As tasters to the Deity' (ll. 75–7) who, as in stanzas 5 and 8 of *The Demonstration*, depends on human senses and human souls for His enjoyment of the world.

In celebrating the mobility and ubiquity of thoughts which, while 'pent within my breast, / Yet rove at large from east to west' (ll. 9–10), Traherne recalls Meditation IV from Donne's *Devotions upon*

Emergent Occasions: 'Enlarge this meditation upon this great world, man, so far as to consider the immensity of the creatures this world produces; our creatures are our thoughts, creatures that are born giants, that reach from east to west, from earth to heaven, that do not only bestride all the sea and land but span the sun and firmament at once; my thoughts reach all, comprehend all.' But Traherne's ecstatic sixth stanza – 'The eye's confin'd, the body's pent / In narrow room: limbs are of small extent. / But thoughts are always free. . . . They know no bar, denial, limit, wall: / But have a liberty to look on all' – contrasts strongly with the pessimistic outcome of Donne's meditative act: 'Call back therefore thy meditation and bring it down. What's become of man's great extent and proportion when himself shrinks himself and consumes himself to a handful of dust? What's become of his soaring thoughts, his compassing thoughts when himself brings himself to the ignorance, to the thoughtlessness, of the grave?'

BLISS

No two poems in the *Thoughts* series are consecutive. Needing a poem to insert between *Thoughts I* and *II*, Traherne excerpted the fifth and sixth stanzas from a longer poem, *The Apostasy* (the complete text of which is found in the Burney MS), and called the result *Bliss* (an appropriate topic in the light of *Thoughts I*, ll. 47 and 56). Readers who wish to compare the two extant versions of this pair of stanzas will discover many differences, which could be accounted for in one or both of two ways. Either Philip Traherne revised (as was his habit) a hypothetical original version of *The Apostasy* containing the stanzas as they appear here, or Thomas, as he transcribed the stanzas into the Dobell MS, revised the version that Philip later used for *Poems of Felicity*. (This is what Thomas did in the case of *The Approach*, an earlier version of which appears as *Centuries* 3.4.)

THOUGHTS II

In *Thoughts I* the speaker's thoughts were portrayed as dynamic, powerful entities: 'machines' and 'engines' (ll. 4, 6). In *Thoughts II*, however, the imagery is organic, emphasizing vulnerability and perishability: a thought is 'delicate and tender' (l. 1); 'It withers straight, and fades away' (l. 11). But this happens only if we fail to display its beauty (l. 12) to God by lovingly nurturing that 'fine and curious flower' (l. 7) conceived in our own souls, which becomes 'the fruit of all His works' (ll. 3–4) when we 'return, and offer' it to Him; this, however, must be done constantly – 'every hour' (l. 8). The initial emphasis on evanescence – on how thoughts are 'So prone, so easy, and so apt to fade' (l. 14) – thus serves to heighten the sense of our own responsibility to 'maintain' (l. 20) by 'continual care' (l. 18) that 'spiritual world within' (l. 43) which constitutes 'our Paradise' (l. 9). Again, the appropriate gloss is *Centuries* 2.90: 'The world within you is an offering returned ... the voluntary act of an obedient soul.' Apropos of stanza 2, on the 'continual care' required to 'maintain a tower' (ll. 18–20), cf. also *Centuries* 2.91: ' ... in the continual series of thoughts whereby we continue to uphold the frame of Heaven and earth in the soul towards God, every thought is another world to the Deity as acceptable as the first ... to continue serious in upholding these thoughts for God's sake, is the part of a faithful and loving soul.' By such careful maintenance, this 'spiritual world within' proves capable of enduring forever while the created world 'doth fade' (ll. 43–7); thus thoughts themselves prove immutable in a paradoxical reversal of the poem's opening stanza. For the temple that David intended to build and why it was built instead by Solomon, see 1 Chronicles 22:7–11 and 28:2–3; this reference occurs again in *The Inference* (see note to that poem, p. 363).

'YE HIDDEN NECTARS' (UNTITLED)

In a return to the ecstatic mode of *Thoughts I*, the poet celebrates the mind's power to internalize its surroundings and in doing so preserve them from decay (ll. 8, 38). Even though thoughts are only 'shades' – images of things – they are superior to 'substances' – things themselves – because spiritual (ll. 6–7, 17) rather than material. The poem actually makes a subtle argument about the transactions between spirit and matter and is thus Traherne's answer to Cartesianism. When Bertram Dobell entitled this poem *The Influx*, he may have been thinking of a passage from *Centuries* 2.87: 'God hath made it easy to convert our soul into a thought containing Heaven and earth.... Which thought is as easily abolished, that by a perpetual influx of life it may be maintained.' In stanza 3, the speaker observes that man is inanimate 'clay', 'stone', or 'dust' (ll. 25–6) without such an influx – that is, unless his senses are 'invaded' (l. 27) and his mind 'informed' (l. 29) by the thoughts, earlier called 'living pictures' (l. 16), that enable his soul to comprise the world around him. For Traherne, however, this power of thinking guarantees not merely existence, as it did for Descartes, but 'blessedness' (l. 24). The image of 'hidden nectars' (l. 1) recalls both *Love*, where the cup that Ganymede shares with Jove contains nectar, and *Thoughts I*, where human thoughts are bees sucking nectar from the world and tasting it on behalf of the Deity.

THOUGHTS III

The theme of the *Thoughts* series is here transposed from epistemological and metaphysical into ethical terms. Recalling once again the bees from stanza 7 of *Thoughts I*, the speaker acknowledges for the first time that both 'the honey and the stings / Of all that is, are seated in a thought' (ll. 22–3). 'Grief, anger, hate, revenge' consist of thoughts no less than do 'pleasure, virtue, worth' (ll. 25–7), and a thought is therefore either 'The very best or worst of things': the source 'of all misery or bliss' (ll. 59–60). But while admitting this duality, which of course reflects our fallen natures, the poem continues to emphasize the positive quality of thoughts, which, as elsewhere in the series, are the 'crown' and 'cream' (ll. 15, 18) of creation and confirm our kingship – though only if 'rightly used' (l. 78). Several lines (ll. 33–50) are devoted to the protean character of thoughts, which differ from matter in not being 'assign'd' (l. 34) a definite form and are thus 'free' (ll. 35, 46) to assume any or all forms; they are 'nimble', 'volatile', 'changeable', 'capacious', 'active', 'voluble' (i.e., mobile), etc., so 'That what itself doth please a thought may be' (l. 36). Yet this very openness means that thoughts possess the capacity for both good and evil.

DESIRE

Calling thoughts 'extensions' in line 16 exhibits the same kind of wit as Marvell's 'my extended soul' in *The Definition of Love*. Both phrases are oxymorons because extension is the property of matter that radically differentiates it from mind in the Cartesian dualism. In the *ubi sunt* passage (stanza 3) the remembered Eden of childhood merges with the pastoral landscape of the 23rd Psalm and the towers (l. 33) of the new Jerusalem (cf. *The City*), but none of these images – being 'material' (l. 38) and therefore dead – is able to satisfy the inborn thirst of the soul. The structure of this stanza is reminiscent of *Paradise Lost* IV.641–56, where Eve, after listing the delightful features of Paradise, immediately recapitulates the whole catalogue only to deny the pleasurable quality she has just attributed to them: nothing is delightful in itself – i.e., without Adam. Similarly, for Traherne, 'not the objects, but the sense / Of things, doth bliss to souls dispense' (ll. 57–8). 'Propriety' (l. 52) means ownership; 'complacency' (l. 60), far from having its bland modern sense, means *delight*. 'All which' (l. 64) refers to the 'the true and real joys' (l. 61). That all such joys 'are founded in desire' – and thus in the very privations of stanza 2 – is an idea expressed in *The Anticipation*, where 'Wants are the fountains of felicity' (l. 64), and in *Centuries* 1.41: 'Were there no needs, wants would be wanting themselves, and supplies superfluous: want being the parent of celestial treasure.'

THOUGHTS IV

The four poems comprising the *Thoughts* series were left unnumbered in manuscript; it was Philip Traherne who later supplied the Roman numerals. For *Thoughts IV*, however, Philip entered a dash followed by the number; the poet himself had used the quotation from Psalms 16:11 in lieu of a title. All modern editors have adopted the title *Thoughts IV*, which probably reflects the intent of Thomas Traherne, who seems to have given special care to the arrangement of poems within this final group contained in the Dobell MS. As a series, the *Thoughts* poems are preceded by *Love* and followed by *Goodness* (a poem about the communication of love among human beings). *Thoughts I* and *II* are separated by *Bliss*; *Thoughts II* and *III* by an untitled but closely related poem, 'Ye hidden nectars'; and *Thoughts III* and *IV* by *Desire*. One intended effect of this symmetrical grouping may have been to invite the reader to make connections between the human capacity for thought and those attributes of the soul – love, bliss, desire, and goodness – that are thereby promoted. Since these qualities are depicted as belonging to a mature spirituality, the *Thoughts* series may be seen as balancing the group of poems on childhood at the beginning of the

Dobell MS and thus imparting symmetry to the design of the volume as a whole.

In *Thoughts IV*, Traherne follows the lead of his epigraph from Psalms by employing his thoughts to imagine himself transported into the divine presence, as Elijah was by the chariot of fire in 2 Kings 2:11 (ll. 3–4). In fact, thoughts, by enabling us rightly to *see*, reveal that we are already in Heaven 'Even here on earth' (ll. 35–6). A story about the prophet Elisha taken from 2 Kings 6:11–19 serves as a parable of our condition. Just as Elisha's servant could not see that he and his master were miraculously guarded by 'mountains, chariots, horsemen all on fire' until the prophet asked the Lord to open his eyes, so we ourselves are habitually *blind* to the joys that 'environ' us in this world (ll. 37–40), which are enumerated in the lines that follow. The poem, and the *Thoughts* series, ends with a prayer as the speaker petitions for grace to transform his soul into a thought so that he might become 'A constant mirror of eternity' (ll. 95–7): a metaphor that sums up much of the content of the series.

GOODNESS

Having established right principles (l. 2) in the poems immediately preceding this one, Traherne now concludes the Dobell sequence by applying such principles to his relationship with other human beings. Just as God finds felicity in our enjoyment of the world, so the speaker emulates the Deity by delighting in the bliss of others. His 'infinity' is the sum total of the blessings he has received from God, which nevertheless would be reduced to a 'drop' (ll. 11–12) were not others similarly favoured. Cf. the quotation from St Gregory in *Centuries* 3.65: 'it was by no means sufficient for *goodness* to move only in the contemplation of itself but it became what was *good* to be diffused and propagated, that more might be affected with the benefit (for this was the part of the highest goodness).' People – and, more specifically, the eyes and lips by means of which they communicate – are represented by metaphors of stars (ll. 19–24, 53–4, 63) and grapes on grapevines (ll. 14, 24, 49–53, 55, 65) responding to the light and heat of the sun (God) by shining and ripening, so it seems, for the benefit of the speaker. 'Bleeding' (l. 24) is apparently an agricultural term referring to abundant fruition or perhaps to wine pressed from grapes – but *not* intended to recall the bleeding vines crushed in the winepress of God's wrath in Revelation 14:19–20.

Poems of Felicity

THE AUTHOR TO THE CRITICAL PERUSER

If Traherne had what nowadays might be called an 'aesthetic credo', this poem would be his statement of it. The poem may have received its title from Philip, who placed the initials 'T. T.' after it to distinguish it (as does the word 'Author' in the title) from the two poems by Philip himself that flank this one at the beginning of the manuscript: *The Dedication* and *The Publisher to the Reader*. The stylistic values endorsed here are similar to those espoused by George Herbert in *Jordan* [2], from which the 'curling metaphors' of line 11 are borrowed, and more ambivalently in *The Forerunners*. Moreover, lines 17–20 may emulate Sir John Denham's well-known lines from *Cooper's Hill* (1655) expressing the wish that his verse resemble the Thames: 'Though deep, yet clear, though gentle, yet not dull, / Strong without rage, without o'erflowing full.' 'Gold on gold' is 'baser' (ll. 15–16) because it violates a fundamental rule of heraldry against superimposing a colour or a metal on itself. *Zamzummims* are giants mentioned in Deuteronomy 2:20; 'Zamzummim words' (l. 21) would therefore be language afflicted with gigantism. *Babel-hell* (l. 22) must refer to the punishment imposed on the presumptuous builders of the tower of Babel when the Lord confounded their language (Genesis 11:7–9). The rivers Tagus, in Spain, and Pactolus, in Asia Minor (ancient Lydia), are 'shining' and 'rich' (ll. 25–6) because their sands contain gold. (According to mythology, it was in the latter river that King Midas bathed to rid himself of his golden touch.) Tagus ('Neptune's treasure-house') and Pactolus are mentioned together at the beginning of Ode II from Abraham Cowley's *Sylva* (1637).

Most of the stylistic excesses repudiated in *The Author to the Critical Peruser* are associated with late metaphysical poetry. Although Traherne expresses here, as in *The Person*, a distrust of metaphor and other kinds of figurative language, it would be a mistake to assume that his own best work relies exclusively on statement. Rather, it is often richly metaphorical (e.g., *The Odour*) and even capable of conducting an argument by developing an elaborate conceit (e.g., *Bells*). Poets who resort to excessive rhetorical artifice exemplify a whole category of people: those who magnify their own works at the expense of God's (l. 43). In its underlying theme the poem is thus an appropriate introduction to *Poems of Felicity*: the 'simple light' (l. 3) by which the soul's objects are best viewed (ll. 7–9) reappears in the opening line of *An Infant-Eye*, which was designed to follow this poem. Philip separated the two poems with his own address to the reader and with the first four poems from the Dobell MS; the present edition brings them back into juxtaposition.

AN INFANT-EYE

In keeping with the stylistic simplicity called for in *The Author to the Critical Peruser*, this poem uses the 'infant-eye' to represent simplicity of vision. 'Visive' (l. 7) refers to the power of seeing, which was sometimes known as the 'visive virtue'. This word is important here, as it is also in *Sight* (l. 23), because it depicts sight as an active faculty, not just as a passive receiver of sense impressions. According to one Renaissance theory of sight, the eye projects beams that illuminate the object on which they focus. The 'animal spirits' (see note to *The Circulation*, p. 334) travel along these beams, or 'visive rays' (l. 7), and convey the image of that object to the mind. Philip, recognizing the importance of this poem to the themes of the whole volume, subtitled *Poems of Felicity* 'Divine Reflections on the Native Objects of an Infant-eye'. These are the 'first objects' (l. 50), enumerated in stanza 6, but subsequently replaced by those objects listed in stanza 8. The latter are specifically the commodities sought by 'wantonness and avarice' (l. 37), results of the Fall. The 'virgin' (l. 3) and 'pure' (l. 8) quality of the light emitted by the infant-eye makes it analogous to 'Those pure and virgin apprehensions I had from the womb, and that divine light wherewith I was born' in *Centuries* 3.1, once again challenging the orthodox Anglican position on original sin. According to the poem's quasi-scientific argument, the visive rays, at first more refined than air and therefore not subject to distracting winds, become 'grosser' (ll. 11, 20, 30) than air and thus, like water, capable of being 'blown' by wind (ll. 29–30). Along with loss of the constancy that once enabled the infant-eye to dispense its light 'unmov'd' (l. 6), there is loss of power as the visive function becomes 'less active' (l. 14), 'feeble and disabled' (l. 41), and consequently capable only of reaching 'near things with its influence' (l. 42) as opposed to 'all eternities' (l. 48).

THE RETURN

The Return carries out the injunction in the last stanza of *An Infant-Eye* and responds to John 3:3: 'Except a man be born again, he cannot see the kingdom of God'; as well as to 1 Peter 2:2: 'As newborn babes, desire the sincere milk of the word, that ye may grow thereby.' Because the emphasis is accordingly on *vision* (ll. 6 and 15) and *growth* (l. 2: 'That I my manhood may improve'), the poem is not escapist, as its second stanza might make it appear to be. Lines 10–11, 'A lowly state may hide / A man from danger', contrast with Andrew Marvell's observation that 'lowness is unsafe as height' (*Upon Appleton House*, l. 411).

NEWS

For the original context of this poem see *Centuries* 3.26, where it appears in the poet's own autograph version as *On News*. Philip, in preparing the manuscript of *Poems of Felicity*, may have taken it from that source and inserted it arbitrarily into the 'infant-eye' sequence. Its last stanza does, however, use the image of the eyeball as an all-inclusive sphere or circle. Unusually for Traherne, the infant here *fails* to appreciate his status as 'the cream / And crown of all' (ll. 45–6). In *Centuries*, the title refers specifically to the good news of the Gospels; taken out of context, the reference becomes more general. Philip made many changes in the text of this poem; the present edition includes both versions for purposes of comparison. For instance, 'I long'd for absent bliss' (l. 38) replaces Traherne's 'I thirsted absent bliss'. Apparently, Philip failed to recognize that the entire poem is a meditation on Proverbs 25:25: 'As cold waters to a thirsty soul, so is good news from a far country.' (Cf. *Centuries* 3.25: 'this thirst of news'.)

FELICITY

As in Herbert's *The Temper* [1], space is here internalized – but with exhilarating rather than disturbing effects. Paradoxically, to look heavenward – i.e., beyond the concentric spheres of the Ptolemaic system – is also to look inward, where felicity is to be found. The poem elaborates correspondences among the spherical shapes of the infant-eye, the human soul, the universe, and the mind of God. The last two lines contain theatrical imagery: a *scene* can be either a stage or a performance; it could also be a formal unit of a larger dramatic work. An *interlude* is an interval between the acts of a play, or a comical or musical entertainment performed during such an interval. The divine mind is being compared to a continuous performance undivided into temporal segments ('No empty space', l. 19) and *above* the level of entertainment provided during interludes.

ADAM

In *Poems of Felicity*, Philip first wrote 'Misapprehension' here but replaced it with 'Adam's Fall'. Margoliouth argues convincingly that the real title of the poem is *Adam*, but his contention that it is not about the Fall seems dubious since the first stanza provides a framework of might-have-been for the poem's vision of Adamic innocence. *Price* (l. 27) means 'value'. For the earth as the Lord's footstool (l. 33), see Isaiah 66:1 (echoed several times in the New Testament). For a fuller development of the idea in lines 41–2, cf. *On Leaping over the Moon*.

THE WORLD

The *theme* introduced in line 25 of *Adam* is here developed, but with the stress on redemption rather than loss. As in *Eden* and *Innocence*, the speaker compares himself to Adam. In this case, however, the comparison involves his mature self rather than his infant self. The heart of the poem is stanza 2, where Christ's blood is seen to have 'sprinkled' (l. 14) 'God's works' (l. 11), thus not only renewing the speaker's joy in them – previously spoiled by sin (l. 13) – but enabling him to enjoy them with even 'greater rapture' (l. 17) than in childhood. This explains the shift from past to future tense in the poem's last line even though most of its stanzas are devoted to a description of the world as perceived by the 'infant-eye' – i.e., in the light of childhood's 'virgin-thoughts' (l. 29). For 'living water' (l. 22), see John 7:38: 'He that believeth on me ... out of his belly shall flow rivers of living water.' Furthermore, lines 20–24 conflate John 4:14 ('But whosoever drinketh of the water that I shall give him shall never thirst; but the water that I shall give him shall be in him a well of water springing up into everlasting life') with Luke 16:24 ('And he cried and said, Father Abraham, have mercy on me, and send Lazarus, that he may dip the tip of his finger in water, and cool my tongue; for I am tormented in this flame'). In the first of these passages Jesus offers 'living water' to the Samaritan woman at the well, and in the second *Dives* (Latin for 'rich man' in the Vulgate version of the Bible) speaks from hell. Images of well and water continue in the next stanza in a passage (ll. 29–36) that expresses Traherne's heretical views on original sin: childhood vision was uncontaminated by 'filth or mud' (l. 36). In line 68, *illustrate* means 'illuminate'. In manuscript, the poem shows much evidence of alteration by Philip.

THE APOSTASY

In *The World*, the speaker assured us of his regenerate state; in *The Apostasy*, he begins a retrospective account of the lapse from original innocence that preceded his eventual recovery. As its title indicates, this poem thus marks a crisis in the quasi-narrative progression of *Poems of Felicity*. Along with the next three poems, it belongs to a negative phase in the sequence, which should be compared with Traherne's personal narrative of his own temporary state of alienation from God and nature in *Centuries* 3.7–23. Here, as there, custom (ll. 50, 60; *Centuries* 3.7–8) is the means of corruption, as Traherne acknowledges no internal source of pollution (ll. 24–5). As in *Centuries* 3.9, hobby-horses (l. 63) – children's toys – actually signify the vanities prized by adults, who are more childish in the conventional sense of the term than children. The 'useless gaudy book' that murders the child's soul (ll. 69–72) symbolizes the false education imposed on him by his elders. It will later be replaced by the Bible in the poem of that title, which begins the next phase of the sequence (as in *Centuries* 3.27), and also by the secular texts of the university curriculum (as in *Centuries* 3.36). Thomas Traherne's autograph version of stanzas 5 and 6 survives as *Bliss* in the Dobell MS; Philip's text is retained in the present edition for the sake of comparison.

SOLITUDE

This poem corresponds to the poet's account of the 'certain want and horror' that came upon him when 'alone in the field' in *Centuries* 3.23. There he finds consolation in 'a remembrance of all the joys I had from my birth'. In the poem, however, it is precisely such remembrance that has deserted him in his continuing state of apostasy. Line 24 – 'I pin'd for hunger at a plenteous board' – epitomizes the entire poem by expressing the speaker's failure to enjoy the world that he inherits and possesses, a failure caused by the blinding (ll. 31–2) of the infant-eye to its own 'native objects'. Philip changed line 24 to 'No welcome good or needed food, my board' after having first copied out Thomas's version, which is restored in the present edition. The line as originally written perhaps harks back to Narcissus' *inopem me copia fecit* ('plenty makes me poor') in Ovid's *Metamorphoses* (III.466), a phrase that became a Renaissance commonplace; Shakespeare's version is 'Making a famine where abundance lies' (Sonnet 1). The bells and churches mentioned in lines 57–80 offer only 'empty sound' (l. 75) and 'external rite' (l. 89) and thus fail to comfort the speaker; nevertheless, these instruments and places of praise point forward to the poems *Bells* and *Churches*, where they contribute to the speaker's recovery from the desolation expressed in this poem.

POVERTY

An indoor counterpart to *Solitude*, *Poverty* recalls *Centuries* 3.16, with its picture of the poet 'sitting in a little obscure room in my father's poor house' and asking, 'how comes it to pass ... that I am so poor?'. (According to Gladys Wade, however, the setting of the poem is an inn belonging to a wealthy relative, Philip Traherne the elder, who was twice mayor of Hereford.) The poem's argument is identical to that of the meditation, but the amount of descriptive detail with which the setting is rendered in its first stanza is unusual. A painted cloth (l. 11) is a 'poor man's tapestry' – a cheap wall hanging, common at the time. Overcoming his blindness (l. 41), the speaker re-learns what he knew in infancy: that '*His* works' are '*my* wealth' and thus acquires a Deity (ll. 54–6), just as in the meditation from *Centuries* a recollection that everything was 'made out of nothing for me' brings the realization that 'then I had a GOD indeed'.

DISSATISFACTION

Line 11 ('I knock'd at every door') seems to echo 'He knocks at all doors' from Henry Vaughan's *Man*, and Traherne appears closer than usual to that poet in his adoption of the quest motif as the speaker, like Vaughan's characteristic persona, becomes a restless searcher for lost light (l. 8). But the specific object of Traherne's quest is, as usual, felicity – the omission of which from the curriculum he regarded as the main defect of higher education (cf. *Centuries* 3.37). Hence the speaker's failure to find it at schools and colleges (l. 13), in the study of philosophy (ll. 59–70), or among the books in libraries (l. 111; *creek* means 'nook or cranny'). *Dissatisfaction* reinforces the critique of university learning in *Centuries* 3.36–45, where Traherne suggests that the secular part of his Oxford experience offered intellectual satisfactions but left him spiritually unfulfilled. 'Roaring boys' (l. 44) are gangs of riotous fellows.

THE BIBLE

The crisis recorded in the poems from the *The Apostasy* through *Dissatisfaction* is resolved by supernatural revelation via the book from Heaven invoked at the end of the latter poem. Why it was not delivered by an angel (as requested) or given to the speaker exclusively is explained in *Centuries* 3.27–34. Traherne's discovery of the Bible in *Centuries* occurs immediately after the poem *On News* and before the account of his experience at the university, so that the sequence of events is different in *Poems of Felicity*. For Traherne, the Bible has many passages confirming truths intuitively grasped in childhood but later forgotten. Among the most important are: that we are God's children and heirs (Romans 8:16–17); that we are made in His image (Genesis 1:27); and that we are kings (Psalms 8:5–6).

CHRISTENDOM

Stimulated by the mysterious word 'Christendom', the child's imagination conjures up an ideal city. The process is analogous to what happens in *Shadows in the Water*, where the child imagines other worlds 'behind' visible appearances, just as here he tries to imagine 'what things did lie behind / That mystic name' (ll. 9–10) –

but with the difference that whereas there the stimulus is visual, here it is auditory: the initial appeal is to the 'infant-ear' (l. 1). (This is in contrast to *Dumbness*, which argues that the intrusion of language on the child's inner solitude begins his fall into corruption.) Nevertheless, the 'conceits' (ll. 42–3) that feed the child's spirit in this poem are almost entirely visual, imagination being a faculty of interior vision or 'transforming sight' (l. 35; cf. the poem *Sight*). 'Things native' which 'mine eye did view' (ll. 51–2) are presumably the 'native objects of an infant-eye' (from the subtitle to *Poems of Felicity*) by which the imagination represents truth to the child's 'virgin-eyes' (ll. 112–13). The image of a 'town beyond the seas' (l. 31) that promises 'a long expected joy' is reminiscent of *News*, in which the speaker wonders, 'What secret force mov'd my desire / T' expect my joys beyond the seas, so young?'

ON CHRISTMAS-DAY

Unusual in its extensive appropriation of a literary model – and a secular one at that – *On Christmas-Day* draws heavily on Robert Herrick's *carpe diem* poem *Corinna's Going A-Maying*. The idea of a refrain may well have come from that poem, and Traherne enriches its effect by using its characteristic rhyme-words – 'sing', 'King', 'ring', and 'spring' – in the second and third lines, as well as the last two lines, of each stanza. Like Herrick's poem, Traherne's is a genre-painting of communal festivity but in a distinctly urban setting. The *minster* of line 120 is presumably Hereford Cathedral, with Traherne's own parish of Credenhill no doubt among the 'remoter parishes' echoing from 'far off' (ll. 109–10) the great service in the city. As in Herrick's poem, streets and houses are transformed by greenery into rural counterparts of themselves. Possibly Traherne's reason for choosing as his model a poem that celebrates springtime and fertility was to reinforce the motif of seasonal transformation: winter into spring (ll. 12, 24, 36, 40–48). His exhortations to his 'drowsy soul' to shake off sloth (ll. 5–6, 13), forsake its bed (l. 29), and attire itself in green (ll. 30–32, 79–82) recall similar rhetoric used by Herrick in urging his 'sweet slug-a-bed', Corinna, to do likewise. In particular, 'Let pleasant branches still be seen / Adorning thee, both quick and green' (ll. 31–2) seems to echo 'Rise, and put on your foliage, and be seen / To come forth, like the spring-time, fresh and green' (*Corinna*, ll. 15–16). But both Herbert and Vaughan, in Christmas and Easter hymns, also reproach their souls for sloth; the latter's *Easter-day* anticipates Traherne's self-accusation of a melancholy mood inappropriate to such a festive occasion. 'Thy lute, thy harp, or else thy heart-strings take' (l. 17) directly echoes Herbert's 'Consort both heart and lute: and twist a song' (*Easter*, l. 13). Like these earlier hymns, *On Christmas-Day* has as its theme the personal regeneration symbolized by one of the two most momentous events commemorated in the Christian calendar. In line 82, the present edition partially restores (at the expense of the meter) what may have been Thomas's own version of a line altered by Philip to read 'A living branch and always green'. The allusion is to John 15:1–5: 'I am the true vine, and my Father is the husbandman.... Abide in me, and I in you. As the branch cannot bear fruit of itself, except it abide in the vine; no more can ye, except ye abide in me.' This reference would seem to explain the horticultural imagery in lines 31–5, where the speaker asks that his soul be adorned with green branches 'inserted [i.e., grafted] into Him' and thus 'laden all the year with fruits'.

In the final stanza, the city becomes a smoothly functioning 'engine' with its magistrate, symbols of office, and peaceful assembly in the minster. If post-Restoration, as seems likely, the poem celebrates the re-establishment of a national church and the re-institution of the traditional Christmas service, banned during the Commonwealth; otherwise, it would have to be based on reminiscences of the poet's childhood before the Civil Wars – or at least before the fall of Hereford to the Puritans at Christmastime in 1645.

BELLS

Bells begins as a kind of lingering echo of the exuberant bell-ringing at the end of *On Christmas-Day*. Since, as Margoliouth observes, Traherne rarely duplicates a stanza form in different poems, the identity of stanzaic form in *Bells* I and II makes this more likely to be a two-part poem than two separate poems; the lines and stanzas are therefore numbered accordingly. (But the case is more problematic than it seems because 'To the same purpose', which shares its stanza form with *On Leaping over the Moon*, is an adjunct to that poem rather than an integral part of it.) However, the conceit of the bells is given different applications in the poem's two parts. In part I bells, refined from common ore and elevated to an exalted position in steeples, are analogous to human souls, rarefied from the clay of mortality to occupy a place in the heavenly choir 'above the starry sphere' (l. 11). The first stanza of part II continues this theme but addresses the poet's own soul: in his ministerial vocation he must transcend his earthy origins and become 'metal pure' (l. 39) so as to 'allure' (l. 44) others' souls to church and salvation. But by the end of the poem the bells collectively have come to signify the whole congregation assembled in worship. 'Those bells are of a piece, and *sound*' (l. 67) – used as an adjective, not a verb, but with a likely pun; their flawlessness makes possible their harmony, which becomes a model for Christian unity (l. 75). The poem is thus in one respect a plea against the 'harsh jarring' (l. 73) of sectarianism and builds to a vision of the ideal solidarity of the Christian community similar to that envisioned in *Christendom* and at the end of *On Christmas-Day*. Yet its public and social themes are intertwined with private and mystical ones.

CHURCHES

The abundance of architectural detail in lines 13–21 emphasizes the physicality of these 'stately structures' (l. 1) in contrast to David's 'temple in the mind' mentioned in both *Thoughts II* and *The Inference*. Traherne is here concerned with the actual embodiment of that archetype. The embossed and gilded 'knobs' of line 16, for instance, may be decorative bosses where the ribs of vaulted roofs intersect. Unlike Milton's Pandemonium in *Paradise Lost* I.710–17, the 'pile' (l. 16) described here is in no way spiritually diminished by its costly extravagance. (Its style is Gothic rather than Baroque.) In the second part (or perhaps the second poem of the pair) the poet imagines what it would be like if there were only one temple, such as that built by Solomon in the Old Testament. Such a church would necessarily be universal and would thus attract 'the Pope from Rome' (l. 11) among other dignitaries. The story of the Queen of Sheba's visit to Solomon (ll. 8–10) is told in 1 Kings 10:1–13 and 2 Chronicles 9:1–12. The lament over the decline of churchgoing in the last stanza looks like a rebuke aimed at nonconformists. But it also anticipates the more general theme of *Misapprehension*, the next poem in the sequence: that the very bounty of God makes us undervalue His

MISAPPREHENSION

Some of Traherne's most familiar themes appear in this poem. The socialization of the child distorts the scale of values taught him in infancy by 'native sense' (l. 42). This blinding of the infant-eye to 'the worth of things' (ll. 11–12) brings on the condition lamented by the poet in *The Apostasy*, *Solitude*, *Poverty*, and *Dissatisfaction* (ll. 5–8). The lost road overgrown by brambles (ll. 36–9) is the road that leads back to Eden. Only when the world is inwardly conceived so that the human heart becomes its 'inclusive sphere' (l. 62) or 'womb' (l. 65) is it rightly apprehended. The image of 'the world set in man's heart' (l. 53; cf. Ecclesiastes 3:11: 'He hath made every thing beautiful in his time: also he hath set the world in their heart') was familiar from popular emblem-books and emblematic poetry, such as Francis Quarles's *Divine Fancies* (1632) or his *Emblems* (1635), where it usually signified the worldly man with his attention fixated on mundane matters. But Traherne's interpretation of the traditional emblem is characteristically his own; cf. *Centuries* 2.66: 'Never was anything in this world loved too much, but many things have been loved in a false way; and all in too short a measure.' The references to the world's *uses* (l. 50) and to its 'united service and delight' (l. 55) lead into *The Odour*.

THE ODOUR

This is Traherne's most sensuous poem, full of olfactory, gustatory, tactile, and visual images. The odour itself is a metaphor for the function of each object that the poet praises. Just as aromatic substances such as myrrh, cinnamon, aloes, or cassia emit their fragrances while remaining intact, so our limbs (for instance) survive the performance of their functions without being consumed in the process (ll. 5–6). Unlike Shakespeare, with whose *Sonnets* this poem seems to have a curious relationship, Traherne does not address the problem of mutability. 'Your uses flow while ye abide' (l. 19), the speaker says to his own body, and 'light communicated' (l. 14) is still light. For Shakespeare in Sonnet 54, however, the essence of 'sweet roses' is distilled at the cost of their lives: 'Of their sweet deaths are sweetest odours made.' (Again unlike Shakespeare, who uses the rose as a metaphor for a certain type of person, Traherne maintains a distinction between man and the lower orders of being; he writes in *Christian Ethics*, 'All corruptible things waste and consume away, that they may sacrifice their essence to our benefit.') The consummation of these roses' existence in their sacrificial deaths is in contrast to the 'canker blooms', which 'die to themselves', or to the 'summer's flower' in Sonnet 94, which 'is to the summer sweet, / Though to itself it only live and die'. When Traherne apparently echoes these sonnets in line 43 – 'Live to thyself' – he seems to put himself at odds with St Paul in Romans 14:7–8: 'For none of us liveth to himself, and no man dieth to himself. For whether we live, we live unto the Lord; and whether we die, we die unto the Lord.' Similarly, Mammon's recommendation in *Paradise-Lost* II.254 that he and the other fallen angels 'Live to ourselves' is hellish counsel. Furthermore, Traherne's advice that the self 'At once the mirror and the object be' (l. 54) contradicts on the face of it the principle of reciprocity that he affirms in *The Circulation*. But this is a poem about self-enjoyment as a particular instance of the enjoyment of the world and, as such, is narrowly focused on its theme. Far from being narcissistic, self-love for Traherne is prerequisite to love of God and of others: 'That pool must first be filled, that shall be made to overflow' (*Centuries* 4.55); consequently, 'we live unto the Lord' *by* first 'living to ourselves'. (Cf. *Centuries* 3.13: 'To live the life of God is to live to all the works of God, and to enjoy them in His image.') Also, it seems likely that just as Traherne remembered the title of Herbert's poem *The Odour*, he would have recalled the Pauline text that served as its epigraph: 'For we are unto God a sweet savour of Christ' (2 Corinthians 2:15) – which is why the uses of the human body are called *sacred* in the poem's last stanza.

Traherne's speaker uses the second person pronoun to denote the members of his own body ('Ye living gems', l. 7) in stanzas 2–7; another person (presumably the reader) in stanzas 8–10; and 'sacred uses' in stanza 11. For honey flowing from rocks (l. 31), cf. Deuteronomy 32:13.

ADMIRATION

The word 'admiration' is used in the Latinate sense of 'wonderment' and describes the tone of the whole poem. In theme and method this poem recalls *The Inquiry*, where the speaker also asked a series of rhetorical questions expressing his amazement that earthly delights are capable of appealing even to angels, who have experienced the joys of Heaven. The angel sipping 'Ambrosia from a mortal lip' (l. 3) may be the 'brisk cherub' who, in Richard Crashaw's *The Weeper*, sips St Mary Magdalene's tears, but the image is also reminiscent of the hyperbolical compliments bestowed by Petrarchan poets on their ladies. Moreover, the extravagant conceits of stanza 3 suggest nothing so much as nature's obsequious attendance on a Petrarchan lady when she walks abroad. While *Admiration* continues the celebration of the glories of the human body begun in the *The Odour* (which is specifically echoed in lines 8-9), it also recalls *The Person* and *Thanksgivings for the Body*. But the blinding (l. 21) of the infant-eye puts this theme in a new perspective. 'Lord! What is man' (l. 43) echoes Psalm 8, one of Traherne's favourite biblical passages.

RIGHT APPREHENSION

The opening line echoes *Centuries* 1.12: 'Can you then be righteous, unless you be just in rendering to things their due esteem?'; and the poem's theme is well expressed in the conclusion to that same meditation: 'The end for which you were created is that by prizing all that God hath done, you may enjoy yourself and Him in blessedness.' For the false (i.e., artificial) lights used by tradesmen to 'set off' shoddy merchandise (ll. 11-13), cf. John Webster, *The Duchess of Malfi* (c. 1613): 'This dark'ning of your worth is not like that / Which tradesmen use i'th' city; their false lights / Are to rid bad wares off' (I.ii). Lines 15-16 refer to the trade in silver shrines to the goddess Diana in Ephesus, which was jeopardized by Paul's preaching there (see Acts 19:23-41). For 'a globe of gold' (ll. 26, 41), cf. *Centuries* 1.14: 'The earth itself is better than gold because it produceth fruits and flowers.' The barrenness of gold (stanza 6; also ll. 74, 84), as noted in Aristotle's *Politics*, was one of the bases for the scholastic attack on usury in the Middle Ages: the natural order is inverted when gold, which is sterile by nature, is forced to bear fruit. Traherne's satirical portrait of the miser or usurer (stanzas 8-10), who so closely resembles his beloved gold, perhaps derives from that tradition. This miser is used as a foil for the 'happy infant' who is truly wealthy (l. 81) in his blessedness. For the speaker, the 'clearer reason' of maturity re-confirms the right valuation of things that 'newness' had once taught the infant (stanza 5).

THE IMAGE

This short poem, first crowded in at the bottom of a page and later marked for deletion, expresses one of Traherne's favourite notions. Although the Bible calls man 'a little lower than the angels' (Psalms 8:5), this difference in status must be negligible since man was created in the 'best of images' – that of God Himself (Genesis 1:27). Furthermore, this great honour carries with it a challenge to '*be* like ... God' (l. 1): 'He hath commanded us to be perfect as He is perfect; and we are to grow up into Him till we are filled with the fullness of His Godhead. We are to be conformed to the image of His glory, till we become the resemblance of His great exemplar' (*Centuries* 2.84).

THE EVIDENCE

In Philip Traherne's arrangement of poems in the Burney MS, *The Evidence* appropriately follows *The Estate*, a poem with which it shares its dominant metaphor (ll. 4, 9, 12). For Traherne, as for Sir Thomas Browne, 'there are two books from whence I collect my divinity; besides that written one of God, another of his servant nature, that universal and public manuscript that lies expansed unto the eyes of all' (*Religio Medici* [1643]). The documentary *evidence* for the speaker's inheritance of his estate is the Bible (stanza 1); but even if the Bible did not exist, nature itself would still affirm the speaker's ownership of the world (stanza 2) by the testimony of its creatures that 'God made us thine' (l. 20). True enjoyment of this extraordinary estate hierarchically comprising 'God, angels, men, fowls, beasts, and fish' must be both 'natural and transcendent' (ll. 26–7), a collaboration of senses and spirit (anticipating the next poem, *Shadows in the Water*, where a child's sensory response to the natural world enables him to intuit the realm of transcendent being). *The Evidence* has affinities with George Herbert's *Man*.

SHADOWS IN THE WATER

This begins a series of three poems based on anecdotes about childhood experiences that, in retrospect, came to embody important truths about human existence; taken together, they illustrate the 'learned ignorance' that characterized childhood in *Eden*, as well as the special quality of seeing with which the infant-eye is endowed. The shadows of the title are reflected images, visual replicas of the three-dimensional world surrounding the child. Because the child does not understand the principle of reflection, he infers from these shadows the existence of other worlds (ll. 10, 16, 29, 36, 42, 44, 70) – a mistake *intending* (l. 3), or pointing towards, truth. By employing imagination or 'fancy' (l. 13), in the absence of a developed adult intellect, the child intuits such worlds, thereby exercising the creative function attributed to him in *My Spirit*. The *antipodes* (l. 38) is the opposite side of the earth (or the inhabitants of that region), conceived here as a mirror-image of one's own immediate locality. Although the world in the puddle may seem a 'phantasm' (l. 44) or illusion, the speaker affirms its reality. This is Traherne's answer to the uncompromising materialism of Thomas Hobbes, who insisted in his *Leviathan* (1651) that 'All is body.' The child's perception of 'things that lie behind' (l. 6) – that is, of 'something infinite behind everything' (*Centuries* 3.3) – corroborates Sir Thomas Browne's metaphor of man as 'that great and true amphibium' who is capable of living in the 'divided and distinguished worlds' of matter and spirit (*Religio Medici*). Like Milton, who speculates 'what if earth / Be but the shadow of Heaven' (*Paradise Lost* V.574–5), Traherne may be playing here with the idea of 'shadow' (sensory manifestation) as opposed to 'substance' (disembodied essence) as in Platonic metaphysics. Comparison may be made between this poem and Eve's recollection of her earliest moments of consciousness in *Paradise Lost* IV.449–91, where 'another sky' appears in a lake, to Eve's 'unexperienc'd thought' (ll. 457–9). Whereas Traherne's speaker anticipates passing through the 'film' (l. 40) or 'skin' (l. 79) of the puddle's surface to interact with his new 'playmates' (l. 73) in the shadow-world, Eve is promised that she will be led 'where no shadow stays / Thy coming, and thy soft embraces'.

ON LEAPING OVER THE MOON

The opening line establishes a thematic connection with *Shadows in the Water*, but the poem proceeds to focus on an experience attributed to the poet's brother Philip Traherne, who edited and transcribed the manuscript of *Poems of Felicity*. Philip was born in late 1640 and was thus about three years younger than Thomas. Throughout the poem, the speaker's inflated rhetoric gives a humorous, mock-heroic tone to his narration of Philip's exploit: 'Adventure strange! No such in story we / New or old, true or feigned, see' (ll. 11–12). Allusions to the archetypal falls of Icarus (ll. 19 and 27) and Lucifer (Satan, l. 59) support this tone. Icarus's wings proved 'deceitful' (l. 28) because he plummeted into the ocean when the sun melted the wax that his father Daedalus had used in constructing them. The syntax of line 14 is inverted: Philip 'went above' Heaven when he jumped over the moon's reflection in the rivulet flowing across the king's highway (l. 21). The experience, though founded once again on a childish misconception about optical phenomena, is 'instructive' (l. 68) because it confirms the poet's belief that we attain felicity by understanding that we are already in Heaven while on earth (ll. 51–4, 69–70) and thus in eternity while seemingly confined by time.

'TO THE SAME PURPOSE' (UNTITLED)

Philip separated this poem from *On Leaping over the Moon* with the same typographical symbol he placed at the head of each new poem in the manuscript; nevertheless, the opening phrase, the omitted antecedent for the pronoun in line 1, the image of the moon, and the stanza form closely connect the two poems. Lugwardine (l. 9), the only local place-name mentioned in Traherne's poetry, is a village some three miles from Hereford, the city where the brothers grew up; Philip was presumably sent there to nurse (l. 2). Again, a 'sweet mistake' made in 'unexperienc'd infancy' (*Shadows in the Water*, ll. 1–2) teaches a lesson: in this case, the familiar one that everything in the world was created to 'serve wholly ... every single person' (ll. 17–19). The 'sense' that we lack (l. 20) is consciousness, or recognition, of this fact about our condition – i.e., what Traherne elsewhere calls 'right apprehension'.

SIGHT

According to Ficino's *Commentary on Plato's Symposium* (1475), the soul 'has two lights, the one natural or innate, the other divine and supernatural'. (Cf. Traherne's 'two *sights*', l. 5.) When 'the instruments of sense have been purged through learning', the soul's natural light 'searches out the order of natural things. By this investigation, it senses that there is some author of this great universe; it desires to see and possess Him; but He can be seen only with the supernatural light. Therefore, the mind, by the searchings of its own natural light, is stirred with a vigorous desire to recover its divine light' (Chapters IV and V; trans. Sears Jayne, Columbia, Mo.: University of Missouri, 1944). The opening lines of *Sight* echo *Felicity*, where the infant, seeking 'bliss above the skies', discovers 'endless space' within his own soul. The relation of the infant-eye (l. 1) to the speaker's third, or inner, eye – the conceit on which the poem is built – is not entirely clear. The 'visive eye' of line 23, like the 'visive rays' produced by *An Infant-Eye*, is an instrument of physical sight. As the child grows to maturity, this organ loses its ability to endow 'natural' (l. 15) and 'earthly' (l. 18) objects with divine light. (For the theory of eyebeams see the note on *An Infant-Eye*, p. 346.) The redeemed adult compensates for the loss of childhood vision by developing intellectual and spiritual insight. As elsewhere in Traherne – especially in *The Preparative* – the soul (identified with sight by the *I–eye* pun) is both a sphere ('ball', l. 21) and a mirror ('looking-glass', l. 50) encompassing and reflecting 'invisibles' (l. 24) or essences, some of which are specified as abstractions in lines 54–5 and in the last stanza. *Sight* is linked to *Shadows in the Water* by the speaker's need for other worlds (ll. 25–7); here, as there, he sought 'new regions' and 'distant coasts' (ll. 30–31) in childhood ('even then', l. 27). As the adult capacity for *thought* (celebrated in the *Thoughts* series of poems from the Dobell MS) replaces the infantile fixation on *things*, the searching beam of the infant-eye gives way to the reflective mirror of mature consciousness.

WALKING

This nature poem, a meditation on God's creatures, continues to develop the theme of *Sight*: the need to see with the mind rather than with physical sight alone in order to 'prize' the world at its true value (ll. 1–2). In line 29 Philip first wrote 'celebrate' and then replaced it with 'praise'. 'Celebrate' is retained here even though it adds an extra foot to the line because it was presumably Thomas's word and because the poem is indeed a celebration of the natural world. Children, 'tumbling' (l. 44) here as in *Centuries* 3.3, perform this celebration spontaneously, but the quality of 'sight' available to the contemplative mind is reserved for 'perfect manhood' (ll. 46–7) and must be approached 'by degrees' (l. 51) – that is, discursively rather than intuitively. For the nature of that 'sight' (l. 46) see *The Vision* from the Dobell MS. In stanza 6, the metaphor of thoughts as bees that 'lade / Our minds [i.e., with images of the world], as they their thighs' recalls stanza 7 of *Thoughts I*.

THE DIALOGUE

The dialogue form, which Traherne could have found in Herbert or Vaughan, makes clear the pedagogical intent of the poem. The questioner's lines are given a naïve tone but are not metrically rough if 'heir' (ll. 3 and 6) is scanned as dissyllabic. The questioner may be a reader who is willing to accept Traherne's argument that each person is the special beneficiary of created nature but who has trouble with the corollary to that proposition: that each of us is 'the heir of the works of men' (l. 3). The answerer supports this case by means of an extended analogy with the sun (ll. 12–34), 'Which doth not think on *thee* at all, my friend' (l. 13) yet none the less by divine design ministers (like everything else in Heaven and earth) to each individual human being (ll. 31–4). Similarly, the labours of other men, working for their own ends, are directed by God to the benefit of the questioner's 'single self' (ll. 35–9). The imagery of lines 19–20 comes from Psalms 19:5, where the sun 'is as a bridegroom coming out of his chamber, and rejoiceth as a strong man to run a race'.

DREAMS

The opening lines recapture the sense of strangeness expressed in *Wonder*, while the poem as a whole reiterates the critique of *experience* (l. 30) found in *Shadows in the Water*. The first three stanzas pose a series of rhetorical questions. Since sight, as defined in the poem of that title, is an interior faculty, then closed eyes *can* 'See through their lids' (l. 7); and that the human 'brain-pan' (l. 14) or cranium *can* (and indeed, must) contain the world is gospel to Traherne. 'Possess' (l. 20) means to take over; the sense of the passage is that the immensity of the cosmos ('magnitude') loses none of its scope when it occupies an active memory. Here, as in *The Circulation*, memory is the storehouse of sense impressions from which fancy or imagination fetches the imagery of dreams. The speaker marvels at the vividness and realism of these 'apparitions' (l. 39; cf. the 'phantasms' of *Shadows in the Water*). For childhood, the dream images *were* real (ll. 24–6), but the blinding (l. 47) of the infant-eye differentiates *things* from the *thoughts* that represent them in the mind. This dichotomizing effect of experience must be undone and thoughts re-united with things because the material world is dead (l. 52) – though not illusory – until conceived in the human mind.

THE INFERENCE

The title suggests that this two-part poem is intended to state a conclusion drawn from premises established in *Dreams*; its opening lines therefore paraphrase the closing lines of that poem. Once again, the poet rings the changes on *things* versus *thoughts*, setting these two entities in opposition but working towards their potential unity. Consequently, thoughts themselves become 'things ... Which I do find / Within' (ll. 32–5). The world might as well be 'yet unmade' (l. 45) for those who fail to conceptualize it and are thus unmoved by it. As in *The Recollection* and several other poems, God's work of creation finds its fulfilment in the human response to it. In part II, David the Psalmist serves as the model not just for the poet (as he is in *Centuries* 3.69) but for anyone who loves and praises God in his mind. If we think of the temple in the mind as the Psalms actually composed by David, then there may well be a secondary allusion to the title of George Herbert's collection of devotional poems, *The Temple* (1633) – a source of inspiration to many seventeenth-century religious poets. On the other hand, the reference may suggest that the unfulfilled intention is superior to its execution, as thoughts are to things. (See note on *Thoughts II*, where David's unbuilt temple is said to transcend the one that Solomon actually built.) Moreover, Traherne (especially in ll. 28–30) may have agreed with Milton's declaration in *Paradise Lost* I.17–18 that God prefers 'Before all temples th' upright heart and pure', which itself echoes Acts 7:48: 'the most High dwelleth not in temples made with hands.' For lines 19–25, see Luke 2:19: 'But Mary kept all these things, and pondered them in her heart'; cf. also Luke 2:51. In line 40, 'them annihilate' means to regard thoughts as worthless, thus effectively obliterating them.

THE CITY

Returning to the theme of *The Dialogue*, *The City* celebrates the speaker's inheritance of 'the works of men', just as *Walking* did that of nature's works. As a child (in Hereford?), however, he drew no such distinction but assumed that his 'Father rear'd' (l. 9) the structures of the city for him: hence the allusion to John 14:2: 'In my Father's house are many mansions' (l. 13); hence, too, the manifestation of the city to the child's 'free soul' (l. 55) as the new Jerusalem (l. 60) from Revelation 21. To the child earth is Heaven, art nature, space infinity, and time eternity (l. 20). In theme and structure, *The City* closely parallels *Wonder*; here, as there, the speaker lapses once into the present tense (l. 1) when recalling his childhood but otherwise adopts an adult point of view (e.g., ll. 10, 19, 23–6, 34–5, etc.). This poem thus harks back to the group of four poems on infancy at the beginning of the Dobell MS; it may be out of sequence in *Poems of Felicity*. There is, however, a link with the poems on thoughts that precede it in context: we cease to be free when 'taught' (by the adult world) 'To limit and to bound our thought' (ll. 69–70). The speaker is ambivalent towards cities in that they feature walls (which were non-existent in Paradise [l. 5]), confine people in 'a narrow pen' (ll. 53–5), and force 'citizens' to 'shut up' their falsely prized material wealth in 'chests and tills' (ll. 71–3). They are not natural, as the child thought, but are products of that same art 'that hath the late invention found / Of shutting up in little room / One's boundless expectations' (ll. 51–3). Nevertheless, the speaker, as a regenerate Christian, understands that the city, through its very concentration of humanity, increases his 'glorious store' (l. 75) of natural wealth but also that he must not let the city confine his soul 'nor be my only treasure' (l. 82). The poem may possibly reflect Traherne's reaction to his new environment when he moved to London with the Bridgeman family in 1669. For the 'everlasting hills' (l. 58) see Genesis 49:26.

INSATIABLENESS

This poem follows logically from *The City* in its reaction against the spatial confinement imposed by artificial structures and property lines as well as the analogous imposition of limitations on the soul's capacity and powers. Its theme is that of *Centuries* 1.22: 'It is of the nobility of man's soul that he is insatiable' – a theme celebrated also in *Consummation* and *Hosanna*, which form a sequence with *Insatiableness*. Far from being alarmed by the explosion of the self-contained Ptolemaic universe into the vast reaches of Copernican space, Traherne welcomed the discovery of a scientific analogue to his own sense of unlimited potentiality within the self. In part I, lines 26–30 are obscure but may mean that the soul experiences intimations of infinity even within finite space (if 'all room' is taken to mean every limited area). Among Renaissance writers, Christopher Marlowe most notably anticipates Traherne in expressing the aspiration that drives the soul in its quest for knowledge, power, or wealth commensurate with its nature. 'Our souls... Will us to wear ourselves and never rest' (*Tamburlaine the Great* Part One, II.vii); cf. the soul's restlessness in *Insatiableness*, part I, line 2, and part II, line 4. For Tamburlaine, however, satisfaction is to be found in 'That perfect bliss and sole felicity, / The sweet fruition of an earthly crown'. Could Traherne have been thinking of this passage when he wrote, 'Not all the crowns... On earth... Will satisfaction yield to me' (part I, ll. 11–13)? In the lines ''Tis mean ambition to desire / A single world' (part II, ll. 7–8), he was certainly thinking of another conqueror, Alexander the Great, who 'sate down and cried for more worlds. So insatiable is man that millions will not please him. They are no more than so many tennis balls, in comparison of the greatness and highness of his soul' (*Centuries* 1.22). Furthermore, for Traherne's speaker, each one of all the worlds to which he aspires must be enriched with the 'infinite variety' (part II, ll. 16–17) of Shakespeare's Cleopatra (*Antony and Cleopatra* II.ii). For Traherne, as for the Cambridge Platonists, the human soul always mirrors the Deity; its boundlessness is therefore an argument for a God of infinite magnitude (II, ll. 23–4). The 'endless expense' that must be disbursed (l. 22) by the soul consists of love and praise in response to God's own endless love and beneficence. The two parts of *Insatiableness* are really two poems, apparently taken by Philip from different places in a hypothetical lost Traherne manuscript and combined under one heading for convenience.

CONSUMMATION

Consummation, as its title indicates, looks towards the fulfilment of the soul's aspirations. With echoes of such earlier poems as *Shadows in the*

Water and *Dreams*, it stands fittingly near the end of *Poems of Felicity*. Moving within an unbounded sphere (ll. 1–3, 13–14), the thoughts generated by the soul enable us to imagine ('conceit' used as a verb, l. 26) sea creatures (i.e., constellations) swimming in the sky (ll. 25–30). The antecedent of 'which' (l. 37) is presumably 'space' (l. 35) – not fully descried as long as the soul remains hidden in the 'darksome dungeon' (l. 40) of the body. Predictable but uncharacteristic of Traherne, this imagery may be due to Philip's intervention. (Cf. Vaughan's 'They are all gone into the world of light', where the soul is compared to a star confined in a tomb.) Because objects (ll. 20, 42) in – and beyond – outer space are indistinct to the soul's vision in this life, we must resort to imagination in order to define them. But just as in *Shadows in the Water* the breach of 'that thin skin' will ultimately admit the speaker to the world he had to imagine in this life, so death (by implication) will 'display' (l. 42) and 'expose' (l. 48) everything in its 'true nature' (l. 54). There will be no further need for imagination (ll. 49–50) as we come to share the Deity's own consciousness.

HOSANNA

A hymn of liberation in praise of the self's transcendence of all limits, including mortality, *Hosanna* welcomes the consummation glimpsed afar off in the previous poem. Impatience with walls, boundaries, and confinement of all kinds is recurrent in Traherne's work and perhaps explains his restless experimentation with prosodic and stanzaic patterns throughout his career, as well as his search for more mixed, free, and open forms as reflected in such later works as the *Thanksgivings*, *Centuries*, and *Commentaries of Heaven*. In *Centuries* 2.81 Traherne argues that infinity 'is the first thing which is naturally known. Bounds and limits are discerned only in a secondary manner.' A man born deaf and blind apprehends infinite space around him: 'He thinks not of wall and limits till he feels them and is stopped by them. That things are finite therefore we learn by our senses, but infinity we know and feel by our souls: and feel it so naturally, as if it were the very essence and being of the soul.' That the liberation celebrated is attainable here and now, not merely after death, is suggested throughout the poem: 'Yea, here the trees of Eden grow' (l. 18); 'Both worlds one Heaven made by love' (l. 30);

'These clouds dispers'd, the heavens clear I see' (l. 47). The clouds that block true vision are 'baubles' (l. 46), the poet's usual term for falsely esteemed material wealth, but clarity of sight (l. 14) enables the soul to embrace 'all things in their proper place' (ll. 51–2) – that is, according to their right valuation – and thereby to reign 'With God enthron'd' (l. 55) even while on earth. In this way the poem reflects Traherne's personal theology more accurately than *Consummation* and may therefore be assumed to have been less tampered with by Philip. The geocentric universe anachronistically evoked in its last stanza is a corollary to the anthropocentric argument of that stanza and of the whole poem (e.g., l. 24).

THE REVIEW

Traherne asks whether the adult capacity for abstract thought is adequate compensation for the loss of the child's affective, sensuous response to material things. The outcome of his 'review' is ambivalent because of the duality of thinking, which can either create or destroy 'a Paradise' (ll. 23–6). In the second part of the poem, the speaker's references to the 'sphere' of his childhood in the present tense suggest that either (a) he has succeeded in his quest to become a child again or (b) his remembered childhood continues to serve his mature self as a reservoir of 'obvious benefits' (l. 10). In either case, the circular pattern of his life is an 'earnest' (l. 11), or guarantee, of immortality. The last two lines echo James Shirley's famous lyric, 'The glories of our blood and state', from *The Contention of Ajax and Ulysses* (1659): 'Only the actions of the just / Smell sweet and blossom in their dust.'

Poems from Christian Ethics *(1675)*

'AS IN A CLOCK' (UNTITLED)

The idea of a clockwork universe has been variously associated with Calvinism, Newtonian physics, and eighteenth-century Deism: perspectives with which Traherne has nothing in common. His simile comparing the world to a well-regulated clock derives not from such scientists as Kepler and Boyle (both of whom had used similar images), but from a popular religious poet, Francis Quarles (in the Second Meditation of his *Job Militant* [1624]). The wit of the passage depends on the *dis*similarity between Traherne's universe, animated by both the human and divine spirits, and the mechanized model offered by some proponents of the new science. (Cf. *Centuries* 2.22: 'But the wheels in watches move, and so doth the hand that pointeth out the figures. This being a motion of dead things. Therefore hath God created living ones: that by lively motions and sensible desires, we might be sensible of a Deity. They breathe, they see, they feel, they grow, they flourish, they know, they love'.) His comparison of the world to a clock is an example of a genuine metaphysical conceit; as such, it conforms to the famous definition by Samuel Johnson in his *Life of Cowley* (1779): a 'discovery of occult resemblances in things apparently unlike'. The poem re-works material from an early 'poem on moderation', mentioned in *Centuries* 3.18 and partially quoted in *Centuries* 3.19 and 21; parallels between the latter quotation and this poem from *Christian Ethics*, of which Traherne was known to be the author, enabled Bertram Dobell to identify him as the author of the *Centuries* and therefore of the poems in the Dobell manuscript.

'MANKIND IS SICK' (UNTITLED)

This is Traherne's darkest poem – his version of Donne's *Anatomy of the World*. As such, it counters the charge sometimes made against the poet that his optimism is founded on a naïveté about evil. In contrast to *Innocence* and *Centuries* 3.7–8, the opening stanza expresses an orthodox view of original sin using conventional images of poison, sickness, madness, and (elsewhere) blindness and captivity: images that are recurrent throughout the poem. The difference may be more apparent than real, however, since even in *Centuries* 3.8 Traherne admitted, 'Yet is all our corruption derived from Adam: inasmuch as all the evil examples and inclinations of the world arise from his sin'; and the images of the poem might be a metaphorical way of saying the same thing. The poem also gives Traherne's ideas on pastoral care. Priests are 'kind physicians' (l. 10) who try to cure the 'sad distemper of the mind' suffered by those benighted souls who live in bondage to sin. Like Plato's philosopher-redeemer in the *Republic* who descends back into the cave (l. 8) from which he had escaped, in order to free his fellow-prisoners from 'chains of darkness'

(l. 41) and lead them towards enlightenment (ll. 37–8, 53–4), the priest runs the risk of being abused and reviled (ll. 13, 29) by those whom he would save. Jesus (stanza 11) therefore becomes his model for meek behaviour in the face of hostility. Although the poem's immediate context is, appropriately, Chapter XXV, 'Of Meekness', in *Christian Ethics*, its true prose counterpart and closest paraphrase is *Centuries* 4.20, where Traherne discusses the way 'to be happy in the midst of a generation of vipers': 'To think the world therefore a general bedlam, or place of madmen, and oneself a physician, is the most necessary point of present wisdom: an important imagination, and the way to happiness.' The 'precious oil and balm' (l. 25) applied by the physician-priest to his patient's self-inflicted wounds are identified in the prose passage as pity and love.

'CONTENTMENT IS A SLEEPY THING!' (UNTITLED)

This poem is built on contrasts: between poverty and riches; rest and motion; idleness and employment; death and life. The overarching contrast, which gives form to the whole poem, is that between the sleepy contentment of line 1 and the 'true felicity' of line 21, which for Traherne is the goal of life. A merely passive state of contentment is lethargic because it fails to employ 'the powers of the soul' (l. 7) to their full capacity. By the end of the poem, contentment has been unexpectedly redefined as life 'stretch'd out' to its 'full extent' – in a position not of repose but of active striving. Margoliouth was probably right in suggesting that the difficult line 2 modifies the 'contentment' of line 1 rather than the 'quiet mind' of line 3. This reading would make lines 1 and 2 grammatically parallel with lines 3 and 4. In line 2, 'alone' perhaps means 'only': the sleep of contentment ends only with death. In its theme the poem is reminiscent of Herbert's *Employment* [2].

From an early notebook

'RISE, NOBLE SOUL' (UNTITLED)

This poem, taken from the 'early notebook' used by both Traherne brothers, is signed with Thomas's initials and is probably the earliest poem included in the present selection of his work. It was crossed through – in Margoliouth's view because its fourth stanza shows it to be 'a physical love poem'. More likely, the poem is a sacred parody of a profane genre: the pastoral invitation to love (cf. the many variations on Marlowe's 'Come live with me and be my love'). Notice that the 'hill, / Where pleasures fresh are growing still' (ll. 3–4), hardly offers the requisite privacy for making love: populated with angels (l. 17) and a welcoming party of 'thousands' (l. 19), it is clearly Heaven. The poem's emphasis on sharing the hardships of the climb (ll. 5–6, 9–10, 13) and its use of sexually suggestive language in its last stanza make it sound like a proposal of marriage (see especially ll. 11–14). There is, however, no basis for such a conjecture in the known facts of Traherne's life; the situation may be entirely imaginary.

From A Serious and Pathetical Contemplation of the Mercies of God *(1699)*

THANKSGIVINGS FOR THE BODY

In all, there are nine *Thanksgivings*, of which *For the Body* is the first. The others are for: the Soul, the Glory of God's Works, the Blessedness of God's Ways, the Blessedness of His Laws, the Beauty of His Providence, the Wisdom of His Word, God's Attributes; and finally – standing a little apart from the rest – *A Thanksgiving and Prayer for the Nation*. Like so much else by Traherne, the *Thanksgivings* are now thought to belong mainly to the years 1670–74: that is, to the period of his residence in London as household chaplain to Sir Orlando Bridgeman. Technically, they are undoubtedly a product of his search for more open forms of writing than the prosodic models of his age offered him. The Psalms and other Scriptural texts, in verbatim quotation (from the Authorized Version of the Bible) as well as in paraphrase and imitation, alternate with passages of free verse, rhymed couplets, prose, and bracketed catalogues reminiscent of Lancelot Andrewes' *Private Devotions* (1648). As in *Centuries* 3.69–96, the quoted material from the Psalms is not clearly distinguished from original passages in a psalmic mode. Although the effect has been described as pastiche, the intent seems to have been to achieve vocal unison with David the Psalmist: 'O that I were as David, the sweet singer of Israel! / In meeter Psalms to set forth Thy praises' (ll. 339–40; cf. 2 Samuel 23:1: 'the sweet psalmist of Israel'). The most important biblical passages incorporated into *Thanksgivings for the Body* and the sequence in which they are deployed are as follows: Psalms 103:1–5 (ll. 1–8); Psalms 139:14–18 (ll. 19–29); Psalms 113:7–8 (ll. 164–7); Psalms 8:4 (ll. 347–8); Psalms 65:8 (ll. 355–6) Philippians 3:20–21 (ll. 424–7); 2 Corinthians 6:16 (l. 463); Psalms 24:7 (ll. 491–2); Romans 6:12–13 (ll. 494–9); Song of Songs 5:4–5 (ll. 500–504); Jeremiah 14:8 (ll. 505–6); Song of Songs 4:9–11 (ll. 507–12); Song of Songs 6:12 (ll. 513–14); Song of Songs 8:2 (ll. 516–17); Song of Songs 8:1 (l. 518). The two paragraphs of prayer and praise at the end of the poem are indebted to Luis de la Puente's *Meditations upon the Mysteries of Our Holy Faith* (1605), in John Heigham's English translation (1619), a fact that links the *Thanksgivings* to other works by Traherne of this period: *Meditations on the Six Days of Creation* and *The Church's Year-Book*.

From Centuries of Meditations

The *Centuries* are written in a small notebook which, according to 1.1, was given to Traherne by the person – sometimes thought to be Susanna Hopton – who is addressed as 'you' from the beginning of the First Century. A presentation quatrain indicates that the recipient of the *Centuries* is female, calls her 'the friend of my best friend' (God?), and invites her to continue writing in the notebook, which Traherne had not entirely used up. The intimacy of these gestures – accepting the little notebook, filling it with 'profitable wonders' (1.1), and returning it to the giver for further entries – places great importance on the physical book itself and on the acts of giving and receiving, writing and reading, as expressions of love. Unfortunately, publication runs the risk of distancing these effects by turning Traherne's second-person addressee into a generalized audience and thus making the intimacy of the exchange seem a mere rhetorical contrivance. The manuscript of the *Centuries* is not, for the most part, a fair copy; deletions and insertions occur frequently, and the book seems to have left Traherne's hands in a rather fluid state of composition. Exceptions consist of the poems and other set-pieces copied into the notebook from time to time. It seems likely that some of the *Select Meditations*, when published, will turn out to be early drafts of certain paragraphs in the *Centuries*.

THE FIRST CENTURY

Like St Paul in Ephesians 3:9, the speaker undertakes to initiate his reader into 'the fellowship of the mystery' (1.3 and 1.5). Knowledge of the *world*, of the *self*, and of *God* (1.16–19) makes plain the truth that 'All the world is yours' and that 'you must of necessity enjoy it' (1.16). The right enjoyment of the world, with a digression (1.32–7) on the folly and ignorance of non-enjoyment, is the theme of most of the paragraphs here reprinted. The selection ends with meditations on wants and needs, in both God and man, as motives for enjoyment.

THE SECOND CENTURY

After a series of passages on the services rendered by the world to the human soul, the speaker is led by way of the Atonement to a consideration of the nature and quality of love (2.40–57; 61–72): the central topic of the Second Century. Because love is identical in its three states – the fountain (love produced in the lover), the stream (love communicated), and the object (love resting in the beloved) – it illustrates the Trinity (2.40). Love is the most natural employment of the soul (2.65) and should be directed towards everyone and everything, not just towards a single person (2.66–8). It is impossible to love the world too much (2.66), but it must be loved in the right way: that is, 'for God's sake' and 'in a blessed and holy manner' (2.69). By so perfecting its love, the human soul converts its powers into pure act (2.73–6) and thereby conforms to the image of the Deity (2.84), as the world becomes 'a valley of vision' (2.94).

THE THIRD CENTURY

The Third Century explores, in terms of Traherne's own spiritual experience, the loss of infantile felicity under the influence of the corrupt customs of the adult world (3.1–13), and the gradual reattainment of felicity in a higher, more mature, and more contemplative mode. Looked at in a broader perspective, this century considers man 'in his fourfold estate of innocency, misery, grace, and glory' (3.43). Because it provides a very rich environment for the poetry in both the Dobell and Burney manuscripts, the Third Century is here reprinted in its entirety.

Although other Centuries quote passages of verse, only the Third has whole poems interpolated among its meditative paragraphs. There are six in all, plus two substantial passages quoted from a lost early 'poem on moderation' (3.19, 21), part of which also found its way into one of the poems from *Christian Ethics*, 'As in a clock'. The six complete poems are: *The Approach* (3.4), a later version of which appears in the Dobell folio; *On News* (3.26), which appears in Philip Traherne's version as *News* in *Poems of Felicity*; 'A life of Sabbaths here beneath' (3.47); 'Sin!' (3.49); *The Recovery* (3.50), not to be confused with another poem by that title in Dobell; and 'In Salem dwelt a glorious king' (3.69), Traherne's tribute to David the Psalmist, his most important model as a poet of praise and thanksgiving.

The sections on sin (3.47–51), which include half of these poems, are clearly a digression or 'parenthesis' (3.51) in the orderly progress of the narrative. By treating them as such and by pointing out to the reader how the very topic of sin 'disorders' his 'proceeding' (3.51), Traherne illustrates rhetorically the disruptive effect on human life of sin and the guilt that it brings with it. The intrusion of sin into the meditator's thoughts, like its sudden entry into his life, is dramatized by the abrupt, monosyllabic exclamations that begin each stanza of the poem on sin (3.49). After *The Recovery* (3.50) and the rhetorical comment (3.51), which explains in retrospect the jarring sensations just experienced by the reader, the return to the interrupted pattern of thought is signalled by the repetition at the beginning of 3.52 of the words that introduced 3.46, the last meditation before the 'parenthesis': 'When I came into the country.' The speaker then resumes his account of his solitary, contemplative quest for the felicity he had once known but had lost.

In its early stages this quest – following a period of confusion, emptiness, and disillusionment (3.14–23) – was impelled by the arrival of good news in the form of Holy Scripture, better than a private revelation (3.24–35). It was furthered by Traherne's Oxford education, despite the defects of the curriculum (3.36–45), and by an ascetic life in the country (3.46, 47, 52–65). Finally, the seeker is brought 'into the very heart' of God's kingdom by the increasing realization that the Bible, and especially the Psalms, confirms his own contemplative insights (3.66–8).

The poem on David (3.69) expresses Traherne's own identification with the Psalmist, who 'most . . . enjoy'd himself, when he / Did as a poet praise the Deity' (ll. 39–40); 'Philosopher and poet too' (l. 45), David 'fill'd his solitudes with joy' (l. 56) so that before his death he was carried 'By secret ravishments above the skies' (l. 73). Finding himself and David 'led by one spirit . . . into the midst of celestial joys', Traherne aspires 'to become what David was: a man after God's own heart' (3.70). Most of the sections that follow therefore consist of quotations, paraphrases, and exegeses of various Psalms attributed to David. Although this material is largely taken verbatim from the King James Bible, quotation marks are omitted here, as in the manuscript, because of Traherne's apparent design to blend his own voice with that of the Psalmist (cf. note to *Thanksgivings for the Body*, pp. 370–71). The following Psalms are recited or alluded to in 3.71–94 in the order given: 8, 19, 22, 24, 28, 33, 35, 36, 45–51, 58, 59, 63, 65, 66, 74, 78, 84, 86, 103–7, 119, 145–50. The speaker's identification with the Psalmist makes it clear that his own soul, like David's, has 'recovered its pristine liberty' (3.95), culminating his quest to regain felicity and enabling him to conclude by expressing his recaptured and intensified sense of communion with the divine (3.97–100).

THE FOURTH CENTURY

In this, the most homiletic of the Centuries, Traherne explains the principles in which human felicity is grounded. He announces at the outset a transition from the contemplative happiness that was the primary subject of the Third Century to 'an active happiness, which consisteth in blessed operations. And as some things fit a man for contemplation, so there are others fitting him for action: which as they are infinitely necessary to practical happiness, so are they likewise infinitely conducive to contemplative itself' (4.1). These 'other things' are the principles to which the Fourth Century is devoted; the ones found in the first half of it are conveniently summarized in 4.54.

Originally, the Fourth Century began with the speaker's declaration that 'I will in this Century supply his place' – the place, that is, of the Third Century's author; consequently, there are references to 'your friend' (e.g., 4.30, 54) and curious phrases such as 'He from whom I received these things' (4.20) as though a third person were writing to Susanna Hopton about Thomas Traherne. The purpose of this strategy must have been to underscore the contrast between the more personal approach taken in the Third Century and the social emphasis of the Fourth; the author is imagining himself as viewed by another pair of eyes.

Meditations 74–8 are taken largely from Pico della Mirandola's *Oration on the Dignity of Man* (*c.* 1487); indeed, 4.75, 76, and 77 consist entirely of Traherne's almost literal translation of a famous passage at the beginning of that work. These sections are included here to show Traherne's indebtedness to Florentine Neoplatonism of the late fifteenth and early sixteenth centuries. The theme of these passages, that the glory of man is his free will, is related to the Fourth Century's exposition of principles because 'By choosing a man may be turned and converted into love' (4.80), which has been established previously as 'the greatest of all principles' (4.61). The closing passages in the selection given here (4.80–84) thus return to the subject matter of 4.55–70 and elucidate the principle best expressed in 1 John 4:16: 'God is love; and he that dwelleth in love dwelleth in God, and God in him.'

THE FIFTH CENTURY

Although so called in the manuscript, this is not really a century because it contains only ten meditations. Since the first of these ends with a statement of the author's intention 'to speak of several eminent particulars', beginning with the attributes of the Deity, and since three such attributes (infinity, eternity, omnipresence) are the only 'eminent particulars' discussed, we must assume that Traherne meant to write more than he did – if not to fill up another whole century. Yet the facts that he returned the notebook to its donor and that he became immersed in many other literary projects before his death suggest that he may have come to regard this most mystical and speculative of the Centuries, truncated though it be, as a fitting coda to the work as a whole.

INDEX OF TITLES

'A life of Sabbaths here beneath' 250
Adam 86
Admiration 121
Amendment 46
Another 57
Anticipation, The 50
Apostasy, The 91
Apprehension, The 29
Approach, The 19, 227 (*Centuries* 3.4)
'As in a clock,' 157
Author to the Critical Peruser, The 79
Bells I 111
Bells II 112
Bible, The 103
Bliss 62
Christendom 104
Churches I 114
Churches II 115
Circulation, The 43
City, The 143
Consummation 148
'Contentment is a sleepy thing' 162
Demonstration, The 48
Design, The 36
Desire 68
Dialogue, The 136
Dissatisfaction 100
Dreams 138
Dumbness 21
Ease 33
Eden 6
Estate, The 40
Evidence, The 125
Felicity 85
Fullness 29
Goodness 73
Hosanna 150
Image, The 125
Improvement, The 16
'In Salem dwelt a glorious king' 261
Infant-Eye, An 80

Inference, The I 140
Inference, The II 142
Innocence 8
Inquiry, The 42
Insatiableness I 146
Insatiableness II 147
Instruction, The 12
Love 58
'Mankind is sick' 158
Misapprehension 116
My Spirit 25
Nature 30
News 83
Odour, The 118
On Christmas-Day 108
On Leaping over the Moon 129
On News (*Centuries* 3.26) 239
Person, The 38
Poverty 98
Preparative, The 10
Rapture, The 15
Recovery, The 54
Recovery, The (*Centuries* 3.50) 253
Return, The 82
Review, The I 152
Review, The II 153
Right Apprehension 122
'Rise, noble soul' 165
Salutation, The 3
Shadows in the Water 126
Sight 132
Silence 23
'Sin!' 252
Solitude 94
Speed 34
Thanksgivings for the Body 169
'Then shall each limb a spring of joy be found' 180
Thoughts I 60
Thoughts II 63
Thoughts III 66

Thoughts IV 70
'To the same purpose' 131
Vision, The 13
Walking 134
'While I, O Lord, exalted by Thy hand' 177

Wonder 4
World, The 87
'Ye hidden nectars' 65

INDEX OF FIRST LINES

A delicate and tender thought 63
A learned and a happy ignorance 6
A life of Sabbaths here beneath! 250
A quiet silent person may possess 23
A simple light from all contagion free, 80
All bliss 62
As fair ideas from the sky, 43
As in a clock, 'tis hinder'd-force doth bring 157
As in the house I sate 98
Bless the Lord, O my soul: and all that is within me bless His holy name. 169
But shall my soul no wealth possess, 40
But that which most I wonder at, which most 8
Can human shape so taking be, 121
Contentment is a sleepy thing! 162
David a temple in his mind conceiv'd; 142
Did I grow, or did I stay? 152
Flight is but the preparative: the sight 13
For giving me desire, 68
From clay and mire, and dirt, my soul, 112
Give but to things their true esteem, 122
God made man upright at the first; 86
Hark! hark, my soul! the bells do ring, 111
He seeks for ours as we do seek for His. 57
His power bounded, greater is in might, 236
His Word confirms the sale: 125
How desolate; 94
How easily doth Nature teach the soul, 33
How like an angel came I down! 4
I saw new worlds beneath the water lie, 129
If God as verses say a spirit be, 221
If I be like my God, my King 125

If this I did not every moment see, 29
In clothes confin'd, my weary mind 100
In making bodies Love could not express 235
In Salem dwelt a glorious king, 261
In unexperienc'd infancy 126
Mankind is sick, the world distemper'd lies, 158
Men are not wise in their true interest, 116
Men may delighted be with springs, 42
Mine infant-eye, 132
My body being dead, my limbs unknown; 10
My childhood is a sphere 153
My contemplation dazzles in the end 50
My naked simple life was I. 25
News from a foreign country came, 83, 239
No more shall walls, no more shall walls confine 150
No walls confine! Can nothing hold my mind? 146
O nectar! O delicious stream! 58
One star 91
Prompted to seek my bliss above the skies, 85
Rise, noble soul, and come away 165
Shall dumpish melancholy spoil my joys 108
Sin! 252
Sin! wilt thou vanquish me! 253
Spew out thy filth, thy flesh abjure; 12
Sure man was born to meditate on things; 21
Sweet infancy! 15
That all things should be mine: 46
That childish thoughts such joys inspire, 19, 227
That custom is a second nature, we 30
That light, that sight, that thought, 29

INDEX OF FIRST LINES

That! That! There I was told 103
The bliss of other men is my delight 73
The highest things are easiest to be shown, 48
The liquid pearl in springs, 34
The naked truth in many faces shown, 79
The thoughts of men appear 148
Then shall each limb a spring of joy be found, 180
These hands are jewels to the eye, 118
These little limbs, 3
This busy, vast, inquiring soul 147
Those stately structures which on earth I view 114
Thoughts are the angels which we send abroad, 66
Thoughts are the wings on which the soul doth fly, 70
'Tis more to recollect, than make. The one 16
'Tis strange! I saw the skies; 138
To infancy, O Lord, again I come, 82
To see us but receive, is such a sight 54
To the same purpose: he, not long before 131
To walk abroad is, not with eyes, 134
Well-guided thoughts within possess 140
Were there but one alone 115
What structures here among God's works appear? 143
When Adam first did from his dust arise, 87
When first Eternity stoop'd down to nought, 36
When first mine infant-ear 104
While I, O Lord, exalted by Thy hand, 177
Q. Why dost thou tell me that the fields are mine? 136
Ye brisk divine and living things, 60
Ye hidden nectars, which my God doth drink, 65
Ye sacred limbs, 38

Visit Penguin on the Internet
and browse at your leisure

- preview sample extracts of our forthcoming books
- read about your favourite authors
- investigate over 10,000 titles
- enter one of our literary quizzes
- win some fantastic prizes in our competitions
- e-mail us with your comments and book reviews
- instantly order any Penguin book

and masses more!

'To be recommended without reservation ... a rich and rewarding on-line experience' – Internet Magazine

www.penguin.co.uk

READ MORE IN PENGUIN

In every corner of the world, on every subject under the sun, Penguin represents quality and variety – the very best in publishing today.

For complete information about books available from Penguin – including Puffins, Penguin Classics and Arkana – and how to order them, write to us at the appropriate address below. Please note that for copyright reasons the selection of books varies from country to country.

In the United Kingdom: Please write to *Dept. EP, Penguin Books Ltd, Bath Road, Harmondsworth, West Drayton, Middlesex UB7 0DA*

In the United States: Please write to *Consumer Sales, Penguin USA, P.O. Box 999, Dept. 17109, Bergenfield, New Jersey 07621-0120.* VISA and MasterCard holders call 1-800-253-6476 to order Penguin titles

In Canada: Please write to *Penguin Books Canada Ltd, 10 Alcorn Avenue, Suite 300, Toronto, Ontario M4V 3B2*

In Australia: Please write to *Penguin Books Australia Ltd, P.O. Box 257, Ringwood, Victoria 3134*

In New Zealand: Please write to *Penguin Books (NZ) Ltd, Private Bag 102902, North Shore Mail Centre, Auckland 10*

In India: Please write to *Penguin Books India Pvt Ltd, 706 Eros Apartments, 56 Nehru Place, New Delhi 110 019*

In the Netherlands: Please write to *Penguin Books Netherlands bv, Postbus 3507, NL-1001 AH Amsterdam*

In Germany: Please write to *Penguin Books Deutschland GmbH, Metzlerstrasse 26, 60594 Frankfurt am Main*

In Spain: Please write to *Penguin Books S. A., Bravo Murillo 19, 1º B, 28015 Madrid*

In Italy: Please write to *Penguin Italia s.r.l., Via Felice Casati 20, I–20124 Milano*

In France: Please write to *Penguin France S. A., 17 rue Lejeune, F–31000 Toulouse*

In Japan: Please write to *Penguin Books Japan, Ishikiribashi Building, 2–5–4, Suido, Bunkyo-ku, Tokyo 112*

In South Africa: Please write to *Longman Penguin Southern Africa (Pty) Ltd, Private Bag X08, Bertsham 2013*

PENGUIN AUDIOBOOKS

A Quality of Writing That Speaks for Itself

Penguin Books has always led the field in quality publishing. Now you can listen at leisure to your favourite books, read to you by familiar voices from radio, stage and screen. Penguin Audiobooks are produced to an excellent standard, and abridgements are always faithful to the original texts. From thrillers to classic literature, biography to humour, with a wealth of titles in between, Penguin Audiobooks offer you quality, entertainment and the chance to rediscover the pleasure of listening.

You can order Penguin Audiobooks through Penguin Direct by telephoning (0181) 899 4036. The lines are open 24 hours every day. Ask for Penguin Direct, quoting your credit card details.

A selection of Penguin Audiobooks, published or forthcoming:

Little Women by Louisa May Alcott, read by Kate Harper

Emma by Jane Austen, read by Fiona Shaw

Pride and Prejudice by Jane Austen, read by Geraldine McEwan

Beowulf translated by Michael Alexander, read by David Rintoul

Agnes Grey by Anne Brontë, read by Juliet Stevenson

Jane Eyre by Charlotte Brontë, read by Juliet Stevenson

The Professor by Charlotte Brontë, read by Juliet Stevenson

Wuthering Heights by Emily Brontë, read by Juliet Stevenson

The Woman in White by Wilkie Collins, read by Nigel Anthony and Susan Jameson

Nostromo by Joseph Conrad, read by Michael Pennington

Tales from the Thousand and One Nights, read by Souad Faress and Raad Rawi

Robinson Crusoe by Daniel Defoe, read by Tom Baker

David Copperfield by Charles Dickens, read by Nathaniel Parker

The Pickwick Papers by Charles Dickens, read by Dinsdale Landen

Bleak House by Charles Dickens, read by Beatie Edney and Ronald Pickup

PENGUIN AUDIOBOOKS

The Hound of the Baskervilles by Sir Arthur Conan Doyle, read by Freddie Jones
Middlemarch by George Eliot, read by Harriet Walter
Tom Jones by Henry Fielding, read by Robert Lindsay
The Great Gatsby by F. Scott Fitzgerald, read by Marcus D'Amico
Madame Bovary by Gustave Flaubert, read by Claire Bloom
Mary Barton by Elizabeth Gaskell, read by Clare Higgins
Jude the Obscure by Thomas Hardy, read by Samuel West
Far from the Madding Crowd by Thomas Hardy, read by Julie Christie
The Scarlet Letter by Nathaniel Hawthorne, read by Bob Sessions
Les Misérables by Victor Hugo, read by Nigel Anthony
A Passage to India by E. M. Forster, read by Tim Pigott-Smith
The Iliad by Homer, read by Derek Jacobi
The Dead and Other Stories by James Joyce, read by Gerard McSorley
On the Road by Jack Kerouac, read by David Carradine
Sons and Lovers by D. H. Lawrence, read by Paul Copley
The Prince by Niccolò Machiavelli, read by Fritz Weaver
Animal Farm by George Orwell, read by Timothy West
Rob Roy by Sir Walter Scott, read by Robbie Coltrane
Frankenstein by Mary Shelley, read by Richard Pasco
Of Mice and Men by John Steinbeck, read by Gary Sinise
Kidnapped by Robert Louis Stevenson, read by Robbie Coltrane
Dracula by Bram Stoker, read by Richard E. Grant
Gulliver's Travels by Jonathan Swift, read by Hugh Laurie
Vanity Fair by William Makepeace Thackeray, read by Robert Hardy
Lark Rise to Candleford by Flora Thompson, read by Judi Dench
The Invisible Man by H. G. Wells, read by Paul Shelley
Ethan Frome by Edith Wharton, read by Nathan Osgood
The Picture of Dorian Gray by Oscar Wilde, read by John Moffatt
Orlando by Virginia Woolf, read by Tilda Swinton

READ MORE IN PENGUIN

A CHOICE OF CLASSICS

Francis Bacon	**The Essays**
George Berkeley	**Principles of Human Knowledge/Three Dialogues between Hylas and Philonoïs**
James Boswell	**The Life of Samuel Johnson**
Sir Thomas Browne	**The Major Works**
John Bunyan	**The Pilgrim's Progress**
Edmund Burke	**Reflections on the Revolution in France**
Frances Burney	**Evelina**
Margaret Cavendish	**The Blazing World and Other Writings**
William Cobbett	**Rural Rides**
William Congreve	**Comedies**
Thomas de Quincey	**Confessions of an English Opium Eater**
	Recollections of the Lakes and the Lake Poets
Daniel Defoe	**A Journal of the Plague Year**
	Moll Flanders
	Robinson Crusoe
	Roxana
	A Tour through the Whole Island of Great Britain
Henry Fielding	**Amelia**
	Jonathan Wild
	Joseph Andrews
	Tom Jones
John Gay	**The Beggar's Opera**
Oliver Goldsmith	**The Vicar of Wakefield**

READ MORE IN PENGUIN

A CHOICE OF CLASSICS

William Hazlitt	**Selected Writings**
George Herbert	**The Complete English Poems**
Thomas Hobbes	**Leviathan**
Samuel Johnson/ James Boswell	**A Journey to the Western Islands of Scotland and The Journal of a Tour of the Hebrides**
Charles Lamb	**Selected Prose**
George Meredith	**The Egoist**
Thomas Middleton	**Five Plays**
John Milton	**Paradise Lost**
Samuel Richardson	**Clarissa**
	Pamela
Earl of Rochester	**Complete Works**
Richard Brinsley Sheridan	**The School for Scandal and Other Plays**
Sir Philip Sidney	**Selected Poems**
Christopher Smart	**Selected Poems**
Adam Smith	**The Wealth of Nations**
Tobias Smollett	**The Adventures of Ferdinand Count Fathom**
	Humphrey Clinker
Laurence Sterne	**The Life and Opinions of Tristram Shandy**
	A Sentimental Journey Through France and Italy
Jonathan Swift	**Gulliver's Travels**
	Selected Poems
Thomas Traherne	**Selected Poems and Prose**
Sir John Vanbrugh	**Four Comedies**

READ MORE IN PENGUIN

A CHOICE OF CLASSICS

St Anselm	**The Prayers and Meditations**
St Augustine	**Confessions**
Bede	**Ecclesiastical History of the English People**
Geoffrey Chaucer	**The Canterbury Tales**
	Love Visions
	Troilus and Criseyde
Marie de France	**The Lais of Marie de France**
Jean Froissart	**The Chronicles**
Geoffrey of Monmouth	**The History of the Kings of Britain**
Gerald of Wales	**History and Topography of Ireland**
	The Journey through Wales and **The Description of Wales**
Gregory of Tours	**The History of the Franks**
Robert Henryson	**The Testament of Cresseid and Other Poems**
Walter Hilton	**The Ladder of Perfection**
Julian of Norwich	**Revelations of Divine Love**
Thomas à Kempis	**The Imitation of Christ**
William Langland	**Piers the Ploughman**
Sir John Mandeville	**The Travels of Sir John Mandeville**
Marguerite de Navarre	**The Heptameron**
Christine de Pisan	**The Treasure of the City of Ladies**
Chrétien de Troyes	**Arthurian Romances**
Marco Polo	**The Travels**
Richard Rolle	**The Fire of Love**
François Villon	**Selected Poems**

READ MORE IN PENGUIN

A CHOICE OF CLASSICS

Matthew Arnold	**Selected Prose**
Jane Austen	**Emma**
	Lady Susan/The Watsons/Sanditon
	Mansfield Park
	Northanger Abbey
	Persuasion
	Pride and Prejudice
	Sense and Sensibility
William Barnes	**Selected Poems**
Anne Brontë	**Agnes Grey**
	The Tenant of Wildfell Hall
Charlotte Brontë	**Jane Eyre**
	Shirley
	Villette
Emily Brontë	**Wuthering Heights**
Samuel Butler	**Erewhon**
	The Way of All Flesh
Thomas Carlyle	**Selected Writings**
Arthur Hugh Clough	**Selected Poems**
Wilkie Collins	**The Moonstone**
	The Woman in White
Charles Darwin	**The Origin of Species**
	The Voyage of the *Beagle*
Benjamin Disraeli	**Sybil**
George Eliot	**Adam Bede**
	Daniel Deronda
	Felix Holt
	Middlemarch
	The Mill on the Floss
	Romola
	Scenes of Clerical Life
	Silas Marner
Elizabeth Gaskell	**Cranford/Cousin Phillis**
	The Life of Charlotte Brontë
	Mary Barton
	North and South
	Wives and Daughters

READ MORE IN PENGUIN

A CHOICE OF CLASSICS

Charles Dickens	**American Notes for General Circulation**
	Barnaby Rudge
	Bleak House
	The Christmas Books (in two volumes)
	David Copperfield
	Dombey and Son
	Great Expectations
	Hard Times
	Little Dorrit
	Martin Chuzzlewit
	The Mystery of Edwin Drood
	Nicholas Nickleby
	The Old Curiosity Shop
	Oliver Twist
	Our Mutual Friend
	The Pickwick Papers
	Selected Short Fiction
	A Tale of Two Cities
Edward Gibbon	**The Decline and Fall of the Roman Empire**
George Gissing	**New Grub Street**
	The Odd Women
William Godwin	**Caleb Williams**
Thomas Hardy	**The Distracted Preacher and Other Tales**
	Far from the Madding Crowd
	Jude the Obscure
	The Mayor of Casterbridge
	A Pair of Blue Eyes
	The Return of the Native
	Tess of the d'Urbervilles
	The Trumpet-Major
	Under the Greenwood Tree
	The Woodlanders

READ MORE IN PENGUIN

A CHOICE OF CLASSICS

Lord Macaulay	**The History of England**
Henry Mayhew	**London Labour and the London Poor**
John Stuart Mill	**The Autobiography**
	On Liberty
William Morris	**News from Nowhere and Selected Writings and Designs**
John Henry Newman	**Apologia Pro Vita Sua**
Robert Owen	**A New View of Society and Other Writings**
Walter Pater	**Marius the Epicurean**
John Ruskin	**'Unto This Last' and Other Writings**
Walter Scott	**Ivanhoe**
	Heart of Midlothian
Robert Louis Stevenson	**Kidnapped**
	Dr Jekyll and Mr Hyde and Other Stories
William Makepeace Thackeray	**The History of Henry Esmond**
	The History of Pendennis
	Vanity Fair
Anthony Trollope	**Barchester Towers**
	Can You Forgive Her?
	The Eustace Diamonds
	Framley Parsonage
	He Knew He Was Right
	The Last Chronicle of Barset
	Phineas Finn
	The Prime Minister
	The Small House at Allington
	The Warden
	The Way We Live Now
Oscar Wilde	**Complete Short Fiction**
Mary Wollstonecraft	**A Vindication of the Rights of Woman**
	Mary and Maria
	Matilda
Dorothy and William Wordsworth	**Home at Grasmere**

READ MORE IN PENGUIN

POETRY LIBRARY

Arnold	Selected by Kenneth Allott
Blake	Selected by W. H. Stevenson
Browning	Selected by Daniel Karlin
Burns	Selected by Angus Calder and William Donnelly
Byron	Selected by A. S. B. Glover
Clare	Selected by Geoffrey Summerfield
Coleridge	Selected by Richard Holmes
Donne	Selected by John Hayward
Dryden	Selected by Douglas Grant
Hardy	Selected by David Wright
Herbert	Selected by W. H. Auden
Jonson	Selected by George Parfitt
Keats	Selected by John Barnard
Kipling	Selected by James Cochrane
Lawrence	Selected by Keith Sagar
Milton	Selected by Laurence D. Lerner
Pope	Selected by Douglas Grant
Rubáiyát of Omar Khayyám	Translated by Edward FitzGerald
Shelley	Selected by Isabel Quigley
Tennyson	Selected by W. E. Williams
Wordsworth	Selected by Nicholas Roe
Yeats	Selected by Timothy Webb